THE GEMINI EFFECT

PAUL KANE

Encyclopocalypse Publications
www.encyclopocalypse.com

PRAISE FOR THE GEMINI FACTOR

'*The Gemini Factor* draws on the twins mythology to create a modern-day thriller of supernatural proportions. The plot is both involving and rewarding while the actual storytelling is quite excellent. Paul Kane manages to create a realistic portrayal of victim/killer/hunter without going over the top as many other writers do… a very well-crafted and rewarding novel which I have no hesitation in recommending.'

SCIENCE FICTION & FANTASY

'What you get within this book are characters who jump off the page, some great dialogue, and a plot that's as twisted as this author's mind can conceive, which only adds to this reading experience. Dressed up as a traditional crime novel, it's the way in which the author has managed to blend Urban Fantasy, a touch of Sci-Fi and mixed it all up with a wicked sense of humour. It's a cracking title and one that I really had a blast reading.'

FALCATA TIMES

'Paul Kane's *The Gemini Factor* breathes some fresh air into the serial killer subgenre… There's no doubt in my mind that readers will think they know where Kane is leading them, only to have the rug yanked out from beneath them time and again. Kane's style is such that you can't help but turn the page to see what he's going to do next, and it's that unpredictability that has earned my readership in the last couple of years. Simply put, the man can tell one hell of an entertaining yarn! If you're looking for a fun summer read, go grab a copy of *The Gemini Factor*, and while you're at it, pick up a couple more of Kane's books. He hasn't disappointed me yet, and I'm guessing you'll enjoy his writing too.'

'Paul Kane has created a brilliantly detailed and utterly believable setting – hopefully one that is revisited in later books. *The Gemini Factor* is a tightly-plotted, well-planned thriller. A disturbing villain stalks a compelling British noir setting, while heroes combine modern forensics and ageless intuition to stop him. Not just something for everyone, but something very good...'

'Kane's no-nonsense writing style makes this book read like a modern crime novel, but anyone aware of his previous work may suspect that there is something more going on than a standard crime thriller, and so there is, although I'll leave what that is for you to discover. The fatal final twists will leave your head spinning... This is such a fun book to read, so easy, it feels like the story just wraps you up. It's like reading those other classic genre storytellers King and Koontz. Kane certainly has the pedigree and this crime/genre novel is marvelously well crafted.'

MORPHEUS TALES

'The reader stays interested from page to page, from beginning to end, as they explore Kane's well-crafted Norchester, and get to know his heroes as they strive to end the spate of brutal killings. Overall, Paul Kane's *The Gemini Factor* offers a very interesting twist on the usual serial killer fiction, with some very, very creepy bits mixed in to keep you thinking about the story for a while afterwards. So, go ahead and pick up this book; get to know a new kind of evil. If you are a twin – sorry; this novel may be particularly disturbing.'

HORRORBOUND

'I was struck first by the dark poetry of Kane's writing. Then I was grabbed by the story and the characters... It's a good story, with good characters and great writing and for all that there is a supernatural aspect, it's the human element in the book that provides the real horror.'

UN:BOUND

'Well-written and very atmospheric, especially towards the end. The characterization was excellent, too. I particularly liked Deborah. I have to say that I have a deep prejudice against books featuring twins. I have written a lot about this but it probably just boils down to the fact that I am the mother of twins and dislike the way twins in books are ALWAYS sinister. It's a tribute to Kane's book that I could overcome this prejudice and enjoy the story.'

For Michael Jason Stokes & Anna Ray Stokes, who kickstarted the new Gemini adventures. And for Alice, without whom this would never have been written.

ACKNOWLEDGMENTS

My thanks to Mark and Sean at Encyclopocalypse for taking a gamble on this one, a sequel to a book originally written over 20 years ago! Your faith in this project, and indeed so many others, has given me faith too. As always, hugs and massive thank yous to all my friends in the writing and film/TV world, for their continual help and their support in the past. A very special thank you, though, to people like Mike Carey, Robert Shearman, Rio Youers, Neil Gaiman, Adam Nevill, Tim Lebbon, Alison Littlewood, Paul Finch, Simon Clark, Joe Hill, Kelley Armstrong, Stephen Volk and *so* many more. Finally, a massive thank you to my family, especially my truly wonderful wife Marie – love you more than words can say, sweetheart.

PROLOGUE

Inside the womb, changes had taken place.

Since seed first encountered egg, energising it with life. It had survived, against all the odds, not just the usual problems that might cause a miscarriage, but the traumas which had occurred outside the body. Then the egg split: a consequence of the conception taking place in this particular city, which had – many centuries ago – been a sacred site for ancient religious sects practising bizarre fertility rituals beneath the light of the constellations above.

Suddenly there were two identical eggs, genetically indistinguishable. Exact duplicates that would emerge in something like eight or nine months' time. Twins. They would be the same in appearance, in looks if not in personality... though they would be more alike than either of them might ever realise. And no matter how 'individual' they grew up to be, the fact remained that they'd started off as one.

Inside that womb the developing foetuses had interacted.

They'd nudged and kicked each other, communicating in their own distinct and secret code. Working out which would be the dominant of the two, who would take the most sustenance from the mother. And also probably trying to get back that which they had lost. The wholeness. Nevertheless, they would share a bond with each other that could never be broken. Not by time nor distance, nor even by the blackness and finality of death itself.

But all that was in the future. For now they were just waiting, patiently waiting.

Because the miracle, the natural marvel that still remains a mystery even in these times of scientific wonder and technological achievement, was only really beginning.

The miracle that some refer to as:

The Gemini Effect.

PART I

CHAPTER ONE

The screaming was still ringing in her ears.

Even now, ten, fifteen minutes since she'd left the rest of them behind – back in the club, doing shots. Screaming and crying out for more. When exactly had she become the boring one? Not that she'd ever really been the swinging from the rafters type, dancing on tabletops. Unlike some of her sister's friends from work (they were known for it in the medical profession, apparently), who weren't far off doing that tonight if they carried on putting it away like that.

But she'd known how to have a good time, of course she had. Especially back at uni, out with her mates till all hours. That's where she'd been the night—

All that seemed like a billion years ago now.

It's called growing up, she said to herself. Having responsibilities. She had an early shift; well, earlyish, around ten in the morning. Plus she was an assistant manager now, had to put her best foot forward, as her dad was always so fond of saying.

Felicity Bailey, 'Flick' to her friends, pulled her jacket tighter around herself until it was almost a hug, and sighed.

Continued walking down the street, the clacking of her high heels accompanying her.

They were just blowing off steam, had a stressful job. Not that hers was exactly walking on sunshine, but you couldn't really compare making sure beds were made and breakfast ran on time to counselling people with PTSD, who'd been through traumatic events. And her sister, Trisha, was perfectly suited to that, having been through a trauma herself when she was younger. One of the worst things anyone could ever go through…

She should be happy for her, especially now. Felicity should have been joining in with the fun and games back there: the giant inflatable penises and male strippers; the Prosecco and Jägerbombs. Their mum had gone home hours ago, after the meal at the Italian place – the more civilised part of the evening – or she'd have gone demented at their hijinks. They'd never really approved of things like that, their mum and dad. It'd taken a lot of persuasion to let their daughters move out and go to uni, and even then it had only been on the other side of town. If they saw that performance back there, regardless of the fact 'the girls' were both approaching thirty now, they'd drag them back home and keep them locked up until they were maiden aunts.

Such old-fashioned views! Although wasn't Felicity the one who'd jumped ship before it was even half-eleven tonight? Was she getting more like her parents the older she got? No, it wasn't that.

Face it, she said to herself, *this is jealousy. Pure and simple.* Felicity knew it, Trisha knew it. That had always been the case, hadn't it. Not just with guys in general, because Trisha had certainly had a few boyfriends – was definitely luckier in that department than Flick – but with one in particular. Danny. Danny Sirk.

Mr and Mrs—

She'd been the one who'd looked after her sister when

they'd split up, not long after they'd graduated. Danny had said they were growing apart, wanted different things from life – at twenty-bloody-one! He wanted to travel more, for instance, get away from that city, and she was staying put, mainly because of the pressure from their folks. But if they were both being honest it was the thing they'd gone through together, that trauma. It had brought them closer at first, and then…

"I don't know what I'm going to do without him. I feel so alone," Trisha had wept into Felicity's shoulder, and she'd held her. Said to her, because it was true:

"You're not alone. You'll always have me."

They'd always have each other; always had and always would. Since birth, as a matter of fact. The strongest bond there could ever be, even stronger than the one they had with their parents. Much stronger actually, because you couldn't share everything with them. She'd seen Trisha through all of that heartache, been proud of her when she went on to become a trainee counselling psychologist at the local hospital, then had built her career up from there. No need for that poxy part-time job at the café now.

And Trisha had been proud of her sister, too, as she'd struggled to put her own art degree to use and ultimately had to rely more and more on work at *The Imperial Hotel*. "You can always circle back to it, sis," was Trisha's sage advice. That or maybe go into teaching, which was something Felicity would have hated. Or art therapy? A failure, was how she saw it, her dreams of having exhibitions and selling her work for a fortune growing dimmer by the year.

Not a bad thing to have money behind you, was her parents' mantra. A stable job, with career prospects. She was luckier than most folk in this day and age, and deep down Felicity knew it. Just not lucky in love. Never lucky with that.

Unlike Trisha, who'd played the field a little – nothing serious, which was why Flick hadn't really got bent out of shape about it – only to bump into Danny again not eight months ago, though whether that had been intentional on his part Felicity still wasn't entirely sure. They'd certainly bumped into each other a lot more since then, and in more ways than one.

"Are you really sure about this?" she'd asked Trisha once on the phone – the phone, because she was seeing less and less of her sister now Danny was back on the scene. "After what happened last time?"

"I'm sure," she'd said emphatically. "We've both done a lot of growing up since uni, Flick."

Felicity harrumphed. Not from where she'd been sitting tonight, as Trisha was oiling up the guy who'd come dressed as a doctor in a white coat (which had soon been discarded in favour of a set of tiny trunks the same colour). Grown up? Hardly. That was what *she'd* had to do when her dreams and ambitions had been shattered.

But that wasn't fair, was it. This was a one-off, a special occasion – and the whole blowing off steam thing. Trauma. Dealing with trauma. With people who were *dealing* with trauma. They were allowed to have a little fun, surely? Especially as…

"I'm getting married!" a drunken Trisha had screamed in her ear a little earlier at the bar. "Can you believe it? I'm getting married!"

Oh, Felicity could believe it all right. She'd had to put up with months of her family talking about nothing else. Plus which, she was the one arranging the reception. Putting those artistic leanings to good use, so Trisha said, helping to sort out what kind of decorations they were having, where to put the tables for the best effect.

"Wass… wassup?" Trisha had asked then, probably seeing the way she'd scrunched up her face.

Felicity had shaken her head. "Nothing. Nothing's up."

And her sister had looked at her sideways, knew exactly

what was wrong. Had known it since Danny had returned. Since she'd announced the engagement. The jealousy thing. Had even told her not to worry, because pulling at weddings was virtually a rule for the Maid of Honour, right? "We'll find you someone nice," Trisha had promised.

Like she needed someone to do that. Like she needed pity. She got enough of that from their parents, her mum already cooing about grandchildren – "I'm glad someone's got their act together in that department. I was beginning to wonder if I'd *ever* get them!" Her dad playing best mate with Danny, off to the football with him every Saturday. And this after they'd called him every name under the sun when he dumped Trisha. Turncoats.

"Why can't you juss... jusss be happy for me?" Trisha had said next, a little sadly.

"I... I am," she'd lied.

"No." Trisha hiccupped. "No you're nosh, you've got a face like a wet bank hol-holiday."

Felicity had shrugged.

Trisha flapped her hand and said, "Aww, bloody piss off then!" She'd done another shot, turned her back on Felicity and danced back over to her friends.

It was a valid question. Why couldn't she be happy for her?

She'd tried, was trying. Would continue to try. But tonight... Tonight she'd just had to bail after that, before they started rowing. At her own sister's hen do, Christ!

Not that anyone would notice, she'd told herself, except that she knew full well Trisha would. Might. If she wasn't under a table somewhere by now, that was.

More often than not knew everything about what happened to each other; always had. Knew if they were injured, if they were sad, if they were sleeping with someone. If they were blissfully happy. Like Trisha was, like Felicity *knew* Trisha was.

Which, when you got right down to it, was the real problem. That and the fact the couple shared that certain something, on that night, when Felicity hadn't been around. When, ironically she'd been the one out having a good time with the art students, getting smashed. While her sister and Danny had been walking back from the café and—

She used to have a dream about it happening to her afterwards, maybe a shared memory or whatever? Maybe something else? But it had been a good dream. That didn't make any sense, obviously; why would you enjoy or want to go through something like that? Had she been jealous of the thing itself? The attack? Hardly. It was more that they'd experienced it together, Trisha and Danny. Not to mention the publicity, being interviewed by the papers, the news afterwards – together. It was something they shared that she couldn't with either of them.

With her twin.

In the dream she wasn't alone, of course. It was her and her sister – before Danny came back, before he ruined everything – and they were walking home from a night out or... Just the two of them. And they would fight off the guy, the serial killer guy who hadn't really been the killer as it had turned out, but rather his little brother. Everyone knew that, knew the tales.

They would fend him off and hand him in to the police, just like Trisha and Danny had done. Her sister had handled herself well that night, had even bitten the twat; she'd heard the account many, many times. Felicity would have known something was wrong herself if she hadn't been...

High? Drunk? she said to herself. Had said to herself many times.

Hadn't even noticed the messages on her phone till the next morning, asking her to come to the police station. Shit.

Shit, shit, shitting shit!

It should have been her with Trisha, should have been

Felicity protecting her. Them protecting *each other*, looking out for each other. Like always. Like it always had been, always would.

Would have been, if it hadn't been for Danny.

He'd done his best to include Felicity, to his credit. Even back then in the station, when she'd finally got inside, they'd all hugged each other. All three of them. But it wasn't the same. Would never be the same.

Would never be the—

Felicity stopped suddenly, looked around. All this stuff, all this crap swirling round and round in her head, mixed with a drink or two, and she hadn't noticed how off the beaten track she'd wandered. How far away from the lights and sounds of the city.

How alone she suddenly was.

Should have rung for a taxi, she chastised herself. But it would cost a fortune at this time of night, on a Friday night. It wasn't far to the block of flats she lived in now, that was why she'd moved there – the proximity to work, to town. To her sister, back then, though Trisha was thinking about moving to the outskirts now, to suburbia. Becoming a Stepford. Getting ready to start pumping out those kids! Leaving her behind in so many ways.

Stop. Stop thinking about all that, she told herself again. *That's what's got you into this situation in the first place. Lost. No, not lost. Just...*

Turned around somehow. Somewhere she hadn't been before that she knew of, a part of the city she wasn't overly familiar with. A quiet part. A darker part. A lonely part.

Except she didn't feel alone.

Felicity trotted on, needed to get to the next clump of street-lights – which had grown further and further apart she now realised. Reaching into her handbag, she pulled out her phone. Felt safer already. Not that the streets weren't safe anymore; they were actually a lot better than they had been all those years ago. The police had been cracking down on crime, and doing a good job of it too. More CCTV, more patrols. The new female mayor had been making a thing of it, that women shouldn't be afraid to walk home at night. Didn't matter what they were wearing (and Felicity tonight had actually gone for an outfit that was, as her mother called it, modest, decent; but that shouldn't even be a thing), there was no reason in the world why they should have to live in fear because of men. And good for her!

Although there were those funny people, weren't there. Weirdos who came here to visit specifically because of the legends surrounding the area. She'd read a piece online about them not long ago, true crime fans, oddballs who were admirers of the nutter who'd once stalked these streets. Who'd once maimed and killed. Everyone had been afraid of him. Men *and* women, he didn't discriminate. All were targets, if you were like Trisha. Like Felicity.

The thought of that made her shiver, pull her jacket even tighter. What the fuck was she doing out here? Her anger, her frustration had made her storm off – not that anyone had seen the storming, Felicity reminded herself. Her blind fury had caused her to tramp on and on until—

You're not alone, she said to herself again. A twisted version of what she'd said to her sister all those years ago when Danny left her high and dry. Wasn't comforting now though, wasn't comforting at all.

Felicity checked her phone, her maps. Her location. She actually hadn't drifted too far away from where she'd been heading. There was the dual carriageway, and... Yes, as she cocked her head she could hear the cars. Signs of life, of civilisation. Of people.

She just needed to cut across the—

Felicity turned sharply, felt sure there was someone... She thumbed on the button for the torch, flashing that around, but of course there was nobody there. Why would there be in this arse end of nowhere? Just her imagination, thinking about that dream after all this time.

Sighing, she continued on, following the map on the phone. The dot that told her where she was, where she'd need to go. Except... The screen started flashing, flickering.

Then it went dead.

"No, come on." Felicity smacked the side of the thing, like their dad used to do with electrical equipment (especially the old TV) to try and make it work. Yet more proof that she was morphing into them if ever it were needed. "Come *on!*" she said more loudly. Felt sure she'd charged the bloody thing before leaving the flat that evening. Or had she? Yes, she could remember plugging it into... or had that been yesterday? Or even the day before? The people at work were always on at her to buy one of those mobile battery things, in case of just such an emergency, but knowing her she'd forget to charge that up too.

Jesus, now she had no map or torch.

Never mind, she could remember roughly which direction to go in. Couldn't she?

You're not alone.

Stop it! she told herself. Now really wasn't the time. She was definitely alone out here, and was glad to be. No patrols, and she hadn't seen any CCTV cameras either so—

Cars... The sound of traffic. She could head in that direction, then she'd just follow the dual carriageway, circle back around – ha! – to get home. Easy. Felicity nodded, she had a plan of action. She started walking again, her heels clacking.

Clack-clack-clack...

Stomp.

She paused. Looked around again. Couldn't see anything, but she'd heard that, right? Above the sound of her heels, the sound of traffic in the distance. She shook her head. Continued on.

Clack-clack-clack-clack-clack…

Stomp. Stomp, stomp.

Felicity stopped again. But just for a second. She'd definitely heard it that time, footsteps. Heavy, like boots.

You're not alone.

Just like in the dream. But it's a good dream, right?

Felicity set off once more, pointing herself in the direction of those cars. *Clack-clack-clack-clack-clack-clack-clack…*

Stomp. Stomp, stomp, stomp, stomp. STOMP!

She speeded up. Needed to go faster. There was definitely someone behind her, she was sure of it. Someone, what, chasing, stalking her?

Come off it.

Look. Take another look.

She cast a glance over her shoulder, but again couldn't see a thing. Even if there had been someone there, it was too dark to—

No. No, it wasn't. There it was… a shape. Definitely a shape. *STOMP, STOMP.*

STOMP.

She could feel her heart beating in her chest, like some kind of animal trying to get out. No, this wasn't what was supposed to happen. Trisha should be here and—

Get a grip on yourself!

She slipped the useless phone back into her bag, reached for something else. The mace she always kept in there. You didn't have dreams, thoughts like those, without doing something about it. Without taking precautions. Anyone came anywhere near her, she was ready for them.

Felicity turned, holding up the spray.

Nothing. Nobody there.

"Fuck," she breathed. "Fucking fuck." And heard her father's voice again, saying, "Language, Felicity." Like that old sitcom with the small bloke wearing glasses they showed repeats of sometimes. "First the 'S' word, now the 'F' one."

Followed by tutting. "Fuck off!" she said then, but wasn't sure whether she was talking to her dad or whoever was out there.

There's nobody *out there.*

You're not alone! More emphatic this time. More insistent.

She turned again, started to run – or do her best in those heels. *Clack-clack-clack-clack-clack-clack-clack...* But then the clacking stopped, and she realised the heels were sinking into something. Grass. Muddy grass even. Making it harder to run.

STOMP-STOMP-STOMP...

You're not alone, you're not alone, you're—

Someone was gaining on her: the boots, those heavy boots.

Right, she thought, she'd had enough of this; spinning around again and holding the mace up – finger on the button to press it. And she thought she saw it then, the shape, the figure. Closer, almost upon her.

Before she began to fall.

Backwards.

Felicity was forever falling down the stairs at home when she was little. They'd lost count of the amount of times she'd done it, over and over. Was lucky to be alive, honestly, because any one of those times she could have broken her neck. But it did mean her body was used to it. Had learned how to cope with it.

Falling. Over and over. Not stairs this time, but down a slope. A grassy, muddy slope. Over and over, down and down. Rolling, rolling. Until she hit something: hard.

She blacked out a little, but quickly snapped to. Or at least she thought it was quick. Might have been hours. No. Not hours. Couldn't have been.

It was noisy now, loud and... bright. There were lights everywhere. Mostly speeding past her, there one moment and gone the next, accompanied by a *Zooming* sound. She was on her side, pressed up against the metal thing that had broken her fall – her roll – and a good job it had. Because she was only a few feet from the road, the dual carriageway. Cars doing about 50, 60, 70 mph. Maybe even more at this time of night, between the cameras. Her side hurt like a son of a bitch, but—

It stopped you, the crash barrier, she mumbled to herself. *A dead stop! Not quite.* And she laughed. *Would have been if you'd rolled onto that road!*

Dead, you'd have been—

Felicity tried to get up, struggled and flopped back down again. Her ribs were killing her. Broken? Maybe. Cracked, almost definitely.

Where was Dad when you needed him, to pick you up when you fell? Where was Trisha? Drunk back there in the club, that's where.

STOMP.

Felicity froze.

STOMP, STOMP, STOMP.

A different kind of sound, the heavy boots – but not following her now, instead making their way steadily down the slope. She had to get up. Ignore the pain and just lever herself—

She cried out in agony, but managed to get a knee under her. Managed to twist around to face whoever was wearing those boots. Suddenly wished that she hadn't.

In the lights from those passing cars, she could definitely see the shape more clearly now. The size of it! Felicity brought up the hand with the mace in, and realised the can wasn't there anymore. She'd dropped it at some point falling down this slope.

Not that it would have done any good, not against—

Christ, the size of—

She turned back to the road, the cars. Reached out a pleading hand. But they were going too fast to see her, to see anything that was happening beyond the barrier.

Dreaming, she told herself. *You're just dreaming again.*

It's only a dream.

And it's a good dream. Not that anyone would want... would be jealous of...

But where. Was. Patricia? She was supposed to be with her. Would always be...

You're not alone.

In that moment, Felicity wished to God that she was. As she was heaved backwards, away from the barrier. Lifted like she weighed nothing at all.

I wish! she thought to herself, disorientated, and let out another little laugh. Then a cry.

She was being lifted by the neck; she could feel the hand there. And as much as her ribs hurt, this hurt more. As she was spun around, to face the person who'd been chasing, stalking her. Not a figment of her imagination at all, or at least she didn't think so.

"But... but you're... You're *dead*..." she wheezed.

"Am I?" he said in a gruff voice, like it was coming from two different places at once. Two different—

Now the screaming. The screaming was still ringing in her ears.

Sadly, Felicity realised, it wasn't because of the people she'd left behind in the club. Her sister, her sister's friends, screaming and crying out for more.

It was closer than that, much closer.

And it was coming from her.

CHAPTER TWO

Screams.

Screaming so loud it woke her up immediately, that instinct kicking in. Not just a parent's instinct, the need to protect your children, but something that had been instilled in her a long time ago. A copper's instinct, a detective's instinct.

She was up and out of bed in moments, stumbling in the darkness but flinging open the door to her room, rushing down the corridor and yanking open another door. The nightlight in there illuminated the scene. Two beds, two boys no more than seven years of age. Both of them sitting up, the sheets gathered around them almost like togas. Both of them crying, both screaming their heads off.

Deborah Harrison was torn; she didn't know which of her two sons to go to first: Jack or James? Both were terribly upset. In the end she went over and pulled James free from his bedding, lifting him up like he was nothing (in reality he was getting heavier by the day, too heavy to keep doing this – but the adrenalin had definitely kicked in). Then, quick as a flash, Deborah rushed over to do the same with Jack, pulling him up and out of his own confinement, placing him in the crook of her free arm.

Drawing them close, heads nestling into her left and right shoulders, soaking the T-shirt she had on.

"Hey," she said gently. "Hey now, what's all this about?"

Jack started to say something into her shoulder, which James continued – none of the words were comprehensible. It was a tag-team kind of talking she'd grown used to. They did it when they were playing, too, splitting up when she was trying to catch them as if giving each other psychic cues.

"I can't tell a word you're saying," Deborah informed them, trying not to let her frustration show. The fact she hadn't been asleep that long – she never slept well these days, hadn't for a while – and that she was absolutely knackered. Thank God Izzy was at a sleepover with her mate, Charlotte from school. At least that's where she hoped her daughter was tonight. "Kids?" she prompted.

Inevitably it was Jack who lifted his head away and began trying to explain. "The...The lady..." he said between sobs. "She... she was... being..."

"Chased," James finished for him, having pulled his own head away from her shoulder to join in. Right at that moment, and not for the first time, the boy looked just like his father. Had that same way of saying something that cut to the very heart of it. Which made her pause for a second, but then Jack took up the thread and she refocussed on him:

"She was... she was falling," he continued. He also looked like his father, as well as James, but then he would do – them being identical twins. Both being *Jack's* twins. But although he shared that man's name, Jack (and she refused to call him Jack Jr. like he was in some kind of American sitcom) had more in common personality-wise with the original James, Jack (Sr)'s brother. From what she'd been told, anyway, because she hadn't really known the man. He'd died before she even met Jack. Killed. Murdered by The—

"And there... there were cars," James added, sketching out the scene more fully, like his dad might have done with his writing; non-fiction, history books, but he still knew how to paint a picture in words.

"Cars?" she asked. "And you both saw this?" It was only now occurring to her that they'd shared this same nightmare, from the way they were telling it. Experienced it at the same time. Not something that had ever really happened before, but then was it so uncommon given the link they shared?

Her sons nodded at the same time. Yes, they'd both seen it. The woman being chased. People being chased in dreams, now that was certainly a common thing. It meant that you were anxious – and both boys suffered from that – meant things were on your mind that you were avoiding, if she recalled her psychology correctly. And falling? A sense of inadequacy, that life was out of your control. They were a bit young to know all this, of course, but both had been having their issues at school recently, so maybe…

"Then," James went on, still crying. "Then the man… Then the man…"

"The bad man," Jack clarified. "He killed her."

Deborah looked from one boy to the other, blinking. Being chased, being killed. She racked her brains trying to think where they might have seen something like that in their waking life, definitely not anything she would have shown them on TV. Izzy then? Had they wandered in while she was watching a horror movie, one of those ones from the '80s she loved so much – and which Deborah loathed? Or maybe they'd been shown something at school on a phone. She'd refused to buy the boys mobiles, but a lot of the parents didn't have the same qualms about the internet that she did, about how much was so freely available. Kids these days could quite easily get around parental controls, knew more about technology than their parents. She asked them about all this and they said they hadn't been watching anything they shouldn't.

Then another thought occurred to her. "You haven't been

in my office have you, looking at the books? Maybe reading some of my notebooks?" Would they have understood a lot of it? Probably, yes, they were scarily intelligent like their dad. "Looking at photos?" She felt sure she'd locked all that away, or put it where they couldn't reach it. Research, but the kind of stuff that might trigger a dream like this one.

Both boys shook their heads at the same time.

"We haven't... haven't been doing anything... anything wrong, Mum," stated Jack.

"Not saying you have, sweetheart," she told him, but a little voice in her head was whispering that perhaps they were lying because they thought they might get into trouble. "Just trying to figure this out." Night terrors, they were common as well with kids of their age, weren't they. Thinking about monsters in the closet or under the bed, things with fangs and horns and—

But some monsters are real, Deborah thought. She'd seen them for herself. Seen what they could do.

"Okay, okay. Well, it was just a nightmare anyway. Only a dream, nothing to be frightened about. The bad man's not coming for you, he'd have to get through me first." She smiled what she thought was a suitably reassuring smile. "And I'm a pretty tough cookie, I'll have you know. I'd..." She began tickling them, fingers running up and down their sides until the sad tears turned to ones of laughter. And they were wriggling so much that she had to sit down on the closest bed, with one of them on either side.

"M-M-Mum," they said in unison. She knew what was coming next: "Can we sleep with you tonight?" broached Jack, the real spokesperson.

She'd been trying to train them out of this, thought she'd been doing a pretty reasonable job actually, not giving in to that particular knee-jerk. Not caving when they were upset and making them stay in their own room, in their own beds.

After all, as she kept reminding them, they also had each other. They'd never be alone.

That thought again stopped Deborah in her tracks. Their father had believed that once, that although they were apart locationally he'd always have his brother. Until someone had taken James away from him.

But her boys weren't the original James and Jack, were they? Regardless of the fact she'd called them that out of loyalty to their memories, because it felt like the right thing to do. Because she still wanted to feel some kind of connection with—

"P-P-P-lease, Mum," chimed in James now.

Deborah sighed; she always had trouble saying no to James. He was the one who needed more help with things, needed more encouragement, needed more... she didn't want to say love, because she loved them equally, but perhaps needed to know that love was there more than Jack did. He'd always been more self-sufficient.

Apart from tonight. They were both asking to come in with her tonight. "All right, okay. Just for the one night, though. Deal?" She held out her hand and they both shook it in turn, and she could still feel the tremble in their grips.

"The bad man won't come when you're around," Jack stated, nodding as if that was that. "Won't be able to find us."

James gazed at her and asked: "I-Is that right, Mum?"

She opened her mouth to answer, closed it again. Then said, "Come on, let's go try and get some kip, shall we?"

As she was ushering them out of the door, James turned and asked her again. He needed that confirmation, it seemed. "B-But you're sure? H-He won't find us in your room? The bad man?"

"I... I'm pretty sure, yes."

James nodded, before adding: "The man with two faces."

Deborah froze once again, stood stock still. "What?" she asked. "What did you just say?"

"The bad man," said James.

Now she couldn't speak at all, was trying to work out whether she'd heard what she heard before, or if it had just been tiredness.

"Mum? Mum, are you all right?" asked Jack, who'd stopped as well and was waiting for them to catch up.

She didn't reply.

Jack came back and took her hand. James did the same seconds later. Now it was her turn to tremble, but they were looking at her, worried. Searching her face to see if everything was okay. Deborah gave a half-nod, then went with them through the door, back along the corridor – the nightlight stretching out into the hall now – and inside her room.

They lay down on either side of her, snuggling into her armpits: mirroring how they'd been when she picked them up. In the safety and comfort of her double bed, it didn't take them long to drop off again. However, it took Deborah considerably longer.

Staring at the ceiling for hours and hours.

Not daring, not wanting to move an inch.

Wide awake in the dark.

CHAPTER THREE

Mornings were always gorgeous here.

No matter what time of year, no matter the season, regardless of how chilly or hot. It was getting closer to the time when the beach she was walking along – still a slight limp noticeable in her stride – would be much more crowded. Wouldn't take long for spring to give way to summer, but in turn that would bring days on the beach with the family, rather than quiet strolls alone. Both had their merits, it should be said.

Long, chestnut hair tied back so it didn't go everywhere in the breeze, Deborah bent down and picked up a pebble. She tossed it casually into the sea and watched it skim the surface. Bounce once, twice, three times as it got further and further out before disappearing into the water.

She'd often thought about getting a dog – and God knows the boys would have loved her forever if she'd done that. Just to have an excuse to walk it along here, throw a bit of driftwood for it to fetch or whatever, splashing out to paddle after it in the sea. But then three kids were enough of a challenge for her at the moment, and who needed an excuse to walk along here? She could please herself, once the school run was over and had the day to do what she wanted. Until she was forced to tackle the washing, ironing, cleaning, shopping...

Luckily she could fit her work in around all that too, and her mum Wendy was more than happy to still lend a hand when she could. Not that she had as much free time these days, now that she lived with Derek down in the village in their cosy little love nest. Like a couple of teenagers those two, sometimes. Actually no – they were *nothing* like teenagers, Deborah could attest to that. She wasn't constantly rowing with them for a start, or having to check up on where they were, worrying about the kind of trouble they might get into. The most those two would be doing was bingo and dance classes.

She thought then about Saturday, when Izzy – her daughter Isobel, fourteen going on pain in the arse, her reddish-brown hair now shot through with 'edgy' streaks – had finally rolled in, at about five when she said she'd be home by two to take the boys out to the park. When Deborah had asked where she'd been all this time, having to ask about three times before the girl finally looked up from her phone, Izzy had shrugged. Time had got away from her, she said, what was the big deal? She could take the boys to the park tomorrow, though she'd even had to be reminded about that in the end and reluctantly trudged off with them.

Deborah could recall the days when she'd been happy to spend time with her little brothers, delighted to play the big sister and take them places. Now they just seemed to be a burden, a chore to her. The same thing had happened when they'd relocated, from the city to the coast. At first Izzy had loved the idea: the sand, the sea, fish 'n' chips, the amusements and funfair. Now this place was soooo boring. Nothing ever happened here, apparently, and she couldn't wait to be eighteen so she could head back to the big lights of urban life.

And if she thought Deborah hadn't noticed the love-bite on her neck when she got home, she was dreaming.

Nope, don't think about dreams. You're having a nice, relaxing walk by the sea.

Deborah, the former detective. The former Detective Sergeant. Izzy would have to go a long way to pull the wool over her eyes, and while they were at it mints didn't cover the smell of alcohol as well as Izzy thought, either.

"You were just as bad at her age, Deborah," Wendy was fond of saying if she brought it up over a cup of tea or coffee.

"At her age? At fourteen?" Deborah would reply.

Wendy would rub her chin then, look down into whatever liquid she was drinking and say, "Well, maybe not fourteen. But they grow up so fast these days, don't they?"

"Only in some ways," Deborah would mutter. Then they'd change the subject to something else more palatable. Usually the soaps, which Deborah was still a huge fan of, though her life was starting to resemble one. If only the writer of this particular storyline would cut to the chase—

No, no mention of chases either.

—move on to something else, preferably in someone else's family, that would be grand. Give the Groves down the road a dose of fraud to deal with or whatever. She didn't mean that, she actually quite liked the Groves. Deborah was just sick of the drama in her personal life, was all.

She thought she'd left all that behind her years ago. Wendy hadn't been so laid back then about things, especially when she'd told her the news about the pregnancy – and about how it had happened. That was to say, she hadn't gone into details about it, just told her the father wasn't around anymore.

"Not around, what are you talking about?" she'd pressed her time and again. She'd known about the events in the underground cells at Norchester, or as much as anyone did who hadn't been there. Just not a great deal about the events leading up to it. About how Deborah had fallen in love with

Jack Foley, former suspect in the 'Twinkle' killings; a stupid moniker the media had come up with. When actually he'd been the brother of murder victim James, and taken it upon himself to trace that man's killer to their city, only to end up dead himself when they confronted…

The Gemini.

That's what the killer had called *himself*. The most vicious, malicious bastard Deborah had ever come across in her life. The events themselves had become a little hazy over time, and especially the more outlandish parts, but she remembered *him* well enough. Mainly because he had the face of her former boss, Detective Inspector Roy Mason. The Gemini's twin, though he hadn't known it until the killer had made contact. Mason had been the subservient twin, which worked out nicely for The Gemini and his plan for the endgame.

Deborah had barely made it out of all that alive. Jack, sadly, hadn't made it out alive at all. And it had been hard admitting that to Wendy.

"How do you mean, it was just one night?" her mother had demanded to know.

"It's kinda all it takes, Mum," Deborah had argued.

"How could you have been so… Didn't either of you think about, you know, precautions?" Her mother had gone red talking about such things and all Deborah could do was shake her head. It had been a spur of the moment sort of thing, her and Jack. In his hotel room, after he'd been attacked trying to save another victim. Something that had been building, yes, but it had taken them both by surprise – especially the depth of feelings that night released.

She'd mourned Jack like she'd known him for years. Felt more for him than she ever had for that shit of an ex-husband of hers, the abusive Phil: Izzy's biological father. Deborah had fantasies sometimes about Jack still being alive, about how he might have adopted Izzy, been there to help her bring up the boys. Because, God knows, Phil didn't want anything to do with his daughter in spite of her going through a period of needing to 'reconnect' with him.

Oh, he'd seen her a handful of times, before he got bored of it all, then he'd disappeared out of her life once again. Out of both their lives, thank Christ. Deborah had tried to explain that this was what he was like, but of course the damage had been done by then. Looking back, it was the start of the rift that was developing between them as the months went by. Izzy, for some reason, blaming her for Phil pissing off again. Probably because it was easier to accept than the truth that her dad couldn't care less about her.

But Jack hadn't been around back then, hadn't been around to help her defend the fact that she was having her babies – twins naturally, because what about this wasn't to do with twins! Hadn't been around for the birth, where Deborah had almost died again due to complications. Perhaps that was what had changed Wendy's mind, made her come around to the notion that these were her grandsons, made her feel ashamed that she'd once suggested – when she was particularly angry with her – that Deborah shouldn't keep them. If ever the boys found out about that...

Because they adored her, and vice versa. As soon as she'd seen them at the hospital, Wendy had fallen in love with James and Jack, just as Deborah had herself, when she'd recovered enough to be wheeled down to the neonatal intensive care unit to see them. They hadn't exactly had a great time of things either during the birth.

But, they were all alive, and in the months that followed actually thrived. Got their feet under them enough to make the move finally to their new home, up on the cliffs, not far from Armitage Bay. Even Izzy had been happy about it all – the boys, the relocation – back then.

Deborah had been given a generous pay-out by her former employers after telling them she was leaving (and after turning down a promotion). Probably so she wouldn't kick up a stink about Mason, that he'd worked in their arm of the Criminal Investigation Department for so long without any of them smelling a rat. Had been helping a serial killer right under their noses.

She hadn't blamed them for that, to be fair. Deborah hadn't spotted it herself till Mason had broken her leg and tried to choke her to death.

Deborah shoved her hands deep into the pockets of her long, dark-green coat, sighed, and looked up at the seagulls circling overhead. The blue sky with fluffy white clouds passing across it. The whole thing was like a postcard; actually she'd seen views like this used on postcards that were sold along the seafront. Here, you could forget all about the horrors of the past, the death and misery.

But there were certain things she never wanted to forget. Jack, for one. She missed him so, so much. It was silly, she'd only known him for a short time – yet it had seemed like a lifetime. That imagined life again.

Her mother had started telling her that now the boys were older, she should get out there again – bit of a turnaround from before. Get on the dating scene (probably inspired by meeting Derek when neither of them had been expecting it). Maybe snag a dad for the boys?

"They have a dad," was her standard response.

"A dad who's around," Wendy would offer next.

Deborah didn't say anything about the fact that he was still around. Sort of. That she still spoke to Jack, even saw him sometimes. That had started when she began feeling low after the birth, and it had helped pull her through. He'd appeared one afternoon when she was sitting in the nursery, shattered and slumped on a chair beside the cots. Just *ping*, and he was standing there looking down on his sons, smiling. That handsome face, the wavy hair that was kicking in now for his children.

Then he'd looked over at her with those grey-green eyes of

his and that smile had grown wider. Deborah had smiled back, tears in her eyes. It was then that she knew everything would be all right. He blew her a kiss and vanished again.

The rational part of Deborah's brain told her it was just her mind conjuring up the image, her exhausted mind. Then and the other times she'd seen him – usually around birthdays or Christmas, but more often when she was struggling. And she never told anyone, they'd have locked her up somewhere and thrown away the key! But she couldn't help thinking 'what if?' She'd seen... something in those underground cells, hadn't she? Something she'd blocked out perhaps, or hadn't been able to comprehend, but... sparks of light, escaping from The Gemini. Tiny lights, like stars.

Like souls?

That was why she talked to Jack, because she felt like he was never far away, and that somehow he could hear every word. He never spoke back, of course, or hadn't so far, but Deborah lived in hope. And really, did he need to? That same feeling everything would be okay that he'd given her in the nursery, always accompanied a sighting. Even ideas sometimes. It was Jack who'd given her a nudge about the line of work Deborah was in now, she felt sure it was. Something she'd be good at, that she could fit around other things.

Still connected to her old job, something she could do with confidence. She'd investigated crimes for a living, so why not write about them? It was something she'd always toyed with – when she was at school she was forever being told off in English classes because her essays and stories were much longer than they should be. When she wrote her reports for the police, she had to hold back on the descriptions. "Stick to the facts," one of her superiors had said when she first started out, but she'd wanted to put in so much more.

Now she could. Now she could let her imagination run riot, although that didn't stop her agent and editor telling her to cut a lot of it out. Jack had been a writer, and she'd collected all the books he'd ever written in the past, before he'd set off on his quest to track down his brother's killer. Historical books, but his style wasn't dry like you see in a lot of those kinds of tomes. They carried you along. Her favourites were the ones about Robin Hood or King Arthur, or explorers like Columbus (his own particular favourite), or even tracing the origins of fairy tales.

So, when she thought about young James developing those skills, maybe he wasn't just channelling his father but also his mother?

Once the idea was in her head, that was that. Crime fiction, detectives solving crimes. She'd wondered about going into true crime, but the idea that everyone and their grandmother wanted her to do something based on what had happened in Norchester put her off. Yes, she would have been paid a lot to hand something like that in (though she had to ask who would believe it!), but Deborah just didn't want to go there again.

In the end she figured it was best to stick to fiction, making up the crimes, her cops and even the locations. The interest in a factual book about her own career had put her in touch with people in the writing world, publishers who were eager to look at anything she sent, including pitches for novels. Some weren't for them, but one caught their eye – all about a father trying to solve the murder of his daughter in a market town not unlike the one she'd grown up in. She wasn't much of a planner, so she'd decided that she would write it as she investigated cases in real life, trying to get to the truth and the identity of the murderer as much of a mystery to her as anyone else till the end. It was a way of working that just seemed right to her.

Although they could get her a much bigger advance if she did it under her own name, Deborah had insisted that they use a pseudonym. If this book was going to be successful then she wanted it to be on its own merits, not because it was written by the woman who'd survived The Gemini.

And it had done okay, well enough to get a second – set by the sea, inspired by where she was living – and even a third. Then she was flying, her readership building, even getting film and TV interest. Enough to keep them afloat at any rate, to eke out the compensation money. It kept them ticking over. She wasn't worried about the boys at all, though. They had a healthy trust fund waiting for them when they were older, courtesy of Jack's will, which stated that any offspring he had would be well looked after. His parents had both died in a plane crash when he was fourteen, and with James also deceased Jack had inherited their estate. Deborah recalled him telling her his family was rich, but she hadn't realised quite how well off until she found out about all that. Money on his mother's side, something about mines.

There were instructions left to help out if they ever needed cash, too, his solicitors had told her. If ever any of them needed it as a family, so the boys would never go short. Maybe he'd been thinking about his ex, Stephanie, when he made that will. About starting a family with her? But she'd done the dirty on him, two-timing with his brother – something that had caused a massive row, ensuring they hadn't spoken to each other ever again. Jack had obviously never got around to changing the will again, or perhaps he'd simply hoped he might have kids at some point so let it ride?

Didn't matter, Deborah hadn't had to touch any of his fortune – and didn't intend on doing so. The boys deserved it, they were his family line, but she... What had she been exactly? Not his wife, certainly, though that might have followed if they'd had the time. More fantasies about him getting down on one knee somewhere romantic, like Italy or Paris, bringing out an engagement ring. She knew him well enough to understand he'd tell her she was being proud not using his money; that it was there for exactly that purpose. To help the living. But it made Deborah feel good to know they'd got by on her own hard work.

She was dreading the day someone leaked who it *really* was writing those thrillers, however. Ironically her agent and editor probably weren't, and she was surprised nobody had let it slip already. The public appearances alone would ensure the books sold in their millions, but at the same time they'd also be asking for trouble. Some of the fans – of The Gemini, rather than her books – could be a little… strange.

No, she preferred it as it was now, their quiet anonymous life.

A life where she could enjoy walks like this one, gorgeous scenery. Living the drea—

What did we say about mentioning dreams, Deborah?

But now it had been mentioned, she couldn't help flashing back to Friday night and that screaming. Her boys having their nightmare about the 'bad man'. The man who'd chased that woman.

The man with two faces.

She'd misheard, that was all. Couldn't have been. Yet she hadn't asked them again about it, hadn't clarified what they'd actually seen in the nightmare. Part of her hadn't wanted to stir things up again, she'd only just managed to get them back in their own beds last night, early because it was school the next morning. And they'd had decent nights on Friday, eventually, and Saturday – which was more than could be said for Deborah.

But wasn't there a large part of her that really didn't want to know? Didn't want confirmation that they'd seen a stalker with two faces. Didn't want to think maybe they were 'seeing' something, like their dad had once done. Said he'd done… She believed that, didn't she? That he'd seen through the killer's eyes, and because The Gemini had stolen James' eye. It was no more incredible than talking to ghosts, when all was said and done. A ghost allowed his twin to witness the murders as they happened.

Wasn't the same, couldn't have been some kind of trace memory anyway, because for her kids to have seen the bad man with two faces it meant they weren't seeing through his eyes at all. Wasn't his point of view, but rather they were watching things like an observer on the side-lines. It just leant credence to the notion that someone had found out about her past, maybe had been talking about it and their own kids overheard – then said something to Jack and James at school. That was worth asking about… discreetly. Wasn't it?

Or perhaps she should just let the whole thing lie, leave it alone and hope it went away. That might be the best course of action, Deborah decided, as she headed for the bleached white steps that would take her back up to the cliff-tops.

That would take her to the lane that wound down towards her house, with its creamy-white stonework and brown roof; far enough back from the edge for erosion to not be a problem… yet, and for the fence around the property to merely be a precaution. But near enough so they could still see the ocean. And a good walk to the nearest house sharing that same space, to give them the privacy Deborah loved and Izzy hated so much.

Privacy, that was, apart from today.

As Deborah got closer, she spotted a blue Land Rover Defender parked next to her own yellow Wrangler. She didn't recognise the vehicle, so was cautious on approach. They didn't get many visitors up here, not that many people knew where they were. Just Wendy, Derek and a handful of others.

Her mind was racing. Press? Fans? Had her secret finally come out? It was only a matter of time, she supposed.

But no. She saw the figure on the doorstep, who'd left the gate hanging open, and was wearing a coat that was only a little shorter than Deborah's, but camel-coloured. She was rapping on the door with the knocker, then realised she wasn't alone and turned.

The smile she gave was at least as wide as Jack's, and when she did so Deborah could see those tell-tale dimples in her cheeks. Face proudly reflecting her one third Chinese genes. Her hair was short now, cut to her shoulders; indeed it was like they'd switched, Deborah having grown hers where once it had been similar to her caller's. Every time she saw this woman, it threw her back to that time – early on in their friendship – when they'd both been at an abandoned factory on Fagin's Row, staring down at a 'homeless person' who'd had his hand lopped off.

"Rosy!" Deborah called out. "How lovely to see you!"

Rosy Lim covered the rest of the distance between them and they both opened their arms for a long hug. When it broke off, Rosy smiled again and said, "Well, if it isn't the bestselling author P—"

Deborah placed a finger on her lips, shushing her, and Rosy couldn't help laughing. "Wha…" she mumbled and her friend removed the finger. "There's no one around."

"You never know," said Deborah, laughing herself.

"Paranoid much?"

"Why, who told you that?" They both chuckled now and it felt good.

"Thanks for the signed copy of the latest, by the way. Haven't read it yet, I'm sorry to say."

Deborah shrugged. "Don't worry, I know how busy you are."

"I'm not the only one, though! What's this now, book five?"

"Six, actually. And they've just sent the galleys over for seven."

"I have no idea what you just said. Sounds like something to do with a ship."

They laughed together again. "It's been, what? How many months? And you've got a new car, I didn't recognise it."

Rosy nodded. "Pay rise. And it was just before Christmas when I saw you last."

"Of course, yeah. The kids loved their presents by the way."

"How are they all?"

"They… we're all good, thanks."

Rosy put a hand on her cheek. "You look tired. Everything okay?"

Deborah leaned into her hand, clasped her own over it and nodded at the same time. "Yeah, all good," she repeated.

Rosy looked at her sideways, as they both dropped their hands. "Hmm."

"Anyway, let's get you inside and I'll make a cuppa."

"Sounds wonderful." Her smiled slipped a little, the dimples fading, and it was Deborah's turn to look sideways at her mate.

"What?" she asked. "This isn't a social call, is it?"

"Not *just* a social call, no," Rosy replied.

"Okay. Should I be worried?" said Deborah as she took out her keys and unlocked the door, holding her hand out now for Rosy to enter.

"Put the kettle on," said Rosy. "Then we'll talk."

CHAPTER FOUR

They talked all right.

Lots of small talk, lots of beating around the bush, going round the houses. As Deborah shrugged off her own coat, took Rosy's and hung them both up – then the pair went into the kitchen and Deborah fetched the kettle to fill it with water. "Have I told you how much I love this place," Rosy said to her, taking in the white walls and wooden work surfaces, wandering down through into the utility nook where the tea, coffee and sugar jars were. "You live in a chocolate box picture, do you know that?"

Deborah gave a small snort, then followed her and placed the kettle back on its base before flicking it on. "I wouldn't put it quite that way."

"I would. You've done all right for yourself, you have."

"What about you? A pay rise, you said. What was it, a promotion?"

Rosy thought for a moment. "More like a bit of overtime."

"Right," said Deborah, but made it sound more like a question. Rosy didn't bite. Instead she was asking again about the family.

"Oh, you know... The boys are okay, not sleeping that

well, hence the…" She pointed at the bags she knew she had under her eyes, the blackness around them.

"What's up?"

"Just a few nightmares. Night terrors, I guess." Deborah shrugged, dragging out a couple of mugs from an overhead cupboard and dropping a teabag in each one. "It's about that time for them, isn't it? Although I don't remember Izzy having those, really. She's more of a terror herself now."

"And how is the young lady, still hoping to be the next Taylor Swift?" When Rosy had been there last, she'd been telling her about going on some kind of TV talent contest, how it was the best way to make it big.

"She moved on to acting, another fad. Wanting to be the next Scarlett Johansson… No, I suppose she'd be a little bit too old now for Izzy's generation, wouldn't she? No offence, Scarlett. Florence Pugh, then. Now I'm just naming Avengers, aren't I."

"Are you?" asked Rosy. "No idea. Can't remember the last time I watched a movie all the way through, or grabbed much time to watch the telly, come to that."

"You're telling me you don't have time for *Emmerdale*? Or *Corrie*? What on earth are we going to chat about?" Deborah chuckled as the kettle at last finished boiling, and she poured hot water over some tea bags, before disposing of them. "You still take it without milk?"

Rosy nodded, gratefully accepted the mug she was offered, which had some cartoon cats on it and the phrase 'Show Us Your Kitties' underneath. Deborah had the much more tasteful one with the unicorn on the side and the legend: 'Bitch, please – I will stab you with my horn!'

They retired to the living room, Rosy almost tripping over a stuck-up bit of rug. "Yeah, sorry about that. Kids."

"You'll go flying on it if you're not careful," Rosy warned.

They sat down on the huge leather couch, Deborah pulling

two coasters towards them for the glass coffee table. "I say again, I love this place," Rosy commented.

"It comes with hot and cold running rows at the moment."

"Izzy again? You mentioned something about her being a terror."

Deborah nodded. "And I thought the terrible twos period was bad. It's got nothing on the teenage daughter phase, let me tell you. There's some party she's on about going to soon, but there'll be boys, drink."

"She's told you that?"

"'Course she hasn't, but I'm not stupid. She's still too young for all that... isn't she?"

"I would have said so, but then I wasn't chasing boys at her age." Rosy smiled sadly. "Quite the opposite. And that brought its own set of problems." She'd told Deborah before about how hard it had been growing up as a gay woman in her household, how difficult it had been to come out eventually to her parents. They didn't really accept that part of her life even today, from what Deborah could gather.

"But you're happy now, with Kiz." Deborah spotted the bristle. The last time she'd seen them both together – which admittedly had been over a year ago, when they'd stopped off on the way back from visiting Kizza's folks in Scotland and they'd all gone for a drink – the couple had certainly seemed that way. Always touching, holding hands, finishing each other's sentences; they'd just moved in together and seemed pretty settled. It made Deborah long for that kind of closeness again, actually. Not that she'd ever really had that with Phil. Or with Jack. Well, they'd never had a chance to do all that kind of stuff. They'd been robbed of it. "Aren't you?" she asked.

"We're... It's complicated," Rosy told her. Deborah waited for more, but her friend was eager to move the conversation on again. She'd tell her when she was ready... probably. "Hey, how's your mum getting on with... what's his name again?"

"Derek? Oh, they're doing just fine. Who'd have thought it, eh? All those years since Dad died and she never really… But now, well, there's no stopping her. Not that I'd want to, I think it's great. A second chance and all that, and he's a good bloke. Looks after her. That's all you can hope for, isn't it?"

Rosy nodded, again a little sadly Deborah thought. "And it never would have happened if you hadn't moved here."

"No, I suppose not. Life's funny sometimes, isn't it."

"Yeah," said Rosy, picking up her mug and taking a sip of her tea. "Funny. Do you ever miss it?"

Deborah frowned. "Sorry?" For a second she thought her friend was asking about being part of a couple.

"Norchester?"

"Oh, right. That's an easy one to answer: No."

Rosy shook her head. "No, right. I don't suppose you would after… How about being on the force?"

Less easy. "Sometimes. I miss making life safer for people, helping them, y'know. But in the end the price was too high. I was putting myself, my family at risk, and that's never acceptable, is it?"

Rosy gave a little shake of her head, but it looked more like she was lamenting Deborah's lost career than agreeing with her. "You were so good at it, though."

"Yeah, well, I'm good at something else now. The writing, remember?"

"Not quite the same, is it?"

"It's better. In a lot of ways, it's so much better, Rosy." She drank some of her tea as well now, growing a little uncomfortable with this topic.

"You ever think about what happened back there?" Rosy asked her next, making things even more awkward.

"I-I try not to." Try, but fail. And people asking her outright didn't help.

"That was some weird shit," Rosy pressed on. "Wasn't it."

A statement rather than a question. "Sometimes it's hard to escape it, wherever you go."

"What do you mean?"

Rosy gave a shrug. "Something went down before you moved to this place, not far from here. You know about that?"

Deborah had heard the tall tales, of course she had. "That thing on the pier, down in Armitage Bay. The guy with the blue eyes. Something to do with some gangsters... Most people don't remember it at all."

"Or don't want to," Rosy replied. "The mind has a way of protecting itself. They ever find out anything about what happened to your cousin?"

More weird shit. Deborah's cousin on her father's side, Gemma, had disappeared some years ago during a strange storm at another seaside location, Willerton Castle. None of the witnesses could remember very much about any of that, either. But some, if you got enough booze inside them, would talk about monsters. Things they may or may not have seen out of the corner of their eye. And you had to wonder... She shook her head, though. Why was Rosy talking about all of that?

Not just *a social call.*

"Some people know the truth. They cover things up, because most folk wouldn't be able to handle it," Rosy explained. "You get to see little bits of it, parts of the whole, in my line of work. Get access to certain things."

"As a pathologist?" Deborah was confused. "What are you—"

Rosy turned to face her friend, put her mug down and told Deborah to do the same. Then she took her hands. "Deborah, last Friday night there was an... incident in Norchester."

"Incident? What kind of incident?"

Rosy sucked in a breath, then came right out and said it. No more small talk, no more houses, no more bushes: "An attack. A murder."

Deborah was beginning to wish she hadn't put down her tea, because she was swallowing dryly; all the liquid in her mouth had gone. She shook her head. No, murders still happened in the world. Happened all the time everywhere. It was awful, upsetting, heart-breaking, especially for the loved ones, but—

"Last Friday night, Deborah, someone killed a twin," Rosy stated. There it was, the thing she'd come here to tell her – and suddenly Deborah didn't want to hear any more. Felt like clapping her hands to her ears so it wouldn't go in; perhaps that was why Rosy had taken those hands in the first place. She needed to hear this, no matter how hard it was for her to process it. Needed to hear the rest because it was important.

"Her body was found by the side of the dual carriageway, had fallen or rolled down the incline. A driver spotted it early on Saturday morning. Time of death was roughly about midnight, she'd been there all night."

Midnight… Chased… Falling…

The bad man. The bad man with—

"She was stabbed with something that had two points."

"A twin-pronged fork," said Deborah under her breath.

Rosy nodded. "And she was missing a foot."

Now Deborah couldn't swallow at all.

"But that's not the strangest part of all this," Rosy continued. There was a *stranger* part? Deborah was finding that hard to believe, at least until Rosy told her the next bit. "You know the vic, Deborah. She was a part of the original investigation into The Gemini. Or rather her sister Patricia was. The victim has now been formally ID'd as Felicity Bailey."

Another whisper, barely audible: "Jesus."

Thoughts were coming too fast, horrible images accompanying them. Deborah pulled her hands away, and stood up sharply. "Would… would you…" She couldn't get the next few words out, the 'excuse me' bit; had to rush off to the downstairs toilet. Only just got there in time, before she felt the breakfast of toast and marmalade she'd eaten that morning come up into the toilet pan. Even after she'd been sick, even after there was nothing left, Deborah still kept heaving.

There was a knock at the door. "Debs? Debs, are you okay in there?"

Okay? Was she serious? How on earth could she possibly be okay after hearing… hearing all that. But the nausea was subsiding, and moments later Deborah felt able to stand and flush the chain. Splashed water on her face and looked up into the mirror, looked at her tired, much older, reflection – her twin – staring back at her. Christ Almighty.

"Debs?" called Rosy again and she opened the door, held a hand up to let her know she didn't need any help.

Then cocked her head back, before asking: "How? How, Rosy? How has this happened? Why is it happening again?"

"I don't know," she answered honestly. "Look, come back with me to the living room. Sit down again. Do you want another tea? I'll make it? Or… or something stronger, if you have it?"

Deborah looked at her watch. "It isn't even midday."

"Hey, it's happy hour somewhere in the world." Rosy sighed. "Sorry."

It wasn't here. Not happy hour at all, not a happy day, week… "Top cupboard on your right as you walk in," she told Rosy. "There's some brandy."

Deborah walked back into the living room like a zombie, stiff and her mind elsewhere. It wasn't racing anymore, if anything it had actually slowed down to a crawl. Rosy returned moments later with a couple of glasses about a quarter full of brown liquid. "Good for shock. Trust me, I'm a doctor."

Deborah took a sip, felt her stomach rolling again, but she

managed to keep it down. "Right, so… a copycat," she said, even before Rosy could sit herself.

Rosy didn't have an answer to that question either, just took a drink. "Like I said, weird shit."

"There are enough people who are obsessed with the case, that someone…" Deborah tried to push the memory of her boys out of her head, the dream last Friday night at precisely the time Felicity Bailey was being – yes, say it! – hunted. Killed. "What the hell was she doing out there at night all alone in the first place?"

"Probably thought it was safe enough. Believe it or not, Norchester has cleaned up its act a lot. More CCTV coverage, more beat patrols. It's one of the safest places in the country now, in fact."

"Tell that to Felicity Bailey," said Deborah, and took another sip of the brandy.

"From what I understand there'd been a bit of a falling out with her sister. Nothing major, just a little jealousy about a forthcoming wedding, I think. Oh, she was coming from a hen do at a club in town, *Flamers* or something I think it's called." Deborah thought back to the older Jack and James now, the falling out about a girl in the past. Surely whoever Patricia was marrying wouldn't have been two-timing her with her sister? "Enough to force her to leave there before the end anyway."

"Oh God, Patricia must be mortified."

Rosy looked down and gave a little nod. "Blames herself, as you would. I mean, it was her twin."

"Yeah. So that was what you came out here to tell me."

"I thought it was a face-to-face conversation, before you heard it from someone else." She raised the glass. "And I think I was right." Rosy had that odd look on her face again.

"There's more, isn't there?" said Deborah. More than another Gemini killing, more than young Felicity Bailey being murdered and having her foot cut off?

More than the dream? Don't mention that, you haven't mentioned that. Keep it to yourself, Deborah.

"You asked about the extra work earlier."

"The overtime," said Deborah.

"Yeah. Overtime." Rosy looked off to the side. "You might not remember, but there was a group who came in right at the end of the stuff with The Gemini." She did remember. The S... something or other. Rosy filled in the other letters for her. "The SCI. Serial Crime Initiative."

"Right, yes." Deborah pointed at Rosy. "Hold on, are you saying that you're working for them now?"

"Sort of. Not quite. I'm being considered. They actually head-hunted me."

Probably not the best choice of words, given the circumstances, the hunting part anyway – although people only had one head, didn't they. Not two. And The Gemini only took souvenirs that came in pairs.

But it triggered a memory, the gruesome sight of that man's body dropping to the floor in pieces; his severed head rolling towards her, revealing the face of the man – other than Jack – she'd trusted most in the world. Roy Mason, her guvnor. She blinked once, twice, tried to focus on something else; a more comforting thought. The Gemini was dead. She'd *seen* him die. This couldn't be him. Deborah realised Rosy was still talking, that she'd missed something, and asked her to go back.

"I was just saying, you should see the stuff they have access to. They're an international cross-border division with specific aims, specialising in unusual crimes or occurrences. Things that can't always be explained by ordinary means. Their headquarters down south is just jaw-dropping, Deborah."

"Was that all in the spiel from the welcome video they showed you there? Sounds more like a cult to me."

"Hardly," said Rosy. "They've stopped a few, though. Are

looking into a few others. There's this one in particular called The Order of the S—"

"If I recall correctly," Deborah interrupted, "they swooped in and gathered up all the evidence from The Gemini case? And it was never seen again. Are they the ones who make sure things get covered up?"

"No, not exactly. I can't say for definite that they don't answer to those who do, though. With regards to The Gemini, it was totally necessary. They wanted to study all the evidence. Study *him*." Rosy rubbed the back of her neck. "I've read his diaries, Deborah. What was left of them after the fire damage; they were found down in the underground cells. Haven't seen the originals, obviously. But the files, the scanned in pages. Makes one of your bestsellers look like... He was something we haven't really encountered before, that guy. He was—"

"I know what he was. He was a butchering psychopath," Deborah said flatly. Yet she remembered the conversations with Jack about all this, about what that 'man' might be. A freak of nature perhaps, Jack speculating that he may have absorbed his own twin in the womb or something – hence the two faces, the incredible strength. Except he hadn't done anything of the kind. Roy Mason had been The Gemini's twin, had *shared* his appearance, and he'd been alive and well and pretending to be a good guy. When all along he was—

The bad man.

One of the bad men anyway. Not the worst of the two, for sure.

Rosy had been talking again and Deborah had missed it. "I'm having a bit of trouble taking all this in frankly," she said by way of an apology.

"Understandable, but you do absolutely need to hear this last bit." Rosy let out a slow breath. "You see, as soon as they found out about the killing the SCI sent a few people to Norchester. They're currently running the investigation."

Wow! thought Deborah. *They really do have a lot of power if they can steam in and do that.* It would never have happened on her late boss Superintendent Bingham's watch. Only it did, she reminded herself. That and more.

"And they sent me here to ask you something."

Deborah touched her chest. "Ask *me*?"

"Yes. Deborah, you're the one who stopped The Gemini last time, why wouldn't they want your involvement?"

"*I* didn't stop him. Jack did that, stabbing him with his own weapon – and he paid the price for it, too." God, how he'd paid the price: thrown across those underground cells like a ragdoll, bones crunching against the wall, where she'd crawled across and found him afterwards. And they'd exchanged those final words that had been rattling around in her brain ever since:

"*I... I had to come... you... understand? You... you think we might... might have had something?*"

"*We* do *have something, always will.*"

She felt tears pricking at the corners of her eyes.

"You were there, you helped," Rosy broke in. "Plus you took down Mason."

Deborah looked away, dabbing at her eyes with the back of her sleeve. "Yeah, I distracted him by letting him cripple me."

"Then you rammed a knife up into his chin."

As satisfying as it was tragic, because she'd still cared about Mason at the time. Because she hadn't yet adjusted to the betrayal, the fact that he'd been involved in the brutal case they'd both been working. It had just been instinct, pure and simple. He was trying to kill her – she defended herself, by killing him instead. Deborah was by no means squeamish, but the thought of that right now was turning her stomach again.

This whole conversation was turning her stomach, honestly. And the next bit didn't do anything to help with that.

"They wanted me to reach out and see if you'd come back.

Come back to Norchester and assist them with their enquiries."

"What? You're kidding."

Rosy shook her head. "You know this case inside out, you know The Gemini."

"But this *isn't* The Gemini, Rosy. He's gone."

"You can say that again," she muttered under her breath.

"What was that?" asked Deborah and even as Rosy was opening her mouth to explain, she wished she hadn't.

"About a month or so ago there was a break in." Rosy paused to pinch the bridge of her nose. "Well, they think it was a break in at the SCI… Might have been an inside job, they're still investigating that. Anyway, the upshot of it is, he was taken."

More rolling of her stomach. "Who? Who was taken?"

"The Gemini, Deborah. Someone stole his remains."

CHAPTER FIVE

It had been a bad day.

Even worse than yesterday, though that had sort of turned into an okay day in the end. Rosy had stayed, walking with her down into the village to meet the kids from school: first the twins, who had been delighted to see their Aunty Rosy again – she was a natural with children and Deborah had told her so on many occasions – then Izzy, who'd torn herself away from her phone just long enough to grunt a hello.

They'd gone out for a bite to eat at the local family pub, *The Seagull*. Deborah's stomach had calmed down by then; she was actually quite hungry, having not had anything to eat since that morning, but had stuck to fizzy water to drink. It had been a pleasant time, surprisingly, and they'd walked Rosy back to her car again and seen her off.

Once she'd gone, Izzy had been on at her about that bloody party again, but Deborah was miles away and told her she'd think about it. That had been her first mistake. She'd just wanted the pestering to stop, frankly. She had a lot on her mind and there wasn't the headspace for parties and boys and all that crap, which to a teenager is all important but to

Deborah, right at that moment, was the last thing she wanted to entertain.

All she could think about was the case, so long ago. The Gemini, the killings, Jack. Rosy and her request. To help that SCI group investigate this new murder, the copycat (had to be). Couldn't be The Gemini, regardless of the fact his body, which was in pieces, had been taken. Could it? That was too fantastical to even contemplate, The Gemini rising from the dead like Dracula or something. Although hadn't she once compared him to just such a creature? That was coming back to her now, the vampire thing. Sucking not the blood out of twins, but, what, their essence?

Their spirits?

And then Jack 'staking' him with his own twin-pronged fork. Slaying the undead monster, only for it to return in the next movie. Good old Christopher Lee had been ash, and he still came back, didn't he.

This wasn't that. This was real life, and in real life people who'd been ripped to bits didn't put themselves back together like Humpty Dumpty and stroll out of facilities to take up their old hobbies. Maybe whoever killed Felicity Bailey had stolen the remains of The Gemini – though according to Rosy, they'd have had a job breaking into that place. Not your average thief, then, but if they were emulating that particular killer they wouldn't be.

But to do what with them? Set up some kind of shrine? Was all this a revenge thing? It was starting to feel personal, certainly, a bit too close to… Not here, Norchester. Her *old* home. She couldn't risk all of this, her new life by the sea. Her perfect life.

Perfect apart from Izzy, that was – but she was just your typical teenage girl nowadays. Much easier to deal with than superhuman stalkers, slashers. It was why she'd had to turn Rosy down, politely decline; wasn't that how they phrased it?

Like she was telling her she was too busy to attend a wedding, a party.

The damned party! Deborah wished she'd never heard that word, wished such things didn't exist. Because after a stressful day of scouring the internet, looking for anything on the Bailey murder – and finding nothing yet, probably because the SCI were keeping it under wraps; how long they could do that for was anyone's guess – and going down rabbit holes concerning The Gemini, she'd forgotten all about what she said the day before.

"You *promised*!" Izzy had snapped.

"I never promised anything," said Deborah. "And you might want to watch the tone, young lady."

"Young lady, like I'm a fucking kid!"

"And watch the language too."

"Fuck you," Izzy had barked, folding her arms over her chest. The twins had retreated off to their room to play a game, getting out of the way of yet another fight that was escalating. Probably not a bad idea, Deborah wouldn't have minded joining them.

"You think that's the way you're going to get what you want? Saying that to me?" asked Deborah.

Izzy paused for a moment, perhaps thinking there was a chance she'd get her way if she behaved. "You said you'd think about it, Mum."

Deborah sighed. That's right, she had. "I did, I have," she lied. "And it's a no, I'm afraid." The second person she'd had to let down in twenty-four hours: both with excellent reasons.

"But whyyy?" Izzy strung out the word, reminding Deborah of that comedy character who'd been so popular at one time, done by the same bloke who'd made Loadsamoney from… Loadsamoney.

"Because… there's going to be boys at this party, right?" Izzy didn't have a reply for that, of course there would be. "And drink?"

"You can't talk, I could smell it on your breath when you rocked up with Rosy yesterday. Boozing in the daytime with your mate! One rule for you and another for—"

"Izzy, you're fourteen!" She didn't want to get into why she'd needed the brandy, why she'd had two or three in the daytime before they'd set off for the kids. Couldn't explain it was because things were getting dredged up that really shouldn't be, that Deborah thought she'd left buried long ago.

"Nearly fifteen! In a couple of years, I'll be able to do whatever the hell I want!" Izzy growled. "No one can stop me."

"Yes, well, until then—"

"You make it sound like you're so holier than thou. Like you've never gone around boozing, sleeping with guys."

"Well, I haven't," said Deborah. She'd had her moments when she was young, but nothing like this, and not this soon. It had only been five minutes since Izzy was tiny, holding her hands up for her mum. Needing her.

Izzy pointed upstairs. "Then how do you explain *them*? Your beloved sons, who you're all about these days. You know, sometimes I wish they'd never been..." She shook her head, but the end of that sentence was abundantly clear. "One night, Mum, and you barely even knew the guy."

Here it was, more of the past coming back to haunt her, just in a different way; the things she'd talked about with Isobel to try and make her understand. Glad that she did, never realising it would be used as ammunition in the future against her. "That... that was different, it was—"

"Yeah, different. Different to *my* dad, who you'd known for ages. Who you married. Knew that other bloke well enough to fuck him though, right? A suspect in one of your cases? I'd like to think I had better taste than—"

Then her hand was up, the slap coming out of nowhere. No, not nowhere – provoked definitely, and intentionally so.

Instinct, like Mason. *Good job there hadn't been a knife around, eh Deborah? Who knows what might have happened then?*

No.

Two very different scenarios, opposite ends of the scale. One, a guy trying to end her life. This... But both wounding her, both a betrayal.

Izzy's hands had gone to her face, covering up the redness. Her eyes wide open, her mouth the same. She hadn't said a thing then, absolutely nothing. Deborah had been expecting an "I hate you!" mirroring that comedy character, but nothing.

"Izzy, I'm so sorry. I—" She didn't even really know what she was apologising for. It had been a horrible thing to say, and about Jack! But she was the grown up here, she should have been able to take it. Might have been able to if it hadn't been for Rosy's visit and the things she'd told her. But what her daughter said next, and said calmly, coldly, eyes narrowed to almost slits, had been so much worse.

"I'm glad he's dead. I wish you were too."

Then she left the room, and hadn't spoken to her since. Eventually, and choking back the tears, Deborah had made dinner – which she'd eaten with the boys, hardly saying a word herself – and left a plate outside Izzy's door for her. A couple of hours later, when she'd checked, the plate was still there untouched.

She'd tucked the boys into bed, and for once they went without any kind of argument – not that they really argued with her about anything, not like the one she'd just had with Izzy. Protest then, might be a better word. They hadn't said a thing, which made her wonder whether they'd heard some of that row she'd had with their sister. Had they heard the nonsense about her wishing they'd never been... born? Izzy hadn't said it, but she'd definitely meant it; in the moment, she'd meant it. Deborah knew it was coming from a place of jealousy, because she was close to the twins and was anything but with her daughter these days – and you had to take into account the hormone situation – but it had still stung. That and—

"I'm glad he's dead. I wish you were too."

That one would stay with her for a long time to come, years probably. Her mother would tell her that people say things in temper sometimes they don't mean, but if anything Deborah had learned that the reverse was often true. Like drink, anger brought out what people were really thinking. Both used to do that with Izzy's *precious* father Philip, at any rate.

None of which stopped Deborah from grabbing a bottle of wine and curling up on the sofa that night, flicking off the lights and flicking through the dross on TV until she finally found one of those satellite channels which showed old episodes of the soaps.

She drank and lost herself in the dramas of Dot Cotton and the Sugdens, the Battersbys and Ken and Deidre's turbulent marriage. Did that till she couldn't keep her eyes open anymore. If the boys wanted her bed tonight, they were welcome to it – she wasn't moving from her comfortable couch.

It had been a bad day. A bad couple of days.

But things were only going to get worse.

♊

Deborah woke when a bright light shone in her face.

Was it morning already? Couldn't be, surely? She still had a bit of a buzz on from the wine, and hadn't drunk all that much – had she? She prised one eye open and looked over at the bottle on the coffee table, only about a quarter full. More than she'd realised then. But that light—

It was too bright and too artificial to be the sun, coming from a different direction anyway: the kitchen and utility nook where she'd forgotten to close the blinds. Deborah snapped herself awake, taking in the TV screen where the channel had switched to some infomercial about fake tanning. Pressing the remote gave her the time, 3:20 a.m. Well into what some people called the 'midnight of the soul' or 'the Devil's hour'.

And something had triggered her security lights outside.

She rose from the sofa a little too quickly, almost falling over sideways. Her head was spinning a little, but she had to focus. The rational part of her mind told her that it was probably just a cat or bird outside that had caused the lights to activate, but there was always the chance that...

The lights went off and she breathed a sigh of relief. If it was anything untoward, they wouldn't do that. But then she realised that the TV had gone off as well, pitching the whole room into darkness.

Everything black.

The electricity had gone off. Or been cut off. Stumbling forwards, she moved towards the window in the living room – lifting the blind there and peeking out. It was a half-moon tonight, which the clouds kept passing across, but it was enough to see the path and the gate by. Enough to see that the gate was open.

Had they shut it when they came back from school? She couldn't remember. Sometimes the boys forgot if they were the last through, and Izzy couldn't really give a shit whether it was closed or open, so it was usually left to Deborah. And she couldn't remember. Shut, closed? Closed, shut? Which one? She'd been in a bit of a daydream anyway, zoning out, which was how she'd been ambushed about the party in the first place. She was damned if she could recall...

Definitely damned, if she'd closed it and someone else had opened the bloody thing!

She made her way through into the kitchen, down into the utility nook. The window in there was next to the fridge and she peered outside, same as she'd done in the living room. Drawing closer to the glass, then closer still.

Something moved out there. Black upon black, but it was definitely a figure. "Shit," breathed Deborah, pulling back sharply. But now she looked again, she couldn't see anything. Her imagination, the drink? No. She was sobering up by the second, adrenalin pumping. Someone was out there, she could sense it.

Her breathing coming in short bursts, she stepped backwards, heading back into the kitchen bit where the knife rack was. Reached out to the side without once taking her eyes off that window down in the nook. Her fingers found the wooden worktop Rosy had been so enamoured with, the edge of the sink... The rack wasn't far away now, if she could just—

Deborah tore her eyes away to look for the rack, for the knives, and saw it through the window in the kitchen off to her right. The face, watching her. The *faces*. Two of them, two sets of eyes. It was only a brief glimpse, and it was still dark out there – if only the floods were still working – but she saw. The person out there had rounded the corner from the nook's window.

She almost screamed, but instead found the rack and pulled the largest knife of them all from the middle slit.

'Bitch, please – I will stab you with my horn!'

Deborah only looked down for a fraction of a second, but when she looked up again the faces, the figure, had vanished.

For long minutes she waited there in the middle of the kitchen, staring at the kitchen window now, holding the knife with both hands; one ear cocked for any noises at the front or back doors. Both locked, that was one thing she did make sure of. But since when had locked doors stopped *him*?

There was nothing.

She retreated further, moving backwards into the living room. Step by step, going back to where her phone was to call the police. Deborah's breathing was slowing, she was calming down and assessing.

Then the TV came back on, the sounds low but the images

casting shadows on the wall. It made her start. The power was back on, then? Not cut off completely. But the floods remained off outside, which meant that either whoever was out there – *whoever? you know exactly who it is! except it couldn't be, it couldn't be!* – was either gone or they'd disabled the lights. She wasn't about to go out and check, not without backup.

It was then that she sensed something else. Not someone outside this time, but someone in there, with her. A figure behind her. The lights weren't being tripped outside because they were in here, with her.

Deborah whirled, bringing the knife around with her. Only she tripped on the edge of the rug, going flying, losing her grip on the knife and banging her head on the floor. She managed to look up, finding it much harder work than it had been on the couch. Thought she saw someone walking towards her.

Then everything went black again.

PART II

CHAPTER SIX

Norchester.

She knew its streets, its people. Its horrors. Or she had done, years ago. All that time since she'd moved away, tried to put the past, those horrors, behind her. Now they had come back with a vengeance. But so had she.

Returned.

Deborah hadn't had any other choice. The horrors were threatening her family, not that she'd told them exactly what they were. Oh, she felt certain she'd seen something that night when she'd tripped on the rug – at the time, anyway. But when morning had actually arrived, and the first thing she'd known about was the kids stomping downstairs, it had seemed more like a dream – a nightmare – than anything, especially in the cold light of day. Had it been? Did she *want* it to be?

"Mummy, Mummy?" the twins had chorused when they discovered her on the floor. "Are you all right?" It was a complicated question to answer. Had she really seen a long-dead serial killer outside their house in the middle of the night? With two faces? Or just one, an effect of the double-glazing's reflection? Had she actually seen the other thing that she'd seen, inside? The other person?

Jack. It had been Jack, she was sure of it. (*Midnight of the soul*... the souls?) Also returning, as he'd done after the boys were born – and other times since. Standing in their living room, scaring the life out of her but not meaning to. Warning her about what was happening, or what was about to happen?

Telling her without even opening his mouth that she had unfinished business. As if she didn't know that already.

Izzy had been there too that morning, downstairs in her pyjamas, probably wanting to know what the commotion was. Deborah was just glad to see they were safe: *all* of them. That the person who'd been outside – had there been a person? (*the Devil's Hour*!) – hadn't broken in and got to her family. "I'm... I'm okay, Mummy just fell." She could see Izzy glancing over at the wine bottle and rolling her eyes, before disappearing into the kitchen and heading back up with a breakfast bar in her hand; she must have been starving.

Deborah probably should have gone and got checked out at the hospital, might've had concussion for all she knew. But instead, she put on a brave face, picked up the knife and hid it behind her back, then went to the kitchen and put it in the sink, before fixing the twins their own breakfast of sugary cereals. They all heard the front door slam while they were eating, Izzy heading off without them. "Have you two fallen out again?" asked Jack.

"They're *always* falling out," James told his brother. Which was true. These days it was true. Although Deborah was beginning to wonder if they'd ever speak again after the previous day.

"Hey, how would you guys like to stay with Gran for a little while?" she asked then.

"Gran? Yay!" said James.

Jack was more: "Why, where are you going?"

"Mummy just needs to take a little trip," she said honestly, because she'd already decided that's what she was going to do. Would be ringing up Rosy after she'd seen the boys off to school, after she'd said goodbye to them and made arrangements for her mum and Derek to pick them up again. To pick up Izzy as well and explain – not that she'd care in the slightest.

"I'm coming on one condition," Deborah had said to her friend when she called her.

"Name it."

"You get someone here to keep an eye on Mum's. Think your friends in high places can manage that?"

"I'm absolutely certain they can, with big, shiny bells on. Something happened?" Rosy asked.

"Not sure," said Deborah, knocking back some painkillers – for the bang on the head or the hangover; they were interchangeable. Because she wasn't sure. Still wasn't, even as she'd packed and caught the first train out. The only thing she was sure of was that something was going on, and it involved her. It involved Jack. And it involved the thing they'd done together all those years ago, the horrors they'd confronted. In Norchester. "I'd just feel much better if they were protected."

"Indeed," said Rosy. "Couldn't agree more."

Even if whoever was doing this had shown up at the coast, they just wanted her back where she 'belonged'. Back where *they* could keep an eye on *her*. If it kept her family out of harm's way, who was she to argue?

Wendy Harrison had wanted to know more, naturally, but Deborah had tried to downplay things. Told her that Rosy needed her help with a case, keeping the specifics out of it. "But why you? You're retired." She saw the face Deborah had pulled at that; it made her sound ancient. "You know what I mean. You quit, and with good reason, I might add!"

"It's just something they need my insight on, that's all Mum. I shouldn't be gone too long." Of course, she had no idea how long she'd be in Norchester for – but she'd cross that bridge when she got to it. Or put off the crossing, stall the inevitable conversation she'd have to have with that woman – though not for too long. It was where she'd got her detective's nose from, Deborah was sure of it. Wendy could sniff out bullshit from a mile away.

She'd taken the train rather than driving, because she didn't like doing that in the big towns and cities now, had grown used to the quieter country lanes and roads. Plus which, it would give her a chance to finish off going through those galleys on her laptop, get the changes back to her editor so she was free and clear of writing work for a while. Until they were clamouring for the next novel, that was, which she'd started outlining until all this had cropped up. Had been planning on getting a first draft down over the next couple of months – but that looked unlikely now. Whatever happened here, it would mess with her concentration. People didn't realise how hard it was to get into that zone with writing, at least it was for Deborah.

Rosy had insisted on picking her up from the station. "The least I can do after getting you mixed up in all this," she told her.

"Any excuse to drive that new car," Deborah had replied.

She'd met her on the platform and they'd hugged again. "I'm so glad you changed your mind," Rosy told Deborah, helping her with her case.

"Yeah, well…"

Rosy glanced over at her as they went up the steps and made for the exit. "Something did happen, didn't it? Oh God, was it my fault?"

Deborah shook her head, then regretted it. Winced and rubbed the back of it, reached into her pocket for another couple of painkillers which she took dry. Rosy was watching all this, concern etched on her face. "I'll fill you in on the drive," she promised.

Which she did, telling her about what she thought she'd

seen (leaving out the bit about Jack, obviously). How she'd spooked herself, then tripped and bashed her head. "I told you about that rug, didn't I. You absolutely should have gone and got that checked out," said Rosy, jabbing a finger at her skull.

"I didn't want to make a fuss."

"Any dizziness, nausea?"

"Had that before I fell," Deborah reminded her. "I'm fine, honestly. Might knock some sense into me." *Although if that were the case, I wouldn't have come at all,* she thought to herself.

"Whatever way you look at it, this *was* my fault," Rosy said. "If I hadn't come to the coast... Bollocks, do you think someone followed me?"

"I'm not even sure there *was* someone out there. I'd been on the 'net going back over stuff from the case, drank a bit too much. A power cut... I dunno."

"Real enough to get you reaching for a knife!" said Rosy.

Deborah said nothing, just stared out of the window at the buildings passing by; some she recognised, others she didn't. But in general, Norchester hadn't changed that much since she'd been away, regardless of what Rosy had told her. It took her a moment to realise they were going in the wrong direction, though. "You said we were swinging by the station," Deborah said.

"We are. Oh, that's right, you don't know, do you? We're not based out of Yardley Street anymore."

"What?"

"That place was declared unsafe not long after you left. It's been sealed off for ages."

Unsafe? That was one way of putting it. "Guess having a murder dungeon in your basement didn't help matters much."

Rosy gave an embarrassed laugh. "No, suppose not. We're on the other side of town now, in swanky new offices."

"Wait a second, if we are dealing with some kind of copycat here, has anyone—"

"Searched the old nick?" Rosy cut in, nodding. "One of the first things they did. He'd have to be pretty stupid to be using the same place as our boy to keep his trophies, though, wouldn't he."

"You'd be surprised what people do," said Deborah. "Especially if they look up to the original, if they're trying to emulate him."

"In any event, they found nothing. Not in the old cells or the building itself."

They lapsed into silence again as Rosy negotiated her way through the traffic that late afternoon. "Come on, come on!" said the woman suddenly, parping her horn at the vehicle in front – and Deborah had a nasty flashback to sitting in a car with Mason, who'd been doing exactly the same thing. "What?"

"Nothing, just remembering my old partner."

"Roy? Jesus, I don't remind you of him, do I? Thanks a bunch."

Deborah couldn't help but grin at that. "Only your driving."

"Hey, I'm a great driver. It's everyone else who— See, look at that arsehole cutting me up!" She held out her hand to illustrate. "That's what I'm talking about right there."

"I think I made the right choice with the train," said Deborah.

Ten minutes later and they'd arrived. Rosy hadn't been joking when she said it was swanky. Deborah craned her neck to look up through the passenger window, at a building that was mainly glass and metal. "Looks like something from *The Wolf of Wall Street*," she commented.

"And less like *The Sweeney*, I know." Rosy seemed to think that was a good thing, but Deborah wasn't so sure. She liked *The Sweeney*. At least you knew where you were with Regan and Carter. This place looked like it would be filled with pencil-pushers more interested in statistics and budgets than solving crimes.

It was secure, however; Rosy had to pass through three checks – including a guard in uniform – just to get to the car park round the back. A far cry from when Jack had tried to get inside Yardley Street with Felicity Bailey after her sister had been attacked.

Poor Felicity, she'd had nothing to do with any of this and yet she'd suffered for it eventually, so many years after the fact. Her, Felicity's sister, her family. So many people's lives ruined by the original killer, and now it was all starting up again.

Unless they could stop it.

Inside, they were issued with lanyards – Rosy's an official one, Deborah's a visitor's badge. Part of her missed having one like her friend's, having access to places like this. Belonging in them. Although she couldn't see herself ever belonging in a building like this one, with its huge foyer and plants, staircases that looked like they reached into the heavens, and all those reflective surfaces. So. Much. Glass!

"This way," Rosy told her, leading them to the lifts: see-through ones, of course. "I should warn you, there's a bit of bad feeling in the bullpen about the way the SCI have muscled in."

"Really? I can't imagine why."

"Well, it's because..." Rosy stopped. "You should work on your sarcasm voice, Debs. It used to be a lot better than that."

As they left the ground – could actually see the ground falling away beneath them – Deborah's stomach lurched again.

"I didn't know you had a fear of heights," said Rosy.

"I didn't till I got in this lift! Bloody hell. Anyway, it's not the heights that kill you."

"It's the ground, yeah. That's an old one, mate."

Deborah shrugged. "If they're clichés, they're clichés for a reason." She'd have been lying if she said she wasn't delighted when it finally arrived at the fifth floor and they could get out. But what she saw didn't resemble any bullpen she'd ever worked in, it seemed much too ordered. More like a call centre or something. "It's all a bit, I dunno, clinical," she whispered to Rosy.

"I like it," she said again.

"'Course you do, you're a scientist." Rosy looked a little hurt at that remark and Deborah smiled. "Sorry, you know what I mean. If it helps, you're the least sciencey scientist I know."

Before she could dig herself in any deeper, Rosy placed a hand on her arm and pointed. "Oh, there he is. Just the man. Come on."

Her friend had been pointing to a guy across the way; tall, broad-shouldered, with short black hair. He was wearing cream trousers and a blue shirt, his tie done up quite loosely, and he had a piece of paper in his hand that he looked like he didn't know what to do with. "Michael!" she called. "Michael..." The man looked up and over, smiled broadly when he saw Rosy. It was the kind of smile that lit up a room, so why did she suddenly feel on edge?

"Deborah, this is Inspector Michael Glover of the SCI."

He held out his hand for her to shake, the one not currently occupied holding the paper. "Or just Mike. Very pleased to finally meet you, Miss Harrison. Thanks so much for coming."

Deborah took his hand tentatively, only shaking it for a moment. "It... it seemed like the right thing to do."

"I hope so. Your assistance will prove invaluable, I'm sure. And thank *you*, Rosy, for the ask."

Rosy nodded.

"We've arranged for the local police to keep an eye on your family, Miss Harrison. They're in good hands."

"Deborah, and much appreciated. It's just a precaution." She exchanged a look with Rosy. "Hopefully just a precaution."

"Better safe than sorry," Mike told her with another big smile. "Deborah Harrison," he said then, clicking his fingers. "The famous Blondie, right? That's what they used to call you on the force?"

Deborah felt a shiver run right through her.

"Er, Mike…" Rosy was making a cutting gesture against her neck, the universal code for 'Shut the fuck up'.

"Have I— Oh no, I've put my foot in it, haven't I?"

"Just slightly," said Rosy.

Who says that? Who hears that name and thinks immediately… Only a handful of people, one of whom was now very dead indeed. She'd even had to explain it to Rosy the first time she'd heard it. A nickname that had followed her around, and which—

"I just meant, I worked with a few people once who knew you, down in… It's what they—"

"It's what *he* used to call me," Deborah said bitterly.

"He…? Shit. Right. Mason. I'm so sorry, I didn't intend… I just… They spoke very highly of you, the coppers you worked with before. I just—"

"Well, that particular copper tried to kill me, so…" Deborah held his gaze until he was forced to look away.

"Like I say, I'm sorry. I had no idea." Mike looked up at her again. "You won't hear that name from me again, I promise."

"Thank you, Inspector."

"Mike," he reminded her. She knew, she just didn't feel like calling him that right now. Could think of a few other names, actually. "Okay, so, I'll let you go and get settled in wherever you're staying. It was nice meeting you. Maybe we could talk more tomorrow?"

Deborah gave a curt nod, watched him hold up a hand of goodbye and awkwardly walk away.

"He really didn't mean anything, you know. Mike wasn't to know."

"So, you'll be working for *Mike* soon, will you? Is that the plan?"

"Debs, don't... I have no idea who I'll be working for, or with, at the SCI." Rosy gave a long sigh. "It's—"

"Sergeant Harrison?" They both turned at the same time, responding to another one of her old names. "I thought that was you!"

Deborah didn't know why she was so surprised to see him, after all there were bound to be some of the old crowd here from her time at Norchester. Bingham had passed away, sadly. Mason...

But him. She just hadn't been expecting to see: "PC Clark!" She surprised herself then by opening her arms wide and giving him a hug and a kiss on the cheek. He smiled, blushing slightly as she put him down. "Look at you, all grown up and everything!"

"Ah, it's DS Clark now, guv." He thumbed himself to show he wasn't in uniform anymore, but instead wearing a navy suit and a tie.

"Really? Wow! That's fantastic. Congratulations!"

"Thanks boss."

She flapped a hand. "You can quit all of that, I'm just plain old Deborah now. No guv, no boss, or even sergeant. I haven't been that in a long, long time. Pleased to see someone taking up the mantle, though."

He beamed again, going even more red. "Hey, my shift's just about over. Don't suppose you fancy a coffee or something? Have a catch up?"

"I..." Rosy looked at her as if to say 'we need to get going', but, actually, Deborah was delighted to see a friendly face here. "Honestly, I'd love that."

"Debs, we should really get you and your stuff to the hotel."

"I don't mind dropping you off afterwards," said Clark, then caught Rosy's sideways glance. "Er, that is if I'm not treading on any toes?"

Rosy opened her mouth to say something, but Deborah got in there first. "Nope, no toes. I think we're just about done here anyway, don't you Rosy?"

Rosy gave a stiff nod. "You'd better come and get your luggage then," she told them both.

"Great!" said Clark, smiling warmly. "Terrific."

Deborah smiled too, he had the kind of smile that was infectious rather than made her uncomfortable. She'd forgotten how excited Clark got about everything, and she could do with a bit of that at the moment.

"There's just one thing," she said as they all began to walk off. "Do you mind if we take the stairs?"

CHAPTER SEVEN

She'd forgotten what a twat Deborah could be sometimes.

It was true that Rosy loved her to bits, but sometimes, just sometimes… What had all that been about back there? What had it *really* been about? Not simply Mike Glover accidentally using her old nickname, surely? He hadn't meant anything by it, and hadn't known it was what Mason once called her. A lot of people had called Deborah Harrison 'Blondie' back when she'd been a cop, it had followed her around. That's what she'd told Rosy when she first asked about it. Mike had just known some folk who'd used it before she even moved to Norchester.

Before The Gemini.

That's what it was really all about, why she was so on edge, and you couldn't really blame her. Rosy had been trying to make allowances for it, after all she'd been the one who'd dragged her back into all this (even though it hadn't been her idea to do so, was beginning to think it had been a mistake). Had got Deborah jumping at shadows outside her own home, unless there really had been someone there – Rosy couldn't rule it out, and felt guilty enough thinking that she might have led them there in the first place.

But the way she'd acted back at the station, that had just been plain rude. She'd embarrassed Rosy in front of her new workmate, colleague, and yes, maybe superior. At present she was just freelancing for the SCI, but she was definitely hoping for a permanent position. The pay alone was amazing, but it wasn't just about that; the resources they had at their disposal were enough to turn any nerd's head. Made the facilities here look like they were still in the Dark Ages.

And Rosy had to wonder whether that had got something to do with Deborah's behaviour as well, the way she talked about the SCI. A cult? Seriously? Fair enough, she had every right to be suspicious after what happened at the tail end of The Gemini case – Rosy had been a little hesitant before she began working for them herself. But at least find out what they were about before slagging them off, before treating one of their investigators like dogshit. They were good people – Mike was a good person, from what she could gather – trying to do a good thing. If – not when – they accepted her on to the team, she'd be proud to serve alongside them.

But then Deborah didn't *want* to serve with them, did she? Had turned her back on that life years ago. Yet it hadn't turned its back on her, it seemed. Yes, the SCI needed her expertise and insight regarding the new copycat case (how could it be anything other than an imitator?) and this was a chance for Deborah to do some good, too. But she and her family might be in just as much danger now as they were back when all this started, from Mason and his brother; more even. So it was in her own best interests as well.

All right, some might head for the hills and hide themselves away – wasn't that what Deborah had done when she'd moved to the coast, in effect? – but things always caught up with you eventually unless you dealt with them. That had been her own experience in life, and she didn't figure Debs as the kind of person who'd shy away from a fight. More like someone who'd confront a situation head-on. Or had been, anyway.

Rosy supposed having kids changed that to some extent; you'd be less likely to put yourself in the middle of things with twin boys in your care. Then again, Deborah had had Izzy when she tackled the original Gemini. Anything could have happened to that little girl as well; Wendy Harrison wouldn't have been able to prevent it. Should have been a detail watching them anyway back in the day, like her family was being watched now.

So, she kind of understood the reluctance to get involved when she'd visited Deborah the other day. Had been more surprised by the call saying she'd changed her mind, and changed it so suddenly; something she'd refused to be drawn on initially.

That was another thing: she'd gone to the trouble of doing that, picking her up, showing her around the new station and introducing her to Mike, only for Deborah to blow her off! Rosy had pictured perhaps a meal after she'd got her booked in, or taking her back to her place so they could all eat together. Only for her to go off with bloody Clark!

Clark, who Deborah hadn't seen in all this time! Who Rosy didn't even know she knew that well! What the actual fuck?

But then it wasn't so much who she'd chosen to spend the evening with, was it? More that it hadn't been *her*. More that Rosy now had to return to her flat without a buffer (what was that about confronting things, again?). More that Kiz would be waiting for her, would probably want to talk some more. By which she meant she'd talk and Rosy would have to listen. For hours. Maybe chew her out again about her new car she'd bought instead of saving the money, even though it was *her* money!

Rosy tugged on the steering wheel of the Defender, swore at yet another driver who could do with digging out his highway code for a refresher; either that or he'd be digging his own grave soon enough.

She let out a long, weary breath. Why couldn't things just carry on the way they'd been going? They'd been happy enough, hadn't they? Rosy remembered meeting Kizza at the bookstore; thought things like that didn't really happen in real life, only in stupid romantic comedies. They'd both reached for the same cookery book at the same time and their fingers had touched, then they'd laughed. They'd got chatting about the book and discovered a shared interest in all things food-related. But for a moment back there, when Rosy had looked at Kiz's face – her skin the colour of milk chocolate; deep, brown eyes you might lose yourself in – she could have sworn her heart had skipped a beat. She thought that only happened in those kinds of movies as well. But God, she was gorgeous.

They'd dated, fast becoming an item. Perhaps a little too fast, looking back. Turns out they were at different points in their lives, Rosy still okay to tick along while Kiz was starting to think about things like having kids, getting a house out in the suburbs. She'd hid that well, Rosy had to hand it to her. Hidden it until they were both pretty invested in the relationship. Until Rosy wasn't sure what she'd do without Kiz in her life.

She'd been simultaneously excited and terrified by the news that Rosy was now working with – for – the SCI. It meant more money, which meant a better lifestyle and more cash for when they had that family and new home. "But won't it be more dangerous?" Kiz had asked.

"No more than it is for me at the moment," Rosy responded. Then she'd trotted out what she always said: "It's not the dead you have to worry about, it's the living who do all the damage."

Kiz had nodded, but she hadn't been convinced. They'd had the conversation before about her working less with the police, so she wasn't involved with high-profile cases. "You mean take more boring gigs?" had been Rosy's answer. "Heart attack on the eighth hole or whatever? Fatty livers and cholesterol."

"What's wrong with that?" Kiz had asked. "You're still giving closure to the loved ones."

Rosy would usually roll her eyes and change the subject (she was doing that a lot lately). Kiz just didn't get it, how could she when she worked in telemarketing. She'd always said she wouldn't mind giving that up and looking after kids. Rosy bet she wouldn't; if she did that for a job, she'd probably end up on a slab herself, having died of terminal boredom. Not that she'd ever say that to Kiz's face, of course.

But you couldn't compare a job like that with what she'd been doing this week. Another Gemini on the prowl, and Rosy had been on hand to do the PM once again. So many similarities it was like going back in time to working on Stuart Redbrook, Haley Archer and the others. Victims of The Gemini, but only the latest ones as they knew now (was that the case here, was Felicity part of the beginning or end game of this?). As Rosy understood, after reading those diary entries.

Maxwell Craine's diary. The Gemini's 'real' name. Or at least the name his adoptive parents gave him; adopted brother of Anton (who'd attacked Patricia Bailey, throwing everyone off the scent), real brother of Roy Mason, though he hadn't known it because the pair had been split up when they were little. Maxwell had been doing this for some time, fascinated with the dual subjects of life and death, with the nature of what he was and what he *felt* as he sensed twins. Killed twins. Could somehow feel their lifeforce being snubbed out, was eventually – if you believed what he'd written – able to conduct it into himself. Make himself stronger. Was intent on becoming the strongest person on the planet that way. Had almost achieved his goal until—

Delusions? Or something more? She wouldn't have even

known this much if it hadn't been for the SCI letting her in. Deborah was focussing on the wrong thing where they were concerned. It wasn't about authority or taking over, this wasn't a pissing contest between departments. This was about getting to the bottom of whether or not all those things in the diary were true. If they were, then…

And if Maxwell Craine had been within a hair's breadth of becoming a 'god', what was to stop it happening again? Indeed, was that what this person was doing? What they *thought* they were doing, at the very least. Maybe The Gemini's remains were part of that process, Rosy pondered. A key ingredient, like when she and Kiz cooked together; something that if it were missing would throw the 'taste' of the whole dish off.

These were the kinds of things she couldn't possibly discuss with Kiz. It was one of the reasons the SCI had taken the evidence back then, because in the wrong hands it could start a panic, especially if it were proved. A person walking around with those kinds of powers… She shivered now, just imagining it. How could you give up working on cases like that for the humdrum, the ordinary? It was one of the reasons her old technician, Eugene the film fan, had moved to the States and was now working with the FBI. It was something she'd been incredibly jealous about at the time, but had now been handed her own chance to do something similar. Something even better, perhaps.

The SCI worked with other divisions and bureaus all the time, she'd been told. She might even get a chance to liaise with Eugene again down the line, on a case out there in the US of A! But not if she was tied down here, like Kiz seemed intent on doing to her.

Rosy parked up in the car park attached to her block of flats, before making her way round to the entrance. She let herself in with the code, nodding to the security guard in uniform that always patrolled the lobby, Bernard, before checking their box for mail. There were a couple of circulars and a letter from one of her relatives in Singapore. Kiz always forgot to grab the post when she got home from work herself, assuming she was back, that was. Which she more than likely was, because Kiz kept pretty regular office hours. It was Rosy who was always on call, ready to spring into action should she be needed at a crime scene overnight or early morning, like she'd had to rush off to last Saturday – having to raincheck the romantic day they'd planned to spend together, beginning with feeding the ducks in the park just opposite their apartments. Kiz had not been impressed.

"I'm really sorry, sweetheart. It's urgent."

"It's always urgent," Kiz had said, sitting up in bed and watching Rosy dress – before pulling up her knees and hugging them to herself. "When *isn't* it urgent? I thought we might, you know? It's been a while."

"I'll make it up to you," Rosy promised, having no idea how she was going to do that – especially as she'd spent the next couple of days up to her armpits in blood and guts and other evidence from the Felicity Bailey murder, thinking about how life was short. And then had been asked to shoot off to the coast to see Deborah, try and persuade her to help, getting back in late but not offering any kind of explanation because, well, she couldn't. Kiz had rolled over in bed, presenting her back to Rosy as she climbed in, too – before mumbling something she didn't quite catch and didn't know if she wanted to. It didn't sound pleasant.

She'd had to say something to Kiz about all this in the end, though, at least about Deborah's visit, because she was bound to make an appearance at the flat at some point. But she'd said it was basically a trip to see the old gang, catch up with a few friends she had in Norchester. That she'd be picking her up from the station.

Kiz had nodded again, said: "Right, yeah. Okay." Like she didn't believe a word of the cover story, because she didn't.

And because she wasn't stupid. Not that she'd think something was going on with Deborah. Kiz had met the woman, knew she was as straight as a pole. No, it was a different kind of jealousy altogether, same as it was with her career.

Rosy reached her floor, then walked down the corridor to the door of her flat, opening it up. "Hey," she called out. "You there, hon?" No answer. Rosy called out again, checking her watch. Definitely way past time Kiz would be home. She walked further in, calling out once more. For some reason she couldn't quite explain, she began to panic a little.

Until Rosy wasn't sure what she'd do without Kiz in her life…

"Kiz?" Her girlfriend was on the couch, just sitting there with her back to Rosy. She reached out her hand. "Kiz are you all r—"

The second her fingers made contact with Kiz's shoulder, the woman jumped a mile. "Holy fuck!" she shouted, a bit more loudly than she probably would have done if she hadn't had her earbuds in. She pulled one out now. "Rosy? Jesus, you scared the shit out of me!"

"I'm so sorry, sweetheart! I didn't…" Rosy's hands went to her mouth, her heart had skipped more than a beat that time – as had Kiz's, probably.

"Wasn't expecting you back yet. I was doing a calming meditation." She looked down at the earpod, then back up at Rosy. "Bloody hell!" But then she couldn't help chuckling.

Seconds later, Rosy was giggling as well. Sheer relief, more than anything. But it was the kind of laughter they'd shared when they first met, and many more times since. Rosy shook her head again, "I'm really sorry."

"I…" Kiz shook hers too. "Figured you'd be off out with Deborah."

"Er… It's like I said, she's here to catch up with people – not just me." Apparently so, and Rosy was doing her best not to still sound pissed off about that. "She's out with a mate tonight, actually. Another former colleague." Not a lie. "So I thought I'd come back and we could have a nice evening in." Totally a lie, but it got her a hug and a kiss, which she instantly felt guilty about. "Maybe make something together like we used to do, a chili or whatever?"

"Sounds good. Are you going to get called away again?"

Rosy knew she looked like a rabbit trapped in the headlights. "Not to my knowledge," was all she could muster. "I'm all yours."

Kiz smiled. "That's great."

That was all she'd been waiting for really, and Rosy felt like such a bitch. "Look, I know things have been a bit crazy the last few days."

"Days?" said Kiz.

"All right, weeks. Months. I'm sorry." There was that word again.

"Come on," said Kiz, making the most of Rosy being at home with her tonight, leading her into the kitchen by the hand. There they made dinner, sat down and ate. The conversation flowed easily and freely and for a little while there, Rosy really thought they could avoid the subject. But just like she'd been waiting to spend some time with her, Kiz had also been waiting to talk again, about the future.

It wasn't that Rosy didn't want to settle down at some point, and she adored kids. Other people's kids anyway. It was just that she didn't know if that was what she wanted right now. Even a dog would have been a big commitment at this juncture. As Kiz had been saying something about options, like artificial insemination, adoption, Rosy had made a joke about having killed off all her goldfish when she little, which went down like a lead balloon.

"You're not taking any of this seriously, are you?"

"Oh, believe me I am," Rosy told her. "Just not tonight." She'd taken Kiz by the hand then, pulling her up and kissing her mouth softly. God she was beautiful, and life was short.

"I thought we might, you know? After all, it has been a while."

Kiz was about to say something, but shut up and kissed her back.

Definitely one of the best ways of changing the subject, thought Rosy, still feeling a little guilty, though that was vanishing by the second.

And then they both headed off towards the bedroom and she didn't feel guilty at all anymore.

CHAPTER EIGHT

Deborah shovelled more scrambled eggs onto her plate, then used the tongs to snag some of the crispier pieces of bacon. She was trying not to feel guilty about second helpings.

What a pig!

Because it was so nice to eat a breakfast that someone else had slaved over for a change. And she was really hungry, regardless of the fact she'd had a big dinner last night – her coffee with Clark having turned into a catch-up curry.

She'd listened as he told her all about his promotions, about working for the CID, inspired more than a little by her example.

"Me?" she'd asked.

"Yeah, of course! You had such a huge impact on my life and my career," he informed her. "I don't think you quite realise. You were an inspiration to a lot of us back then. It was a sad day when you left, gu—" Clark saw her watching him to make sure he got it right. "Deborah." The young man grinned again. Except he wasn't all that young anymore, not as old as her – or as old as she felt certainly – but old enough. Hairline receding, putting a bit of weight on, though it suited him. "Heading towards the big three-oh!" as Clark put it.

"Sod off! You wait till you're past the big four-oh, mate," she said with a snort.

"No! You don't look a day over—"

Deborah pointed at him with her fork. "Choose your next words very carefully."

Clark laughed himself. "You don't look any different, honest."

"Well played," she told him.

"So, how're you doing, bos... Deborah?"

"You'll get there in the end, Clark. I also answer to Deb or Debs."

"If you're Deborah, then I'm definitely Robert, or Robbie – whichever you prefer."

"Okay, Robbie... I like that name. Though I tell you, it'll take some getting used to."

"You'll get there in the end," he said with another chuckle.

She realised he was still waiting for an answer to his question. How *was* she doing? And she told him about her life now, about how the kids kept her busy. About her writing.

"No way, that's you?" Clark whistled. "The girlfriend loves those books! Wait till I tell her I know you."

Deborah held up a hand. "It's kind of a secret, Robbie. For now, anyway."

"Right, gotcha. I can keep a secret, I'll just be vague about it."

Then she realised what he'd just said. "Wait, girlfriend?" Not that she'd thought anything of all this: the coffee; the curry. Just old friends having a natter, no more to it than her and Rosy; the fact that when she'd last seen him he'd looked about twelve helped. Maybe that's why the girlfriend thing had surprised her so much.

"Yeah, Helen. Haven't known her all that long, but, well, she's something pretty special, I reckon."

"That's... Robbie, that's so nice. I'm really pleased for you. But, just a tip that'll help moving forwards, whether she likes my books or not, I probably wouldn't be telling her you were out on a date with an older woman."

He looked shocked at that, panicked even, and she couldn't help roaring with laughter – and not long after that, he was too. It was nice, felt like the first normal thing to happen to her in days. She didn't even mind when he brought up the inevitable subject of why she was here, not that he hadn't guessed already. He was CID, was bound to know about Felicity, about the new Gemini killer. "I mean, I just assumed when I saw you fraternizing with the enemy," he said.

"Oh, is that what I was doing?"

Clark gave a small titter. "I'm just joking; he's all right is Glover. But some of the others aren't too happy about the way him and his mob just butted their way in. They do that a lot apparently."

"Hmm, can't say I'm too impressed myself," she admitted.

He gave a shrug. "Whatever works, I guess. And they do have an excellent track record for putting the bad guys away. Hopefully that's what'll happen here. Especially now you're on board, too."

Deborah held up her hands. "Whoa, I'm just an observer. Rosy seems to think it'll help, my being here. I'm not so sure."

"It'll definitely help, gu— Debs." He went quiet for a moment or two, looking down at the remains of his tikka. "Do you ever think about it? You know, being down in those cells?" Clark looked up then. It was the most serious she'd seen him all evening.

"I try not to. That's what I say to people, anyway. But yeah, of course I do."

Her dining partner nodded. "I still miss him. Peel."

"Yeah, you're bound to. You guys were really close."

Another nod. This was why it felt so right to be out with Clark, with Robbie – why she'd said yes in the first place. Not just to hack Rosy off, and she still didn't really know why

she'd done that. Hadn't been her fault Glover had called her…
that name. Hadn't been his really, and she felt guilty about the
way she'd handled it – would say sorry herself to both of
them tomorrow. No, the real reason she was here having this
meal was they'd shared something that nobody else on earth
could possibly understand. They'd been there in those
underground cells, had witnessed the end of The Gemini. And
the more time she spent here, the more time around people
like Rosy and Clark, the more she was starting to remember.

They'd saved each other. The only ones who had walked
away from that confrontation. Some people hadn't been as
'lucky'. Jack, Peel. An officer with his whole life ahead of him,
he'd probably be right up there with Clark by now, a DS too.
She'd been the one who'd roped them into this, ordered them
down there as backup. It was her fault when all was said and
done, just another thing to feel guilty about.

"That bastard Mason," Robbie said shaking his head,
naming the real person who was to blame.

"Yeah, I know," said Deborah and reached over for his
hand. Held it for a few moments before saying, "Definitely
don't tell Helen about this." They both laughed again and she
squeezed his hand tighter.

After arguing about who was paying for the bill, and
agreeing to split it, they'd found themselves outside and she'd
found herself saying: "I don't know if I said this to you back
then, but thank you, Robbie."

"What for?"

"Well, for my life. My boys' lives. If it hadn't been for
you—"

"I did nothing but get my arse handed to me," he said
sadly. "You're the real hero."

"Naw," she replied. "That was Jack." She'd cried then, and
Clark had held her, and she'd put her head on his shoulder.
But strangely she felt better afterwards.

Then he'd given her a lift back, as promised.

Back to another place she'd known in a different life. Back to *The Imperial Hotel.* It still looked pretty much the same from the outside: tall, with an air of majesty. Standing firm against the elements, against time. But inside she noted, as Clark carried her case in for her – always polite, ever the gentleman – through the pillars and revolving door, the hotel had had work. Didn't she remember something about it being taken over by a major chain? Not a lot that could be done structurally, but a lick of paint and new furniture had worked wonders for the place. Spruced up, Wendy Harrison would have called it.

"Thanks Robbie," she'd said again to him in the foyer, "for everything."

"My pleasure."

Deborah had given him another peck on the cheek, watching him turn a deep shade of red once again before saying goodnight. Then she'd wandered over to the reception desk and rung the bell. A man who looked sort of familiar, and more than a bit worse for wear like he hadn't slept in months, appeared through the door behind the desk. His name-badge bore the legend 'RALPH'.

"Hello, and welcome to *The Imperial,*" he said, in a kind of *kill me now* voice. The kind of voice that said he'd worked here a long time and it had taken its toll. He made a half-hearted attempt at smiling, but looked thoroughly miserable. "Do you have a reservation?"

"Hi, yes. I've got a room booked under the name Harrison."

The man consulted the computer on the side of the desk. "Harrison… Harrison… Here we are." Was it her imagination or were his words slowing down even more, as he became increasingly bored repeating actions he'd probably done a million times? "You requested a specific room."

"That's right. 307, if it's available."

Ralph nodded, and even that was in slow motion. "It is.

Do you know how long you'll be staying with us, Miss Harrison?"

"I-I'm playing it by ear," she told him, then went into her handbag and fished out her purse for the credit card he'd requested. She was disappointed when he handed over a card in return, rather than the actual keys this place used to use.

"Do enjoy your stay," Ralph told her as she turned towards the lifts; thankfully enclosed rather than glass.

She doubted that very much. As she was about to walk off, she spun back around, the lifts having reminded her of something. "Er, Ralph?"

"Yes?" he replied.

"How long have you worked here?"

He gaped, obviously not used to guests taking such an interest. Then he gave her a look that said 'too bloody long', as she'd suspected. "Why do you…?"

Deborah jabbed a finger over towards the empty lifts. "There used to be someone who worked here, worked on the lifts. Albert." She remembered that man fondly, a man who'd helped Jack – even driven him to save a life when The Gemini had targeted a priest, so Jack had told her afterwards. Lovely fella, but he'd had to have been in his seventies or eighties even back then.

Ralph smiled again, only this time it was warmer, more genuine. "That's right. Albert. It was a sad day when he went." The second time she'd heard that in as many hours.

"He… he passed away then?" she asked, fearing the worst.

"Oh no," said Ralph with a shake of the head. "He's… *he's* not dead. Just retired. Alive and well, last I heard."

Deborah let out the breath she'd been holding. Along with Clark's promotion, that was another piece of good news. Probably the only good news there'd been in the last week. "Excellent, thanks."

"Pops in occasionally," Ralph went on. "I think he misses it. Between you and me, they got rid of his post so he didn't have a choice in things, otherwise he'd probably still be around." He said that last bit like he couldn't really understand why you would be if you had a choice in the matter, but then added: "This place was his life."

"Yeah," said Deborah, looking up and around in the foyer. She knew exactly how the old man felt. She hadn't spent as much time here as Albert – or even Ralph, though he probably hadn't wished to – but her entire life had changed because of the night she'd spent in *The Imperial*.

The night she'd spent in the very room she was heading to, 307.

And it was funny, because as soon as she walked in she'd felt it – in spite of the fact the room had changed more than a little, too. Even as she'd unpacked, got ready for bed, she'd felt closer to Jack than she had in so long. Hadn't seen him, but as she'd climbed into bed finally, she'd almost felt him beside her. Could imagine his arms around her, especially as she recalled that time they'd spent in this space together. The time they'd created James and Jack.

She'd slept more soundly last night than she had in a good while as well, even dreaming about being with Jack, making love again, holding him. Being *held*. She'd woken early but rested, and the first thing she'd done was ring her mum, checking to see if everything was okay – because it had been a bit late by the time she arrived here.

"Absolutely fine," she reported. "At this end, anyway." Deborah hadn't gone into any more details about what was going on with her, just asked to speak to the boys. As she'd expected, Izzy didn't want to speak to her.

"When are you coming home?" they asked.

"Soon," she said. "I've just got some stuff to do first."

"What kind of 'stuff'?" Jack had asked next and she hadn't known how to answer that, so had just told them she loved them more than anything in this world – and that she would see the pair before too long.

Then she got dressed and headed down for breakfast, where she was now apparently having seconds. There were only a handful of other guests eating that morning: a man and woman in their fifties who weren't talking to each other, either they'd had a row or were that kind of couple who never communicated or had simply run out of things to say; a bloke in a sharp suit, looked like a businessman of some kind, sipping his early morning coffee and tapping away on a tablet; a family, whose kids were tearing around the table instead of eating their toast; a middle-aged woman on crutches with her leg in a cast; and a young couple who looked like the opposite of the older one, gazing into each other's eyes and speaking in whispered tones of love, smirking at each other and blowing kisses.

Deborah finished up her second plateful, drank some more of her tea, and headed back out into the lobby area. It was there that she saw a woman sitting on the end of a row of chairs, gazing into space rather than into someone's eyes, then gazing out of the nearest window.

Like Ralph, she recognised that woman and went over. "Felicity?" The name was out before she realised, then she thought: *Christ, no. Not Felicity...*

Patricia Bailey. Her twin.

Who looked up and over in her direction, looked at Deborah through eyes that were red-raw, and frowned. "S-Sergeant Harrison?"

"I... I'm not..." She didn't want to get into all that right now, just felt those waves of guilt again. Felt the overwhelming urge to say: "I'm so sorry. I thought... I didn't expect..."

Patricia shook her head. "It's okay. You were half-expecting to see my sister here, right?"

Deborah remained silent. Had she been? No. She hadn't been expecting that, because she knew Felicity was dead, *of course* she did. Just hadn't been expecting to see Patricia here instead. Had maybe thought that this was some kind of ghost, perhaps? It happened. She sat down next to the woman she'd last seen all those years ago, after Anton Craine's attack. There hadn't been a trial, because that man had killed himself, spurred on by the words of Mason – the real brother of The Gemini.

"What are you…?"

Patricia shook her head. "I thought perhaps Ralph might be around? He worked with Flick, y'know? To be honest, I think he kind of liked her. But she didn't feel the… feel the same way."

"He was in last night," said Deborah absently. Now she thought about it, that was probably what had been wrong with him. His tired eyes, like he hadn't slept. His look:

Kill me now.

What he'd said about Albert: *He's… he's not dead.*

Someone was, though, weren't they. If Deborah hadn't been so wrapped up in her evening with Clark, with getting to room 307, she'd have realised. Some bloody detective she was!

"I need to talk to… Flick was sorting out the wedding arrangements, she…" Tears were flooding Patricia's eyes and she bent her head. "I'm sorry, I'm being stupid."

Deborah placed a hand around her shoulders and rubbed them. "Not stupid at all. I can't begin to understand what you might be going through." Although she could, couldn't she. She'd lost someone to this madness before. Not a sister, but—

"I just keep going over and over it in my mind. If there hadn't been that bad feeling maybe… If we hadn't… If she'd had someone like Ralph, perhaps all this would have been easier on her, the stuff with Danny."

"You're marrying Danny?"

"I was," said Patricia. "I don't know what's happening now. And my folks are… I've… I've lost her, Sergeant Harrison. I've lost my only sister. And he can't possibly—"

"I know," said Deborah.

"Do you know what the last thing I said to her was? I told her to piss off. Can you even— My own sister!"

"You didn't mean it, I'm sure."

"I didn't mean for her to… And now she has. Gone, and I'll never see her again." *Only when you look in the mirror,* mused Deborah, but it wasn't a helpful notion. "I don't really know what I'm doing, to be honest. I'm in a bit of a state." She paused, suddenly switching to another subject. "Have you found anything out? I spoke to someone called Glover at the station, a colleague of yours, when I gave my statement, but I don't really… Do *you* know what happened yet?"

"I…" Deborah shook her head. Patricia was still assuming she was with the police, like no time had passed at all, and Deborah still wasn't correcting her. What was the penalty for impersonating a police officer these days?

"Then why— How did you know I'd be here?"

"I didn't," Deborah answered honestly, then said: "I'm just—"

"You're talking to people from the hotel," Patricia finished for her, nodding. Deborah was grateful that she didn't have to lie. That she didn't have to get into why she was staying here, why she was back. Patricia clearly didn't know she'd even left, and it was better that way for now. "Oh my God, you don't think someone here had something to do with it?"

"No. No, that's not what we're thinking at the moment." For all she knew it might have been someone here; wasn't beyond the realms of possibility. But this conversation did at least tell her that nobody had spoken to Patricia or her family about The Gemini, or a possible link with that case. Wasn't a bad thing, either.

'Just' that Felicity had been killed. 'Just' that someone had killed her. Because the next thing Patricia said was: "Promise me something, though. *Promise* me, Sergeant Harrison."

"I-I will if I can, Patricia."

"Promise you'll get whoever did this." She looked at her

again with those red eyes, those pleading eyes. "Promise me that they'll pay."

Deborah hesitated for a moment. Then she answered. What else could she say in reply to that but:

"I promise."

CHAPTER NINE

A car was dispatched for her that morning.

Couple of uniforms in a squad car, which she was told about via a text from Glover. Rosy had obviously given him her number, but the woman in question wasn't answering her phone that morning. And she wasn't at the station to greet Deborah either, so she was escorted upstairs to an interview room by the young officers who'd driven her – who actually reminded Deborah a little of Peel and Clark back at the start of their careers.

"Thanks," she said to them, as she'd got into the habit early on during her time as a cop to always treat PCs with respect and courtesy. The backbone of any police force, who worked as hard as – often more so – than plain clothes.

Glover, she was rapidly deciding to show far less courtesy to.

After vowing to apologise the previous evening, she'd changed her mind completely today – not least because he hadn't even bothered to show up. And because she'd basically been treated like some kind of suspect; several hours in that room, being asked questions by a minion of his called

Fleming, a fussy little woman with the abrupt manners of an old-fashioned hospital matron.

"I'm not sure how all this is relevant," Deborah had said at one point. There was stuff about why she went into the force, her time at other nicks – and every time she brought up perhaps taking a look at the reports and evidence about Felicity Bailey, Deborah was stonewalled. She thought that was why they'd sent for her in the first place?

"Everything is relevant, Miss Harrison. No small detail can be overlooked." She expected Fleming to say next: "Besides, it's good for you! Now take your medicine like a well-behaved little girl. Then you'll get a treat!" Which turned out to be a limp sandwich and luke-warm coffee from the canteen. Good job she'd loaded up at breakfast.

By mid-afternoon, and by the time they were getting into more personal questions about her marriage, her family, about her relationship with Mason and Jack – with still no sign of Glover – she'd more than had enough. "That's it, I'm done here." Deborah had got up and begun walking out of the room. For a second she thought Fleming might try and stop her – good luck! – but all she did was rise with her, glance over to the mirror, and nod, stopping the recorder at the same time.

If this is the way the bloody SCI operates, you can stick it, thought Deborah. They'd asked *her* to come, for God's sake! She told the woman she'd find her own way out, and when she couldn't spot either Rosy or Clark around, she'd done just that, dumping her visitor's pass on the desk downstairs.

It took several deep breaths once she was outside the station to calm down. Then she'd walked to the main road and hopped in a taxi. She'd considered just going back to *The Imperial* and packing, but she'd made a vow that morning. A vow she somehow intended to keep. So instead she found herself somewhere else entirely, somewhere she hadn't expected.

Somewhere that had also changed quite a bit.

Fagin's Row was no longer the cesspit it had once been, full of abandoned factories and buildings on their last legs. These days it was filled with industrial estates and new build houses. As she walked around the neighbourhood, Deborah was amazed at how things had turned around here. It was barely recognisable as the place they'd found a murder victim almost eight years ago, dumped, head lolling on its chest, legs out in a V shape – and with its right hand missing. Indeed, the building where the corpse had been discovered by some homeless people, just off Arndle Street, was no longer an old factory at all. It was an 'activity hub' whatever the hell that meant, complete with 'rock climbing', 'go-carting' and 'paint-balling'. Deborah couldn't think of anything worse, though the boys would probably love it in there. The neon letters on the outside alone were doing her head in, making her want to take another painkiller – but she resisted. Absently, she wondered if the folk in there shooting each other with paint, pretending, had any clue that a real dead body had once been found inside? There'd been some activity that night, definitely.

As she was staring at the building, lost in memories, she became aware of someone directly behind her. Someone who'd approached while she'd been wool-gathering, and was inching nearer by the second. She whirled, bringing up a fist.

"Hey, easy! Don't shoot! I come in peace!" said the man with black hair, in the suit with a loose tie dangling, holding up his palms in mock surrender. "Friend, friend!"

Deborah almost punched Mike Glover anyway. "What are *you* doing here?"

"I could ask you the same question."

"Why not, I've been bloody well asked all the others today! Are you following me?"

"Not following, exactly."

"Then what?"

"It's not safe for you to be roaming around the city on your own, Miss Harrison. That's why I sent a car for you in the first place this morning."

"Not safe?" she spat. "I can take care of myself."

"I can see that." He lowered his hands slowly, and she finally unballed her fist. "But you're also my responsibility. I was the one who requested you come."

"And then sat me in a room and asked me ridiculous questions all morning."

"They weren't— All right, maybe some of them might seem a little pointless to you, and DS Fleming can come across as a little brusque."

"A little?"

"But they're standard SCI operating procedure. Getting to know a person's character to begin with and—"

"Fuck the SCI," she told him. Then she looked at him sideways. "You were in that other room, weren't you. Observing, through the two-way?"

Glover didn't answer.

"I'm not a lab-rat, Inspector."

"I never said that you were. Look, we've gotten off on the wrong foot here. I'm just trying to figure out what happened all those years ago, and what bearing it has on the incident that occurred the other day."

"You won't find out by asking me crap about me and—"

"Roy Mason? Jack Foley?" asked Glover. "Are you quite sure about that? The way Foley kept showing up at The Gemini crime scenes, what he was doing in those cells when you confronted the killer."

Her number wasn't the only thing Rosy had divulged then, chatting to her new friends. And she had to wonder whether that Blondie titbit hadn't been something else Rosy'd let slip. Something Glover had said on purpose, to gauge her reaction. Deborah started to walk away. The DI just trailed her, as he'd apparently been doing since the station. So she turned and faced him again. "You said you needed my help."

"We do. You were there, throughout the whole thing. There are… gaps. Things we don't know."

"And I just bet you couldn't wait to get me here to plug those gaps, right? Events other people weren't around for."

"I realise this is hard but—"

She jabbed a finger at him. "You don't know a fucking thing about me!"

"So tell me."

"You've got to be joking."

"I'm serious. I want to know all about you… It. The case. Everything. No formal interviewing, no questioning by Fleming, just you and me. The whole story."

"After… You think that…" Deborah was actually lost for words.

"You've got to trust someone at some point, Miss Harrison."

"If I do, it won't be you, pal. The bloke who let the remains of The Gemini slip through his fingers." She paused for a second, wondering if she'd said too much. Whether that comment would cost Rosy professionally. Wondering if she even cared now.

Glover cocked his head. "Actually, that wasn't technically me, but I take your point."

Deborah gaped at him. "Are you for real?"

"Very," said Glover. "Miss Harrison… Deborah, can I call you Deborah?"

"No."

He sighed loudly. "We've got to work together here. I want to stop whatever this is as much as you do."

"I doubt that." It crossed her mind to tell him about her promise to Patricia Bailey then, but she held her tongue. "And it works both ways, Inspector. Trust that is, wanting to know about a person's character."

Glover stayed silent once more.

"Like I said to Fleming, I want to know what you guys know. Especially about what happened last weekend."

"Some of it is highly sensitive material, and you're just a civilian, Miss Harrison."

"Just? Piss off!"

"I didn't mean… I can't do right for doing wrong, can I?"

She prodded his chest now with that finger she had up. "I'm a civilian whose assistance you desperately need, apparently. That *you* specifically requested. So think about that."

Glover nodded. "You're right. But there are protocols, there's red tape. I can't just—"

"Goodbye again, Inspector Glover."

She began walking off a second time, turning and holding that finger up in case he dared to follow once more. He didn't. Instead he called after her: "You never answered my question. Why you were here?"

"Okay, all right. But you should already know. This is where it all started. For me, anyway." Deborah called back over her shoulder. "I was hoping to see a ghost or two."

"Right, right," Glover said. And something else she only just caught because she was heading away from him, but it sounded like: "We've had some experience with those ourselves."

Then he was out of earshot, and she was flagging down another cab.

♊

This time she'd ended up back in the city centre.

Thought maybe a little retail therapy might help take her mind off things, calm her down a bit. Deborah couldn't remember the last time she'd been out shopping in a city, as opposed to just ordering something online or popping into the pitiful selection of shops they had down in Armitage Bay.

She'd ended up wandering around a few clothes stores, picking up some tops, looking at dresses for special occasions she definitely didn't have coming up. Standing staring into mirrors and holding up lengths of sequins or satin against herself, catching how tired she looked in her reflections.

There were plenty of other shoppers around, and she said to herself: *There you go, Glover – I'm not wandering around on my own.* But she'd be lying if she said it didn't make her feel better to be around other people, chatting to each other, getting on with their ordinary lives. Not knowing a thing about what else was going on around them.

Deborah had also gravitated, inevitably, towards the bookstores. In one, probably the biggest they had in Norchester, she was delighted to see a display of her crime novels. She even looked over her shoulder, and stealth-signed a few. It wasn't something you were supposed to do as an author, but Deborah always thought to herself it would be a nice surprise for anyone picking up a copy to see a message from the author inside hoping they'd enjoy it. She'd also be screwed if anyone saw her, the cat about who she was would be firmly out of the bag then – probably much to her agent and editor's delight.

After wandering around a bit more, she drifted past another place from her past – which was also coincidentally filled to the rafters with books. Norchester central library had been one of the last places she'd visited with Jack towards the end. Though they'd both been separately before, they'd headed there again together after that night they'd spent in Room 307 at *The Imperial*. It had been closed then, too early for actual punters, but they'd been let inside and made a startling discovery when they were taken down to the archives section.

Deborah ventured in, and was happy to find that unlike some of the other places she'd visited on her return, not a lot had changed inside here. A few more computer terminals, a rearrangement of the tables here and there. Rather than heading for the crime section, Deborah had made for the non-fiction aisle. They'd had one or two of Jack's books – under his writing name, John Foley – on the shelves way back, and she wondered if they were still there.

She couldn't find any, so went off to ask one of the librarians – a tiny blonde woman in a cardigan who did a search. "Oh, I'm sorry. I'm not picking up anything by that author. We could try requesting it from another neighbouring library, though?" She looked at her watch. "We are closing soon, however, so perhaps if you came back some other time?"

"Don't worry about it," she told the woman. Deborah had long since tracked down all of Jack's books she could find. "Oh, but before I go, there used to be a librarian here. I was wondering if…"

"What was the name?"

She grinned. "Hole. With a 'H' not a 'W'."

"Oh yes, of course!" She giggled as if recognising how the man introduced himself to people. "Marvin! He still works here. Come with me." The woman led her across the floor of the library, over to where a man was rearranging some titles on a shelf. Even with his back to her, he looked wrong. Marvin Hole had been thin, reedy, while this bloke was a good few stone heavier. Taller too. And, when the woman called his name and he turned around, this guy was definitely younger. "Marvin? There's someone here asking after you. I'm sorry, I didn't catch your name."

He frowned, and when he did that Deborah could certainly see a vague look of the other Marvin Hole about him. More than just a look, actually; he could have been that man's younger twin. Then he smiled and said: "Oh God, of course I know who this lady is! It's Harrison, isn't it. 'Inspector' Deborah Harrison."

♊

She'd returned to the hotel.

It was already starting to feel like her safe place, her place where she could think. Where she'd spent that special night with Jack – and even just dumping her shopping back in the bedroom, Deborah could feel him around her.

There had been too many shocks today. Patricia after breakfast, the interrogation, Glover showing up at Fagin's Row, and then the library. She'd felt the same way about that as when she'd seen Theo Redbrook, the brother of the murdered Stuart: the victim they'd finally identified from Fagin's Row. She'd taken Peel with her to let the family know, only to be confronted with Stuart's doppelgänger answering the door. His twin, who'd looked exactly like him. Not a younger version of, but *him*.

She'd be fooling herself if she said she hadn't been thrown when the man 'pretending' to be Marvin Hole had recognised her, in spite of the fact she'd never seen him before in her life. But then she would hardly have been able to, given he'd been too young before. Only graduated four years ago, he told her, but his father had put in a good word for him there. Had shown him the ropes, even given him the keys to his precious archive downstairs.

"Father?" said Deborah, the penny dropping. "Right. And is he still…"

The man's face fell at that. "Regrettably, no. Heart attack last year, I'm afraid. He'd be sorry he missed you."

"I'm sorry too," she told him. "He was a good man."

Marvin – named after his father, just like little Jack was – nodded. "Yes. Yes he was."

He'd gone on to tell her that assisting them had been the highlight of his dad's career, that he'd told everyone about his part in helping to catch The Gemini! It was at this point Deborah had started to become a little uncomfortable with the subject matter, because when all was said and done it was the information Marvin Hole Snr. had provided that steered them down into those underground cells. Yes, it had led to The Gemini being stopped, but had also resulted in Jack's death.

"Dad became a bit of an expert on it all, and it sort of rubbed off on me, I suppose," Marvin admitted. "I've been researching the subject for a while now, continuing his work. If you have the time while you're here, maybe—"

"Oh, I'm not sure about that," Deborah cut in. She'd been interviewed enough recently.

"I just meant, maybe you'd be interested in taking a look at some of the findings. There's some fascinating historical stuff that's been—"

"Maybe next time," she said quickly. "I'm only here visiting friends. Thought I'd say hi."

"Yes. Yes, of course."

She'd made her excuses and left, not least because the library was closing anyway – but felt a bit sorry for bailing on the young man. Deborah hadn't wanted to lie about being here, but if the real reason got out... And this Marvin shared his father's enthusiasm, excitement – he'd been a fan of Jack's books, if she remembered rightly.

"Riveting, absolutely riveting... You know I dabble myself a little bit. Nothing in your league, but perhaps sometime you could have a look at a few of my ideas..."

Ideas that had been passed on from father to son? Which included The Gemini? The last thing she needed was to get sucked into all that. Goodness knows what would happen if he found out she wrote as well! Some kind of collaboration, presumably. Wouldn't be the first time someone had suggested that in the past, via her publisher and agent of course.

After dinner at *The Imperial*, which had been a lovely roast in the hotel restaurant – their chef really was excellent – she'd decided to adjourn to the bar area, figuring a gin might help her to put this particular day to rest. No early morning school runs, no chance of being discovered with a mostly empty wine bottle by the kids. Not that she did that often, and not that she should. Not that she wanted to make a habit of all this, because it was far too easy to go down that road.

But just for tonight...

She checked her messages, finding none from Glover, Rosy or Clark, who she *had* given her number to. Just a couple from her mum asking if she was okay, which she answered, asking in turn if the kids were all right. Deborah did think about ringing again, but really didn't want to field any more problematic questions today.

One gin turned into two, turned into a few, especially as the TV in the bar was screening the soaps. But she stopped before things got too fuzzy, making her way to the lift and then to her room. She managed to change into her vest and shorts, wash her face and clean her teeth, before finally climbing into the comfy bed.

"Night sweetheart," she said to Jack. Then she'd fallen into a dreamless sleep, only to wake, panicked and sweating in the middle of the night. Sitting up, and in the light from the window – coming in through the curtains she'd left open a crack – she saw the shadowy figure at the end of the bed.

Sitting on the end of it, the edge. He had his back to her, but even in the darkness Deborah could tell who it was. The fact he was naked helped with that, and she could see the contours of his muscles outlined by the moonlight. He was looking down, the same way Patricia Bailey had been doing, except he had his head in his hands. When he realised he was being watched, he sat up, then turned.

Jack Foley stared at her, with such grief and sorrow in his eyes it made Deborah want to cry. He missed her, the same as she missed him; wanted to be with her, she knew. But it wasn't just that.

Same as last time, he'd appeared because he had

something to tell her – even if he wasn't using words. Jack had been the reason she'd actually returned to Norchester, not Rosy or Glover. Not even the thought of Felicity, murdered, left by the side of a dual carriageway.

But now she was sensing that might have been a mistake. Jack was scared about something, frightened. Frightened for her. For—

It was at that point her phone started buzzing. She looked away to the bedside table for just a moment, and by the time Deborah returned her gaze to the end of the bed Jack was gone.

She grabbed the phone, trying to focus, head pounding now – from either the knock the other night or the alcohol, she couldn't tell, didn't care. Decided to flick the green button across anyway and answer. Then she realised why Jack had visited, why he looked so sad.

And by the time dawn arrived, yet another police car was arriving to pick Deborah up.

CHAPTER TEN

It was called Valentine Avenue.

But the only love letter or card that had been written and sent here recently was one addressed to death, penned in blood, and carved on human skin. The only flowers would be ones that mourners brought and laid down in time.

Deborah was more than familiar with the scene: the CSIs, blue and white tape cordoning off the area, the men and women in uniform on crowd control. She'd been thinking about one just like it the previous day. Instead of an old, abandoned factory, though, the setting this time was a clump of trees up the far end of a broad road. The victim had been left there, having been beaten and stabbed.

Another future ghost to add to the list.

"Wasn't beaten," said Rosy eventually, getting up after examining the body. That's what the person who found him had assumed, as the man's face was covered in blood. A mugging gone wrong or something, then the person being robbed had been dragged and planted – if you'd pardon the use of the word – under the cover of those trees. You could see the smears now that it was light, or lightish. The blood streaks from the pavement to the patch of grass. It was a useful cover story for what had really happened here, so they'd let the witness think that. A mugging gone wrong, *horribly* wrong for the poor guy on the receiving end. Very right for someone else: the person who'd done this. "His nose is missing," Rosy stated, turning to face the assembled audience as if waiting for applause in a theatre production.

DI Glover, DS Fleming… and Deborah.

If only it was a play, thought Deborah. Then that man would be getting up now after acting his socks off, taking his final bow. Unfortunately, he'd taken his final ever bow overnight. At around the time she'd received that video call.

Hadn't been the police, it had actually been her mother – and sometimes Deborah wished that she'd never shown her how to do those. Sometimes you just didn't want to be seen, or to see what was happening at the other end of a call. On this occasion it was the screaming and crying of James and Jack, who just needed their mummy.

"I didn't know what else to do," said a distraught Wendy Harrison, turning the camera on the two boys in one bed, hugging each other for comfort. "Look, here's Mum. She'll make everything all right again."

I wish! she'd thought, still barely able to focus. "W-What's happening, you guys?" she asked tentatively. Aware that she probably looked a sight, not least because she'd just seen Jack. Because he'd been so upset. Also aware that she was slurring her words a little.

"We… we… we had a bad dream," said Jack, words punctuated by sobs.

"About the… the bad man…" James chimed in.

Deborah felt a shiver run down her spine. "Oh no, not again. I'm really sorry."

"W-Where are… are you, Mummy?" they screamed in unison, still crying.

"I really wish I could be there, but—"

"H-He was… he was hurting that man," James was screaming.

"Hurting… hurting his *face!*" added Jack.

"What the hell's going on?" Deborah heard next, another voice entering the fray. Entering the room, she saw. Isobel. "I'm trying to get some sleep!"

"Aren't we all," Deborah heard her own mother say.

Regardless of how she was snapping, both boys ran to Izzy, clutching at her. "What… what's going on?" she said more softly this time. "Gran?"

"They had a nightmare."

"Oh," said Izzy. "Is that all? I thought someone was dying, all the racket they were making."

"C-Can we come in with you, Izzy?" asked James.

"Pleasssssse!" begged Jack.

"God no," Izzy told them.

"Isobel," said Wendy and even though Deborah couldn't see it, she knew her mother was giving the teenager one of her 'bloody well do it' looks.

Izzy let out a long-suffering moan. "Oh, *all right*. But you'd better not elbow me in the ribs this time, either of you!"

Deborah heard the kerfuffle as Izzy led them off to spend the rest of the night with her, where they would feel safe. It was the next best thing to her being there and letting them in to her bed. When the coast was clear, Wendy switched the camera back on herself. "It's a good job Derek's deaf as a post! What on earth have you been letting them watch?" she asked.

Here we go, it'll be something I did. "Nothing. I've been racking my brains about it."

"Racking your— This has happened before?"

"Just the once, but… I even thought maybe they'd got into my research or—"

"Your… Good Lord, they haven't, have they?"

"No. No, I don't think so."

"You don't *think* so?" There was a vein popping out on the

side of Wendy Harrison's head. "Why can't you have a nice job? I thought when you quit the police... But anyway, it's a wonder you know what they're getting into these days."

"What's *that* supposed to mean, Mum?"

Wendy clammed up.

"*Mum?*" pushed Deborah.

"Just something Izzy told me the other day, about you smelling of booze when Rosy visited."

Deborah gave a groan to match her daughter's from before. "That was... I wasn't—"

"Then falling down drunk the other night."

Cheers Izzy, you shit-stirrer! "I tripped," she replied by way of an explanation.

"Right, okay."

"Mum, look I can—"

"You're drunk right now, aren't you?"

It was Deborah's turn to keep quiet. She knew exactly how she sounded: still pissed.

"*Aren't* you?" Still no reply. "That Rosy's a bad influence on you, you know."

Bloody hell, anyone would think she was the teenager here. Deborah was willing to bet Izzy hadn't told her grandmother about the party she was so keen to attend. "If you must know, I haven't seen her all day."

"I think you should get yourself back home, where you belong."

Deborah shuffled further up the bed. "I can't."

"Why ever not?"

"This... What I'm doing, it's important, Mum."

"More important than your kids?" That was a low blow, but then it wasn't the first and wouldn't be the last, Deborah supposed.

"It's not like that," she said angrily.

"And what *are* you doing there exactly?"

"I can't tell you."

"Your family needs you."

"Other people need me, as well." She thought about Patricia Bailey, what she'd said to her.

"I see. Well, I suppose that's that then." Her mother hung up.

Deborah slumped forward, letting the phone go. "Arse," she whispered. In the space of less than a week her entire world had exploded, or imploded – however you wanted to look at it. Whichever way was worse, she guessed.

Her head was still thumping, and she thought about taking some painkillers but that probably wasn't a great idea. Didn't want to add OD'ing on drugs and alcohol to her repertoire as a bad friend, bad daughter and bad mother.

Bad dream, about the bad man.

So she'd laid back, at least tried to rest her aching head, and somehow – probably the gin still in her system – she'd fallen asleep again.

Until the vibrating of her bed woke her, the ringing of her phone. This time it really had been the police, Glover letting her know they'd caught another one. "I'm sending a car to bring you to the crime scene. Oh, and by the way, this is what trust and letting someone in looks like."

Deborah issued another low moan, hauling herself out of bed and slapping water on her face. Getting dressed and grabbing a coffee from the restaurant, risking those painkillers now because if she didn't her head might simply burst open.

Might look just like that poor guy Rosy had been examining. Except it was his nose that had been torn apart apparently. "And I can tell you this with a degree of certainty, he was stabbed with a double-pronged weapon. In the side to be precise, through his jacket and T-shirt there." She thumbed back to the victim.

"So, our man again," said Glover. "But I thought, I mean, the nose. We only have one of those, last time I checked."

"We do," Rosy answered. Then she tapped both sides of

her own. "But we have two nostrils. Our copycat took one of those, cut it right off. Presumably he either had one already, or is going to acquire another."

"Ah, thank you. Good work, Rosy," said Glover, who walked forward to have a further look himself – taking Fleming with him, thankfully.

Why don't you just throw her a frickin' treat, thought Deborah, then felt bad about thinking it. Especially as Rosy wandered over then, nodding the greeting she'd skipped on the way to examine the dead man. "You look like shit," she told Deborah.

"Thanks. I feel worse than I look, if it helps," she replied. "Didn't get much sleep."

Rosy nodded, looked back at the victim. "Well, sleep is overrated." Facing front, she asked: "How'd it all go yesterday? I heard you walked out."

"It was more a sort of storming out."

"Okay…"

"Didn't like the line of questioning."

The pathologist shrugged. "We've all been on the receiving end of Fleming's questions, it's just routine. Especially when they're vetting—"

"Rosy, I don't work for them. Never going to, either."

"They were just trying to get some additional information."

"The stuff you hadn't already told them about me, you mean."

Rosy's face screwed up. "I haven't said anything that wasn't already on record."

"You sure? About Mason? About Jack?"

She didn't answer that.

"I'm just not mad keen on the way your new friends go about things, is all," Deborah said eventually.

"They're good people, trying to do some good," argued Rosy.

"By following me around town?" She jabbed a finger in Glover's direction. "Creeping about, stalking people, like your inspector there."

"I'm sure he was just..." Rosy's sentence trailed off. Deborah could tell that even she thought that was weird.

"Doesn't matter, they're your work colleagues not mine – thank God! You trust them."

"I do," Rosy said, but had a slight hitch in her voice.

"Just – and I say this as your friend – just watch yourself, okay? There's something fishy about all this. About Glover."

Rosy shook her head. "Are you sure that's not just a hang-up from Mason?"

"Probably. But can you blame me?"

She didn't have an answer for that one either, she simply cast her eyes back in the direction of the latest body. "I just want to get to the bottom of this," she told Deborah.

"Believe it or not, me too."

"Made a real mess of him, of his face."

"H-He was... he was hurting that man..."

"Hurting... hurting his face..."

"I thought someone was dying, all the racket they were making."

Deborah swallowed dryly, pushing down those thoughts. But the timing, of last Friday's attack, of last night's—

"Rosy, if I tell you something, would you—"

Glover returned and Deborah shut up again, Rosy looking at her with a puzzled expression on her face. "So, any thoughts Miss Harrison?" asked the inspector.

It was Deborah's turn to shrug. "Not really, just that it's all very familiar territory."

"Been there, done that, bought the T-shirt, right?"

"Something like that."

"Okay, you're welcome to tag along for the post-mortem though." Glover looked at Rosy. "Miss Harrison *is* welcome to sit in, isn't she?"

"Of course," Rosy confirmed.

Deborah held up her hand. "I'm good, thanks."

"Right, yeah. Not everyone's cup of... You need a strong..." He patted his stomach.

"I'm not squeamish, if that's what you mean," snapped Deborah, thinking back to when she used to attend PMs and scoot when the bone-saws came out and internal organs were being removed. She'd done the same at Stuart Redbrook's, though hadn't been as much of a wuss as—

Fuck! Fuck his name, and fuck *him*.

"Are you sure that's not just a hang-up from Mason?"

Hadn't been a wuss at all, can't have been to be involved in— He'd just been pretending, like he had with everything. Making sure she didn't get near to the truth, making sure... Making her care about him.

Fuck.

"Of course not," said Glover, the SIO on this case. Was he being sarcastic? It was hard to tell. Indeed, Deborah was having a really hard time reading this guy altogether.

"I've just seen enough in the past, that's all. And I doubt it'll give us anything useful."

"Hey!" said Rosy. "Thanks for that."

"You know what I mean. Stab wound with the fork, two puncture wounds. A part of the body that comes in pairs missing. It's the same MO, you know it and I know it. Cutting up that poor guy over there's not going to tell us anything we don't already know, and if this is like what happened before the perp's too smart to leave any DNA or evidence behind. And I'll just bet he's a—"

"Sir, sir!" They were interrupted this time by Clark jogging towards them. "We've confirmed the ID."

"Excellent," said Glover.

"Name's Geoffrey Whittaker, lives not too far from here. Porter at the local hospital, he was probably coming back from a shift."

"Jesus," said Glover.

"There's more," Clark told him, just as Fleming came back over too. "He's a…" The DS looked at them all in turn, stopping when he reached Deborah.

"He's a twin, isn't he?" she finished for him. "Another twin."

CHAPTER ELEVEN

The past and present were starting to blur.

Colliding, running into each other. There was certainly a sense of déjà vu to everything that had happened recently, and was continuing to happen. When Glover had made that crack about buying the T-shirt, he'd been more right than he knew. It was like she'd visited not just this place before, but this time. Or rather she was watching a movie of it play out again, some schlocky horror flick where the bad guy—

The bad man, the man with two faces…

——just kept coming back and back. Didn't matter that he'd been killed before, didn't matter that you thought you were done with it all. He needed to return for the series to continue, for the franchise to carry on. A franchise with its fans, she was starting to realise.

Uniform had continued to canvas the area where the Whittaker murder took place (Geoffrey, identical brother of Graham), going door-to-door, but Deborah knew they'd turn up nothing. If this killer was anything like the last, he'd be meticulous. Would know exactly when and where to strike, might have been trailing the victims for some time; might possess even more details about them in this age of digital information. Same went for the CCTV in the area, regardless of whether there were more cameras than ever in Norchester – all part of the clamping down on crime thing – it was a lost cause.

Indeed, some of the closest surveillance footage near Valentine Avenue was either corrupted or blank. "This happened with the original Gemini," she'd told them back at the station during one of their meetings – in a long room, with an equally long table and a presentation screen at one end showing the mangled images. "There was some talk that he might have jammed or blocked the CCTV feed. Personally, I just figured that it had been messed about with by… by his brother."

There was certainly a case to be made that the footage which had been acquired from the multi-storey, where they believed Stuart Redbrook had been snatched and/or killed, had been tampered with by Mason.

"Our IT people have been working on what we have," Fleming told them, "and did manage to clean this up a little." She pressed a button on a remote control and played another clip of a shadowy figure running across the frame, dressed in dark clothing. At one point the person even looked up at the camera as if knowing it was there, just not caring, but the face looked… strange, glowing almost.

"What is that?" asked Glover, scratching the back of his head. "Some kind of facial distortion mask?"

"There was a theory that maybe The Gemini had some sort of effect on electrical equipment. You know, like people who are prone to static shocks and such, but perhaps he could control it? Direct it?" Deborah gave a shrug when a bunch of people around that table she didn't know all gaped at her. "I dunno. It was just a theory."

A crazy theory, though was it any crazier than Maxwell Craine 'absorbing' twins to feed himself somehow? Fairy tales to frighten children. No more insane than what she'd told

Clark when he gave her a lift back to the station after the Whittaker murder; he'd insisted on giving her a lift actually, though both Rosy and Glover offered.

"You okay?" he asked as they drove through the streets.

"No. Are you?"

The young man shook his head. "It does all feel like history repeating itself, doesn't it."

"Same shit, different day," she said under her breath. "Let's hope it ends a bit differently."

"Yeah," Clark answered.

"Robbie? Can I tell you something."

"'Course," he said, glancing over. "Anything, bos—Deborah, er, Debs."

"Keep working on that," she told him, with a slight smile. "This might sound a bit odd, but then what doesn't about all this."

"Tell me about it."

It was just a saying, but she did. She told him about it, the thing she'd been about to broach to Rosy before Glover returned. The thing that had been on her mind since she'd received the message about the murder, since she'd seen Geoffrey Whittaker's corpse. "I think… I think my boys are dreaming about the killings."

"*What?*" he said, staring at her, and the pool car he was driving veered off track slightly. She pointed at the road ahead and he refocussed.

"I don't know for sure, so promise me you won't say anything to anyone about this."

"I—"

"Promise me, Robbie."

He nodded. "I promise. But what do you mean, they're dreaming about it? Do they know what's going on here?"

"Of course not!" Deborah realised that had sounded more defensive than it needed to be. Like he was the one accusing her of being a bad mother this time. "I'm sorry. No, they don't. I'm not talking about dreams after the fact."

Clark frowned. "I don't follow you."

Deborah sighed. "Okay, to put it into context: Jack could 'see' the killings when they happened last time."

"What?" repeated Clark, sounding like a stuck record.

"He saw the murders – as they happened. Said that his brother James was showing him what The Gemini was doing."

"His brother…? But his brother was—"

"Dead. Yep, I know."

"That was why he was tracking The Gemini, wasn't it. Because he'd killed his brother."

"Correct again. But didn't you wonder how he was so good at that? What he was doing at the crime scenes when we got there, sometimes even before us?"

"There was…" He paused, looked over again apologetically. "There was some talk that he was the killer himself."

"I know," stated Deborah. "I know there was."

"That he might be involved in it all."

"Oh, he was involved all right. Up to his neck in it, just not in the way people imagined."

"I mean, I know now… Jack was the one who… And I'm sorry again that happened, Deborah… Debs."

"We're getting there," she said, then when he looked confused, "with the name, I mean."

"Right," said Clark. "He was— So he couldn't really have had anything to do with the killings. Could he?"

"Robbie, Jack was one of the kindest, sweetest men I've ever known. He was trying to end all this." She shook her head. "I'm not even sure he was out for revenge, he just wanted the killings, the deaths to stop." Deborah brushed away a tear from the corner of her eye. "Pity it took his own death to do that."

"And Peel," Clark reminded her.

"And Peel. Thing is, the boys are Jack's sons. I-Is it beyond the realms of possibility that they've, I don't know, inherited something from him? Some kind of psychic ability?"

"Bloody hell," was all the response she got from him this time. Then: "Who else knows about all this? Feels like something you should be talking to Rosy about."

"Rosy knows about Jack," said Deborah. "Or at least what he told me about his... visions. Is that the right word to use? I'm not sure she believes it, even after all these years. But she knows. Which means Glover probably does too, as she seems to be in his pocket."

"You really don't trust him, do you?"

Deborah shook her head more emphatically. "Not in the slightest. Which means I can't trust Rosy either at the moment, unfortunately. Hence the..." She put her finger to her lips when he glanced across. "Nobody knows about the boys, only you."

"Wow. I mean, well, thank you, first off. But, like, wow."

"None of the rest of the old lot are around, and you're not under the SCI's thumb," she explained. "But also, well, you're you. You're Clark."

He smiled at that. "Thanks, is what I'm trying to say. It means a lot."

Deborah placed a hand on his arm. "Thank *you*." Once she'd started, she told him the rest. About how the dreams coincided exactly with both Felicity Bailey's murder and Geoffrey Whittaker's; about what had happened on the video call the previous night. "Some of the things they were coming out with, it makes you wonder. Makes you think."

"Deborah, if what you're saying's right, then we might be able to use it. Might be able to get to the victims before—"

She held up her hand. "I'll stop you right there, because I know what you're about to suggest. You think I haven't thought of it myself?" Deborah let her head drop to her chest.

"I can't have my sons getting tangled up in all this, it's bad enough that I let myself get drawn back in. I can't let *them* be used." She emphasised that word, to drive home the fact they were people, that they were just children. "Used as some kind of early warning system! Holy shit, my mother thinks I'm the worst person in the world as it is."

"She already knows something's going on, by the sound of it," said her companion.

"Mum knows they're having nightmares, yeah. But I'd like to leave it that way. What's happening with them – if it even *is* happening – is very different to Jack anyway. He wasn't dreaming, it happened when he was awake. And the twins, they're both... both still alive." She looked up and over, speaking through gritted teeth. "I plan on keeping them that way."

"Of course," said Clark.

She wiped away more tears. "Even after everything, even after all that chasing, all that torment he went through, Jack only ever saved one person from The Gemini. And he was badly injured in the process. I should know, I patched him up. That was the night we—" Deborah paused, stopped herself from opening up a bit too much, oversharing. This wasn't Rosy after all.

"Jack didn't have the resources. The means to reach the target in time. He was just one man," Clark reminded her. "Maybe if we'd had more bodies down in those cells, some firepower..."

"You saw him. You saw that... that *thing*, the same as I did. Do you think guns would have stopped him, Robbie?"

"I... We'll never know, I guess."

Did she detect a hint of resentment there, that they hadn't gone down to the sewers mob-handed? Did he blame her for Peel's death, now that he knew everything about Jack? Had she been wrong to trust him with this information, with the stuff about the boys' dreams? "Robbie. You promised."

"I won't say anything, Debs. I gave you my word."

"Then that's good enough for me," she said, having made a promise herself recently. There was silence for a while, before she added: "It couldn't have gone down any other way." But Deborah wasn't sure even she believed that. If she'd known about what was going to happen, what they were facing in those cells... Did Jack have to die? Had there been a way to save him?

Was there a way now to save others?

It was something that she was still thinking about during all those briefings afterwards, during the days that followed – and especially when during one Glover said explicitly: "If only there was some way of knowing what this creep's going to do next!"

She and Clark had exchanged a look, both pleading in their own way – Clark for her to tell someone, Deborah hoping that he'd keep her secret – a glance she felt sure Glover spotted. But then they'd all moved on to other things.

Like the fact that Mayor Tierney was demanding to know what the hell was going on. Two murders in the space of a week, in her city? Outrageous! Clark pointed her out when she came to visit, a woman who looked a little like the ginger lady from that quiz show who was always putting people down. Reminded Deborah of a mayor character she'd created for her first thriller, as it happened; the one set in the market town. Tierney had disappeared into a side-room with Glover where raised voices could definitely be heard. When she exited, she did not look happy – had obviously decided who the weakest link here was – but then again neither did Glover.

Deborah knew that pressure was probably being put on the inspector, not just from the Mayor – as he'd taken over the case from the local lads, probably elbowing some quite senior officers out of the way in the process – but also his own higher-ups. The SCI would have a hierarchy, same as any other organisation, and right now they'd be demanding results. And as all-powerful as they were supposed to be, even they'd have a job keeping a lid on this for long – especially where the press were concerned – and then the shit would really hit the fan.

Nevertheless, Deborah still felt she was being blocked. Included in meetings, asked her opinion on things, but not fully involved. She always got the sense that she was being excluded from things, especially when Rosy was on the scene. She'd notice papers being passed back and forth between Fleming – who was still giving her filthy looks for that storm out – and Glover, but she still wasn't being granted access to anything important.

Fair enough, she wasn't a copper anymore. What right did she have to access what Glover called 'sensitive materials'? But at the same time they'd brought her into the mix for more than just this, hadn't they? To sit around doing bugger all while the killer followed their own devices and desires, executing their own plans. Not even the twins' nightmares would help them figure all that out. Yet she needed to justify, at least to herself, all the earache she was getting from her mother about not coming home yet.

Deborah might not officially be police anymore, but that didn't mean she couldn't investigate off her own bat. Let's face it, she told herself, as she sat in the bullpen being ignored once more, left with some magazines and a coffee, who would notice she was missing? Not even Glover this time, and she doubted he'd bother to trail her with all this on his plate. Things had escalated, and Deborah decided that if she was really going to help then she should get off her arse and do it. She'd never been one for spectator sports.

So, glancing around a final time to make sure nobody was watching, she got up and left.

Left, knowing exactly where she was going.

And who *she* was going to ask for help.

♊

He'd been delighted to see her, the same as last time.

"Inspector!" Marvin Hole said when she found him in the library that late afternoon. "I didn't expect to see you again so soon."

"Hello Marvin."

"Actually, I prefer Vinny," he told her with a big smile.

"Then I'm Deborah. I-I'm not really with the police anymore, you see."

Vinny flapped a hand. "Oh, I know that. It's just how Dad used to refer to you, and I sort of… But Deborah. Right, yes." He was a bit like a puppy dog, Marvin – Vinny – she found, the more time she actually spent with him. Very friendly, extremely eager to please.

"I don't want to interrupt your work," she said, looking around her to see if anyone else was watching. They weren't. "It's just that you said, if I ever had the time…"

"The research. Yes, yes of course! Oh, don't worry, I pretty much finished my cataloguing for the day this morning. They're happy for me to take breaks down in the archive, as long as the work gets done."

"Excellent, thanks Mar— Vinny." It suited him more than his father's name, and she soon found herself calling him that without even thinking about it.

"Okay, so follow me then." He took her through the library, a route she recalled from last time, down a set of steps into the records section – flicking on the lights – to the archive that had been his father's pride and joy. "Dad made quite a dent in it, scanning things in, and I've been doing my best to continue the good work, but there's still so much to do. Hasn't helped that this particular topic has been occupying my time of late." He turned then and tapped his nose. "Our topic." Vinny trudged on, taking her past dusty books on shelves and some open under glass. There were microfiche machines down here, a couple of photocopiers, but mostly it looked the same as she remembered. "It was down here, in these archives, that Dad uncovered most of the stuff about Norchester's history. You know about the rituals and all that?"

Deborah shook her head. "Rituals?"

Vinny laughed. "Yeah, the reason why Norchester has more than its fair share of twin births. It's not a fluke, didn't happen by accident. Do you know you're almost forty percent more likely to conceive twins here than anywhere else in the world? Even higher than the African country of Benin. They have nearly 28 twin births per one thousand."

Deborah was beginning to see that she'd come to the right place. And it definitely explained a few things about her own sons. "You're saying that has something to do with some old rituals?"

"Oh yeah, almost definitely. A lot of people dismiss that kind of thing as mumbo-jumbo, don't they?"

"Most people," she admitted. But not her. Not anymore.

"And the majority of people don't even know about that side of Norchester's past. There was a concerted effort in fact to wipe it from the history books by the Church, lumping it in with all that witchfinder nonsense from the seventeenth century. But it goes back much further than even they realised, almost to the beginnings of Norchester, when the place was just a tiny settlement. To a particular tribe who worshipped a god who was a twin himself, and who wore many faces – though never more than two at a time. A bit like the Roman god of beginnings, transitions, duality and doorways, Janus. Some say our fellow was the descendant of a man – as legend has it – who could absorb the power of other creatures. A man who once absorbed a wolf he came across in a cave when he was sheltering from the elements. The First Wolf, which gave him the ability to shapeshift. It's where the notion of werewolves first came from, according to a few sources."

Deborah let out a whistle. She wasn't one for mythology

and legend, just knew bits and bobs from her research as the original case was unfolding – derived from books she borrowed out of this very library; information about Castor and Pollux, especially. But even she had to admit this particular one was a doozy.

"Here, check it out." Vinny scanned the shelves, snapping on a pair of latex gloves as he did so, the noise making Deborah jump. He mouthed an apology, then reached down one particular leather-bound volume with patterns on the outside. It looked like the one that called up demons in the movie with the chainsaw-handed guy. He placed it on a special foam cushion resting on a nearby table, then pulled a light cord to switch the bulb over. Everything went red, like a darkroom, and he carefully opened the book. Using tweezers, Vinny turned the pages as Deborah watched, fascinated, over his shoulder. She couldn't understand the writing, but the pictures told this particular story for her.

One showed a group of robed figures, hooded figures, dancing around a fire, holding hands. Another depicted a priest of some kind, with a chain around his neck, a symbol dangling from it – two horizontal parallel lines joined by two vertical ones, the sign of the Gemini – drawing a knife across the palm of his hand. Yet another showed symbols on the ground, patterns not unlike the ones on the bound book, while a further one displayed an altar with two identical people on it, that same priest with the Gemini chain standing above them – wearing a rudimentary mask now with two faces – about to plunge a dagger into their hearts.

"They did all of this on what they called sacred ground, in one particular location. Nobody really knows the exact place. Dad and I were trying to find it for years. The real power was in the sacrifices, as you can see. Sometimes they even killed members of their own family, the ultimate offering. Ah, here, this is why."

The final image Vinny stopped on was a representation of

the god he'd been talking about. Huge, muscular, and naked. The artist had drawn faces on the skin, all over that body from the neck downwards. Screaming faces; trapped faces. She had a flash of something, a memory – memories she'd pushed down, buried – and had to look away.

Burning, blackened flesh. Then that same skin healing, faces underneath, constantly shifting, in a perpetual state of flux. Two sets of eyes opening, two lots of teeth shining white as this person grinned.

"Oh yes. *Now you understand. I am The Gemini... I am The Gemini!*"

Deborah felt woozy, her vision swirling. She staggered backwards, head pounding once again.

Past and present, starting to blur.

Running into each other.

CHAPTER TWELVE

"Oh, hey, are you all right?" asked Vinny, realising what was happening.

Deborah couldn't answer, couldn't even speak.

He reached for her, steadying her. "I think we should get you sat down," he said. "Do you need water or anything?"

Deborah gazed at him, then gave a half-nod. Vinny led her away from the book, a bit further down the corridor.

"I've got water in my office." He tittered. "I call it my office, it's basically a broom cupboard they let me use down here." Keeping hold of her to make sure she didn't keel over, he unlocked a door and led them inside, snapping on another – much brighter – light.

In this small room there were a couple of computers on a wooden desk, a huge scanner next to them; clearly where he digitised the old texts. An office chair was pushed under the desk, but there was another cushioned one behind it which Vinny led Deborah towards and lowered her onto. He rushed off to the side where there was a mini-fridge, which he opened and took out a bottle of water. Vinny proffered it to her. "Here you go."

Deborah took it gratefully, digging around in her handbag

for her painkillers – knocking a couple back with the water, and ignoring the fact Vinny was watching her. "I'm… I'm okay," she told him.

He nodded. "Oh, I have coffee, tea? Would you like—"

"Tea would be lovely," she replied, then watched as he bent into the fridge and took out a half-empty milk bottle, opening the top and sniffing it before pulling a face. "Black's fine," she told Vinny and he gave a relieved smile.

As he went over to another table and turned on the kettle – Deborah couldn't see a sink in here, so she assumed he used the bottled water when he wanted a brew – she looked around her. The dull thumping in her skull was dying down a little, allowing her to focus on the walls and what was plastered to every spare inch of them.

She noticed the newspaper clippings first, recognised some of them, yellowing with age: headlines like 'POLICE NO FURTHER WITH MURDER CASE' and 'FAGIN ROW DEATH, POLICE BAFFLED.' But later ones as well: 'CANAL VICTIM IDENTIFIED AS HALEY ARCHER', 'TWINKLE STRIKES AGAIN, CITY LIVING IN FEAR'.

It did nothing to take her mind off what she'd seen out there, the flashbacks to those underground cells – the culmination of that particular murder spree – coming back sharper and sharper. There were photos on Vinny's walls too: of Mason; of her. Some from the papers, same as those reports, but one she recognised from when she'd spoken to the media for the first time about the case outside that old factory on Fagin's Row. Some kind of screenshot from the news reports.

"Now, I know what you're thinking." Vinny was suddenly beside her and she started, but then he gave her the tea in a nondescript white mug with a chip in it.

"T-Thank you. Ah, what am I thinking?"

Vinny chuckled. "*Conspiracy Theory*, right? Mel Gibson." Him and Rosy's old movie-obsessed assistant Eugene would make a good pair, thought Deborah.

"Can't say I've ever seen it," she confessed.

He giggled again. "I told you it was a bit of an obsession for Dad, and I've kind of picked up the pieces. It was more than any other members of our family were willing to do. I wanted to do him proud, y'know?"

Deborah nodded.

Vinny walked around in front of her, folding his arms. "What happened back there, if you don't mind me asking, Deborah?"

She opened her mouth to speak, then simply shook her head. "I-I don't know," she lied.

"Something to do with that image? You've seen it before, haven't you?"

"I really don't want to talk about this, Vinny." It was one of the reasons she'd bailed the first time, but then Deborah remembered why she was here. She needed help, and the SCI were cutting her out again. She sighed. "Okay, yeah. Things are a bit hazy still about what happened at the end of everything. But you're right, that did spark something."

Vinny nodded firmly. "I thought so. The Geminites used to—"

"Wait, hold on a second. The what? The Geminites?"

"It's what they came to be called. Followers, worshippers of The Gemini."

"Worshippers... Holy shit," she breathed.

"Those were some of the rituals in that book they used to try and consecrate this ground, the settlement that eventually became Norchester."

"Consecrate. You make it sound like a religious thing."

"It was, to them. Holy shit indeed." He giggled again at that, then said more seriously, "They were paving the way eventually for his return."

"Like... like Jesus, you mean."

"I guess. There are certain parallels."

There were no bloody parallels as far as Deborah was

concerned. But she could see what he was getting at, people still thought that the Saviour would come back eventually. These nutters just believed that would be in the form of The Gemini. "So, let me get this straight. They were performing these bizarre rites, sacrificing people—"

"Sacrificing *twins*, to be specific," Vinny broke in.

"Right, yeah. It was in the picture. Twins. To make sure that if you conceived in Norchester you had more chance of giving birth to a twin yourself?"

"That's about the size of it. In the hopes that someday the one, true Gemini would rise, and then he'd have a fertile hunting ground."

"Hunting ground? Dear God." Deborah took a sip of the tea, which was more than a little brackish. "But Maxwell Craine was killing people – killing twins – all over the place. They still haven't located half of his victims."

"Maxwell Craine wasn't his real name. He was adopted, taken away from this place when he was only a baby."

"While..." She refused to say the name. "While his brother grew up here."

"Adopted by the Masons," Vinny confirmed. "You should read his diary sometime. The Gemini's, I mean. It's fascinating!"

"You've got—"

He nodded. "I've been doing a bit of research into the family line, which you can trace right back to the beginning of all this activity in Norchester centuries ago."

"You've been... hellfire, this is all..."

Vinny pulled out the chair at the desk and moved the mouse to bring his computer to life. He typed in a password, then started bringing up folders. "Here, look. Their mother was only a teenager, fifteen, sixteen, when she was violently raped. Gina Carlyle her name was."

"Raped?" So the Gemini twins were conceived in violence,

thought Deborah. It certainly explained a lot. And their mother was only a little older than Izzy... Dear Lord.

"Yeah. You can't really blame her for giving up her kids. Whether or not they intended to send the Alpha so far away, I don't know. Maybe not. He found his way home again, anyway. But the whole thing was arranged, orchestrated. From beginning to end," Vinny continued. "By the Geminites. She was murdered not long after the adoptions went through. They were getting rid of loose ends, I suppose."

Deborah put down her tea. "Loose ends? Who else knows about all this?"

"Not many people. Took us a while to dig it all out, but there are places on the dark web where you can—"

"Do the authorities know?" Deborah rose, rubbing her head. Trying to stop the thumping from coming back.

"You mean the SCI?" Vinny asked.

"You know about them?"

He gave another shrill laugh. "Oh yeah, 'course. How they tried to stop the X killer is a classic. Charles Mansfield and all that."

"The X..." Deborah walked around in the small space. "But do they know about all this? *How much* do they know?"

"I'm not sure," Vinny admitted. "Probably not as much as me and Dad, I have to say. Especially if they asked you to come back to fill in the blanks." He spun the chair around. "I mean, that's why you're here, right Deborah?"

She stopped in her tracks. "What?"

"Why you came all this way, from the coast. From Armitage Bay? Leaving Wendy, Izzy, Jack and James behind?" He stated it all simply, like it was common knowledge. "It's happening again."

Her mouth fell open.

"They're not the only ones happy to see you, though," Vinny went on. "I'm really glad you're back."

Deborah's head was beginning to spin again. "Wha—"

Something in that water, that awful-tasting tea? It was then she realised where her jaunt in that small space had taken her. To a curtain. A partially pulled curtain. Something was poking out from behind it; she didn't want to see, but needed to at the same time.

Reaching out, she grabbed it, yanked it back.

Behind there was a dummy, a mannequin. The kind you might find in any shop window, the kind she'd seen walking around the shops the other day, before she ended up here. Before she'd even met Marvin Hole's son. But on this one was a suit, dark clothing. Pitch-black. It was a bit like the outfit a cat-burglar might wear, designed so that they could sneak about. On its hip was a tool belt, with compartments: the sort Batman might favour. The mannequin itself was wearing a mask, which reminded Deborah of something.

Reminded her of the mask Anton Craine had once worn when he was pretending to be The Gemini to throw them off the scent. Two masks stitched crudely together, to give the effect of *two* faces. Just like the priest had been wearing in that picture when he was murdering the twins.

And hanging on the wall right alongside all this was It. The It. *His* weapon, the dual-pronged fork. The same weapon that had ended so many lives, before and after she came along. Stolen, presumably along with *his* remains. Along with all this other crap.

Stolen by Vinny – or someone working with him?

"Shit," she breathed. "*Shit…*"

"Deborah." He was standing now, behind her. She didn't have long. And didn't have much of the element of surprise left.

She threw herself backwards, hitting him, unbalancing him. Shoving him sideways, and making for the door – which she hoped he hadn't locked again behind them. She'd assumed this place was locked up because of all the research, the *Conspiracy Theory* material that would make his colleagues think twice about him. But it was actually locked because this was his lair, his underground lair – same as the cells were for the original Gemini.

The copycat. Whether he was for real or not, whether he was... like The Gemini – probably not if he needed a mask – didn't matter.

He was dangerous. And she was down here alone with him.

Deborah tugged on the door handle.

It didn't budge.

CHAPTER THIRTEEN

"Deborah!"

She heard him call out to her from behind, righting himself. He'd be on her in moments. She tried the handle again, the sweat on her hands making it hard to grasp. It shifted, finally, and she flung the door open, flung herself out through the gap.

"Deborah! Deborah, wait! Come back!"

Fuck that, she thought, shaking her head to clear it. Trying to shake loose whatever drugs he'd given her. Running, stumbling. Almost falling to the floor.

Red. That's all she could see. Redness, like Hell. Like—

The blood, so much blood. It had been at all the crime scenes where the twins had been killed – murdered by The Gemini. Dead now himself, but with pretenders to the throne.

The man 'pretending' to be Marvin Hole.

Pretending to be so much more besides.

She was down here in Hell, with *him*. The killer they'd been trying to catch this time. Fulfilling her promise to Patricia Bailey, regardless of the cost to her own family's lives.

To *her* life.

Faces, trapped beneath the surface.

Trapped, down here. In the hole with Marvin… Vinny *Hole*. Jesus! Not quite. She was aware that her mind was racing, not making much sense. Her muddled brain, her thumping head.

Phone! Even as she ran, she dug around again in her handbag. Trying to locate her mobile. It was in there somewhere, had been near the top but then she'd been scrabbling around in there for her pills – painkillers and whatever drugs he'd given her, probably not a great combination.

Where was it, where was—

Deborah risked a look over her shoulder. He hadn't set off yet. What was he doing, what was—

Her fingertips brushed the edges of the thing, the square bit of plastic and aluminium that might just save her. She dragged it out and thumbed it on, even as she stumbled onwards. Banging into a bookcase, which toppled over. Surely someone up there had heard that!

No. She was down in the archives, probably soundproofed. Phone. Phone. She needed to ring Clark, had him in her contacts thankfully, which she brought up, pressing the button at the same time.

Nothing. No dial tone, no "Deborah, where are you? What's that? You need my help right away? Of course, I'll be there in seconds like Superman!" Clark, in more ways than one.

None of that.

Because there was no signal down here. Of course not. And no internet either, unless you were logged in to whatever system Vinny was using. The same as the library's? She didn't even know what the password for that was!

Up, get your arse upstairs! she shouted at herself.

She couldn't even see the stairs. No, wait, there they were. Deborah almost tripped on the first one, catching her foot on it. Clumsy, like she'd done with the rug Rosy had warned her about.

Her bum leg, the one that had been broken by... by The Gemini's brother – don't say his name! – was letting her down too. She'd need a stick in a few years, they'd warned her about that. Once the arthritis kicked in, when she was getting older. *Even older* then. If she ever made it to that point, if she ever got out of this.

Then she was at the top, but she could hear the footfalls behind her. He was coming.

Breaking out into the library itself, she spun around and wished she hadn't, because it just disoriented her more than ever. Deborah cried out for help.

No-one answered.

It was only then that she noticed the lights had been dimmed. There were no people milling around, nobody looking at the shelves. No staff around either. It had closed, while she was down there in the archives – the dungeon, the cells? – it had closed up for the day. They'd left Vinny to it, probably did that all the time. And why not, they used to leave his father here after hours too. Everyone else had much better things to do than obsess about a case from ages ago.

Than plan more murders to lure her back to Norchester, knowing the SCI would probably ask. Or somebody would. *Should have stuck with your first instincts*, Deborah told herself. *Not come within a million miles of this place!*

But then there had been the figure at the window – hadn't there? The figure, and Jack (who she hadn't seen since the night of the Whittaker murder; who certainly hadn't warned her about all this). Jack had 'told' her to come.

Jack's dead!

She'd be joining him soon enough, unless... The doors, she needed to find the doors. Bloody hell, where were they? She'd only been in here twice since she'd packed up and left the city behind all those years ago. Hadn't been taking a vast amount of notice of the layout, then or now. Was more disorientated than ever, fighting the effects of the drugs.

This was like one of those dreams – don't mention dreams, don't mention Mas… – where you're being chased but you can't wake up. Chased by someone, something relentless, unstoppable. *Wake up, oh please let me wake—*

Where were the main… Didn't matter, because off to the left of her, behind another lot of bookcases, was a clearly labelled Fire Door. That would do. That would get her out of this place, this mess. Get her to freedom and away from—

Deborah lumbered towards it, head spinning worse than before. She more or less crashed into the bar that opened the door, practically fell through the gap. She was dimly aware of some kind of alarm going off, but ignored it.

It was just as dim out here as it had been back in the library. Night had also fallen while she'd been underground. Evening at least. And she had no idea where she was, where the Fire Exit door had taken her. It wasn't a populated place, that was for sure. Somewhere out behind the library.

There were those footfalls again. He'd be following her any moment, so she had no option but to go up the sidestreet ahead of her. Deborah ran, as fast and as well as she was able, considering.

At the same time she thumbed her phone back on, checking for a signal. Still none. Still too close to the library, probably. Did they have a blocker to stop folk using them in there? How far did it extend? Or was this just one of those blackspot areas of the city?

Didn't matter. It was of no use right now, she had to get away from her pursuer. Find some people! Christ, how hard could that be in bloody Norchester? *Dunno, let's ask Felicity Bailey, shall we?*

But she wasn't in the middle *of the city*, Deborah answered back.

Next to a dual carriageway, and nobody had stopped to

help. He killed her next to a busy road. Killed Geoffrey Whittaker on his way home from work.

She wondered if her kids would see this, or didn't it work that way? She wasn't a twin, so… She was their mum, though, wasn't she? What about that bond? Who'd take any notice of them, anyway? Not enough to get help here in time, that was for damned sure.

Deborah kept throwing herself forwards, hit a junction and couldn't decide which way to go. Left or right? Right or left? Like the decisions you make every day in life. Left: don't come to Norchester; right, come to Norchester and get stabbed to death by a maniac.

The footfalls decided for her, and she went right. Which led her to another sidestreet. She was getting more and more lost by the second, easy prey for someone who knew these streets better than she did. Who could take their time while she went up and down, round and—

"I'm not a lab-rat, Inspector."

Not a rat in a maze. She still didn't trust Glover, but she'd take his help over nothing right now. A shadow moved across the wall ahead of her, and she pulled back. He'd caught up. He'd found her. Deborah ducked down another alley, almost falling over some bins there. "Deborah!" She heard him call out her name again, struggled to keep quiet – her breath coming in painful gasps.

She whirled, backed up.

Then backed into something. Not a wall, because it was too soft. But a person. Someone standing there, waiting for her. She tried to move forwards, but hands grabbed her. Hard. She tried to elbow backwards, catch her captor in the ribs, or even the face, but there was no chance of that. He was holding her fast.

So she leaned as far forward as she possibly could, then brought her head back sharply. It probably hurt her more than it did him, but the grip relaxed. Not completely, but enough to be able to wriggle free.

Deborah fell forward now, but somehow managed to keep upright. To fling herself on again, to try and escape. Looking down at the phone she'd managed to keep hold of, she saw that the signal bar had returned.

Here, in the back-streets and back alleys, there was a bloody signal!

She pressed the line with Clark's name on it, heard it ring once, twice, three times and then get picked up. "Clar—" That was all she had time to say before the phone was wrenched away, her attacker grabbing her wrist with one hand and snatching the thing out of her fist with the other. The black square was sent clattering away into the shadows.

"Get… get the fuck off me!" screamed Deborah, trying to wrestle free again. But the figure in black took no notice. The figure, she saw out of the corner of her eye, that had two faces. That was wearing that bloody two-mask abortion, just like Anton Craine!

She managed to gain enough leverage to swing a punch: the same move she'd almost floored Glover with the other day when he'd sidled up behind her. It landed, but awkwardly. And the response was to wrench Deborah's other arm, almost out of its socket.

Another scream followed, but this time of agony.

Then he shoved her to the ground. This shadowy figure, this shadow thing. Looming over her, ready to finish the job. Completing what his predecessor couldn't manage. This was it. Death had finally come for her. She'd been living on borrowed time since the cells, and now that time had run out.

She half-closed an eye, but not before something else happened. Not before Deborah saw someone else there in the alley. Clark? He'd got her message after all. Had come here faster than a speeding bulle—

No. Not Clark, someone tackling the figure though, from

behind. Getting him in a headlock, cutting off the air-supply. The trapped figure reached up and batted at the arm doing the damage, but the person behind adjusted their position, pulling back tighter and tighter, until the figure in black started to go limp. Until they began to drop to their knees.

Deborah just caught a glimpse of the person who'd saved her, and didn't know if she could believe what she was seeing. "You...?" she moaned.

Before her other eye shut. The drugs, the effort of the struggle catching up.

Having their effect.

PART III

CHAPTER FOURTEEN

History repeating itself. Again.

Only she was on the other side of the glass this time, the other side of the mirror. Made her sound like Alice, going through the looking glass – ready for more adventures in Wonderland. Norchester had been called many things in the past, but never that.

Yet here she was, back once more. Different nick, different coppers in that interview room, including another uniformed one in the corner, but an eerily familiar subject being questioned. Squint and you might be looking at an older version of Anton Craine sitting, handcuffed, on one side of the table. Someone about eight years older than Craine, say. The man was broad, muscular, clean-shaven, short hair – though it wasn't spiky – but the same dark eyebrows and intense stare. He was wearing a black T-shirt instead of a white one; black, to match the rest of the outfit he'd been wearing before.

An outfit that had been topped off with a hood and two masks stuck together, making it look as if the wearer had two faces. An outfit very similar to the one Deborah had seen back in the library, but also different. For starters it was more of a robe-like affair, the hood loose rather than skin-tight as it had been with the adopted brother of The Gemini. Not a cat-burglar style, more elaborate than that, more… ceremonial, religious.

More like a priest.

On the other side of the table were Inspector Glover and DS Clark. Fleming had so desperately wanted to sit in on the interrogation, but Glover had – quite rightly – gone with the arresting officer. Besides, he'd wanted someone local there, maybe to appease the Mayor? Didn't matter, he'd made the right decision anyway, Clark was a good copper and was proving an equally good wingman for the SIO on this occasion.

Did she want to be in there with them, perhaps instead of Clark? Like she had been last time, like she had been with Craine? Yes and no. Deborah couldn't help thinking back to that interview, where her boss had lost control, played the bad cop – definitely the 'bad man' – a bit too convincingly. So convincingly, she'd had to virtually hold him back in case he went for Craine and blew the case.

Of course, she knew now that the hatred he'd felt had been more to do with the fact Anton had grown up with that man's twin, had spent his childhood in The Gemini's company when it should have been…

Deborah couldn't help but feel sorry for that poor sod Anton Craine in some ways, dominated and manipulated by such a monster. By an older brother who he looked up to, who he'd do anything for. Even kill, or attempt to. Even take the blame for a series of murders he didn't commit. A scapegoat to buy The Gemini time to finish what he'd started so long ago. A scapegoat her old guvnor had taken great pleasure in taking out of the equation. Removing him from the board like he was a pawn in a game of chess.

Memories, more memories. But this was the here and now, and what was happening in the present was in so many ways very different. For one thing, they had absolutely no idea who this fucker was.

"Your name," said Glover. "Tell us your name."

The man simply stared at him, saying nothing.

"We'll find out sooner or later, you might as well tell us now and save everyone a lot of trouble."

The staring continued, except now it seemed to be saying: will you? Will you really find out later? His fingerprints had been burned off, probably with acid, Rosy had told them. So they couldn't run those through any databases. No matches so far either for the photos they'd taken of him when they booked the guy in.

"You do realise the seriousness of your situation, don't you?" Glover said then.

More staring.

Glover sat back in his seat, blowing out a puff of air. It was about the millionth time he'd asked all this, or at least it seemed that way to Deborah.

"You're going down for assault for starters." Clark took over now, tag-teaming it. "Assault of..." He thought for a moment, perhaps not sure how to describe her: consultant, friend? "...an associate of ours."

The stare switched to the DS.

"Assault, possibly murder as well." They had no evidence of this, but couldn't rule it out. When all was said and done, someone was running around out there copying The Gemini's MO. But they'd been wrong before, about Craine.

She'd been wrong more recently too, about Vinny Hole.

In Deborah's defence, you couldn't really blame her. It all added up. Underground lair: check. Gemini costume and weapons: check. Obsession with the subject matter: check. An orgy of evidence in fact; no court in the land would think twice. Except they should. Because it had been Vinny Hole who'd saved her, who'd come to her rescue when she was being attacked by the guy currently being sweated by Glover and Clark.

It was the last thing she'd seen, before she lost consciousness. Hole, behind her attacker, having placed him in a choke-hold. She remembered thinking, how could he be in two places at once? Chasing and attacking her, yet at the same time helping her? Because he hadn't been. He'd been chasing after her to try and explain, and a good job he'd caught up, because she'd run head-first into some real trouble with this other joker.

Deborah woke up in the hospital, where she'd been taken, groggy but alive. Rosy had been there, by her bedside. Had explained what happened after everything went black – but not before Deborah had seen the worry on her face, the concern there. "Shitting hell, Debs," was all she'd said when the patient woke, though, shaking her head for good measure.

Apparently Clark had received her call, tracked her location and turned up with several squad cars in tow. He'd found quite the scene when he got there, Deborah completely out of it on the ground and two men nearby. One dressed in black, also unconscious, the other holding him down and claiming he'd made a citizen's arrest.

Not taking any chances, and not knowing what the blazes was going on, Clark had nicked both of the blokes and called an ambulance for Deborah. An alarm was also going off at the library, but one of the men – a Marvin Hole – said that was because he and Deborah had both come from there. Assured them that the head librarian could vouch for him, and also would be able to turn off the sirens.

"He's the one… I thought that he might be… but then he —" Deborah had started to get out of bed.

"Oh no you don't," Rosy had warned. "They still need to run some tests, finish checking you over." Which they'd done, but found Deborah was fine. She hadn't been drugged, but the painkillers she'd been taking were probably the cause of her disorientation. "How often have you been popping them anyway, they're only supposed to be for short-term use."

"Erm…"

"You haven't been mixing them with alcohol, have you? Or taking them on an empty stomach?"

All Deborah could do was shrug at that.

"Didn't you read the warnings that come with those?"

"Who reads those?" she asked.

"All meds have side-effects, Debs. Especially painkillers that strong! And they're addictive. They were probably *causing* your headaches in the first place."

"Yes Mum," she'd said, then noted the way Rosy had twitched at that. More to do with the use of that term, it seemed, than because of the nagging. Looked like she'd touched a nerve. And Deborah regretted saying it the moment the words were out, not least because she knew how it felt to be on the receiving end of that with Izzy.

But anyway, the tests had come back normal and so she was released under Rosy's supervision. "We need to get to the station," Deborah had told her. "So I can sort all this out. Talk to Vinny."

"In the morning," Rosy had replied.

"Now," she'd insisted, putting on her own mum voice and folding her arms to show she wasn't going to budge on this. She at least needed to know what was going on with that room Vinny had in the archives, the outfit.

Turned out they were just replicas based on the actual Gemini clothes and equipment. "You should see my flat, it's full of geeky collectables," he said when Deborah was finally allowed to see him down in the cells – and there'd been just as much relief on his face as Rosy's. Relief that she was okay, but also that she was here to get him out of that place. "The fork's blunt, a 3D plastic rendering. I know it's kinda weird, but having that stuff in there helps me focus on the research. I feel like I'm closer to him then, like I might be able to get into his head."

"Trust me," Deborah told him. "You really don't want to be doing that."

"I never even thought… I realised what you must have assumed, but by then it was too late. I tried to get you to come back, tell you it was all just a misunderstanding. I'm a bit… my social skills aren't great, you see." As for what he knew about her, about the fact that the killings had started again, that was merely down to his own detective skills, which she couldn't really criticise as she was conducting her own investigation outside of the SCI. "Dad kept tabs on you, and I guess I just carried on doing that. I think it made him feel better to know you were okay. I think he thought you'd come back one day, maybe need his help with all this at some point."

There were too many people who knew things about her they shouldn't for Deborah's liking, but she could at least see that Marvin Hole Snr's heart had been in the right place. "I'm sorry I never came back to see him when he was still alive," she said finally to Vinny.

"Are you really sure you can trust that guy?" Clark had asked her, when she talked to them about getting the librarian released without charge.

"If he hadn't been around, who knows what might have happened," she said. Plus he'd offered to share his research with her, let Deborah have a look at that diary; it was more than anyone here was willing to do.

"Just because he stopped that other freak, doesn't mean he's okay." Clark had a point, she supposed. It could have just been for show, they might have been working together for all she knew – but Deborah really didn't think so. There had been genuine concern on Vinny's face when he tackled the robed figure. And as for that choke-hold! A martial arts move learned in lessons he'd been going to since he was very young. There'd been no faking the panic, the desperate need to prevent that man from harming Deborah more than he had. He'd almost crushed the guy's windpipe! Needed to get the once-over from the medics as well, and there was still a redness around his neck.

Didn't account for the silence, of course. That he was doing on purpose, because he could definitely speak now they'd been told. Was just choosing not to. She couldn't take her eyes off him; was mesmerised by the way he was just sitting there, like a statue.

She jumped when the door opened behind her, turning to see DS Fleming enter and give her a curt nod. "Anything?" the woman asked, peering past Deborah through the two-way mirror.

"Nope."

Fleming came and stood beside her, hands behind her back, rocking on her heels. "Listen, I think I owe you an apology. For the other day."

"Oh?" said Deborah.

"I know I can be a bit forthright. But I really didn't mean to upset you, I just had a job to do."

"It's… fine. I don't blame you."

"You shouldn't blame Glover, either. He's just doing the same. We were both very sorry to hear what happened to you."

Deborah turned to face her. "I appreciate that, thank you."

"And I want you to know, I have the greatest respect for what you did all those years ago. It was very brave."

Deborah couldn't tell whether Fleming was being patronising or not, but decided to give her the benefit of the doubt and thanked her again. There was nothing brave about what she'd done back then, though – or at least she didn't think so.

They lapsed into silence once more, carried on listening as the detainee was questioned. Watched as Glover opened the folder that was in front of him, started getting out photographs of the recent victims: of Felicity Bailey; Geoffrey Whittaker. Describing what he was doing for the audio recording, for the cameras. It was the same thing they'd tried with Anton Craine so long ago. This guy took about as much notice of the pictures as he had, but at least he hadn't started laughing. Deborah was beginning to wonder if he was some sort of robot.

"You understand that at this moment in time, you're our number one suspect in these murders?" said Glover, spreading the photos out more. The man still didn't look. "That we think you might be a copycat, a wannabe. A pale imitation of a serial killer known as The Gemini."

There! She wouldn't have seen it if she hadn't been gazing so hard at the man who'd followed, who'd attacked her. But there had been a twitch of the lips, the corner of the mouth. "He doesn't like being called that," she said under her breath.

"Excuse me?" asked Fleming.

"An imitation. A copycat."

"Come on, at least look at your handiwork." Glover tapped the photos with his finger. "You want recognition, right? You want credit? You're starting up the work all over again, aren't you. His work? Only right you should get some kind of kudos for that."

Another twitch.

"Isn't that what you want?" Glover leaned back again. "Otherwise why do it? Or are you attempting the same thing he was? His crackpot scheme to become some kind of superbeing by killing people and chopping them up. How ridiculous!"

More twitching.

"As if anyone would ever bow down to that looney," Glover continued. "Barking mad, he was. Who would ever worship someone like that as a god, eh? Only more idiots, like him. Only—"

The man rose then, lurching forwards as if not able to take any more. "You dare!" he screamed. "You dare talk about *Him* like that!" Spittle flew from his mouth, the only thing stopping him from reaching Glover and Clark were the handcuffs tethered to the table by a length of chain – and Deborah wasn't at all convinced those would hold.

Clark stood, gesturing for the uniformed officer in the room to back off. "Easy mate." He came around the side of the table, and the suspect glared at him.

"Imitation? Wannabe?" His intense eyes shifted from Clark to Glover. "You know nothing." Then back again, only this time he did spit *at* Clark. Spat right in his face.

Clark pulled out a tissue and wiped it off, then covered the rest of the distance and stood face to face with the man. "All right. Enough," he said. Clark made to push him back down again and the suspect batted his hand away.

"You know nothing of his splendour!" he said, snarling. "You ask who would worship him, the one, true Gemini?" He reached up and pulled down his T-shirt, ripping it to reveal something on his chest. At first Deborah thought it was a tattoo, but then she realised it wasn't ink at all.

It was a brand.

The puckered skin was raised, burned. And in exactly the same place that the chains had been in that illustration from Vinny's book. The same symbol in fact, those parallel lines. The sign… The *mark* of The Gemini.

"I know what he is," she whispered, then when she saw Fleming's mystified face. "I-I think he's a Geminite priest."

"A what?" she asked, still baffled. For all their resources, it seemed the SCI were completely in the dark about those guys.

"I am His!" yelled the man, once again resisting any attempts to be seated by Clark.

"Right, okay," said the DS. "Whatever you say."

"You know nothing," he shouted again.

"So tell us," demanded Glover, trying to get his attention.

"I will tell *her*," growled the man, and he looked sideways at the mirror. Looked through it, at Deborah: locking eyes. Felt like he was looking through her as well. He can't have known she was standing there – for all he knew she was still in the hospital, or well away from here at the very least. Was probably just a total guess. "The whore of the one who felled him."

So much for the guessing theory. "Rude," she said, but there was very little humour in the remark.

"I will talk to her, and her alone," repeated the Geminite. It was only then that he sat down again.

And Deborah realised what side of the glass she suddenly preferred to be.

CHAPTER FIFTEEN

When he'd said alone, he meant it.

Not just that he'd only talk to Deborah, he wanted to be on his own in that room with her. "Uh-uh," said Glover. "No way. Not happening."

"If it's the only way to find out what's going on, then I don't really have a choice," she told him as they all stood in the observation room, watching the seated figure.

"There's always a choice," added Clark. And, indeed, as she was going in – having made her mind up – he'd said to her again: "You don't have to do this, you know."

She'd patted his arm and then walked inside the room. The uniformed officer was still in the corner, keeping an eye on things, and the Geminite had stared at her, then him, and she knew what she had to do. "Would you mind..." she said to the PC. "I don't think he'll say a word with you in here."

The officer frowned, then looked at Glover through the gap in the door – and he'd nodded. "I'll be right outside, though," he informed her.

"Of course." She'd expected no less, and to be honest – although if the man really wanted to do something, she doubted the PC would be able to get to them in time – it comforted her to at least know the 'guard' was out there. And that the others were behind the two-way mirror, including Rosy, who'd joined them now and had also had plenty to say about Deborah going in there alone. "You've got to be kidding me?"

"I'm the only one he'll talk to," she'd told her friend.

"None of this'll be admissible, you know."

"That's not why I'm doing it."

"No, there's got to be some other way," Rosy said.

Deborah had shrugged. "I'm open to suggestions."

But there hadn't been any, because what could any of them suggest? She either did this or didn't, there was nothing else to it. Yet, as she took a seat opposite the man she really wished there had been some other option. Some miracle to save her from this.

It wasn't until Deborah was this close to him – uncomfortably close – that she understood how wrong she'd been. He bore only a superficial resemblance to Anton Craine, the nostalgia aspect – if you could even call it that – filling in those blanks. The strange sense of déjà vu she was still experiencing, yet things were playing out very differently this time than they had the last. A red mark she could see now, where she'd caught him on the nose, which matched the ones at his throat. "All right. I'm here. You've got my attention," she said, hardly able to hide the crack in her voice as she spoke.

It was only now that he laughed, more accurately a repugnant snort. "I'm honoured," he said, in a way that made it sound like he felt anything but. "Do you have any idea what you did? Back then, back in those cells?"

"We stopped a demented psychopath from killing anyone ever again."

"Please do not call him that, stooping to their level." He thumbed over to the mirror, where Glover and co. were no doubt glued to the scene. "You and I both know how inaccurate that description is. There was no insanity, nothing psychopathic about what He was doing. There was only purpose."

"Well, if his purpose was to slaughter a bunch of people and ruin their families' lives, then congratulations. He succeeded."

The 'priest' sighed. "He was almost there. He had returned to his home, his ascension was almost complete. Then you and your fucking boyfriend showed up." It was the first time she'd heard him swear and there was something even more chilling about that, about the hatred this man clearly had for Jack Foley. But then she realised there had been a reason for using that word other than the usual. "Fucking. Having been *fucking*. The result of which were two bastard offspring."

"Hey!" she aimed a finger at him. "Call me what you like, but leave my kids out of this."

"Leave them out? How can I, when they are so obviously involved? When certain parties have involved them."

"Parties? What parties?"

Nothing.

Deborah changed the subject, needed this conversation to be steered away from James and Jack. "Why were you there, in the alleyway? Were you following me?"

"No," he stated flatly.

"Then how did you know where I was?" She was getting a little tired of people keeping tabs on her.

"We always know," he said and his face broke into a crooked smile. His teeth were the colour of soggy cardboard.

"We? So there's more than one of you? Makes sense, The Gemini never operated on his own. Always had helpers."

"We are more than just helpers. We are *His*. We are everywhere," he informed her. Another thumb towards the mirror. "Your friend in there knows. The policeman."

"Glover?" she asked and he simply smirked again. "How

long have you been following me? Was it you at my house? Outside my house, with your silly little mask on?"

"You would do well not to mock."

"One of your friends, then?"

"We are everywhere," he repeated.

"Including in the SCI," said Deborah. "You stole his remains, didn't you?"

"You only delayed His plans," said the Geminite. "He will rise again."

"On the third day, right? Eight years is a bit longer than that. What's the problem, performance anxiety?"

The Geminite grimaced.

"Is that what all this is about? You're sacrificing people – sacrificing twins – to him? Trying to resurrect him?"

"He *will* rise again."

"Yeah, well, I'll believe that when I see it. He looked pretty fucking dead the last time I saw him. In pieces, by the way, like he left his victims."

"You understand nothing."

"Isn't that why I'm in here? So you can explain it to me?"

"I have explained."

Deborah frowned. "Have you? I must have missed that one."

That chilling grin again. "Nevertheless…"

"You know what, I'm so sick of all this. The prophecies, the folktales and all the mumbo jumbo. I thought I was done with this horseshit."

He cocked his head. "Did you?"

"You don't scare me. I've done research on cults, I've written about them before. The cult of personality, how some people can make you believe anything. Make you do anything. You're just wrapped up in all that. I actually feel sorry for you."

"Feel sorry for yourself, for your family. His wrath, his vengeance, will be unlike anything that's ever been seen."

"Yeah, right. I've heard it and heard it."

"You know. You *know*. You're trying to forget, but you've seen it: His magnificence. You've seen it up close and personal, and for that I am envious."

"Uh-huh, and we stopped him."

"You merely postponed the inevitable, as I said. His destiny."

"Destiny." Deborah was the one snorting this time. "He's bloody well dead! Deal with it. *He* failed. *You* failed."

"Yet you are here. I am here." He sort of had a point, in a roundabout way. This was still going on, even after The Gemini's demise. Something was going on, that was for damned sure. People were still dying.

"Who are you working with? Working for?" She couldn't help herself, her eyes flicked over to the mirror again and she thought about Glover.

"We are everywhere," he repeated. Those mantras were really racking up.

"Yeah, so you said."

"The fate of the world hangs in the balance," the man cautioned. "Nothing less than humanity's future."

"If humanity's future rests with sad wankers like you and Twinkle, then we really are doomed!" she told him.

"Do not use that name!"

"What, wanker? Or Twinkle?" She'd been hoping the moniker the press came up with for The Gemini – a shortened version of 'Twin-killer' – might rile him. Provoke some kind of reaction. "Both sound about right to me. Lame."

The Geminite shot up again, same as before, reaching out with those cuffed hands. If she stayed where she was, there'd be no way he could reach her. But Deborah got up herself, leaning across the table. She could imagine people's hearts in their mouths behind that mirror.

She grabbed him by the wrist, pulling him in close. "Ah-ah-ah, you can't do anything to me, remember? His wrath and all that? I'm assuming He'll want to take care of me when he 'returns'. You'll probably even get into trouble for grabbing me back there in the alley, right?"

He paused, stopped struggling, the anger vanishing from his eyes. Suddenly realising she might be correct. "I did not mean you any harm." It sounded like Vinny's apology, when he put it like that. "I would not harm you now – not physically. You are His. But there are other ways to hurt people."

"What do you mean by that?" Deborah squeezed the wrist she had hold of, digging in with her nails. "What the hell do you mean?"

That crooked smile returned, and she couldn't help herself. She brought back her free hand and punched him in the mouth, felt something give as he spat to the side. Then she scrambled across the table, reaching for his throat, wanting to wring the information out of him. He just started to guffaw, a tooth missing now, one of his molars.

"Tell me!" she barked. "Tell me, you bastard. Who're you working with? What are you going to do next?"

But then hands were on her, dragging her off the Geminite. The uniformed officer, Clark, Fleming. All pulling her away from the man whose face was bloodied. Not as much of a mess as Geoffrey Whittaker's, but not far off. "Deborah. Debs, that's enough." Clark was echoing what he'd said before to their prisoner. "That's enough."

Then she was being dragged from the interview room kicking and screaming, and into the corridor. "Let go of me!" she cried out. "Let me go!"

"Are you going to behave yourself?" asked Fleming.

Deborah didn't answer. Then reluctantly she nodded. They let her go and she immediately tried to get back inside.

"Get her out of here," she heard a voice say. And, as she was being virtually carried off down the hallway, she saw Glover watching her. Watching and rubbing his chin. And the words the Geminite had said were going round and round in her head:

"*Your friend in there knows. The policeman…*

"*We are more than just helpers. We are His.*

"*We are everywhere.*"

CHAPTER SIXTEEN

They were everywhere.

People, other kids from her school. Watching, staring. She'd just had to get out of there. Felt like everyone knew – but how could they? – that everyone was judging her. Some because she hadn't given in, because they were jealous, some because she'd let it get this far.

Shouldn't have got this far, but she'd listened to her friends. Listened to her heart, or had it been her hormones? It was hard to tell one from the other these days. She didn't know what she was doing from one minute to the next, to tell the truth. Angry one moment, so full of love she felt like she'd burst the next. The latter had been how she'd ended up in this situation: the love stuff.

And it was – had been – love. Hadn't it? Izzy thought so, at least. Love. *In love* with Adam Ryan, the boy she'd had a crush on for, like, forever. Since they'd been little kids, since she'd moved here with her mum and her nan. Far away from everything she'd known, and not for the first time. They'd moved a lot before Norchester, her mother always moving around with her job, the career coming first. Not that she'd minded, not really. Izzy had always found it hard to make friends at whatever school she'd ended up in. Didn't really bother honestly, because what was the point? You'd just end up saying goodbye after six months, a year.

She'd had a couple of mates in Norchester, but nothing to write home about. Wherever home was. Then what had happened, happened, and suddenly they were all off to the coast. Mum was no longer a detective, she was a writer suddenly, and they were heading to Armitage Bay – to stay this time, Deborah Harrison had promised. Definitely to stay.

Because there was another little surprise, she finally revealed to Izzy. Her mum was pregnant with twins – twin boys – and she'd need to quit the force to look after them properly. Find another job that meant she could spend more time with them, to put it another way. More time with *all* of them. Be a proper family for once.

Apart from Dad, that was. For the longest time she'd wanted to meet him, get to know him. Her biological father, her real father. She'd built him up in her mind, making excuses for why he wasn't in her life and – if she was being frank – blaming her mum massively for that. Hating her for it sometimes, for denying her the chance of a dad. For dodging the subject and keeping them apart so long.

She'd tried to warn Izzy, sugar coating it to start with; telling her that he was just unreliable, selfish. She hadn't listened. Then, when she was old enough to hear the truth, her mum had told her about the addiction, the abuse. It still hadn't put Izzy off. If anything she figured her mum was exaggerating (she was a writer after all), that there were two sides to every argument. Until she'd seen it for herself, when her dad had got back in touch.

Her mum had said it was Izzy's decision to see him if she wanted to, that she wouldn't get in the way of that this time. And he'd been all sweetness and light to begin with, taking her out for day trips, making up for lost time, she thought. Fuelling the notion that it was Deborah who'd been the unreasonable one, that she'd been the problem in their marriage and when it came to him and Izzy.

Then it had all dried up again. He'd taken on some work that would see him travelling a lot, he said. But not to worry, he'd still be back as often as he could to spend time with her. He sent a present and card the first birthday, the first Christmas. Then just a card, then… nothing. She'd tried calling him, messaging him, texting. More often than not he wouldn't pick up or reply; if he did it was short, clipped. One time he even told her to stop hassling him, that he was busy. And Izzy had had to come to terms with the fact he'd abandoned her. Again. She made excuses for him a second time, but the more time passed and the more he didn't give a shit, the sadder and angrier she became. It wasn't something she could talk about with her mum, or her nan, because they'd warned her, hadn't they. So, because she was there, because she'd *always* been there, her mother bore the brunt of her frustration.

She hadn't deserved such treatment, the rational part of Izzy's mind understood that. But this wasn't about being rational, was it. This was about lashing out, venting. It was just the start of the problems between Izzy and her mum.

And in spite of what she'd said before the woman left for Norchester – to 'consult' with the police over something, apparently – she loved her brothers. Always had done. Especially when they first moved, and it was explained to her that they'd need their big sister to look out for them. It made her feel important. Made Izzy feel special, wanted. The way they looked up to her, in some ways more than they did with their mum. Izzy was always teaching them stuff, spending time with them.

When did that become a nuisance? A chore? When had it become a drain on her life, something that was *interfering* with her life – in particular her social life? (*Stop hassling me, I'm busy!*) Only over the last couple of years, but it was there, and the feelings about it were growing stronger by the day. Should have stuck with her first instincts, about how everything would change when they came along. About how... how her mother might love them more than her. She'd never given Izzy any cause to think that, not in all these years, but it still niggled. The thought festering.

If anything, they had something in common. Both she and the boys had lost their fathers, but theirs hadn't had a choice in the matter. He'd died. Had been killed, though her mother had never really gone into detail about that; something to do with her last case as a copper. Whereas Izzy's dad totally chose to leave her behind and move on. Twice. It wasn't their fault, but she couldn't help hating the boys a little for that too.

Not to mention the bloody way her mother talked about their dad, like she was still in love with him! Fuck's sake! Like they'd had this big love that nobody else could understand, when they'd only been together for a very short time. How? How could they have loved each other *that much*? She didn't understand. And, quite frankly, Izzy was jealous of it.

She'd loved people. Probably as much as her mum had loved Jack. But getting them to love her, that was something else entirely.

She loved Adam. Loved him *so* much. The way his fringe fell across his eyes sometimes and he'd brush it back. The way he smiled, the corners of his mouth rising just the right amount: no more, no less. And when he played football at lunchtime with the lads, she'd pray for Adam to be on the skins team for just a glimpse of him without his top on. It would send tingles through her she couldn't control or explain.

Izzy had loved him for a long time, as a friend first, then something more. She was starting to get somewhere, as well, felt like they might end up officially as boyfriend and girlfriend at long last – especially now that he'd seen the error of his ways and dumped that cow Dani Wyatt. Whatever he'd been doing messing about with her was anyone's guess, she was as thick as pig-shit with a laugh like a hyena. Pretty enough, Izzy supposed, in an obvious sort of way. But she was out of the picture in any event.

Which left the way clear for Izzy, and Charlotte was going out with his mate Kevin so she asked him to ask Adam if he fancied her. Which he said he did. And it had all gone from there really. They'd spent time in the arcades, double dating, hanging out on the seafront. There wasn't that much more to do here, one of the things that always drove her mad. They'd hung out at Charlotte's, at Kevin's, though always with the parents around. And the other week, when she'd said she was on the sleepover, they'd gone down to the pier – under the pier to be precise – and got drunk on cheap cider Kevin had brought from his dad's garage.

That is, they'd got drunk. Izzy had been taking sips, until she felt a bit dizzy and then stopped. The others had looked at her funny, but she'd said she didn't feel all that well and got out of it. In all honesty she'd been scared. Scared that Adam had wanted to go further than the kisses they usually stole when they were on their own. Charlotte and Kevin had 'done it', so they said, as had quite a few of her classmates. Izzy knew she couldn't put it off forever – and didn't want to, really, not where Adam was concerned – but also didn't want her first time (and it would be, absolutely, her first time) to be under the pier when they were pissed out of their heads.

"Never mind, the party's coming up," Adam had said, and she'd nodded. The party at Kevin's while his dad was away, and his big brother was in charge who didn't give a flying fuck.

It was one of the reasons she was so adamant about going, because she didn't want to let Adam down. The main reason she'd got into the fight with her mum about it all, and said those horrible things she didn't know how to back down from. Didn't know how to apologise for afterwards, either; her pride not letting her. Then her mum had been gone and she couldn't, though not before they'd found her rolling around on the floor after downing that wine.

Izzy's first thought had been that the woman was so upset because of their row, she'd necked the alcohol and passed out. She couldn't really talk about Dad, had lost the high ground completely about drink. But she'd felt guilty, as guilty as she'd felt when her mum had left the dinner outside her door after the fight. Then immediately mad again when she remembered the woman had vetoed the party, that it might mean the end of her and Adam. The end of her world! *Sod her*, Izzy thought, leaving without saying goodbye that morning. Then not getting the chance later because her mum was already AWOL.

"Had to rush off back to the city," Nan had explained – without really explaining, and Izzy got the impression not even she knew why. "So you'll all be staying with us for a little while."

Izzy couldn't help grinning at that. Here was her opportunity. If her mum was away, she wouldn't be breathing down her neck about the party – which she still fully intended to be at – watching her like a hawk. Her first thought was that she'd tell her nan she was going to Charlotte's for a sleepover again, because she was always doing that. Her mum *let* her do that. But then again that might get back when they were talking and her mother might twig what was going on. She was far from stupid.

Which left Izzy with only one alternative. There was a lock on her door at her nan's place, so she'd say she was going to bed early because she had a bad headache, a migraine even, get ready and just head out through the back window. It was easy enough to climb down, what with that extension sticking out under her room there. Izzy was just praying the boys didn't have another nightmare or something, or want to come in with her. Even if her nan knocked, she'd either assume the girl was asleep or listening to something on her headphones as she did that a lot. Her nan often joked, "Those things are so big, you'll be as deaf as Derek soon!"

She felt bad just sneaking out like that, but what option did she have? Izzy had been told in no uncertain terms that she *couldn't* go, and as much of a soft touch as her nan was (with her at any rate, even after all this time) she wouldn't go against her own daughter's wishes where her child was concerned.

This was too important to miss, Izzy knew that. So she'd clambered out and made her way to Kevin's place while it was still relatively light, yet arriving fashionably late. A boy she didn't really know that well called Tony answered the door, releasing the *boom-boom* of the music inside, and she could tell by his reaction, his jaw dropping, that she looked good. Izzy had certainly made the effort, spending time on her hair and make-up, wearing the new dress and jacket she'd saved up for and bought a couple of weeks ago in anticipation of this one, special night. Even if his reaction hadn't told her, Tony's "Chuffing hell!" had been confirmation enough. "Izzy, you look... Chuff me!"

She'd smiled, politely thanked him. Then asked if Charlotte, Kevin or – especially – Adam were around. "Yeah, yeah. Come in, come in," he said, hanging up the jacket she'd given him; eyes all over her. "They're in the kitchen somewhere."

Kevin's dad's place – he was a single parent, as well – was an old converted farmhouse, quite big with lots of different rooms. As she made her way through she saw familiar faces, all nodding to the beat of the music – if she didn't have a headache before she might get one here – and all nodding hello to her. Some couples were in corners, already in serious lip-locks with partners.

She spotted the trio she was looking for even before she got to the kitchen doorway, all with plastic cups in their hands. There were bottles of all sorts on the kitchen counter,

Izzy noted, including vodka and gin. Not far away, she also saw Dani – in a skanky mini-skirt and vest-top – leering across at Adam, watching him as if waiting for her moment to swoop in. Izzy wasn't about to give her the chance.

"Hi!" called out Charlotte when she saw her, bouncing around with excitement. "You made it!"

"'Course," Izzy shouted back in reply. "Why wouldn't I?" She caught Adam looking her up and down approvingly too, grinning. Izzy threw him a smile back.

"Come on, let's dance!" Charlotte said, grabbing her hand and leading her off to another room, the dining room, where people were jumping up and down to the drums. Izzy was looking over her shoulder the whole time, looking for the boys. She needn't have worried – they trotted along after them soon enough, bringing more drinks.

After dancing for a while, the room getting warmer and warmer, Charlotte and Kevin peeled off, then vanished. Which left Adam with Izzy. He put his arms around her, rocking to the music, whispering in her ear and kissing her neck. "W-Where have they gone?" she asked.

Another smirk. "Where do you think?"

It wasn't long before Adam was gesturing for her to come with him, which she did. Izzy thought they were going outside for some air, passing through another room where people were playing Twister, but he was actually leading her to the foot of the stairs. Izzy hesitated. "What's the matter?"

She gave a half-shrug.

"Come on." He smiled again, and it was the kind of smile that had been melting her heart for some time. "Come on, it's okay."

Izzy went with him up the stairs. It *was* okay, she kept telling herself. She'd known Adam a lot longer than her mum had known Jack, regardless of all that stuff about having only spent a night together but loved each other a lifetime – she'd got it from some cheesy SF movie, Izzy felt sure. This was different. They were boyfriend and girlfriend. Would spend the rest of their lives together, if she had anything to do with it.

She looked up and the height of those stairs was making her woozy, making her head spin. Izzy had only been sipping the drinks again, putting them down half-full when nobody was looking, on tables or sideboards, so it wasn't that. This was some other intoxication, her stomach doing somersaults at the same time.

Then they were at the top, moving past the queue for the toilets, moving towards the rooms at the end of the corridor. Adam checked a couple, found they were occupied. "Sorry," he said each time.

Before finding one that was empty. A spare room for guests, by the looks of it. Adam pulled her across towards the bed.

This was different, she kept saying to herself, over and over. Different from her mum and Jack. Because this was happening to her and not her mother. More real. But that only made it scarier, didn't it?

And all she could hear inside her head were her mum's words:

Don't let a boy rush you, if he's serious he'll wait. If he's worth it.

Don't let a boy ruin your chances for a good future, a good job... (for that career in the sciences she was starting to lean towards; not the acting, that had never been a serious thing).

You're still very young, there's time enough for all that when you're ready.

And as different as all this was from her mum and Jack, she might still end up with a surprise at the end of it if she wasn't careful. A surprise like the twins were.

"What's the matter?" Adam was asking her again, his words slurring more than they were downstairs. "It's okay, come on."

He was pulling her down onto the bed, hands suddenly everywhere at once.

When you're ready... When you're ready...

Kissing her, sucking, biting her neck like some kind of vampire.

When you're—

"I'm... Adam, I'm not sure I..."

He wasn't listening, wasn't stopping either.

"Adam, no."

No means no. Another one of her mother's pieces of advice, back when she'd been willing to listen.

When you're—

No. No way was she ready, she realised. Not in a million years. "Adam, stop."

He wasn't stopping.

Izzy shoved him off, rolled him away from her, panting. "What? What are you talking about?" snapped Adam. "You've changed your mind?"

"I-I didn't... I never said—"

"Fucking leading me on!"

If *he's worth it.*

"I wasn't, I'm just not... Please. Please don't be like that."

"Be like what? Fuck!" he shouted. "Silly cow!"

Tears were welling in Izzy's eyes, she couldn't believe what he was saying. Couldn't believe how contorted that pretty face of his had become. "Adam..."

"I'll go and find Dani," he barked. "She's always up for it."

Izzy was crying freely now, shaking her head. Someone burst into the room, she didn't know who it was, didn't care. She got up off the bed and raced towards the door just as they were apologising. Raced past them, ignoring the calls from Adam behind. Ignoring the stares from people on the landing, people everywhere.

She'd almost tripped heading down the stairs, cast a look sideways for Charlotte, but couldn't see her. Wasn't sure she wanted to see her, to be fair. Certainly didn't want to talk about all this. Izzy pushed past the people in her way, swimming through them, not caring if she elbowed someone to get them out of the way. Was aware she must look like a mess, her make-up smudged, mascara running.

The door. Her jacket.

Her phone in the one pocket of that new dress was going off. She took it out, saw it was Adam, and quickly turned the thing off. There. There it was, the front door. Freedom.

Grabbing her jacket from the hook, she bowled outside and into the fresh air.

Then she began to run.

♊

Night had fallen while she'd been inside.

Inside, being humiliated. Izzy had no idea what the fallout from all this would be. Wouldn't find that out until she was at school again, unless she turned on her phone (not happening) and she had a feeling the headache she'd faked might last a few days now, turn into a *real* migraine.

She rubbed at her eyes, trying to see where she was going. Head for home. Her nan's place anyway. But she couldn't tell her about this. Couldn't tell her or her mum, although she desperately wanted to. Needed to. Needed her.

What a shame you said the things you did.

All because you wanted to go to that stupid party! How'd that work out for you, eh?

Not all that well.

All those eyes, people watching. People judging, one way or another; but they wouldn't know yet. Couldn't. It would spread throughout the year like wildfire, though. Maybe even beyond that. Izzy choked back more sobs, stumbling on down the path. She'd have to be quiet when she got in, would probably be all cried out by then anyway. No more tears left.

Oh, who was she kidding? There would always be tears left, more to shed about this over the coming weeks. Yet another disappointment. She'd just have to push it all down tonight, hide it as best she could tomorrow – although migraines make you cry, don't they?

All those eyes, all those people everywhere.

She was alone now, though. Alone and walking back, had slowed up after sprinting the first leg. She'd wanted to get away from Kevin's dad's place as quickly as possible, but soon ran out of steam. She'd never been the most athletic of girls, always the one hanging around at the periphery of netball games; never picked first. And walking, strolling, meant she could wallow in her misery with only the stars above for company.

She was alone now.

Wasn't she?

Izzy's head whipped sideways. She felt sure someone had been there. Just out of the corner of her eye, a flash of something moving. There were fields not far away, so it was probably an animal of some kind. A rabbit or something. You got used to that kind of thing out here in the countryside, far from the hustle and bustle of city life. A different kind of nightlife.

There was a light breeze, and she relished the feel of it on her face as she walked. But there was no doubt it was getting colder. Spring had only just sprung, and it was nowhere near summer yet. Then it would be warm all night long! Sweaty even, uncomfortable – hard to sleep. But the holidays did at least mean no school, and she wouldn't have to face—

Another noise, off to her left, made her jump. It was the wind rattling the slats in a fence. "You're just scaring yourself now," she whispered. But she'd be lying if she said she wouldn't be glad to get back, to get into her pyjamas and pull the covers over her. It would be the closest thing to climbing under a rock she'd get at the—

Izzy felt the first spot of it on her forehead. Then her cheeks, joining the tears, tickling her nose. Fucking hell, that was all she needed. More of it fell, water spattering her face as she looked up. She hadn't even brought a handbag with her, not even a little clutch, let alone an umbrella. Wasn't like Derek, obsessed with the weather and what it was going to do tomorrow – he'd been wondering if he should put the bins out the other day in case the wind took them – but maybe he had a point. If she'd been more aware of that, she'd have known it was going to rain.

Not just rain, but piss it down. Seconds later, it was pouring; washing her tears away. Izzy looked around for somewhere to shelter, but she'd be lucky out here. And the houses were few and far between, not that she'd be knocking on strangers' doors in the middle of the night to let her in. A sure-fire way to get into trouble, in more ways than one: you never knew who was going to answer; but also it was a sure-fire way of things getting back to her nan, her mum. Izzy really didn't want to explain all this to them, she didn't have the energy.

Movement again. Not far away.

Izzy looked, saw shadows through the rain. Something, some*one* out there. She stopped, frozen to the spot, swallowed in what sounded to her like some kind of cartoon gulp.

People everywhere, staring.

No. Not people. One person.

That shadow moving now, she could see rain bouncing off it – him? Izzy tried to focus, but the rain was making it more difficult, causing her make-up to run. She was getting drenched, probably looked like a drowned rat. Why would anyone choose to be out here? Unless…

Unless they were following her.

Her mum had warned her about this kind of thing as well. Not to go anywhere on her own – certainly not the middle of nowhere! – because there were men who stalked girls like her.

She'd had to deal with them when she was on the force; you always think it's not going to happen to you and then—

The snapping of a twig or a branch.

The city. That's where she needed to be right now, where there were streetlights, CCTV cameras. Not fields and cliffs and—

Phone! She should fish out her phone and turn it on again, might be lucky enough to get a signal out here; then again, might not. But at least she could turn on her torch. She dug into her pocket, rooting around.

That shape was heading towards her, the 'someone' who'd been watching her. Staring, judging. Izzy began to run. Again. Ran as fast as she could, but of course the rain was turning the path to mud. To slush. She skidded, almost going flying into a ditch, the phone flying out of her hand into the darkness. Didn't have time to search for it, would never find it anyway and couldn't just stay here wondering what to do.

Should have stayed at the party, she said to herself. (Warm and… safe. Had she been safe?) But how could she? There was nothing for her there now, hadn't ever been it turned out.

If only she'd listened to her mum. If only she hadn't—

Footfalls. Is that what she could hear behind her now? Someone coming after her, someone chasing her? Maybe they'd been watching her since the farm, since Kevin's dad's.

Izzy scrambled to get herself upright and nearly ended up doing the splits. That would have been unfortunate, she thought to herself, because she wasn't a gymnast either. Had never mastered that kind of thing like some of the other girls, throwing themselves around on the ropes and the parallel bars, rolling around on mats, while she watched at the edges of the gym again. Never picked first for teams. Always on the outside, looking in.

Always wanting to be wanted.

To be loved.

Whoever this is might love you in a way you really don't want, she thought to herself and it spurred her on. Could sense someone behind her, risked a look over her shoulder but couldn't see a thing.

Had been so focused on what was behind her, she didn't face front again until it was too late. Until she'd run into someone. Someone whose arms wrapped around her tight. Suddenly there was light, noise.

And Izzy realised the person who had hold of her, the person who'd grabbed her – who was probably in cahoots with whoever was behind – wasn't alone.

People, everywhere. Watching, staring.

Judging.

CHAPTER SEVENTEEN

Into every life, a little rain…

And it had certainly done that: fallen. Especially recently, last night and this morning, turning into a storm, in fact. A storm that had been a long time coming, it seemed. Leaving that strange ozone smell in the air, reminding Deborah of the crime scene by the canal years ago, cyclist Haley Archer's body being examined, the rain pitter-pattering on the roof of the tent.

There would be more crime scenes like those, like Felicity's, like Geoffrey's, unless they got to the bottom of all this. Unless *she* got to the bottom of it.

Wasn't as if the authorities were helping much; if anything they were giving her more of the cold shoulder than they had before. Okay, she shouldn't have lost it like that back in the interview room – shouldn't have let that bastard Geminite (whose identity still hadn't been confirmed) get to her. Made her old boss look like an amateur in the rage stakes, it had to be said. Fair enough they'd been forced to drag her off him, because she was ready to tear the fucker apart, but they'd treated her like the criminal, not him.

Had taken her off to the visitor's room, where Glover

eventually came and found her, with Rosy in tow. "Well, that wasn't very clever, was it?" he said.

"I didn't realise I was going in there to be clever," she replied. "Just to get information, which you were having trouble doing."

Glover folded his arms. "That's what you did, is it? Get information? Looked like you were auditioning for *GLOW* to me. He could press charges, you know."

Deborah scowled. "I'd like to see him try. As for information, I found out that he's working with people on the inside."

"Working with lots of people everywhere, if he's to be believed," Rosy chipped in.

"Seemed to think you knew something about it all, didn't he," Deborah continued, never once taking her eyes off Glover. "What exactly did he mean by that?"

Now the inspector threw his hands into the air. "How the hell should I know? The guy's clearly a nut-job."

"He's a fanatic, there's a difference. They're focused, and although it doesn't make much sense to us he definitely knows what he's doing. And he – they – have a plan."

"I think the best plan for now is for you to go back to the hotel and get some rest," said Glover. "Don't you think, Rosy?"

Her friend nodded. "That's exactly what I told her when she left the hospital."

"You mean stay out of the way?"

"I mean stop putting yourself in *harm's* way, Miss Harrison. Running about pretending to be Batman and Robin with your librarian friend."

"I wasn't— And if it hadn't been for Vinny, you wouldn't have that guy in custody right now."

Glover held up his hands now in a gesture of placation. "We're very grateful for your help, truly we are. As we... as *I* have been all along. I'm very grateful for you even coming."

Funny way of showing it, thought Deborah.

"But I'm beginning to think it was a bad idea. That I might have put you in great danger."

You think?

"Please, just go and get some rest."

There didn't seem much point in arguing and she wasn't sure she had the energy for it anyway, after the scuffle in the alley and coming down from the adrenaline of facing the Geminite. "Just do me a favour," she said, saying it to both Glover and Rosy because then she knew it would probably get done. "When you put him back in his cell, have someone watch him. Make sure he doesn't bite off his own tongue." She wasn't done with him yet, not by a long chalk.

So Rosy had run her back to *The Imperial*, made Deborah promise not to take any more of those pills or have a drink that night. "Tell you what, we'll have some champagne when all this is over. Deal?" she said. "But you make me a promise, as well."

"Name it," said Rosy.

"You double-check that they're keeping an eye on my family."

"Of course, I'll get Glover to—"

"Not Glover. *You.*"

"Still don't trust him, eh?"

"I trust him even less now, Rosy! That guy just implicated him in all this, weren't you listening?"

"That wasn't what—"

"'I don't know what he's talking about'," said Deborah, lowering her voice to imitate Glover. "'He's a madman!' Yeah, right."

"You're going to have to trust someone else at some point," her friend told her. A mirror of what her SCI co-worker had said when he'd surprised her at Fagin's Row.

"I think the best plan for now is for you to go back to the hotel and get some rest. Don't you think, Rosy?"

"You mean stay out of the way?"

She had no intentions of doing that at all, and there *were* people she trusted. Clark. Rosy, who regardless of everything was one of her oldest friends. One of the few that had stuck around, anyway. She trusted her at least to check on the security of her kids, her mum, which she agreed to do.

They of course had no idea about all this, how much danger they could potentially be in. The Geminite's words had really shaken Deborah.

"There are other ways to hurt people… We are everywhere."

Not an out and out threat, but implied. Enough to rattle her, to have her messaging her mum that evening to check everything was all right. 'We're fine,' had been the response. 'Apart from Izzy having a bad headache. She's taken herself off to bed.'

Deborah had nodded. Fine, yes. That *was* fine. Better than what had been going on in Norchester, anyway. Then an email had come in, distracting her. From Vinny Hole. She wasn't in the least bit surprised that he had her private email; probably had her mobile number as well.

He was apologising once again, saying that he hadn't meant to frighten her. And that he hoped this made up for it a little bit. Oh, and to not share because he hadn't exactly obtained it by legal means. Friend of a friend of a friend, and all that. He sounded more like his father than ever then, even by email.

Deborah had hesitated, wondering what on earth it could be. But her curiosity had got the better of her and she'd clicked the private link he'd sent that would be accessible for the next day. Only to find…

Pages from the diary of Maxwell Craine! She remembered now Vinny mentioning that, saying something about having read the extracts, asking her if she wanted to as well. 'Fascinating', she believed was the word he'd used. When she started to pore through the scanned pages, sitting back on the bed in her room, she couldn't agree more.

Parts had been burned away by fire damage from what happened in the underground cells, but there was enough to build up a picture of young Maxwell and what made him what he was. Someone who felt alone – mostly because he'd been robbed of his 'other half', his twin – and been placed with a family who, although they could provide the creature (interesting choice of words when talking about the future Gemini) comforts in life, couldn't fill that void. It detailed the way his mother had never really warmed to him – something that had resulted in him murdering her, and covering it up – how he'd discovered that he could 'sense' the presence of other twins, even if they didn't know it themselves, and his experimentations into how he might channel their lifeforce so that it wouldn't be 'wasted'. When Rosy had called him a unique individual, something no-one had seen before, she hadn't been joking. He considered himself to be some sort of mutant, the kind that do appear in nature. But whether his killings were actually making him stronger, or it was just all in his mind – psychosomatic, believing it to be true – was anyone's guess. She supposed that's what the SCI scientists had been trying to find out with his remains. Interestingly, he thought himself to be some sort of superhero, that this was his origin story. That eventually he'd be the one to fix the world's problems. To fix everything.

It also showed just how much abuse Anton had endured, to the point where Maxwell had even ordered him to go and play on a main road and he'd obeyed, only to be pulled back out of the traffic by a neighbour just in time. That man had been totally under his control, mesmerised by his older 'brother'. If she hadn't understood it fully before, this totally explained why Anton had done the things he'd done in Norchester. How much influence his sibling had on him, and might have on others.

Of course, Maxwell had no idea about the cult that had worshipped him for centuries. Who had engineered this whole thing, apparently. Had they been watching him even then? They must have been. Tracking him as his murderous tendencies emerged, as he tore through twin after twin, stabbing them with a weapon based on his musician father's tuning fork. Figuring himself to be a detective of sorts, as well. Enough of one to evade the police when it came right down to it. Until, finally, his collection of twin body parts which he thought amplified his connection to the people he'd killed, was almost complete.

The diary ended where he'd just discovered that he had a brother, and was about to contact him. Ended as 'The Gemini' was rising.

"You only delayed His plans… He will rise again."

Deborah had mailed Vinny back, thanking him. Giving him the broad strokes of the interview with the Geminite priest, telling him what she thought was going on: that they were trying to resurrect their 'god' somehow.

She hadn't slept much. The rain kept her awake (into every life, but not *this* much…) the thunder and lightning, plus a general feeling that something bad was happening to someone close, not to mention the fact that entries from the diary were swirling around in her brain, all mingling, merging into one.

I had that weird dream again last night, the one I've been having ever since I can remember…

I'm standing, gazing into a mirror. But the reflection isn't really me, at least not the me I am right now. More like the me I want to be. My reflection is… more confident-looking, doesn't wear glasses (I've had them since I was seven); I'm standing prouder, taller, instead of slumping…

I've felt restless ever since. Like there's something I should be doing. I need to do.

I overheard them last night. Mother and Father... "You can tell just by looking in his eyes," Mother said, voice lower but still full of hatred. "He's different... That... that stranger upstairs masquerading as our boy."

Both the dreams and 'Mother' were right. I'm not a nobody, and I am different (though I didn't have anything inside me, not back when she said those words). Pieces of the puzzle are starting to slot together...

Anyway, back to the first one I... hunted. Yes, I suppose you could call it that. I tracked him, at any rate, got his scent in my nostrils. Followed him, planned it all in advance: what I would wear – all black, including the mask – what I was going to do, where I was going to do it.

I had to share this one with you. The latest addition to my collection.

Matt Wilson (names to faces now, faces to names), fitness instructor in a gym. I followed him for four days, the posing twat. I did so enjoy our little 'altercation' out in the car park when he was leaving work late. And he was strong; a real challenge...

When the phone started to vibrate beside her on the bed, she'd started awake.

Snatching it up, she saw the clock, saw that she'd only had a couple of hours sleep at most, unsurprisingly. But another message had come in from Vinny, this one marked urgent. An answer to *her* message, but also saying that he'd doubled down on his research, called in several favours and finally tracked down some information he thought she should know straight away. Information that might be relevant to the case. Eager to please, once again.

Bleary-eyed, Deborah had read what Vinny had to say. Then she'd sat bolt upright. Relevant? That was the understatement of the century!

Because what Vinny had sent over that morning,

ridiculously early, was probably the most important thing anyone had ever shared with her. Something that would change everything.

On his travels, Maxwell Craine had fathered twins. Twin sons.

And Vinny knew where one of them lived.

CHAPTER EIGHTEEN

If they were lucky, they'd reach him in time.

Before he got wind they were looking for him, before he had a chance to bolt. Not that he had an inkling anyone was looking for him, did he? That anyone was coming for him? If this person – by the name of Luke Simpson – was still where Vinny thought he was, then he couldn't possibly be responsible for the murders in Norchester. It was simply too far away; the drive over was telling them that, because it was taking forever. But what about his brother? What about *his* twin? Both sons of Maxwell Craine, The Gemini.

Was he working with his sibling? Was this all about revenge? At the very least Simpson was someone they should probably have a talk with, all part of the ever-expanding mythology of this legend.

Deborah glanced across at Clark, who'd barely said a word since they exited the motorway and he'd told her that the back roads were probably going to be the fastest way to get there. To get to the outskirts of a town called Kamton, which, honestly, Deborah had never even heard of before. If he was keeping a low profile, then this Luke Simpson had definitely picked the right place to do it.

Bored, Deborah took out her phone, but she hadn't been able to get a signal for ages. Probably a consequence of being out among the rolling hills, particularly lush after having a proper drink the night before, sheep and cows dotted about the place. She used to be quite excited by that, when she first moved from the city, from Norchester. But Armitage Bay and the surrounding areas had their fair share of countryside, with all the animals which accompanied that. It was no longer an exotic thing, and today she had other stuff on her mind.

Like the fact Clark was probably hacked off with her. It had been a big ask, she knew, and at a time when he was already on thin ice with Glover for hanging around with Deborah too much – or so she'd been told in no uncertain terms when she rang him up. Probably why the inspector had taken him into the interview with the Geminite rather than Fleming, trying to bring the DS more to heel. Was he dangling the promise of a position at the SCI as well? Would Clark even be interested?

"Deborah, I can't. I really can't."

"But this is *huge!*" she'd told him, having woken him up at the crack of dawn.

"I agree. All the more reason you should tell Glover."

"I… If he goes in all guns blazing, then we could lose our only shot at finishing this once and for all." She didn't want to bring up the trust thing again, she'd harped on about that enough to Rosy.

"Please. If the shoe was on the other foot, I'd do it for you."

"Debs—"

"You said last week that I was an inspiration to you, that I'm one of the reasons why you decided to join the CID. Well, my gut's telling me to go in quietly."

"Look, I'd like to help, but—"

"If you don't, I'll just go anyway. You know I will. I'll jump on a train or a bus or whatever and go there on my own."

"Debs, you can't."

"Then come with me, Robbie. *Please*."

There was a pause and a long breath down the line. "I'll swing round and pick you up, I guess."

"What are you going to tell the station?" Tell Glover is what she really meant.

"I'll pull a sickie or something."

"Oh thank you! Thanks so much!"

But he hadn't been best pleased about it, and she couldn't really blame him. No-one liked to be strong-armed into something, especially as it might get them into trouble at work. Deborah didn't want that, the force needed people like Clark. At the same time, she didn't know who else to ask. Rosy would just go straight to Glover, Vinny had already done enough – though would probably jump at the chance of a road trip to talk to the son of The Gemini – and she needed someone with clout on her side.

Someone with a badge, even if he would be off his patch here.

Still, she didn't want it to come at the expense of their friendship – and it wasn't until she saw how mad he was with her, that she realised how much she'd come to rely on that. Eventually, after miles of silence, she attempted some small talk. "How's Helen?"

At first she thought he wasn't going to answer her, then he just said: "Hmm?"

"Helen? You know, your girlfriend. I didn't wake her up too, did I?"

Robbie's eyes softened. "Oh, no. No, you didn't. I'm not seeing her till the weekend. She's fine."

"Ah, right. For some reason I thought you guys might be, y'know, living together."

Clark shook his head. "Not yet. Maybe, someday. It's just easier at the moment, what with work and everything."

She almost asked 'hers or yours?' but then she knew the

answer to that already. It was a hard life being the partner of a cop. "Yeah, makes sense," she answered, leaving a gap. Then: "Definitely don't tell her you and me went on a trip together." It was a stab at humour that fell completely flat.

"Wasn't planning on it."

Another lapse into silence, which she broke with, "I can always sort out a couple of signed copies of my books for her. If she's—"

"Deborah. Debs. Look, I know what you're trying to do. And I appreciate it. But, well, this is really awkward for me."

She hung her head. "I know. And I'm sorry."

"I try and do things by the book, is all. This maverick stuff doesn't come easy to me. Keeping info from superiors, going behind their backs to—"

"I said I'm sorry." She hadn't meant it to, but her words came out with an edge to them. It was their first real lead since she'd been brought into all this, apart from the vague talk about Geminites that Vinny had come up with, and the priest now in the cells at the nick, who'd clammed up again since she'd attacked him.

"You're coming across as a bit…" Clark shrugged. "When you went for that guy, I mean. I get it, I really do, but—"

"Oh, do you?" she asked, the tone still there.

"You weren't the only one there when The Gemini was taken down before, remember?"

"I remember," said Deborah. "I'm remembering more and more each day." And was it her imagination or did she see a wince at that, as if he was doing the same. They'd both blocked it out, but now those memories were coming back with a bang. "You weren't the one dragged back into this, though. Who put her family at risk because of it. Hell, Robbie, I'm not even job anymore. Not even on the force, I shouldn't even be—"

"No, no you shouldn't. That's what I was trying to tell you

back there on the phone, let the others handle it. Let Glover—"

"Fuck Glover," she snapped. "I'm sick to death of hearing about bloody Glover! I've done more for this investigation since I've been back than he's… Why is that, do you think?"

"He's not Mason," stated Clark, glancing over.

"Don't ever say that name to me, Robbie."

"Mason," repeated the man, on purpose probably, "was a complete and utter… You weren't the only person he let down, Deborah. You weren't the only one who lost somebody."

"Not the same."

"No, but I… I did love Peel. He was like a brother to me. We came up through training together, watched out for each other."

She'd known they were close, but Deborah hadn't realised quite how close until then. "Robbie, I'm sorry. I really am."

He nodded, and she could see he was trying to control his emotions. Teeth gritted, attempting to hold back the tears. "I just wish…" Now he shook his head.

Her hand was on his arm again, another squeeze like back in the curry house. "Yeah, me too."

Clark laughed suddenly. "He told me about that time you know, with you and him in the car. When he dropped the sweets."

Deborah couldn't help herself, a smile broke on her face when she recalled that memory. Unlike some of the others associated with this case, it was a nice one. They'd been on their way to do a horrible thing, to inform Stuart Redbrook's family about his death; deliver the 'death knock' as they called it on the force. But the car journey, a bit like this one now, had been nice. Funny even. "He looked like a little kid with those sweets, and then he dropped them all over the floor of the car."

Another chuckle from Clark. "I shouldn't laugh, he was mortified. Thought he'd made a bad impression."

Deborah joined in with the laughing. "He thought I was going to report him, didn't he."

Clark nodded.

"I told him, if I reported every copper who scoffed sweets on duty—"

"You'd be doing paperwork from now till doomsday."

She turned and smiled at him, and he smiled back. To think that Peel had remembered exactly what she'd said, and then Clark all these years later… "He was a good bloke."

"He was."

They tailed off into silence again for a few moments, but it was a comfortable silence. The silence two friends can share without having to say anything at all. But then Deborah remembered something else. "Allsorts."

"Sorry?" asked Clark.

"The sweets. They were liquorice allsorts."

Clark gave a nod. "Those were his favourites." He leaned forward and put on some music, some woman with a terrific voice accompanying a set of furiously played strings. It wasn't the kind of thing she'd pegged Clark for, but Deborah was glad of it as she watched the greenery go by, the faint outline of a rainbow in the distance.

A nice journey, but with something horrible at the other end.

♊

After stopping off at a pub for lunch, one of those really out of the way traditional places called *The Wanderer's Rest*, where they were served by a burly barkeep who introduced himself as Abraham Bamford, and said they did the "Best shepherd's pie you'll ever taste!", and after Clark consulted the map he always kept in his car, they arrived at the outskirts of Kamton mid-afternoon.

It took them half an hour or so to find the place they were actually looking for, however, through a combination of asking people and just blind luck: a block of flats that looked like two concrete Lego bricks on their sides stuck together, and was totally out of place, just a hop, skip and a jump from all that nature. Not to mention being equally at odds with its own name: Meadow Hill.

Wasn't hard to figure out why Kamton council had stuck the place here though; out of sight, out of... From the graffiti that covered the walls, to the smell inside the lifts – of vomit, or pee, or possibly a combination of both – it was a billion miles away from apartments like the one Rosy inhabited, in more than just distance.

They spotted youths with caps on, wearing hoodies, hanging about round the stairs that they took, a couple of which eyed Deborah up like she was an option on the menu back at *The Wanderer's Rest*. Her response was to stare back until they looked away; it was something she'd learned very early on walking the beat. They also didn't seem too impressed by Clark's suit and tie, the whiff of police coming off him in waves.

"Not exactly somewhere I'd expect a criminal mastermind to be living," muttered the DS.

"Or the perfect place to lay low," Deborah countered.

They reached the level they were looking for, which took them out onto a walkway with a rail separating them from the inevitable drop. "Flat 401, just down here," said Clark, gesturing along the corridor. Deborah tried not to look to her left as they walked.

Someone was just coming out of their front door ahead of them. He was thin – too thin, really, because his jacket, T-shirt and jeans hung off him; even his dirty-white trainers looked too big – and he had that stooping stance of someone who was either hung over, or was looking to be. A drawn expression, pale skin and bulbous eyes, with a goatee beard, it wasn't until they got a little closer that Deborah spotted the resemblance. The man locking up his door had the look of a younger version of Maxwell Craine. Of Maxwell's brother, too.

That was to say, he bore more than a passing resemblance to The Gemini.

If The Gemini had been a washed-up druggie. If he'd been a weakling, which was about as far from the truth as you could possibly get. Even as he turned to see them, Deborah was wondering if this man's father had known about him. Probably not. Wondering also if this man knew about his father? That remained to be seen.

And to get the answer to that question, they'd need to talk to him. They'd need to—

His eyes went wide, his hand trembling as he finished locking up his flat. Deborah looked across to see that Clark had taken out his warrant card, was flashing it – always by the bloody book! – and that alone was filling this bloke (who *had* to be Luke Simpson, couldn't be anyone else but one other person) with complete dread.

That was when it happened, when he turned away from them and bolted. "Stop! Police!" shouted Clark, which Deborah couldn't help thinking wasn't the smartest move to make around here, either. The badge, the warning… Nothing would guarantee a chase more than that.

They set off after him, Clark ahead of her because he had longer legs, because he was more physically fit. What with this and the stunt in the alley, she was beginning to feel her lack of time in a gym. That and her years, her bad leg. Simpson was pelting down the walkway, elbows going up and down like some kind of well-oiled machine. Weakling he might have been, but he clearly made up for it in speed.

Clark was gaining, though. Would have caught up with

him there and then if it hadn't been for the sudden appearance of more of those youths. Might have been the same ones from the stairs, might have been some others – they all seemed to look the same here – but the intent was clear. There was no love for the law in Meadow Hill, and if someone was trying to escape a copper then they'd definitely get help.

They barrelled into Clark, sending him spinning. Sending him back into Deborah, who was knocked towards the railings. Sent backwards over them, her top half flying off into space. She had seconds, and would have gone over completely if it hadn't been for Clark grabbing her and pulling her back.

"Oh no you don't," he said, setting her upright again. "You okay?"

Deborah nodded, but she felt far from all right. It had done nothing to combat her recent fear of heights at all. "Go! Get after him!" she said.

Clark nodded, set off again. The youths looked to have scampered, but as soon as Clark was out of sight, they suddenly appeared again. Deborah had barely got her breath back, was still shaking from almost going over the edge. But there was a new thing to panic about now, a new threat. Three of them, stepping closer.

"All right," she managed. "Who's first?"

♊

Clark caught sight of his target just as he was vanishing round the corner.

Heading for a set of stairs. Would he go up or down? that was the question. He was left no choice, really, when a woman with a baby coming up to this level cut him off. Simpson began upwards, with the policeman hot on his heels.

Clark pelted up the steps, taking them two at a time to try

and catch up with the person he was pursuing. This was important, he couldn't let him get away. Wasn't about to.

Clark rounded one turn, then another. And… lost him.

Had he gone out onto the walkway at this level, out through the door there? Must have done, Clark couldn't hear him on the stairs now as he craned his neck. Then suddenly he was being struck again, shoved into the wall, which he hit and then slid down. Simpson had been hiding in the well between the stairs and had shot out like a missile.

Clark was aware of being kicked while he was on the ground, once in the side, once in the face. But the next time he saw a foot, he grabbed it. There was a noise which was like a cross between a yelp and a war cry, and the man pulled his leg back, leaving the filthy trainer in Clark's hands.

Limping away, Simpson started racing upwards again.

Clark scrambled to his feet, tossing away the shoe and shaking his head to clear it. Then he was off in pursuit once more.

♊

Right, thought Deborah.

Here she was, no baton, no backup – because she hadn't wanted to tell anyone about this, had she, stupid mare! – and a bit wobbly from almost falling several storeys to her death. She was also, though, not in the mood for this shit. The three youths had really picked the wrong day to mess with her.

Kicking out, she got the nearest one in the crotch. He fell to his knees, holding his privates like they were about to drop off. One of the others reached to grab hold of her, but her self-defence training was coming back to her now – Vinny wasn't the only one who'd been taught that – and she took his arm, levering it over her shoulder to throw her opponent. He ended up on the ground in a puff of concrete dust and dirt, completely winded. The third she elbowed in the face, hearing and feeling the satisfying crunch of his nose. It made up for not having managed the same to the Geminite with the back of her head.

Without thinking twice, Deborah stepped over the fallen youths and made her way to the corner, following Clark's trail. There was a woman and her baby just standing there, staring upwards, frozen in time. "Did you see— Doesn't matter," said Deborah, because she knew exactly where they'd gone.

Knew where she needed to follow them, as well: up and up.

Which she did, knackered by the time she'd done a few more flights. But there was still no sign of the pair. No sign of Simpson, nor Clark. Then she heard voices, further up, coming from an open doorway above her.

Deborah put on a spurt, clambering up the last few steps, using the handrail to drag herself to the door. Panting, she stumbled through – thinking that the rest Rosy had advised wouldn't come amiss right about now – and out...

Onto the still-wet roof of the block of flats, one side of the roof, anyway. Her head started to spin at the view, at suddenly being confronted by the height she was at. There were no railings up here, no walkways.

She took a few breaths, trying to steady them. There wasn't time for this, she had to catch up with Clark.

More voices, then a loud piercing scream. "Christ!" she mumbled, setting off again, rounding the side of the building.

There she saw her friend, standing a good way from the edge. He turned when he noticed she was there, face bloodied. There had been a struggle at some point, but up here or—

"Robbie? Robbie, what happened?" she asked as she got closer.

He shook his head, made his way to the edge and looked down. Against her better judgement, Deborah joined him, but only managed a quick peek.

There she saw a body, limbs out at odd angles, blood pooling from a head wound, it looked like. Simpson.

Clark was still shaking his head. "He… I tried to get to him, but… He was walking backwards, slipped and—"

Deborah didn't hear the rest. She was too busy pulling back, away from that view. Away from the dead body. Dropping to her knees, head spinning once again.

Then throwing up her shepherd's pie.

CHAPTER NINETEEN

What a mess.

What a complete and utter shitshow! Deborah, sitting sideways on the passenger seat of Clark's car with the door open, legs sticking out, looked around at the people and vehicles that had gathered outside Meadow Hill since they'd called this in. Ambulances, cop cars, local plod. They'd already arrested the youths that had attacked her, were using the whole thing as an excuse to go through the block of flats like a dose of salts and weed out the drug dealers, the fences. But that was never what any of this had been about.

They'd probably have to give statements soon, explaining themselves, but where would you start? Right at the beginning – and which one, the centuries ago one? – or what they were doing here today? Lie perhaps, about why they'd come? She had a feeling, or maybe it was a hope, that once the SCI arrived they'd just take over everything and no explanation would be necessary.

Except to them.

Clark was already doing his best to try and explain to Glover right now. She watched him in the back of the ambulance, cuts on his face stitched up, shirt untucked where they'd had a look at his ribs – which had thankfully not been broken – rubbing the back of his neck as he spoke into his mobile.

They were in so much trouble.

Her eyes flitted over to where the cordoned-off body lay now. Luke Simpson. He was in more trouble, or perhaps his troubles were over. Depended very much on whether you believed in ghosts. Did she feel sorry for him? Deborah wasn't quite sure, that depended on whether he had anything to do with the events back in Norchester. But then how were they ever going to find that out now he was dead?

Hadn't been lucky. Hadn't reached him in time.

Correction, *she* hadn't reached him in time.

Maybe she'd have been able to calm him down, talk him back from the edge – assuming she'd been able to get near it herself. But he hadn't jumped, had he; just an accident. The wetness of the roof, the fact he was trying to get away from the police. Why? Just because he was some junkie on the wrong side of the law, or something else? Something more sinister. Something involving his brother?

Bollocks.

Deborah had been so wrapped up in her thoughts she hadn't noticed the noise at first. Coming from her handbag, which was in the back seat. A vibrating sound, her own phone. She reached around and grabbed it, rooting around inside for the mobile and freeing it.

She looked at the caller ID. Her mother.

God, that was all she needed right now. And another videocall, damn and blast. Deborah thought about just letting it ring off, then felt guilty and accepted it. "Mum," she said.

Wendy Harrison filled the screen, and she looked upset. "Deborah," she answered, voice thin and reedy, then suddenly higher-pitched. "Oh, thank the Lord! I've been trying to get hold of you all day. Well, since the power came back on from the storm and the phones started working again… Where have you been?"

"Signal was rubbish, and then… What's happened? Mum, what's wrong?"

Wendy sucked in a breath. "It's Isobel."

Deborah's mind immediately brought up the parental rolodex of things it could possibly be: that she'd had an accident herself; that she was sick with some mystery virus; the headache had got worse, perhaps, something brain-related; that someone had kidnapped her and was demanding a ransom; that she'd run off with some older man who'd taken her abroad to be his slave.

But it kept coming back to one thing and one thing only: The Gemini.

That she was—

"M-Mum?" was all she could manage.

"Oh, don't worry. Sweetheart, please – she's okay." Wendy Harrison could obviously see the look on her face, just like Deborah could read hers. "Well, I say okay."

"Mum, please tell me what's happened."

"Last night, I'm…" She sighed. "Izzy slipped out. I'm really, really sorry."

"Slipped…" Then it clicked. She'd been so preoccupied with the case, with that bastard diary of Maxwell Craine's, that she hadn't realised the date, was hardly aware of what day of the week it was anymore because this whole thing was consuming her again. "The party," she said, spitting out the words like she had a hair on her tongue.

"The party," her mother confirmed.

"I totally forgot. Mum, I never even warned you about—"

"No, no. This is on me sweetheart. She was in my care and I dropped the ball."

Deborah knew she should be mad, but it was only something she would have done herself at that age – okay, maybe a bit older; a *lot* older – if she was desperate to see friends. But her first thought was still to find out if her daughter was all right. "What happened?"

"From what I can gather, because she was in a bit of a state, some boy upset her. She's not saying too much about it."

"Right." Some boy. They could deal with that, standard teenage behaviour – teenager 101, in fact. "Okay."

"But that's not all."

"Not…"

"Deborah, she was brought back here by the police."

Now she was thinking, what on earth had Izzy got herself tangled up in? Was the boy a criminal or something? Deborah looked up at Meadow Hill and couldn't help thinking: were there drugs involved?

"They found her out in the rain, apparently. Running around in the rain. She was on her way home, said someone was following her or something, or she thought there was someone…"

Fuck.

Not a boy. Someone else.

"There are other ways to hurt people…

"We are everywhere…"

A Geminite or —

"Lucky they happened to be there, wasn't it?" continued Wendy, one of her eyes narrowing. It was a tell-tale sign that she was scrutinising the reaction of her offspring.

"Yeah," said Deborah. Now she understood exactly what had happened, why they were out there, especially after she'd asked Rosy to check on the security detail. Had probably clocked Izzy leaving the house, followed her at a discreet distance. Had they lost her, or followed her to the party? Either way, they'd caught up with her as she'd been walking home alone, and before anything could happen to her. "Lucky," Deborah said, repeating her mum parrot-fashion.

"The strangest thing, though. They're still out there,

outside our house. Parked a little way down the street. Deborah, what's going on?"

She wanted to fill her in. Tell her so, so desperately.

"Are we in some kind of danger? Is it something to do with why you're in Norchester?"

Well, I'm not in Norchester right now; I'm at a scene of crime where I was attacked and a guy fell off a roof and died. But yes. And yes.

"Deborah, is this something to do with—"

Her mother was interrupted then, screaming and shouting in the background. The sound of kids screaming and shouting. Her kids: Jack and James. Wendy turned, the screen showing the ceiling for a second. "What in heaven's name? Boys, boys what—"

"Mummy! *Mummy!*" they were both crying out in unison.

"Mum?" said Deborah. "Mum, what's going on? What's—"

Wendy's face filled the screen again, but the image was jerky – either signal trouble again or she was just trying to do two things at once: talk to Deborah and calm down her grandchildren. "Hold on," she heard her say. Then there was muffled talking, she could barely hear a word of it.

Deborah was suddenly aware of someone behind her in the back seat. She didn't turn, because she knew instinctively who it was. Her eyes flicked up to the rear view and she saw him there, staring back. Eyebrows furrowed, worried. She knew that look all too well.

"Mummy! Is that Mummy?" Jack, she thought, her attention diverted.

"We need to talk to her!" James now.

Wendy, looking more than a little confused, said: "Did you hear that?"

"What's the matter with them?" asked Deborah, panic rising. All she wanted to do was be there with her kids, to scoop them up in her arms and hold them tight.

Wendy held the camera towards the twins and offscreen said, "Here you go."

"Boys?" Her voice cracked when she saw how shaken they were.

"Mummy! Mummy! The bad man…"

She didn't even bother asking Jack who he was talking about. "What about him?"

"You have to stop him. He's… He's going to do something to the man with the books." James' pleading face.

Deborah frowned. "The man—"

"The man in the place with all the books!" Jack clarified. "He's waiting for him."

"No," said Deborah, looking up at the rear view again. Jack – the ghost of her Jack – had vanished. "Boys, I have to go. But I'll call you right back, okay?"

They both nodded, Wendy's face hoved into view but Deborah didn't even have time to say goodbye to her mum. She'd ended the call and was levering herself out of the car, striding across to Clark in the ambulance – almost colliding with one of the uniformed officers policing the scene as she went.

If they were lucky…

He saw her and gave a curt nod. "She's here with me right now." Then he put his hand over the mic. "Did you hear all that? I assume you did the way he was shouting. We're bloody amateurs, and he's going to have my balls in a sling."

"Never mind about all that," Deborah retorted. "Give me the phone."

If they were lucky…

A bewildered Clark gaped at her. "What?"

"The boys, they've… seen something." She didn't have to say any more than that, because Clark knew about the visions, the—

"They were asleep?" he glanced at his watch. "Dreaming?"

She hadn't even thought of that, they definitely wouldn't

be in bed this early. No, this had been a waking vision. Like Jack's had been. She'd deal with that revelation later, she decided, and stuck out her hand. "Robbie, please."

…it wouldn't be another mess, a shitshow.

They'd reach him in time. Had to!

Clark handed over the phone to her. "Glover. You have to get some people to the library, *right now!* I know who his next target is. He's going after Vinny…"

"He's going after Vinny Hole!"

It had been a long day.

A long night before it. Ordinarily, he'd have been down in the archives for a good while yet, still scanning in documents, or doing more research, but Vinny was tired. He'd barely had any sleep – thought he might be spending the night in jail for starters, until Deborah had got him out of there.

Then there had been the chasing up, pulling out all the stops to get her that information. Wanted to make amends for scaring her. He'd been well on his way to tracking it all down anyway, just needed a final push to get the job done, and working with her had done that.

Working with the police. Sort of.

Just like his dad had done all those years ago, helping with The Gemini case! It was his turn now. And though Vinny hadn't done any of this for the credit obviously, for the kudos, it would probably end up being an unexpected side-effect if today was anything to go by. The way the staff had looked at him, the rumour mill in full effect. Vinny's boss had given him the option of a few days off, but where else would he go? This place was just as much a home to him as, well, home. More so, perhaps. And the people, who now thought he was some sort of hero... Something about saving some woman, though a lot of it was still under wraps; he hadn't even given a formal statement to the authorities yet. Even so, the way his colleagues had been looking at him...

The way Andrea looked at him now.

Andrea. Small, blonde, pretty Andrea. Perfect Andrea. He'd loved her since the moment he'd started working here, just hadn't had the guts to tell her how he felt. Wouldn't have been able to stand the rejection, because she could have her pick of guys – why would she be interested in him? So, not enough guts to say, 'actually, I think you're wonderful'.

Let's face it, didn't have the guts to say more than 'hello' or 'goodbye' to her most days.

Except... except today she'd sought *him* out, as he'd been catching up stacking the shelves. Today she'd come over to talk, to chat. That never, *ever* happened. As he'd told Deborah, he was quite socially awkward; had been all his life. Inherited it from his father, who'd been exactly the same. However that man had met Vinny's late mum was a miracle, but met they had. Met, married, and had children.

Marvin – him – and his brother, Marcus.

His twin brother Marcus.

Who'd been the exact opposite of him, and indeed their father. Had more of their mother in him, rest her soul. Rest *both* their souls now, but at least his folks were back together again, that was how Vinny had to look at it. At least there was that.

At school, Marcus had always been the popular one. The lucky one. Good at sports, listened to the right bands. Always the one who wasn't afraid to talk to girls. Might not have done well academically, but that was only because he was out having fun. Having the time of his life, as a matter of fact. While Marvin...Vinny, as he preferred to be called, much to his dad's chagrin – an attempt to try and make himself sound more cool, when he was anything but – well, he hit the books. He was a chip off the old block, off the old man; a bookworm just like him. Could read so fast – he'd get through a huge tome in just a couple of hours – learning, always learning, and his grades were so high some of his teachers thought he might be cheating. His dad went in to argue his case about that on one occasion, saying how proud he was of Vinny and that the boy didn't have a cheating bone in his body.

Vinny found the odd friend or two here and there (and, sometimes, they were really, *really* odd). Nerds, mostly, who were into role playing, comics, computer games, that kind of thing. But even they didn't stick around for very long. So, when Marcus took off to travel the world after he left school, Vinny found himself getting closer and closer to his dad. Even taking up his interests. One in particular, of course: his father's 'claim to fame'. Not that it had made him famous at all; he was massively overlooked when it came to news reporting about The Gemini.

But without Marvin Snr's help, they'd never have found those underground cells at Yardley Street. They'd never have stopped the serial killer that was terrorising this city back then. Didn't seem very fair to Vinny, not at all. Hadn't been Deborah Harrison's fault, Vinny knew that. She'd had her own problems to deal with, not least the death of the man she loved.

Yet his father never complained, was always very happy he'd been able to assist. It had led to his interest – obsession was more apt – with all things 'Gemini'. Vinny recalled his dad showing him the research he was doing down in the archives, in addition to his actual duties at the library, and he'd been in awe. Had been delighted to take it all over when his father passed away, saw it as more than just a legacy – it was something important. Vinny had completed his degree at Norchester Uni first, then trained as a librarian and followed his dad into working here. Had his father known even then that he didn't have long left? You could never tell, he was so private about, well, private things.

Marcus had returned for the funeral, naturally. Had been more than a little hacked off with Vinny because he hadn't let him know sooner about the illness. "It all happened so fast," had been Vinny's response. "Plus I wasn't sure where you were."

His brother had been pretty useless at keeping in touch, and he was probably more angry at himself than anyone for being too late. They hadn't really spoken since, which made Vinny sad, but what could you do? He was used to being alone, being in his own company, though he had to admit he missed his dad something fierce.

Was that the real reason he'd continued to keep tabs on Deborah and her family? To make up for not having one of his own anymore, and with little chance of having one later in his own life? Vinny's father had always said how nice Deborah was, how kind to him. He'd felt it was his duty to keep an eye on what was occurring, just to make sure she was safe and happy. So Vinny had done the same. Nothing weird about it, nothing stalkery – although maybe it had come across that way to the woman herself. Just one of the reasons why she'd freaked out when he brought her to his 'office'. That and the replicas! Should have gotten rid of all that stuff ages ago, but like he'd said to her, it focussed his mind on The Gemini. Helped Vinny to figure him out.

Thankfully, he was making it up to her. He'd not only helped when she got into real bother back in that alley, but was also stepping up and giving her intel she might not have access to. The diary, the stuff about The Gemini's children. He hoped it helped, because if anyone was going to uncover the truth it would be Deborah. One of the best detectives he'd known, according to his father. Okay, probably the *only* detective he'd known, but still...

Aiding Deborah had not only made Vinny feel better about

himself, it had also made him feel like he was truly carrying out his father's wishes. Plus it had resulted in that conversation with Andrea, who'd told him she'd always hoped he would talk to her since he started working there. And who would have guessed it, she was actually into some of the same things as him! Was more than a bit geeky herself, with an interest in gaming, comics and even the same movies, more or less. How fantastic was that? Not only perfect, not only kind and lovely and... but also on his wavelength, whatever that was.

They'd made plans to see the next comic book movie together the following Friday night. "It's a date then," Andrea had said.

Vinny had simply nodded, not wanting to mess anything up at this stage. It had been a struggle not to yawn while they'd chatted, as he didn't want to give the wrong impression – she was anything but boring! Didn't want to put her off. Of course, he'd be worrying about messing things up anyway between now and then, but for the first time in forever he was happy. Ecstatic, even. Tired, because it had been a long day, a long night before it, but it had also been potentially life-changing. Hopeful, at least.

So, as he'd locked everywhere up – still the last one in, even though it was early for him – there'd been a spring in his step. A spring in it even as he made his way across the carpark, tugging on his jacket, his red Fiesta the only one still in there; under the light, where he always parked, because inevitably it would be dark when he clocked off, even in the summer.

Content, lucky and—

Then he saw it. The figure.

It had risen out of the shadows around his car, the ones just beyond it. At first he didn't realise it *was* a figure, because it was so hunched over. But as it – he – began to straighten, it was obvious that this person had just been crouching. Waiting.

And now that he was standing tall, even at this distance Vinny could see the size of him.

His first thought was that this was another Geminite, maybe out to take revenge on him for what he'd done. Incapacitated one of their number, responsible for his capture by the police. Vinny hadn't even thought twice about doing that, because Deborah Harrison had been at risk. Hadn't thought about any potential repercussions, not until he was being put in a cell, too.

Certainly hadn't been worried about someone attacking him, because his dad had sent him to those martial arts classes when he was still at school. Had thought it best that he knew how to handle himself, because of the bullying. And he'd picked that up fast, as well, learnt quickly. The first time he'd thrown someone in the playground, a youth twice his size, using their own body weight against them as he'd been taught, the others had learned their own lesson. The bigger they are... They all left him alone after that.

Hadn't worried about Andrea, because they'd only just started talking today – although moving forward, he might want to think about some protection for her. If they got close. And he should be so...

Lucky. Had never been the lucky one, that had always been Marcus. Vinny had had his father's luck: the cancer that killed him had been a rare one. Only one person in so many million, he'd been told.

The same went for this, here, happening now. In a way it was lucky, sort of, like he was sort of working with the police. How many people got to see this, got to meet *Him*? Not a follower, a worshipper. Not even one of those priests from the book he'd shown Deborah.

But Him. *The* Him. In the flesh.

Because not only could Vinny see the height of this individual now (not merely twice his size, but maybe three times!) and who else could possibly be dressed like that –

dressed in the outfit he had a copy of, a twin of in his office – but he could also see that face, especially when the figure turned it up towards the light to look across at Vinny.

That face. Those faces.

Two, more accurately. Not a mask, not special effects like you might see in one of those movies he was planning on taking Andrea to. But real. Two faces in one, on one face. Crammed into the area like they were competing for space. Two sets of eyes, two noses, two mouths – though actually, when the figure grinned, it just looked like there was one mouth stretching all the way across.

The Gemini. In person.

He should have turned then; turned and tried to run away. After all, he could guess what this monster wanted from him. Not revenge as such, something more personal than that. Instead, Vinny carried on walking towards him. His curiosity was overcoming his fear – and wasn't there just a part of him wondering if this was a dream or something? His obsession, inherited from Marvin Hole Snr, creeping into his nightmares. The only surprising thing was it hadn't happened already. He'd fallen asleep at his desk, running a search program or talking to another person with an interest in this particular killer on the dark web.

The dark—

No, this was real enough. Wasn't it? Wasn't that what dreams felt like when you were experiencing them: totally real? He'd wake up in a moment and would feel foolish. Would feel—

"I hear you've been looking for me," said the figure. The sound was so strange, echoing, coming from two people at once like a weird kind of stereo.

Not looking for, as such. Looking *into* would be a better description. "I heard you were dead," answered Vinny.

The figure cocked his head. "Do I look dead to you?"

Vinny shook his own head. This person certainly didn't.

But then The Gemini had sons, didn't he. Just like Marvin Hole had sons. Deborah had gone off to search for one of them, but this could well be the other. Was almost definitely the other, unless you believed in those old resurrection fables. Like him, the child carrying on his father's work. "I guess not."

"You're an… admirer of my work."

"I-I don't know if I'd put it quite like that. I would like to understand it."

The Gemini smiled that bizarre smile again. "It's always nice to meet a fan. And, trust me, I'd love nothing more than to stay a while and chat."

…to talk, to chat. That never, ever happened.

Only a few people had ever had this opportunity. "Wait, I just—"

"But time is running out. And I must complete my task."

"Wait," said Vinny again, realising he'd stopped walking towards this figure. Hadn't needed to, because The Gemini – this Gemini, anyway – had covered the distance himself. So quickly, Vinny hadn't even noticed. Quicker than he could read a page from a book!

"Wait," he said a third time, but the figure wasn't doing that. Wasn't waiting at all. Couldn't, it seemed, because he was eager to finish his work. The weapon – now that really was famous! – the twin-pronged fork, detached from the belt and out in front of him. Aiming squarely at Vinny's torso. He angled himself sideways, narrowly avoiding the blades, but losing his balance in the process. Vinny toppled over, hitting the ground and then rolling – which at least had the benefit of putting him out of that fork's reach.

Stumbling to his feet, his momentum carried him forwards now. Vinny had no desire to remain here anymore, didn't care what he might find out. What secrets would be revealed to him. He just wanted to get the hell away from this predator, whether he was the original one or not. "Where are you going?" he heard the 'man' ask from behind him. "You can't escape me."

I'm going to do my best, thought Vinny. *I'm going to do my absolute—*

There was a rush of wind, so powerful Vinny felt it brush his hair. Something landed in front of him. Something that had been behind him only moments ago. A leap that should have been impossible, but wasn't for this person. The strength that must have taken!

There was no option now but to fight. To tackle this one, final bully if he wanted to live. The thrust came again, the fork seeking its target. Vinny gabbed his arm, tried to throw his opponent like he had all those years ago when he'd been in the school yard. Grabbed the arm and attempted to use this person's weight against them. But he couldn't shift The Gemini. It was like trying to throw a stone statue, immovable unless they wanted to be moved.

Vinny punched and kicked, any one of which would have taken down an ordinary person, but had little to no effect here. The Gemini's response was to grab him, by the shirt, his jacket still open at the front. He lifted Vinny easily, like he weighed nothing. Then he threw him. Back towards his own car, where he slammed into the windscreen of the Fiesta, splintering it, creating a spider's web of glass.

Even as he struggled to remain conscious, Vinny was aware of the noise they were making. Surely someone had heard all the ruckus! A man being thrown casually across a carpark, hitting his own car... and now sliding off the front of it. He'd let out a cry, hadn't he? Wouldn't someone have heard that, if nothing else?

But no-one came. Nobody was coming to his rescue like he'd raced to Deborah's. Didn't have anyone monitoring what he was doing, keeping an eye on him. Apart from The Gemini, of course. He'd been watching. Must have been, he always did that with his victims. Had probably been watching and following Vinny for a good while.

The heavy footfalls now as that person walked across the empty carpark. Vinny opened his eyes to see the boots just inches away. The Gemini had halted, was bending down. Bending over Vinny to pick him up again.

Lifting him with one hand, fork ready with the other. "Don't worry. You're about to understand everything," the person with two faces promised. "To learn it all." He wasn't sure whether this was a reference to what Vinny had learned himself over the years, from his martial arts lessons to the research on the history of this being, or just because of where he worked; his love of those books inside it. Didn't matter either way, because the result was the same. The price he'd have to pay for this lesson, which didn't, to him, seem fair. Not now he had Andrea, sort of had her. Might have been able to build a future, have a family.

Not anymore, though, not once that fork went in. And it was funny, because it didn't really hurt. Not like it had when he hit the windscreen. Maybe his body was already shutting down? Just felt cold, freezing almost.

Then something even more bizarre happened. He felt like he was leaving his body. Like they did in all those out of body experience flicks, except he wasn't going on anywhere. To Heaven, to Hell, wherever – or whatever – came next. It felt like he was being drawn into that blade, then into—

From his time in some of those chatrooms and on message boards on the dark web, he'd learned of another mythos. One that totally explained why things weren't fair, why good things happened to bad people and vice versa. Humans being manipulated by one-eyed creatures who controlled every aspect of a person's life. Before you ended up in a giant, floating eye called The Beholder. Trapped inside it, helpless. Feeding it. Some people believed that, Vinny wasn't so sure.

But if it was real, if those... Controller things did exist, then joining all those other souls might have felt a little like this.

Trapped, inside The Gemini. Empowering him. Inside...

"I feel like I'm closer to him, then, like I might be able to get into his head."

"Trust me. You really don't want to be doing that."

Deborah's words to him, and Vinny had to admit she'd had a point. You really didn't want to be inside this head, except now he didn't have a choice. It was happening with or without his say. The only positive being that, yes, he was starting to understand. About how all this was coming to an end, that it was nearly time.

Just a couple more parts, that's all he needed: including Vinny's right kneecap, which he was working on now with a knife; bone and flesh, the whole – Hole – thing! It had taken time to build everything up again, but he'd had help. Lots of help.

He couldn't make out much now, was fading, the absorption almost complete. But Vinny could swear he heard sirens. Someone coming to help him at long last. Too late sadly, but the thought was there.

Time to rest, though, now. It had been such a long day.

And he was so, so tired.

CHAPTER TWENTY-ONE

There'd been no getting away from the fact.

No hiding it, either, this time. Not after the latest victim had been killed. Poor Marvin – Vinny – Hole. Following a tip-off, the police had gone in there tooled up. Armed response units, dogs… They'd got there too late to save Vinny, but had spotted his attacker running away. One or two of the armed officers got off a shot or several, even claiming they'd hit The Gemini as he'd fled. But they never found any blood on the scene, and the trail had run cold a few streets away, even with Alsatians in the mix.

They'd also used drones, the SCI's contribution to the hunt. Thought they'd picked up the person they were tracking a couple of times – a large, dark shape, moving so fast he was practically a blur – but in the end it had amounted to nothing. And, not unlike what had happened with the CCTV footage, the drones had suddenly ceased responding to commands and crashed. Not just figuratively, but literally.

No covering up what had happened, the press finally putting it all together and spreading the word, flying in the face of Glover and the SCI's efforts to 'control the narrative' as he put it. The Gemini was back and he'd killed three people already in the city – that they knew about. They weren't saying it was the original killer, how could they when all the newspapers, TV stations and online sources had reported that he'd been killed eight years ago? So they were going with the same assumption the police and the SCI had been making, that this was a copycat. A *very good* copycat, but someone who was emulating the original Gemini.

Deborah wasn't so certain anymore.

Thank Christ none of the reporters had linked it to what had happened back in Kambury with Luke Simpson, another tipoff that had actually come from Vinny Hole. But the SCI now knew what Deborah and Clark knew, a DNA match confirming that the young man was indeed Maxwell Craine's son. They still didn't have any evidence that he was a twin, because the boy had been put into the system on his own. "No wonder he had a distrust of authority," Glover had mused when he read Simpson's file. "He'd been in and out of state-run homes and foster care since he was small, getting into all kinds of scrapes. Then getting in with the wrong crowd afterwards, the kind that get you hooked on whatever you shouldn't be hooked on. Then you two come along and start shouting 'stop, police!' and the next thing you know he's falling off the roof of Meadow Hill flats. Good work!"

Clark himself was looking at suspension, possible dismissal, pending an investigation for his part in the 'accident', but Deborah had at least managed to put that right. She'd had to come clean herself about where she'd got her information from, not the stuff Vinny had given her, but the reason she'd known the librarian was in mortal danger.

"Your kids?" Glover had said, smoothing back his dark hair so forcefully it looked like he was going bald. "Your *kids?*"

"Not all of them, just Jack and James," she'd confessed.

"Now, let me see if I've got this clear. They dreamed about the other attacks?"

"I… I think so. I wasn't sure to begin with, thought maybe it was all just a coincidence, but, well, yeah."

"And you didn't think to mention this little nugget, that it might be something we could exploit?" His voice was rising by the second.

"I didn't *want* anyone exploiting my sons, thanks," said Deborah, hers rising to match the inspector's.

He shook his head. "No, no. You're right. That came out… I didn't mean it to… But now. Now that we're pretty sure. We *are* pretty sure, right?"

She told him about what they'd said, about the man who worked in the 'book place' – sounded a lot like Vinny to Deborah. Enough for her to put the authorities on alert, though a fat lot of good it had done them. "You should have got there quicker," she replied, and perhaps was implying something, too. Deborah still didn't trust Glover as far as she could toss an iron girder.

"What are you trying to… We did our best! Got there as soon as we could. Do you know how hard it is to scramble ARUs without anything more concrete to go on? I guess you do, you've been in this situation yourself. You'd have taken them down into the cells with you, if you'd had the time, yeah?"

Deborah felt the sting of that one. Touché. Not having armed officers with them back when they confronted The Gemini before had meant life and death – mainly death – for half their number. Though would it even have mattered? she had to wonder, same as before. Would bullets have stopped him? "You should still have got there quicker," was all she could muster in response, feeling overwhelming guilt about Vinny. She had just been starting to warm to the guy, might have been friends for quite a long time if this hadn't happened. Brutally murdered himself by the person he'd devoted his free time to studying; him, and his father before that.

She'd been feeling bad enough about it, but bumping into his brother Marcus at the hospital where they'd taken the body (before transferring to Rosy's morgue) had made things a hundred times worse. As she'd done in the past, she mistook the twin for Vinny to begin with – part of her forgetting that he'd been killed. Wanting it not to be true. Only it was, and this was Vinny's identical brother: Marcus Hole. The spitting image of his brother, yet more confident and forthright. The 'dominant' one of the pair, presumably.

"I'm too late again," was what he'd said when she introduced herself as a friend of Vinny's. "Same as I was with Dad. Too late."

"There's a lot of that going around," had been Deborah's reply.

"But you don't understand. I… and this is going to sound really bizarre, but I heard him. I heard my brother. As plain as I'm hearing you now."

"What? How do you mean, *heard* him?"

"It's hard to explain, but I thought I heard his voice. Must have been around the same time he died."

That connection again, you could never underestimate it. Where James had *shown* Jack those murders years ago, it appeared that Vinny had been communicating with his own twin in a different way. "And, if you don't mind me asking, that is, what did he say?"

Marcus shook his head, but she wasn't sure if it meant he minded or not. Then he answered: "'It's Him. It's really *Him*. He's here.' I assume whoever killed him?"

Deborah just nodded. But she knew exactly what Vinny had been talking about, what he might be referring to. The person who killed him was the real Gemini. Not an acolyte but the real deal.

She'd passed on that information as well, obviously, though she wasn't sure what good it would do now. Only that they were facing someone, something that was equally as dangerous as The Gemini had been almost a decade ago. Brought back from the dead, or reincarnated maybe? But Him, definitely *Him*.

So Glover had been feeling under pressure, and another visit from the Mayor hadn't helped matters either. More shouting in a side room, then this time when she emerged, the Mayor had looked over at Deborah, walked over to her – sticking out her hand. "Mayor Tierney."

"Deborah Harrison."

"Yes, I know who you are," the woman said, and for a moment Deborah thought she was going to start chewing her out, too. "I wish you were in charge around here," the Mayor continued. "Instead of all these... outsiders."

She didn't know how to answer that one, so she gave a half-nod. Deborah knew what she meant, however; ever since the SCI got involved in all this, it had made things much more difficult than they'd needed to be. If she'd been SIO on this operation, maybe Geoffrey Whittaker might still be alive, or Vinny Hole. And then they'd have another resource at their fingertips.

As it was, the only resources Glover seemed remotely interested in were her children, which he stressed again not long after that meeting and in the same side-room – a place rapidly beginning to feel like 'the argument room' from that old Python sketch. "I need to do something, and quick. Especially now the cat's out of the bag with the press. And the Mayor—"

"I thought the SCI didn't answer to anyone," Deborah said to him, hardly able to keep the snarky tone from her voice.

"We don't," Glover confirmed. "But she can make life difficult for me while I'm here. While I'm *still* here, that is. There's talk of my being replaced."

Deborah would be lying if she said she was sorry about that, and he could tell exactly what she was thinking without her having to say a word.

"You might not be so glad about who you get instead," he told her.

"The devil you know?" she offered.

"Something like that, though I take exception to being called a devil. The real devil's still out there, Miss Harrison. And we're no closer to catching him than we were when you came on board. Less so now one of our best leads is dead."

"Not to mention the man who gave us that lead," she reminded him.

"Though if we'd known about this thing with your sons…"

"I didn't even know if it *was* a thing," she told him again, but then looked down. "I wasn't sure that—"

"We need them here. Closer," he stated. "It's as simple as that."

"What?"

"You heard me. If there's even a chance they could tip us off about the next attack…"

"No way!" Not only did she not want to put her children in jeopardy, she didn't like demands – especially where they concerned members of her family. First they lured her back to Norchester, now…

"They'll be safer here than where they are, even with the Armitage people keeping an eye out. Oh, I heard about what happened the other night with your daughter; of course I did. They couldn't find anyone who'd been following her, but…"

She was forced to concede he had a point about that, there were people out there who might wish her mum and Izzy harm, those Geminite gits – and they were still getting nothing from the priest – but this wasn't the solution. "Then put them all somewhere safer. Somewhere a million miles from Armitage or Norchester." She couldn't see that going down well with either her mother or the kids, and she missed them something chronic, but if it meant minimising the risk to them, then wasn't that worth it?

"The twins need to be here. With you, preferably."

"At the hotel, you're joking!"

"Maybe not there. We could arrange for a safe house in Norchester, or on the outskirts where—"

Deborah folded her arms. "No fucking way. Not happening, Glover."

There was a knock on the door at that moment and they both welcomed the interruption. It was Rosy bringing the autopsy results from Vinny Hole's PM. "Thought you might want them in person." It was the same thing as before, though. Might as well have been Haley Archer's results, as The Gemini had to get on with things quickly that time as well, because people were around. Of course in this instance it was police people on the scene, but it made no difference to the outcome. Death by that bloody twin-pronged fork again. Followed by rough cuts, detaching the knee. The new collection coming along nicely.

As Glover was reading, he kept glancing up and eventually he clicked his fingers. "Rosy!"

"What?" she asked, maybe thinking she'd done something wrong.

"No, no. Don't worry. We were just talking about how we could bring Miss Harrison's twins here safely, so—"

"No we weren't," Deborah broke in. "*You* were talking about that."

"So they'd be nearby in the case of another attack," Glover persisted.

"Okay…" Rosy strung out the last bit, not quite grasping what he was getting at. Deborah got there first.

"He's talking about them staying with you."

"Well, why not? Just till we sort all this out. You know the family, right? Do you have security at your place?"

"Erm, some, but—"

"Perfect. We could bolster that, obviously." He put down the report and turned to Deborah, opening his palms wide as if to say, 'that's the best deal you're going to get'. "At least they'd be with someone they know. And you could be with them anytime you wanted."

"They don't know Kiz. No offence, Rosy."

"None taken, on her behalf. They *don't* know her. I mean, she'd probably be delighted to get to know them. Would jump at the chance of having kids around. Only—"

"Then it's settled," said Glover.

"Whoa, whoa. Nothing's settled," Deborah maintained. "Far from it."

"I'd rather do this the easy way than the hard way," was the inspector's answer.

"You have no idea what hard is, mate."

"Hold on, hold on." Rosy was stepping between them like some kind of referee in a boxing match – or wrestling. *GLOW*, wasn't it? Deborah would bloody well show him *GLOW* if he wasn't careful. "Look, what's this about? Why are you bringing the kids here in the first place?"

That was right, she hadn't told her friend yet. Hadn't confided in her, just Clark. And now Glover. Shit. Deborah did her best to explain it without sounding like she'd been keeping something from Rosy, but the hurt on the woman's face was plain.

"I see," she said eventually.

"Rosy…" Deborah reached out to place a hand on her arm, but the woman moved back just far enough so it couldn't land.

"Bottom line, this will help. Not just us, but other people. If we can identify where and when our boy might strike next…"

"We can get there just after he's finished?" Deborah said bitterly. But she knew he was right, and she was rapidly losing ground. It was starting to look like she was keeping the one thing that might crack this whole thing wide open to herself, as if she was a selfish child with toys she didn't want to share.

"If it'll save lives," Rosy said with a shrug of the shoulders, "then I don't think any of us have a choice." She looked pointedly at Deborah. "Do we?"

"The twins certainly don't. They didn't ask for this."

"Neither did Jack, but he helped anyway. Did all that he could to stop more deaths."

Deborah felt like raising the point that he'd done it at the cost of his own life, but they'd be going round in circles. Rosy was right. "Okay," she reluctantly agreed. "All right."

Glover clapped his hands together like he'd just won a prize. "Splendid. We'll make the arrangements then, and—"

She raised her hand. "Wait a second, there's a condition."

"Name it," said Glover.

"You get off Clark's back about what happened with Simpson. That was all my fault, he was only there because of me. Didn't want to be there, as a matter of fact, so back off."

Glover stared at her for a moment or two, holding her gaze. Then he nodded. "He's a good copper. It would be a shame if a… misunderstanding was to leave a mark on his record. Good enough?"

"Good enough," said Deborah.

Before they all started filing out again, Deborah feeling more than a little sick about the decision she'd just made – had no option but to make – Glover stopped her by placing a hand on her arm this time. She looked down and he removed it. "You're doing the right thing," he told her.

"Am I?" she replied. "I wonder."

But there'd been no getting away from the fact, this might save lives.

No hiding from it either.

PART IV

CHAPTER TWENTY-TWO

Getting away from it all.

That's what they were doing. That's *all* they were doing. It was what she'd said to her granddaughter, Isobel, what she was trying to tell herself – though it wasn't really working. For one thing, they lived at the coast. Wasn't that where people *went* to get away from everything, from the towns and cities, from the stresses of modern life? Bills, work, all of that. Rushing off to the seaside to reconnect, enjoy some much-needed peace.

They lived in a paradise already. The kind of place Wendy Harrison's own mum and dad used to bring her to for day trips, fish 'n' chips and paddling in the ocean. It was all they'd been able to afford in those days, a cheap break. Wendy had always said that if she had the money she'd try and do better, which was why they took Deborah abroad to France, Spain, Italy, as well as some of the lovely places closer to home.

They'd even visited Armitage Bay a couple of times, all three of them. She had fond memories of buying Deborah candyfloss on the seafront, of her and her late dad going on the rides along the pier – including the huge Ferris Wheel they still had there. Nice memories.

She'd always hoped, but never dared dream, she'd end up somewhere like that when she retired. Not that she'd worked for a long time, not that the stresses of bills or employment had bothered Wendy for many decades. Her husband Stan had made sure of that, worked hard. So hard it had put him in an early grave, sadly.

When she'd pictured herself in those later years, he would always be there. The 'old farts on a beach' thing. They'd chuckle at that one, imagine a future when they'd be sat on a bench watching the waves rolling in and out. Suddenly he hadn't even been there in the present, snatched away from her.

Part of her had to wonder whether the worry about Deborah and that piece of work Phil Croft had contributed. Stan had never liked him from the get-go. "Just something about him," he'd always say to Wendy, though she'd thought the man was pleasant enough. Which of course he was around them, around other people. It was behind closed doors she now knew that the trouble was brewing.

It made Wendy so sad to think of her little girl being abused like that. Never thought it possible, as strong and feisty as she was. But they do a number on you, men like that. Make you rely on them, erode your confidence. Use phrases like 'if you loved me, you'd do what I want'. Separate you from friends and family. They'd had to wait till the relationship had hit rock bottom, of course. Till Deborah came to them, turned to them for help, which must have been one of the hardest things she'd ever had to do.

But Stan had worried and worried in the meantime, probably imagining scenarios where he'd be visiting the morgue after Phil had done his worst. Bad enough Deborah was in a line of work that saw her facing danger on a daily basis, although Stan was actually quite proud of her for that. Standing up for what she believed in, doing what was right, helping people. Then Stan was gone, but he'd made sure his wife was well provided for.

Wendy was on her own, and so was Deborah. On her own, apart from Isobel, that was. A pregnant Deborah had needed Wendy now more than ever and she wasn't about to let her daughter down. Wendy had been there for the birth, had helped out with Izzy when she was a baby. They'd ticked along as a kind of family unit in their own right, and for a while things had been okay, apart from all that moving around for Deborah's job. Her daughter had managed to push down how lonely she was, and so had Wendy. They had more important things to worry about, like making sure Izzy felt secure. Making sure she felt loved – because she absolutely was.

Wendy couldn't have loved her more if she'd been her own child. Was maybe a bit softer on her than Deborah, even, because she was her granddaughter. That was just what you did, wasn't it, whether you were hands on or not. She recalled visits to her own gran when she was small, how she'd give her tubs of ice cream, sweets by the bucket load, regardless of how Wendy's mum complained. "They'll rot her teeth, she'll get too used to them!" Her gran had taken no notice whatsoever, and for that Wendy was grateful. They made for comforting memories when she looked back.

Then Norchester had happened. If Stan hadn't died when he did, that would have finished him off! His daughter on the trail of a serial killer, and a particularly brutal one at that. Wendy had continued to look after Izzy, naturally. Kept the worst of it all away from her, during the late nights and the obligatory snapping Deborah would do when she got home from work – understanding that it was hard to face death and misery on a daily basis and be dancing a jig when she got home to her family. At the same time, Wendy was always worried about what effect that would have on their relationship – Deborah's and Izzy's. Did that little girl think her mother was putting all this before *her*? And weren't there times when Wendy worried her own daughter might be doing that, as well?

It was during this period she'd got involved with one of the suspects in the case. A certain Jack Foley. The irony of it all being that, from what she could gather, Wendy would have really liked this man. He was apparently kind, loved Deborah to bits, he was educated – a writer no less – and he was well off. *Really* well off. Not that money was the be all and end all, but you couldn't get by without it, could you?

Unfortunately that case ended… well, it ended the way it did. Jack had been killed, had actually given his life to try and protect Deborah – which just made Wendy like him even more; what a pity they'd never met. And her daughter had been badly injured. The only positive being that they'd stopped that monster for good.

At least she'd thought that was the only plus side. Wendy could still recall the moment she'd told her about the twins, Jack's little 'going away present'. Felt ashamed now of thinking: here we go again, single mother time. Would need Wendy more than ever now! And at a time when she was looking forward maybe to slowing down, when Izzy was off doing her own thing and perhaps they could both do theirs: Deborah *and* her.

'Course, it never really worked out like that, anyway. Wendy was still heavily involved in her daughter's life, just as they both would be with Izzy probably, moving forwards. People do stupid things when they're young (when they're older too). And the more time that passed, the more Izzy was starting to take after her mum.

But the twins, she couldn't imagine life without them now. Felt mortified about the fact she'd even suggested getting rid of them! Hadn't been able to imagine life without them since they were born (and she'd almost lost Deborah again on the operating table that time); since the connection had been formed between them and their mother, but also them and their grandmother. Now she'd do anything for them, *absolutely* anything – same as she would for Izzy.

Which was why she'd taken them at short notice when Deborah asked her to. When Deborah had seemed so desperate again. Telling her that 'the powers that be' wanted her to return to Norchester, to consult on some case or other. Wendy had been concerned again, because Deborah had left all that behind, the police work and that damned city. Stan would have been proud of the way she'd found her feet at the coast, built up another successful career – a much less terrifying one – and Wendy had to say she couldn't be prouder herself. Whatever this was, surely they could find someone else to ask? She'd thought that, whilst also being proud again that they'd come to Deborah for her advice.

It meant she'd be away for a few days, however, but actually that had worked out well for Wendy as she'd been saying she hadn't seen enough of Jack and James recently. Partly her own fault, because Derek was on the scene now—

Derek. That was another story. She hadn't expected to fall for someone again at her time of life, hadn't wanted to. Who would ever compare to Stan? But Derek didn't need to, he was very different to her late husband. Something had just clicked when she met him in that coffee shop. She'd been having a quick tea after doing the shopping, indulging in a scone as well because she thought she deserved a treat after a particularly hectic week… and he'd just been there. Standing there by her table, talking, asking her if she wouldn't mind some company.

Wendy's mouth had fallen open. Mind? Did she mind…? And before she could answer, Derek had been sitting down with his coffee and still talking, then asking her about herself. Ordinarily she'd have been horrified, would have told him to bugger off! There was just something about him, though (the kindly eyes, that smile) which made her listen, made her want to open up. Some might have been wary, might have called him a charmer – and indeed Deborah had issued a few warnings about strangers, like the roles of mother and daughter had been reversed or something – but it had worked out in the end.

She'd seen more of Derek, more coffee dates, the pictures when they were having seasons of old movies, dances on the pier. Gradually, before she even realised it was happening, they were together. A couple. Inseparable, actually. Not only had Wendy realised she didn't mind the company, she'd grown attached to it. To him.

It had been one of the hardest decisions she'd ever had to make, to move out of Deborah's place and into Derek's. Hard to tell her daughter as well, after all this time they'd been together. Yet strangely it had been one of the easiest things in the world to do, and she'd never looked back since.

Not only had Derek taken to the grandkids like they were his own, he looked forward to their visits. Hadn't said a word about them all coming to stay for a while because Deborah was out of town on work. Had only asked: "Is she all right?" Bless him.

It had been a good question. One that Wendy didn't know if she could answer properly. *Was* her daughter all right? No, she didn't think she was, if she was being honest. And those niggles hadn't been helped by finding out Deborah had been drinking too much in Norchester – before she left, too, if Izzy was to be believed! Coinciding with that Rosy coming back into their lives. Moving backwards rather than forwards.

Rosy: an unwelcome reminder of a time in her life they'd all sooner forget, surely. A time that, yes, had included Jack. And while Wendy could admit, like Deborah, she wished the father of her boys was still on the scene, he wasn't – and that was that. A sad truth, but the truth nonetheless. What Deborah needed was a 'Derek' of her own, someone to share the good times and the bad with. You couldn't do that with a ghost, hanging on to the past.

And this whole Norchester thing had just set her back, as far as Wendy could discern. Might even have been one of the reasons the twins were having nightmares, before and after she left. Why Deborah and Izzy were at each other's throats. Except there was more to all of that, as she'd found out.

Wasn't just the past coming back to haunt her, it was replaying back in Norchester, Wendy had discovered. A Gemini copycat, so the news places were saying; three victims in Norchester alone that they knew of. She could sort of understand why Deborah hadn't told her that was what she was doing there; indeed wasn't there a part of Wendy that already knew? What else could it have been? But still, she couldn't help being angry with Deborah for keeping her in the dark, particularly as there seemed to be some kind of threat to her family as well. People working for – or with – this copycat, was her understanding.

"Mum, I couldn't… There were things I wasn't allowed to tell you, for a kick-off. It's an ongoing investigation, you know the score."

"But some sort of nod would have been nice. There we were going about our lives as if—"

"Why do you think the police brought Izzy back? They've been keeping a watch over you since I left. It was all arranged."

At least that was something, and Wendy *had* been the one who was in charge when Izzy snuck out of the house. "Who's keeping an eye on you, though? Rosy?"

"There are… I have friends here."

"Let me ask you this, have you been hurt yourself? Put at risk?"

The silence told her everything she needed to know. Of course she'd been at risk, this was Deborah. "I'm going to need to ask another favour," had been the way she'd broken that silence.

"Don't like the sound of that." Wendy definitely hadn't liked the sound of what came next. Dragging the twins to Norchester? What for?

"It wouldn't have been my first choice, trust me," Deborah had informed her. "But… There's more, I need you to head off with Izzy. Maybe the three of you can go to Penny's?" Penny was one of Wendy's oldest friends; she hadn't seen her in a while in spite of multiple invitations. She'd been talking about visiting and Deborah knew that. "Just keep it to yourself. Don't tell anyone where you're heading, okay?"

"Deborah, this is ludicrous."

"Yeah, I know." Sounded very much like she hadn't had a say in the matter, so there really wasn't much point in arguing the toss about it. Probably just wanted the twins with her, that was all. Nothing to do with why she'd had to hang up so suddenly and rush off the other day, or those dreams about the 'bad man'.

Nothing whatsoever.

Same as Wendy would tell Izzy they were getting away for a while, that was all. She'd expected there to be an argument about that – but maybe the girl had thought twice about pushing it after what she'd done. Or she wanted to get away herself, seemed to love the idea of being off school for a bit. Miles from her friends, the further the better. "What about Jack and James?" she'd asked, and Wendy had told her they were going to be with her mum. Izzy had hidden it well, but there was hurt there when she'd said that. Prioritising again. Putting the twins first this time, not just the job.

There was one problem with the plan: Derek, as lovely as he was, as understanding as he was, didn't get on well with Penny. Maybe there was a bit of jealousy on her friend's part, Wendy figured, or just a clash of personalities, but whatever the case he would flat out say no to visiting the woman, Wendy knew that. But she also didn't feel comfortable about leaving him alone, even if there was protection around (and unlike Deborah, she had come clean to her partner; she owed him that much and he'd never trust her again if she hadn't). So she'd suggested he take his brother up on *his* invitation to go and visit. Wendy wasn't mad on Neville, so it seemed like the perfect opportunity to kill two birds with one stone.

Kill…

Wendy shook her head. *Two birds, two boys. No, don't even think about it!*

She was desperately worried not just about Deborah now, but James and Jack – last seen heading off with Rosy, who herself had an escort of two men wearing suits in a black car. Friends from a division she'd just started working with apparently. The lads had been happy enough to go with the woman, because they were off to see their mum, but had looked back sadly to wave at Wendy. Even Izzy had given them hugs that threatened to break them in two before they left the house. The girl hadn't been able to face waving them off.

When Wendy had returned indoors, Izzy had thrown herself into her arms in turn. Floods of tears followed, Derek heading off to make some tea. And it had all come out about the boy and what had happened when she went to that blasted party. As she'd told Wendy the story, she'd thought again that this girl was going down the same path her mother did. Being drawn to guys like Phil – which she supposed was a phase all girls went through, except it seemed to have passed Wendy by. All she wanted, really wanted, was for Deborah to meet someone nice. For her granddaughter to do the same, when the time was right. When she was old enough.

"We'll have a lovely time away and forget about everything, just us girls together, eh?" But that was easier said than done, wasn't it. How could Wendy forget about everything, stop worrying about things she didn't even really know much about?

As she looked over at the passenger seat, at Izzy turned towards the window – the cars passing her by on the motorway – Wendy could see her gloomy face in the reflection. Knew that she felt the same way. Felt that even given what she'd told her, spilling the beans about the party and such, there was more the girl was itching to say.

"You all right, love?" she asked finally, echoing Derek's question about Deborah.

Izzy faced her, mouth downturned. But it wasn't any of the other stuff bothering her now, something had been on her mind since Deborah had sent for the boys. "I-I said some horrible things to Mum before she left. Wouldn't even talk to her. And about Jack and James." She hung her head. "I don't know why."

"It's okay," said Wendy. "She knows you didn't mean them."

"Does she?"

"I'm sure she does."

It didn't seem to do anything to help with her granddaughter's distress. "I love her, you know," she said, looking up again.

"I know."

"I love them all, very much."

"Yes, I know that too. Your mum knows it as well."

Izzy nodded, but tears were forming in her eyes.

"Tell you what, when we get settled in at Penny's we'll see if we can get hold of your mum, eh?"

Another nod.

"And you can say all this to her yourself."

Izzy nodded a third time, then shifted about uncomfortably in the seat. "I just... Why do I get this feeling, like I'm never going to see them again?"

Wendy drew in a sudden breath. The words had shocked

her, but Izzy was only saying what she was thinking herself. "I… I really don't know. You'll… we'll see them soon. I…" She was going to say 'I promise' but for some reason didn't feel like she could; Wendy had always prided herself on not making promises she couldn't keep. She shifted about herself in the driver's seat. "I'm sure that we will. Let's just try and enjoy ourselves, eh. We're getting away from it all."

Only she couldn't help thinking now that, like her daughter Deborah, they were never going to get away from any of this. That it was tied to them, would follow them around like a bad smell for the rest of their lives. That far from getting away from it all…

It would be with them. Here forever.

Here to stay.

CHAPTER TWENTY-THREE

She shifted about in the seat.

Couldn't get comfortable on the couch, was wondering how long they'd have to stay. Wasn't that this place was horrible, quite the opposite: it was lovely. For an apartment it was really, really nice; stylish whilst still being homely. Wasn't that the sofa was hard or anything, no, it was extremely comfortable. It was more the reason she was there – and Deborah had to wonder how much of it Rosy had told Kiz, how much her partner was *allowed* to know. That, apart from anything else, made her feel like she was on edge. Walking, sitting, on eggshells.

Deborah had tried to time it just right. They'd sent a car for her, to take her from *The Imperial* to this place, around the time that the twins would be getting back from Armitage Bay with Rosy. She hadn't gone with her because as much as she'd have loved to see her mum and Izzy, she didn't want to flag what they were doing any more than was necessary – and she'd wanted to avoid any strained face-to-face conversations.

Which was more than she was doing right now. After passing the nearby park and the cars outside watching the building, which had armed undercover officers sitting in them trying to look inconspicuous and failing miserably (which might not have been a bad thing as far as deterrents went), Deborah had used the code she'd been given to get inside. That tripped an alarm if anyone tried to get in without it, and Deborah noted the uniformed security guard in the downstairs lobby. On Rosy's floor she pressed the bell at the correct door, which had a peephole so you could check who was on the other side. Her friend had been right, it was pretty secure here.

"Deborah!" said the beautiful dark-skinned woman who opened the door, kissing her on both cheeks. She was wearing an oversized shirt and skinny jeans, or leggings – jeggings, they called them, didn't they? Stupid name, like coatigans and shackets. "Come in, come in."

She'd only met Kiz the once, but had got on fine with her. Knew her about as well as you could get to know someone passing time in a pub. Had got the sense that she was a nice person. Back then she'd been looking out for Rosy, making sure she was with someone who was worth her time – not that Deborah would be able to do anything about it if she wasn't. But today it was because the boys would be staying here with her. "Kiz, really good to see you again."

"Take your coat off, please. Make yourself at home."

Kiz was already walking through the short hall into the living room, so Deborah followed after she'd taken off her coat and hung it on the peg next to the door. The tall woman looked back over her shoulder, caught Deborah eying the kitchen which was just off to the side of that room, with no door separating it. "Oh, don't worry. We've put anything hazardous out of the way in the high cupboards. Bleach, knives… chainsaws, that kind of thing." She laughed, but there was a nervous inflection to it Deborah hadn't noticed the last time she'd met her.

"I really appreciate you doing this, Kiz. Thank you."

The woman flapped her hand. "Happy to. Look, I had

some time due off from work – if I can't use it doing something to help out, then…"

"Still, it's really good of you. Thanks."

"Honestly, please. You don't have to keep thanking me. You and Rosy are like family, so… Oh, come and have a look at this, see what you think."

Deborah followed her through another little corridor, with two doors. Kiz opened the first one, which was clearly the spare bedroom. "Oh, wow… I…" The woman had gone out and bought a matching bedspread and pillowcases, covered in little comic book figures. In addition to that, there were toys scattered about the place: Lego bricks; a remote-controlled car; some action figures. "This is…"

"I wasn't sure what they liked to do. I also dug out the old games console for the living room, in case they like playing stuff on those. Haven't used it in years, so it might be a bit too old school for them, I dunno."

"Kiz, this is *amazing*. You've gone to so much trouble, I can't even begin to… There are some grown-ups I can think of who'd love all this." That made her pause for a moment, thinking about Vinny and his talk of collectibles at his place. She pushed that aside and changed the subject: "It must have cost a fortune."

She batted this comment away with a hand as well. "We want the boys to feel at home while they're here."

Deborah picked up one of the books on a desk nearby. It was a bit young for the twins, but she appreciated the thought that had gone into all this. Wondered if there was more to it than just looking after a friend's children for a few days (hopefully just a few days).

"She'd probably be delighted to get to know them. Would jump at the chance of having kids around."

Rosy's words when they were talking about doing this back at the nick, and suddenly it clicked what was the matter with her friend. With this relationship. What Kiz said next only confirmed that suspicion. "I mean, you guys are going to have your hands full with work and everything, right?"

"I..."

"Rosy's always working. She works so hard." Now there was a touch of resentment in there too.

"Well, she's taken on those extra duties with the SCI and all."

Kiz sighed. "Yeah, I know. Doesn't leave a whole lot of time for family stuff, though."

Family stuff, not private stuff. Not her and Rosy time, although that was probably another bone of contention. "It can be tough juggling all that."

"Right. Yeah. Oh, listen, do you want a tea or something?" Kiz didn't wait for the answer, was already heading back out again towards the living room and kitchen. Was filling the kettle by the time Deborah got out there. "They shouldn't be long before—" And right on cue, Kiz's phone pinged. She took it out of her 'jeggings' pocket, though she had trouble getting her long fingers inside. "Aww, looks like they're going to be a little late. Traffic on the motorway, apparently."

Late? Deborah couldn't help bristling at that, wondering if something had happened. Wondering if someone else had got hold of Rosy's phone and—

"Sit down and relax," said Kiz, nodding at the couch.

Yes, she did need to relax. Calm down. Traffic would be a bit of a nightmare at this time of day. Traffic was just traffic. There were more SCI people escorting Rosy, who'd gone with her to the coast to pick up the boys. It was fine. Absolutely fine.

Except it meant that it was just the two of them for a while. Having tea. Sitting there, virtual strangers, having tea. Which was why Deborah couldn't get comfortable, which was why – even though Kiz had gone to so much trouble, making this place so nice for the boys – Deborah was thinking about how long this would all be going on for. How long they'd have to stay here. If anything, the way that spare room looked (like they'd be here for months rather than days) made her feel worse. And Kiz's comments about working – they applied not just to Rosy, but her, too.

Ignoring the twins, neglecting them. Putting this first.

Silly really, when they were now as much a part of it all as Deborah. Being used like some kind of early warning detection system. By Glover. By *her*.

To try and save Vinny, though it hadn't done much good. Maybe next time, though. That's why they were doing this. It might save lives. It might help them catch—

"Deborah," Kiz began, something that usually preceded a question in her experience.

"Yeah."

"You've known Rosy a long time, haven't you?"

She nodded, still waiting for the question. "Since we worked together here."

"Do you think..." Kiz shook her head, drank some of her tea. It was like a mirror of the morning she'd spent with Rosy, like she was now doing the same thing with the other half of that pairing. Being a therapist or something. Her friend had glossed over what was wrong back then, wanted to get to the nitty-gritty about The Gemini, but Kiz was definitely more keen to chat about it all. "Okay, I'm going to come right out and ask. Do you think she's the, y'know, maternal type? Not maternal, but, well, the 'wanting kids' type?"

Deborah put down her own steaming drink. "Kiz, I don't... I've known Rosy years, but you *know* her. You're closer to her than me." You *should* be at any rate, thought Deborah.

"I guess." Kiz looked sad, then. "It's just we've been talking about the future, y'know?"

She nodded again. "I do." The future was never far from her mind, especially at the moment. Wondering if she even had one, for starters. Wondering if any of them did, if the

Geminite's prophecies were correct. "It's hard. Take it from someone who wasn't expecting to have any more after Isobel. Total surprise, and I certainly wasn't expecting two!" Though apparently there were reasons for that, according to those books of Vinny's.

"They change your life, right?"

"They certainly do. But in the best ways, as well as... I don't know what I'd do without them now, honestly I don't. I've missed them so much. I love them so..." Deborah realised she was getting off topic. As much as she really didn't want the boys anywhere near this city, and all the shit that came with that, she was also desperate to see them again. Why weren't they here already?

"That's what I'm talking about. That's what I had when I was growing up. I'd like that as well, with the right person."

"With Rosy." Deborah wasn't sure whether it was a question or a statement.

Kiz looked her in the eye. "Yes. With Rosy."

"Well, I won't pretend it's been easy. It takes up a lot of your time, obviously. And if I hadn't had Mum to help, bless her. After Jack... I know there are women out there who cope on their own, and I take my hat off to them: they're incredible. But I'm not sure I would've coped alone with the twins, or with Isobel. You think I might be a bit all over the place at the moment, but I was a special kind of mess back then after Phil."

"Phil?" This was obviously something Rosy hadn't discussed with her, and for that Deborah was grateful – but it did mean she had to give her the edited highlights herself.

"Jesus," whispered Kiz. "And for the record, I don't think you're all over the place at all. I really admire what you've done with your life, what you're *doing* with it."

"Thanks, I appreciate that."

"And it's great you had your mum and everything. My folks are up in Scotland, I know, but they'd help out where they could. I wouldn't be on my own, though. Rosy would be…" She let her sentence tail off.

"Oh, I wasn't trying to say…" *Balls*, thought Deborah. *Open mouth, insert foot. This is why you shouldn't be talking about all this, giving out advice. You're the* last *person who should be doing that.* "She's terrific with the twins, you should see her. Actually, you will see." *You're babbling now, Deborah.* "I just meant, her job is quite…"

Kiz nodded. She knew exactly how demanding Rosy's job was, and it would only get worse with her new responsibilities that was for sure. Kiz might not be a single mum, but there would be times when she'd feel like one. "Level with me," Kiz said then.

Oh no, what now?

"How much danger are you guys in?"

"What?"

"Chasing this guy." Kiz shrugged. "I've seen the cars downstairs, the Men in Black keeping watch. They wouldn't do that unless it was serious."

"Er…" Deborah wasn't sure how to answer that. Her mother had asked the same question and she'd tried to dodge that, too. Again, she wasn't sure how much this woman was *allowed* to know beyond what the press had already reported. Thankfully at that moment the buzzer went. *Saved by the bell!* she thought.

It was Rosy, at last – who else could it have been, they wouldn't have let anyone else through other than maybe Fleming, Glover or Clark, but she'd told them they needed this space to adjust. "I've got a couple of bundles of trouble here looking for their mother," she called through, and Deborah rushed to the door.

What she saw were two boys who looked anything but trouble. Shy, nervous, wondering what they were doing here, probably wondering where the hell their mum had been the last week or more. James was looking up at Kiz, who'd just been introduced to them, unsure what to say or do. But when they both saw Deborah, their whole appearance altered. They visibly relaxed, then set off like runners in a race, going from standing beside Rosy to almost reaching her in the blink of an eye.

Deborah was used to this, however, and had already started bending. She was pretty much on her knees, arms open wide, when they hit home – ploughing into her with a force that nearly toppled her over. James took the left, Jack the right, and she enveloped them, pulling them tighter and tighter to her.

She was crying freely now, as it also hit home how much time she'd missed with them. "Oh boys, I'm so happy to see you," she whispered.

"Mummy!" they both chorused.

She never wanted to let them go ever again. But of course she had to, they were in the way of everyone getting to the lounge for one thing. It was only now that she saw Rosy and Kiz together, holding each other and pulling back, kissing. They'd missed each other as well, even though it had only been a few hours. When you loved someone, it could get you like that.

"Come on, let's go inside," said Kiz, not even waiting, just stepping over them. "I've got ice cream, cake. Whatever you guys want, really."

Deborah glanced at her watch. "Oh, I'm not really sure..." Then she looked at Rosy. "They won't sleep tonight if you give them all that sugar."

But the twins were gazing up at her pleadingly, frightened they were going to miss out on the delicious treats. Rosy just gave a shrug. "I'd better not mention the chocolate they've already had in the car, then."

"Muuuum," They sang together now. "Pleeeease!"

Deborah couldn't help grinning. "Okay, just this once. To

celebrate being together again. But if you're sick, it'll all be your Aunty Rosy's fault."

"And your Aunty Kiz," the woman called out happily from inside the apartment. Now there was a woman who'd definitely got a maternal side, or at the very least knew how to get kids on side. They were already rushing in to see what was on offer.

"Everything go all right?" Deborah asked Rosy now.

"Yeah, no problem." Her friend looked at her. "Sorry I was late, we got in a few horrendous jams. And here, everything okay?"

Deborah opened her mouth, closed it again, and gave a little nod. Then she went through into the living room herself, to the kitchen, where Kiz was dishing out the goods like a female Willy Wonka. She'd already turned on the TV, set to a random cartoon network. This was the fun side of it all, but Deborah had to admit she thought Kiz would be good with the harder aspects as well. Rosy, on the other hand…

The kids retreated with their bowls, leaving Rosy to join Deborah and Kiz. "So, all okay?" the woman asked again, this time both of them. Kiz exchanged a look with Deborah, and they both nodded together. One of Rosy's eyes turned to a slit. "Why do I get the feeling I've missed something?"

They both shifted about now, probably wondering how much they were *allowed* to say, so instead moved off into the living room to join the kids. Where hopefully it was a bit less strained. Uncomfortable.

A bit less like walking on eggshells.

Being on edge.

CHAPTER TWENTY-FOUR

Pots.

Specifically watched ones. Apparently no-one at the SCI was familiar with that concept at all. Not judging from the amount of times they were checking on them, and in the end had sent Fleming round in person, to be present in case anything happened.

When all they could really do was wait.

Deborah had been glad of the fact there'd been nothing to report, because if the boys hadn't dreamed about – hadn't 'seen' – anything then that meant another potential victim was still alive. Meant that the monster out there who had the same skillset as his predecessor, might even be the same person, hadn't made another move. Perhaps he wouldn't, although that was a slim hope, Deborah realised. What had started here would need to finish, one way or another. But the breathing room was welcome at least, it had allowed them to get back to some kind of normality, her and the boys.

Enjoy each other's company, anyway. That wasn't to say they hadn't had fun with Rosy and Kiz – and, as predicted, their Aunty Kiz had fast become a favourite – it was just that she'd wanted to be around as much as possible too, maybe overcompensating for not having been there previously. She'd tried to explain to the boys that what she'd been doing was important, that it was helping people – that they were all doing that now, whether they realised it or not – but Deborah wasn't sure how much of it the kids understood.

About the bad man, the bad man with two faces. About how they needed to stop him.

But that had soon been forgotten about anyway, at least as far as they were concerned, when they settled in and made use of the toys and games Kiz had provided, often with the woman herself joining in. They even ventured outside to the park to feed the ducks in the pond there, under the watchful eye of the officers nearby, of course. "I hope you know I'm calling on you in the future if we need a babysitter," Deborah had said to her with a wink.

"You'd better," she told her.

"Both of you, obviously," she'd added when she felt Rosy come up behind her. There were still some unspoken things going on about that, about the conversation Deborah and Kiz had had while Rosy fetched the twins. And she felt bad about hanging around so much, about the boys even being here when it was obvious the couple needed some time and space to work out what they each wanted from this relationship – once and for all. But at the same time, Jack and James were here, with her, for the first time in what seemed like decades, not days.

They'd stayed up late watching stuff on that first night, until the boys passed out and Kiz had given her a hand putting them to bed. "You were wrong about them not sleeping."

"Well, yeah, they crash out sometimes after the sugar high – especially when they've had *this* much. Did you not see them riverdancing before?"

Kiz chuckled and nodded. "How could I miss it?"

"Hyper doesn't even begin to cover it."

"Look," she'd said then. "Why don't you stay over tonight. The sofa's surprisingly cosy, I've fallen asleep any number of times myself on there at the weekend. I'm sure the boys would be delighted to find you here in the morning."

Might have been a confidence thing on her part, not yet sure whether they'd be all right waking up in a new place, with this woman who'd been shovelling ice cream and M&Ms into them – though she had nothing to worry about on that score. They had taken to Kiz pretty quickly, and that would only build. Maybe it was just the hour, the thought of having to make her way back to *The Imperial* at this time of night, in spite of the fact they could just get a squad car to transport her. But yes, actually, Deborah didn't feel like leaving anyway so accepted the kind offer.

Rosy had already gone to bed when they returned to the living room, so Kiz just got some spare blankets out of the airing cupboard, passing more cushions over so that Deborah could hit the sack as well. Though not before Kiz had given her a hug and another kiss. "Thanks again," Deborah said, "for everything."

"Thank *you*," Kiz told her.

As she lay there, with just the table lamp on, Deborah had promised herself it would just be for the one night, this. But one had turned into two, then three – and Kiz had made her feel very welcome there, providing a spare toothbrush (she'd bought an extra when she got toiletries for the boys) and some clothes for her so she didn't have to go back if she didn't want to.

But at night she could hear the raised voices coming from the main bedroom. Probably hadn't been about her staying, or the twins – more likely just tension about the 'having a family' thing in general – but it still felt like this was intruding on someone else's life when she shouldn't have been.

Those hadn't been the only arguments of the last couple of days, however. Her mum had video called her from Penny's, and they'd done the whole 'how was everything and everyone?' routine, then she'd put Izzy on, who apparently was eager to talk.

"Hey sweetheart, how're things?" Deborah had said.

Looking sheepish, the teen had apologised – a kind of blanket sorry for everything. "I just, I wanted you to know that, Mum. I love you."

"It's much appreciated, I love you too. *So* much." And if they'd stopped there, that would have been fine. But true to form, they'd slipped into that mother and daughter at war act that seemed to just be a habit most of the time these days. Something as simple as "I'm glad you're safe, after the party and everything" had set Izzy off again. And they were back to square one, doing battle without even realising it.

"I'm okay. I can look after myself. I would have been all right anyway, you know, without those people checking up on me."

"Right." Deborah couldn't help herself. "Not the way I heard it."

Izzy let out an exasperated groan. "I don't *care* what you heard."

"This is why I didn't want you going in the first place. I've tried to warn you about all this stuff, it's only because I've been through it. You're too young for boys, for—"

"I handled it," snapped Izzy. "Give me some credit for that."

"I do, really I do."

"You just didn't want me to go because you don't trust me. Like, *at all!*"

"That's not true, I just wanted to—"

"I don't know why I bothered with this. You sent for the boys, but not me. It's obvious who you love more."

"That's… Izzy, how could you—"

"You can all just go to hell!"

There was blackness, the phone had clearly been dropped

on the sofa. When it was picked up again, her mum's face filling the screen, Deborah could hear sobbing in the background. "Hi again, love," her mum said.

"What did I do? What did I say?" asked Deborah, exasperated.

"Just give it some time," were Wendy's wise words. "Give her some time."

Yeah, thought Deborah. *Maybe give her till she's eighteen or twenty and starts to get her head on straight.* "Sure. I'd better go anyway, Mum. Love you."

"Love you too. Be safe."

And wasn't there just a twinge at that, the rebellious teen inside Deborah rearing her ugly head as well; the part that whispered *her* mum thought she couldn't take care of herself either. That she didn't trust *her*. It was all a process, Deborah guessed.

Then there were the rows with Glover over the phone, about how they still hadn't gotten anywhere questioning the Geminite. "I don't know what you expect us to do, if he won't talk he won't talk," the inspector had told her.

"I'd make him talk," she offered.

"We're not allowed to use torture, it's against the Geneva Convention." Meant as a joke, but like all of Glover's jokes it missed its mark. "Look, we're trying. In the meantime is there anything from the boys?"

"No. Nothing. I can't just activate them like radar."

"I understand that, I just thought maybe... a dream or something? I was just wondering."

A dream or something. He didn't understand a thing; it wasn't as if Deborah understood it much more. "You'll be the first to know, I'm sure," she'd said. But he hadn't left it at that, checking constantly, and that evening he'd even sent Fleming over.

Pots. Watched pots.

It was the last straw really, that woman being there to spy

on them. She'd grown used to her, but still didn't trust or like her that much. Not this much, anyway. Deborah had been thinking about grabbing some stuff from *The Imperial* anyway because she felt like a homeless person, maybe sneak in an hour on her own with a change of scenery – she was still paying for the room, after all – and give the others some space at the same time. Even the boys were showing signs of getting antsy, being a bit ratty – though they had nothing on Izzy. She made sure they were okay with her just popping out though, otherwise Deborah wouldn't have gone. They were so busy playing some platform game they barely even heard her. She smiled and kissed them both on the tops of their heads.

"We'll arrange for someone to go with you," Fleming had told her.

"No need, Robbie... DS Clark is picking me up," she said, and the woman had raised an eyebrow at that. No doubt it would all get reported back to Glover. She couldn't give a shit.

Deborah had waited in the lobby, got chatting to the security man down there and found out his name was Bernard, and then climbed into the car when Clark arrived. "Hiya," she said, "thanks for doing this."

"I think it's me who should be thanking you," he replied. They hadn't had a great deal of contact since Luke Simpson died, not alone anyway, so this had been the first opportunity for him to say that. "For making sure I wasn't out on my ear."

"You're kidding, aren't you. It was my fault you almost got canned. I'm sorry."

"No need to be, you were bang on the money with Simpson. I'm sorry I..." Clark shook his head and she placed a hand on his arm. It was becoming a familiar action. When he looked up at her she smiled. "All right then, to *The Imperial* it is, m'lady," he said, doing his best *Thunderbirds* impression.

Deborah played along. "Thank you, Parker."

They both chortled. Once he'd set off they began chatting again, falling into that easy rhythm. Deborah was starting to think she was closer to Clark these days than Rosy. "Must be nice to be with your lads again."

"Oh, it is, Robbie. You've no idea."

"Yeah, mums and their sons. You can't beat that bond," he replied. "And there's been nothing…"

"Don't you start," she said to him, then laughed to show she wasn't being serious when she saw his face. "Sorry. It's just that Glover's been non-stop with all this."

"He's being put under some serious pressure to get things sorted now," Clark told her. "Even more than before."

"I'm still not convinced he's not involved in all this somehow," Deborah confided.

"Naw, I don't think so." That was just Clark, he always saw the best in people. "But yeah, he should lay off a bit where your kids are concerned. Hasn't he ever heard of that thing about kettles boiling?"

She knew the phrase he meant, but she'd grown up with the pot one. They never boil when they're being watched.

All they could do was wait.

CHAPTER TWENTY-FIVE

Waiting was the worst.

Worst thing about these kind of assignments, hands down. DC Craig Gough rubbed his leg again, which had gone to sleep. He felt like joining it, he was so bored. He glanced over at his colleague in the driver's seat, DC Hickey, whose head was lolling back, eyes like slits as the man fought to keep them open. Once or twice his mouth had *fallen* open so far that he'd started to snore, waking himself up, and he'd always look over at Gough and say: "I wasn't asleep."

Yeah, right. But Gough could hardly blame him.

There had been a match on earlier, they'd listened to it on the radio – would have watched on their phone but neither of them wanted to drain the battery. That had kept them going for a while, staved off the tedium. Then Hickey had challenged him to a game of 'I spy' (what were they, ten?), where the only things they'd been able to come up with were 'S' for Street, 'W' for windows and 'D' for Doors. Gough had ended the game with an 'F', watching Hickey's face contort as he tried to guess, his brain working overtime.

"Fruit?"

"Where's the fruit around here?" Gough asked him.

"Erm… All right, all right, I give up."

"Oh, that was an easy one. It was 'F' for 'Fucking hell let's stop playing this game!'"

"There's no need to be like that about it." Hickey had folded his arms and not spoken for about an hour. It had been a blessing.

Gough couldn't decide which was preferable, a protection gig or stakeout. There's wasn't much to choose between either, really, both involved waiting. There was a chance you might see some action, of course, on this kind of duty. Have to stop someone who was trying to get to the people you were guarding, that got the old blood pumping! And of course you were allowed to carry; Gough could feel the comforting weight of the gun in the shoulder holster beneath his jacket, nestled just under his armpit. He'd absolutely loved firearms training, pulling the trigger, firing his pistol and hitting the target. Still got as much practice in at the range as he could.

On a stakeout, you might see a different kind of action, mind. Sitting there with your binoculars or telephoto lens camera, if it got dark and the subject went to bed without drawing the curtains or whatever.

And they weren't alone.

Not that he was a perv or anything. Not that he got off on any of that, like some people he could mention – like Hickey, for example. But it did no harm to look, did it. They were being paid to observe, right? To watch. Surveillance. He was only a red-blooded man, after all. Men were visual, weren't they. Couldn't help it.

Not that he looked at porn or anything. Not at all. Well, *hardly* ever. Not as much as some. Not as much as Hickey, he was always on about it. Sniggering like that cartoon duo that used to be on the music channel. Did you see this or that on ShagHub? X-Rodent? The positions those people got themselves into… But there was something to be said about watching a live 'performance', wasn't there. He wasn't doing anything wrong.

Maybe he'd go back on the firing range again tomorrow, let a few off.

Jesus, he really needed to get a girlfriend.

Gough's last few attempts at dating had been disastrous, but then what could you expect when you were swiping left or right, dredging through photos of people sticking their tongues out, sticking up 'V' symbols, or pouting like they were constipated? Not that he was any great shakes. Didn't profess to be an Einstein or whatever, but God Almighty…

First there had been the 'Influencer' who was more concerned about taking photos of her meal than eating it, and when she did eat kept rushing off to the bathroom – "'S'cuse me, babe!" – where she was probably bringing it back up again. What a waste of time and money that night had turned out to be. Then there had been the hairdresser, who kept telling him what kind of style he should have: "It'd look lovely if you grew it out, maybe swept it over. Who does it at the moment?" He didn't like to admit that he popped into the men's barbers in the precinct and just told the guy "Short". Five minutes tops, and cheap as chips!

Finally there had been the girl who worked on the make-up counter, only part-time she kept telling him, while she started her own fake tan business up. The strange orange colour of her skin competed for his attention with the hideous dayglo colours of her eye-shadow and lipstick.

There had to be better pickings out there than that. Someone easy-going, on his wavelength. Gough knew there was, because he'd been with one. A girl called Victoria who he'd known from school, but got together with after she returned from uni. They were going out for a couple of years all told, but her parents had never really liked him. Her dad especially, kept saying that she could do better (ironically). In the end it had torpedoed the relationship, but

Gough had really, really liked Victoria. Hadn't just been about the fact she was pretty – those stunning ringlets that cascaded over her shoulders, they'd have kept the hairdresser occupied for months – or about the... physical side of things, though that had been terrific, he had to admit. He'd come as close to loving someone as he ever had done with Victoria; they'd got on, had fun. She'd been his best friend.

He'd even stupidly started to think about a future with her, maybe even marriage – a honeymoon abroad (believe it or not Gough had never even been on a plane, never flown). Perhaps a family down the line? Kids, that sort of thing.

Shit. He really missed Victoria.

Hickey was nudging him now, breaking into his thoughts. "Hey, look. Clarky's picking up that Harrison woman. Been spending a lot of time together, so I heard."

Gough watched as she got into Clark's car and they sat there a few moments, then she touched his arm, and they shared a private joke. They did look close. "So what?" said Gough. "Good for them."

"Bit of a toyboy situation going on there, don't you think?"

Gough shrugged. He couldn't care less. Someone might as well be happy with their love life. "Probably just getting out of the way of Fleming." They'd seen the woman enter a while ago, just before it started getting dark. Now there was a real piece of work, the DS from that SCI department – the one that had come in dishing out the orders and bossing them all around. Like Janet Street-Porter and Ilsa of the SS rolled into one, she was. Might be nice on the inside? If so, she hid it very well.

"Yeah. Bitch," was Hickey's contribution to that debate.

It was kinda their fault, the SCI, that the two of them were out here freezing their arses off tonight, instead of at home watching a good action flick on TV. Something with Gerard Butler blowing things up and shooting everyone in sight (something had fallen, or whatever); though Gerry was getting a bit old for that kind of thing these days.

There was a bang on the window and Gough jumped. "Fuck's sake!" he said when he saw DC Maple standing there wetting herself. She was in the other car not far away behind them, along with Constable Peters.

Gough wound the window down. "Couldn't resist," she said, leaning in and grinning, her eyes twinkling. "You were miles away."

"I was thinking about shooting people," he told her. "Maybe starting with you."

She laughed. "I see."

"Seriously, I could've shot you." Gough patted his chest. "With my lightning reflexes, you shouldn't sneak up on people like that!"

It just made her laugh even harder. "All right, tiger, calm down. I was just about to do a coffee run, maybe grab some muffins or something. There's a place a couple of streets away."

Hickey perked up at that. "Ooh, I could murder a flapjack and a hot chocolate."

Gough sighed. "Okay, since you're offering. Just a flat white for me." The caffeine would certainly help him stay alert. He started to rummage around in his pocket for his wallet.

"S'okay, this one's on me, hotshot," she said, beaming, then looked over at Hickey. "*You* can pay me later."

They both watched her head off down the street, then disappear round the corner. "You should go for that," said Hickey.

"Go for what?"

"Her. Maple."

"What?"

"Hell's bells, mate. She's sooo into you." Again, what were they, ten?

"No," said Gough. "*Is* she?"

"Oh yeah, has been for a while. Haven't you noticed, the banter and everything?"

Gough couldn't say that he had, but then he'd never been good at noticing when women were flirting with him. "No," he said again.

"Yep. You could do worse than that, tough cookie she is. And gorgeous, in case you hadn't noticed that either." Hickey shook his head. "If I wasn't married…"

He didn't need his partner to tell him he could do worse, Gough knew from experience he could do worse. *A lot* worse. Might even end up being another Victoria situation here, you never knew. Only without the breakup this time.

"If I was you, I wouldn't wait around," Hickey added, a weird thing to say when that was exactly what they were doing at the moment. Then he clarified it with: "Life's definitely too short."

♊

He's been waiting.

In the park opposite the apartment block, hidden from view behind some bushes, peering out through the iron railings. *He's* been watching and waiting, observing the police officers even as they watch the building. *He* saw the other car pull up, watched as the oh-so familiar woman got in. As she laughed and played around with her driver, the car pulling away again.

It's now or never, the time to strike. But wait… wait again, as the female 'undercover' – what a joke – cop leaves her car, her partner, and goes over to the first one. Chats with the men inside, then moves away to go down the street.

Now then. Strike now.

The waiting is over.

♊

Bernard 'Bernie' Noble didn't mind the waiting around.

He'd got used to doing that in the army, dug out in foxholes in some foreign land. This wasn't so bad, hanging about in a posh foyer with a comfy seat off to one side if his legs started to ache. Drinks or snacks on demand from the machine next to the stairs (he had the code). Plus one of the perks was he got to live here rent free on the ground floor. Life could be worse.

Had definitely been worse during his time serving, when he'd put his life on the line for his country. He'd seen colleagues – friends – get blown to bits, shot up, crippled. You don't just walk away from that unscathed. Sometimes you didn't walk away at all. Had it been worth it? Bernie wasn't sure, couldn't be certain it had really been appreciated. More wars had followed, there was still no sign of peace in the regions he'd been dispatched to.

Necessary at the time, though, he understood that. Bernie had been a tearaway when he was younger, falling in with the wrong crowd; stealing, car-jacking, even some mugging, he was ashamed to say. He'd had to become a shark swimming in these urban waters. What else was a latch-key kid like himself supposed to do? It was fend for yourself or— His parents hadn't given a toss about him, his dad had been blind drunk most of the time, and Bernie wasn't the cleverest. Used to tune out at school, when he could be bothered to go. College or uni was never an option for him.

Wasn't stupid by any stretch of the imagination, just not academically-minded. Wasn't a crime, unlike some of the stuff he got up to. Sometimes when he looked back he was amazed he hadn't ended up in jail. Just hadn't got caught, that was all. Had been lucky in that respect.

One of his mates hadn't been, but he was offered the option of signing up instead of prison and had taken it. He'd talked Bernie into tagging along with him, said it would be 'fun'. "Free holidays, and we get to run around with a gun!" That was how he'd put it, but the reality had been something very different.

What it *had* taught Bernie, however – regardless of how tough it had been – was discipline, honour and respect. Self-respect, more importantly. That and to be ready for anything. It had at least turned his life around, set him on the straight and narrow. Taught him valuable life lessons he would never have learned anywhere else. Even his dad was proud he was doing something valuable with his life. Finally stepping up. Noble by name, now...

When Bernard's tours were over, when he left, he had to admit he'd been a little lost. Wasn't quite sure what to do with himself. Some of his old friends had come calling, trying to rope him back into that dodgy life he'd escaped from, but he'd had the strength to say no now. Say "Go fuck yourselves" essentially. The very reason why they wanted him back, could use his muscle, his fighting ability to their advantage, meant that they hadn't asked twice.

There were legal ways to use his skills, he just needed to find them. Something that put them to use, rather than taking just anything like a few of his buddies had done; Keegan, for instance, in the construction trade, though he seemed to have disappeared off the face of the Earth after that business at Willerton Castle... So Bernie had worked as a bouncer for a little while, standing on the door of various nightclubs, but that had grown more and more dangerous as the years went by. Never knew when some prick might try it on with a knife or a smashed bottle (weapons he was familiar with from his youth, more's the pity) and all it would take would be a lucky punch. Conversely, you had to be so careful when using force, because people would sue you soon as look at you these days.

But, as with crime, or like the army, it was a small world. A friend had recommended him for a security job, and he'd been good at it. More gigs had followed, then this one: a cushy little number, something that might just suit him as he got into his 40s.

And back in a uniform, of sorts.

He liked it here, liked the people. Sometimes he'd chat with them, if they wanted to that was, and keeping folk safe here was definitely worthwhile. Certainly appreciated, he even got Christmas presents from some of the residents. Bottle of 20-year-old single malt last year from that nice Mrs Baker.

His job was even more important at the moment, what with everything that was going on. Bernie wasn't privy to all the ins and outs, of course. But he knew it had something to do with that lady Rosy Lim, because she worked for the police. And that other lady who was staying with them for a bit, Miss Harrison (those kids he'd spotted with Rosy had to be hers). Also a cop, or had been once – you never lost the look. At one time of day, they'd been his adversaries, but he'd been on the right side of the law for a long time now.

Even felt a kinship with those officers out there keeping watch from their cars. Comrades in arms, just like before.

Waiting, just like he was. For what? Bernard had no idea. But he'd be ready. Ready for anything.

He always was.

♊

Hickey yawned again for the millionth time.

Gough yawned too, couldn't help it; yawns were infectious. Where was Maple with that coffee? Wasn't just that he needed the caffeine hit now, he'd been thinking about what Hickey said, about not hanging about. Was looking forward to seeing her actually, coming round that corner.

Then the tapping on the window came again, but it only made him jump a little. *Must've gone around the block and come back the other way*, he thought. *Never mind, at least she's here. At least—*

The tapping turned into a crash, a smashing sound. The glass breaking, the bits tinkling as they fell inside. "Wha—" Gough managed, before looking across and up. Seeing that huge figure, seeing the faces staring at him: two sets of eyes. They'd all talked about this, mentioned it in meetings and during conversations about The Gemini, but that really didn't look like a mask at all. Two faces stitched together, yes. But real faces. Moving, mouths twitching, eyes blinking.

Immediately Gough reached into his jacket for the gun. Another hand closed around his own, preventing him from drawing it out. It squeezed, and he heard a cracking sound. Seconds later, he felt the pain as the bones in his hand were crushed like they'd been placed in a vice.

Before he had a chance to cry out, he was being dragged through that broken side window. Something caught on his trousers; Gough had a vague notion of them being ripped by the jagged glass. Except it wasn't just his trousers that were caught, his legs were being raked by those shards too. Gough could feel the wetness as he was thrown to the ground.

Hickey was finally free of the car, clambering out of the driver's side, his weapon already drawn. That had stopped his yawning, the adrenaline that must have been pumping through his system. Gough would be all right now; Hickey would get this bastard before he did anything else. He'd—

In the time it had taken even to think this, their attacker had skirted the car and grabbed Hickey's gun arm by the wrist before he could fire. Yanked it up so hard the limb popped out of its socket at the shoulder. The huge man dressed in black let the arm go and it flopped uselessly by Hickey's side, the pistol dropping to the ground with a clatter. A backhander put a stop to Hickey's cries, snapping his head sideways.

Gough tried to get his gun out with his other hand, but he

was in a bad position. Better to just try and get away, crawl away – the only option open to him since his legs were shredded. Where the fuck was their backup? Maple was at the coffee place, sure. But her partner, Peters? Where the fuck was—

Then he saw it, the blood covering the windscreen of the car behind them. Obscuring his view of what had actually happened to poor Constable Peters, and for that Gough was grateful. It was about the only thing he *could* feel grateful for at the moment.

Now, he was hoping that Maple took her time. That there was a great big queue of people waiting to be served in that coffee place, because if she came back here...

She'd end up like the rest of them. As dead as—

Even as he was thinking this, Gough was aware of the giant behind him. Standing, towering over him. Bending over him.

"D-Don't—" he began, but then he was being lifted up.

Way up, further than he was expecting. Up above the giant's head. This person, The Gemini – it couldn't be anyone else – was hefting him like he was lifting weights. Holding him there for a moment. Gough wasn't quite sure what he was going to do with him next, just drop him on the ground again, shattering more bones? Before stamping on him?

No. That wasn't it at all.

At the last moment Gough spotted them, the railings that bordered the park. The tall iron bars that came to a point at the top. They didn't look that sharp, but if someone were to fall on them from enough of a height...

Say the height Gough was being thrown, up and over towards them. Had never been in a plane, but didn't need one to fly now. He was flying, all right. Then falling. His weight carrying him downwards, down onto the spikes.

They punctured him in several places; he couldn't move even if he wanted to. Couldn't lift himself off the railings, even if his hand hadn't been mashed, his legs already torn to pieces.

All he could do was watch, as The Gemini made his way across the street.

Watch and do nothing, not that they could ever have done anything to stop that… that *thing*. Just watch, just wait.

Wait for the end to finally come.

♊

He doesn't usually kill aimlessly.

Not even for fun. Life is precious, it's a waste to kill indiscriminately. It has to be *useful*, help to complete *His* mission. Serve a purpose. Not long now to wait, not long at all, then it will all be *His*. The power. Power over life and death. Such *power*!

All that stands in His way are these people. The police officers, the man He's heading towards right now in the lobby of this building. Doesn't like to kill, especially when they're not twins – as none of these people are. *He* can tell, sense it.

It gives *Him* no satisfaction, but needs must. Explaining it wouldn't help, that would take too long and they wouldn't understand anyway. Most of them don't even think He's real.

This man ahead of *Him* probably doesn't think *He* is either.

They believe in the killer, the man who did all this. But they don't believe in what *He* is becoming.

What *He* will become. *He's* waited so, so long.

Watched and waited. Not much longer now.

Almost there.

♊

Almost there, the huge figure Bernie had just witnessed taking those officers apart was almost at the door.

He took out his phone. That was strange, it didn't seem to

be working. He could usually get a signal here, ring the authorities if there was trouble, not that he'd ever really had to. Once or twice when some thugs were loitering – they reminded him of himself at that age, to be fair. Thankfully they'd pissed off by the time the cops got there. Bernie had held up his phone, mouthing what he was doing, and it had been enough to scare them.

Wouldn't do any good with this guy. Bernie wasn't quite sure what *would* scare him. Maybe nothing. And as he looked up from tapping in 999 again, trying to summon backup, he realised the huge figure – no, call him what he was, The Gemini, the guy from years ago who'd been in the papers this week – was already inside the lobby.

He wasn't quite sure how. Couldn't see any damage to the doors, the glass hadn't been broken and no sirens were going off. No alarms. Must have broken the locks, though, somehow. Must have—

The figure was massive. Even bigger the closer he came. Like one of those American wrestlers or something, the ones that spend all that time in the gym pumping iron. Larger than that, perhaps. Solid with it. Bernie wasn't exactly small, but at the side of this bloke…

"Now, you stay back. I've called for the police and they're on their way."

The man shook his head, and there was something wrong with that head, wasn't there? Something wrong with his face. Faces, plural.

Because he had two of them.

"*Fuck,*" breathed Bernie. But he had a job to do, protecting these nice people in here. Had to step up. Noble by name… "I'm warning you, the police will be here any second."

"No they won't," the huge man said in a kind of stereo voice, the words coming out of two mouths at once.

"They—"

The man moved forwards, so fast Bernie didn't even see

him do it, same as with the doors. That didn't stop the security guard throwing a punch – might land lucky, you never knew. And he certainly didn't care about being sued this time. Bernie's fist connected with the man's torso, and it was like he was punching a breezeblock. Did more damage to his own knuckles than to his opponent; what he wouldn't give for a machine-gun right about now. Or even a knife or a smashed bottle.

The Gemini smirked.

Bernie pulled out his baton, struck his opponent. He'd seen guys almost as big as this go down when they were whacked with one of those. This bloke didn't go down. What happened was the baton broke in two.

"They're coming, I'm telling you!" screamed Bernie. An empty threat, he hadn't been able to get through. "The—"

"Police! Don't move! Stay where you are!" Nobody was more surprised than Bernie at that. As if by just willing them to appear, the cops had arrived. His backup had arrived. Comrades in arms.

When The Gemini turned, standing to one side, Bernie saw who this actually was. One lone police officer, a woman. She looked like she'd been crying.

"I said don't move, you motherfucker!" she roared at him. One woman, on her own.

But she had a gun drawn, had a bead on their enemy. He'd done it himself, usually in some desert in a faraway land. "Do it!" he shouted. "Shoot him now, before—"

He didn't need to worry, she was already pulling the trigger. Already firing, the slugs pumping out through the barrel accompanied by tiny flashes of fire. Didn't matter how fast this fellow was, he couldn't outrun a fucking bullet. Wasn't fucking Superm—

That wasn't his intention, though. The Gemini was just standing there and letting the bullets hit him. The hero Bernie had been thinking about was also known for letting them bounce off him, a bit like that punch had. Instead, what happened here was the bullets disappeared. They hit him all right, just didn't do anything.

Kevlar under all that black clothing, had to be! A bullet-proof vest. Or maybe his clothes were lined with it, like that assassin with the beard who seemed pretty indestructible himself. Which meant the cop needed to go for a headshot to down him.

Too late. The Gemini was on her, slapping the gun from her hand, slapping her back out through the doorway and into the street.

Bernie peered past him. The woman wasn't moving. So much for the backup, the comrades in arms. It was down to him now. This was what it had all been building towards, his purpose. He made for the pistol, getting down on his belly and sliding across the shiny floor.

The Gemini rounded, saw what he was doing. Began to race towards Bernie.

Almost there, almost... His fingers were touching the handle, he was scooping it up. The Gemini was above him, swooping in. And suddenly Bernie had the gun in his hand.

Had his finger on the trigger. The Gemini's head in his sights. He was Roy Scheider now and the real urban shark was tearing towards him. Coming at him. Smile you son of a—

Bernard pulled the trigger and fired.

CHAPTER TWENTY-SIX

"He's coming!"

The scream echoed throughout the apartment, probably louder than it should be because it was coming from two places at once. James and Jack, who'd been playing their game – so wrapped up in it, they'd hardly twitched when Deborah had departed. It was amazing how quickly they'd settled into life here, Rosy thought. But then kids were adaptable.

Just a couple of weeks ago, they'd had their ordinary life by the sea. Living with their mum, going to school, putting up with their big sister teasing them, she was willing to bet. Then, since her visit, since Rosy had talked Deborah into coming back to Norchester – and was there a part of her that was wishing now she hadn't? knowing that it had been the point when things had gone to hell in a handbasket? – they'd been shoved from pillar to post. First staying with their gran, then ferried here to the city. More adaptable than Rosy could ever be.

Or wanted to be?

She'd agreed to all this, 'course she had. Was happy to, she loved those twins to bits. The chance to spend some time with them was always welcome. Fun Aunty Rosy! Plus, as Glover had said, it might help save lives, give them a heads up about any potential Gemini activity – something Deborah had been keeping from them, it appeared, that connection. Keeping from her and Glover anyway; she'd since discovered that Clark knew, which had rankled. Crystallised just how far apart they were growing, her and Debs. How little trust there was these days.

And Kiz had been delighted, as Rosy knew she would be. A little too delighted, for Rosy's liking. Saw it as a chance for them to experience life as a 'family', with children around. Had gone out and bought all that stuff! There was no high ground about the new car now, not since Kiz'd gone so overboard (different league, Rosy, different league).

"It'll be good practice," she'd told Rosy.

Wasn't something she particularly wanted to practice, though, because she still wasn't sure she wanted kids of her own. Liked her life as it was. For Rosy, this was just about being in the right place at the right time to facilitate a solution. That scientist's brain of hers coming to the logical conclusion once again, the *only* conclusion. But it had definitely given Kiz ideas.

Had led to words between them. Not the ideal time or place to talk about such things, to row about them – especially with Deborah in the next room, and especially as she could tell those two had already been discussing it – but they were used to being on their own, talking about things whenever they wanted to (another advantage, to Rosy's mind). Used to not having to keep their voices down, either. She'd been accused of being selfish, but if she was that then she'd never have offered up their flat in the first place.

"Not about that," Kiz had said. "About the idea of having kids in general."

There was nothing to say to that, because it was probably true. They just wanted different things from life, moving forwards. Or were at different points in their life. One or the other. They'd let it be eventually, agreed to talk about it again when all this was over, when Deborah wasn't around all the time. But the spectre of it hung over them. The spectre of a possible break-up.

When really they should have been worrying about a very different kind of spectre altogether. The reason those kids were in the apartment in the first place.

"He's *coming!*" the twins cried in unison again, both children breathing quickly – so fast Rosy thought they were going to pass out. Was even looking around for a paper bag or something, because this had the definite makings of a panic attack.

"W-Where's Mum?" This was… she wanted to say Jack, but it was so hard to tell them apart.

Kiz was doing her best, instinctively going to them and rubbing their shoulders – one hand on each of the boys. Ever the mother in the making. "She's just popped out, remember?"

"Muuum!" bellowed… James, Rosy thought it was. Kiz looked over her shoulder at Rosy, and all she could muster was a shrug. Logic wasn't going to do a damned thing here.

"What's… what is it?"

"*He's* coming!" they both shrieked again. "The bad man!"

"This is it, isn't it?" Fleming had joined Rosy, watching the performance. "This is what we've been waiting for." Up till now she probably hadn't even believed in all this, a connection: the woman seemed far too pragmatic for that. But it was hard to ignore the evidence, hard to block out the fact those twins were seeing *something*. Fleming brought out her phone, tapping away on the screen. "Come on, come on!" Then to Kiz, as if she was some kind of translator, as if the kids weren't just a few feet away from the DS herself: "See if you can find out where he is, where he's going to be."

Kiz looked a bit confused, not quite sure what was being asked of her. But then neither Rosy nor Deborah had really gone into any detail about why the twins were here. She knew they needed to be somewhere safe, somewhere close to their mother. Trying to explain some kind of psychic link between them and the killer might have been a bridge too far.

"Ask them!" snapped Fleming, which just made the kids cry all the more. "Ask them what they can see!"

"Boys… Boys, what is it? What's the matter?" Kiz said in a soothing voice, still not fully grasping what was happening here.

"He's coming!" they just kept repeating. "He's coming, he's coming. He's *coming!*"

"Dammit, I can't get through to Glover," grumbled Fleming. "He's not answering."

"T-The man with the gun," said one of the twins, Jack or James, Rosy didn't have a clue by this point. "He tried to…"

"But…" said the other one, taking over. "But he couldn't…"

"Man with the…" Something clicked. They had to be talking about the officers downstairs, one of them anyway. Someone who'd tried to stop The Gemini. "Fleming," she said, clutching the woman's arm. "Fleming, I think we need to get out of here."

"What? Oh blast, the phone's dead. I can't get a—"

"Right now!" It was Rosy's turn to snap, but the woman was still looking at her blankly. "We need to leave, right now!" Wrong place, definitely at the wrong time!

"It's not the dead you have to worry about…" Or was it?

"Wh—" the DS began, but was cut off by a knocking sound. A loud thumping.

Coming from the front door.

"He's *here!*" the twins hollered now, spittle flying from their mouths. "The bad man… He's—"

And that's when things really went to hell.

♊

"Pull... pull over!"

Deborah was clutching her head, then clutching the dashboard of the car. They hadn't even made it across town, certainly hadn't made it to *The Imperial*. And they wouldn't now, because, "Something's wrong, Robbie. Something's..."

"Deborah? Debs?"

"Pull... over, I... *'He's coming!'* Oh my God, oh my God! *'He's coming!'*" She could hear parts of what she was saying, the parts that weren't really her speaking. That she was channelling from somewhere else.

"What? Who?"

Through clenched teeth she managed: "*'The... bad... bad man.'*"

"What?"

She was vaguely aware of Clark looking around for somewhere to do as she'd asked, to pull over. But the traffic was awful tonight, it was hard to find a gap. "What are you talking about, Debs?"

"*'He's coming,'*" she said again.

"The Gemini? He's coming for us?"

She tried to shake her head, but it hurt too much. This made those headaches she'd had after the fall seem mild by comparison. And her vision was swimming, blurred. Instead of the road, the lights of the cars – reds and yellows all blurring into one – she was seeing something else entirely. Channelling sights as well as sounds.

Seeing:

He bursts in – "He's here!" – smashing the door to pieces. Fleming approaches, having given up trying to reach Glover. Her gun's drawn, but it doesn't faze *Him*. The huge man... thing... with two faces. *He* doesn't even pause, simply disarms her, grabs her by the neck and lifts. There's a cracking sound as *He* flicks *His* wrist sideways, snapping that neck.

Fleming's eyes go wide, her tongue lolls out of her mouth like a panting Labrador.

Rosy looks around for something to use as a weapon and fails miserably. She resorts to throwing things at the giant: a cup, a book. That's not going to stop *Him*. She's an annoyance at best, something to be charged out of the way like a rugby player tackling a defender to score a try. Rosy goes flying over the sofa, rolls away out of sight.

Which leaves the prize. The reason *He's* here, what *He's* come here for. The boys, the people she's seeing this through. Seeing through their eyes, but as one. It's a weird sensation, and she wonders if it is anything like what Jack – her Jack, dead Jack – experienced when he witnessed the—

No, please God. No...

Not the boys. Not Jack, not James. *He* will only want one of them, she knows that. Somebody help them, *please*.

And somebody does. Someone tries, at least. Kiz stands between *Him* and the twins. She's shaking, terrified. Little wonder, because the mass of blackness in front of her is a good few feet taller than her – and she's tall. Tall for a woman.

Tall, strong. It still won't do any good. Won't help, or make any difference. But Deborah appreciates it all the same. Kiz stands in the way as if they're her kids, as loyal to the twins as if she'd given birth to them. Here is a woman who should *absolutely* have children, who would fight for them.

The Gemini regards her with *His* two faces, shifting faces. Changing all the time. Deborah's seen this before. It is *Him*!

It's *Him*, from the cells. It's the person who killed Jack. It's—

The person who is going to kill Kiz. Because even now she's trying to stop *Him* from getting any further, fuelled by the screams, the terrified cries of the children.

"Leave them alone!" Kiz yells, and for a second, just a second, it looks like The Gemini is going to do just that. Reacting, responding to something. A mother's tone, the one

Deborah would use herself if she were there. Oh, why isn't she there? Why did she leave them?

The moment is gone, and The Gemini clamps a hand down on the top of Kiz's head. *His* fingers squeeze, there's another cracking of bones. A skull this time, rather than neck. She lets out an almighty howl as *He* lifts her off the ground that way. Lifts and squeezes; squeezes and lifts.

Then there's silence. Kiz stops crying out, her body goes limp.

The Gemini drops her and she collapses into a puddle on the living room floor, like she's returning to primordial liquid.

He steps over the prone shape on the floor, steps closer to – Deborah – the boys. Leans in, reaches in.

The connection is severed.

The car has stopped, jerked to a stop as Clark tugged on the handbrake.

"Deborah, Debs?"

Deborah looked over at him, head still aching though nothing like it had been a few minutes ago. "I..." she managed.

"What? What is it?"

"The boys," she answered. "James, Jack. *He* has them."

"What?" Clark sounded like a stuck record.

"They're gone." Deborah began to cry, tears flowing down her face. "Oh Robbie. I've lost them."

Clark shook his head. "No."

"I've lost them." Her turn to repeat something, and she'd never believed anything more in her life. Even though she hadn't been there, not physically anyway. Even though she hadn't had any kind of confirmation or anything, she knew.

"I've lost them," she said one last time. "They're..."

"They're lost."

CHAPTER TWENTY-SEVEN

She felt lost. Was lost.

Did that mean *all* was lost? They had certainly lost the battle, the fight against The Gemini – a battle they hadn't even known was coming. Never, in all this time, not back then or now, had he done something like he did that night. So blatant, so openly. His work was usually conducted in the shadows, down back alleys, in car parks, creeping into people's homes.

Nothing like this. Nothing approaching this carnage.

The place had looked like a war zone by the time they returned, having fought more traffic – including a jam that pinned them in for a good twenty minutes. Deborah hadn't been at all surprised to see the ambulances, the police cars. To hear the helicopters overhead still searching for any trace of the person who'd done this.

They wouldn't find him, not until he wanted to be found. But it did prove this much, if he didn't care about being seen – about being caught – then the 'game' was almost over. There wasn't much time left. The difference between rising and risen.

Between risen and ascending, whatever that meant.

"Ten fatalities on the scene," Glover had told them when

they found him, "including some residents as he made his way through the building, and members of the protection detail outside. The security man, Noble, he was torn limb from limb. Fleming's—"

"Dead," Deborah had mumbled.

Glover nodded. "Yes, regrettably. Broken neck. Twenty more injured, some severely."

"Rosy," she'd ventured. "Kiz?"

"From what I've been told, Miss Lim got away lightly – some cuts and bruising, possible broken collarbone. Her partner..." Glover shook his head, which she took to mean there was bad news on that front, but then he suddenly added: "She's in surgery right now, but it doesn't look good."

"Bloody hell," was all Clark could say, running a hand through his hair.

"She protected the boys," said Deborah.

Glover gave another nod, took that as a guess. "Yes, I suspect she did. I'm sorry, Miss Harrison. We didn't find any trace of your sons."

She felt like hitting him then. Felt like punching him in that stupid face of his, asking where the hell had he been? Why he had suggested that they bring Jack and James here – though she knew the answer to that one – and what he was going to do about it now they were missing. But she knew the answer to that as well: fuck all. What *could* be done?

They were gone. They were lost.

Which meant she was lost too.

The next few hours passed by in a blur, but Clark had stayed by her side throughout all of it. She'd made him promise again not to say anything about what had happened in the car, at least until she figured out what was going on. But she hadn't even told *him* that she'd 'seen' the incident in the apartment, just that she'd had a feeling something was wrong; that the boys had been taken. Call it a mother's intuition, but she knew the truth. It had been much more than that, of course, like they'd been able to *show* her what was happening.

First their ability to tap into what The Gemini was doing, whether they realised that was what they were doing or not. Now this? Deborah had no idea what it meant, or how it could be used – not now, anyway.

Instead, she'd demanded to see the Geminite priest again. "You're kidding, the last time we did that you almost killed him," Glover told her.

"I just might this time, unless he tells me where I can find my kids."

"Not helping your case, Miss Harrison. But I do sympathise." Oh, well, that was all right then – as long as Glover *sympathised*. "I've been trying to get through to him for days, though. He just won't play ball."

"He might with me," she said. "It's worth a shot, right? One last try? You owe me that much."

"Guv," Clark had pleaded on her behalf.

Glover let out a strangled breath, said he'd see what he could arrange. "I'm pretty much done here anyway, they'll definitely take me off the case now." No controlling any narrative at that point.

What he'd been able to organise, off the record, was a trip down to the cells to see the man. To talk to him through the grille in the door. "What has he done with them?" she came right out and asked. "Tell me, what's he done with my children?"

The Geminite priest sat on his bunk in the small room, hands on his knees, head down. Didn't even acknowledge her presence.

"Tell me you piece of shit, or—" Glover had placed a hand on her shoulder and she'd immediately shrugged it off.

"Easy Debs," Clark had whispered.

"Tell me what you know, *please*." Deborah was crying again, didn't know what else to do.

The man had turned in her direction, looked right in her eyes. Then he stood, bolt upright; it made them all start. He walked towards the square hole in the door, peering through it. He grinned. Laughed. "Your children are already dead," he informed her in a chilling tone.

Deborah snarled, and tried to stick her arm through, to grab him by the collar, but both of the men she was with pulled her back. Had to drag her back down the corridor and out of the cells. "That went well," Glover said when they got outside. "Clark, would you be good enough to escort Miss Harrison back to her hotel, please."

"Yes, guv."

It was what he'd been doing while her kids were being threatened, attacked. She should have been there, should have stayed. Maybe then The Gemini wouldn't have come at all, if he'd been waiting for her to leave.

Then again, perhaps he'd just have crushed her skull like he did with Kiz. "They're not... They're not dead, you know," she said to Clark as he drove her once again across town.

"I know," he told her. "I know they're not, Debs." But there was a flutter in his voice, a waver that said he wasn't really sure he believed that.

Did *she* believe it? She wanted to. Wanted to feel them, as she had when they were taken. But that might just be desperation, because it would break her if what the priest had said was true.

Clark had pulled up outside *The Imperial*, peering up and down the street – commenting that at least the press hadn't got wind of where she was yet. That was likely to change in the days ahead, though. "Do you want me to come in with you?" he asked.

She hesitated, frowned. Then answered: "No, no. I've taken up enough of your time already, Robbie."

"It was my—' He stopped shy of saying pleasure,

switching at the last moment to, "I was glad to help, Debs. Honestly."

Then she'd given him a peck on the cheek again, like the first time they'd met recently. She had no idea what made her do it, another need probably – not to be alone – but her lips were sliding sideways, connecting with his suddenly. She hadn't realised quite how much she'd come to rely on Clark, and for a second he responded. He'd felt it too, that spark between them. But this was wrong, all wrong. So many kinds of wrong. He had a girlfriend for one thing. Helen. Yet, she did want him right at that moment. Needed not to feel all the hurt, the pain. Clark could take all that away.

But he was the one who broke it off, probably quite rightly. Before things went too far. "Debs, I… It's not that I don't want to, it's just…"

She smiled at him sadly. "I know. I know. Don't take any notice of me. I'm all over the place, Robbie."

"Of course you are." That was just one of the reasons, but what he said next didn't make her want him any less. "You'll see them again, I promise." Like her, this man didn't make promises he couldn't keep.

See them, more than likely. But alive or…? That was the question.

"Your children are already dead!"

Deborah took Clark's hands in hers, pulled them to her lips and kissed the knuckles. "Thanks, Robbie. I mean that. Thanks for everything."

"Try and get some rest," he told her. She waved him off, turned, and made her way up the steps. Deborah almost collapsed against one of the pillars there, tears coming again. But she wiped them away with the sleeve of her coat, stood upright and managed to somehow negotiate her way through the revolving doors.

She was stumbling towards the lifts when she heard someone calling out her name. "Miss Harrison. Miss

Harrison!" As with Clark, her first thought was the press, in which case she might just batter someone. But it was Ralph, beckoning her over now. She really wasn't in the mood for inane chatter tonight, but then she saw someone emerge from the back office. Someone she recognised.

"Albert?"

He'd aged, of course he'd aged – it had been so long since she'd last seen him. Since he'd been telling her about what had happened the night he and Jack had saved that vicar, making an official statement once she'd recovered from her own wounds. Had she ever really recovered? Deborah was beginning to wonder.

But all things considered, and given he'd been as old as God when she first met him in that lift she'd been heading for, he looked pretty good. Walked with a stick now, but that was all.

"Been popping in the last few days, haven't you," Ralph clarified. "Hoping to see you."

The old man skirted the desk and ambled towards her, clearly having trouble. "Hello Deborah," he said. He had such a kindly face, had gone to so much effort to see her again she didn't want to just dismiss him.

She motioned for them to sit on the chairs nearby, the ones she'd seen Patricia Bailey on just the other morning. "When I saw the reports in the paper, I knew you'd be back. And I knew where I could find you."

"Albert... I..." She was fighting back the tears again.

"Whatever's happened?" he asked, and she told him. Told him about what had happened with her boys. With Jack's boys. Then he hugged her, though it took some effort on his part while they were still seated. "Oh my, I'm so sorry. I really hope..." Albert shook his head. "You stopped all this once, with Jack's help. You can do it again. Evil never triumphs, not really."

"I think it did tonight," she told him.

Albert moaned softly. "If only Jack were here," he said. "He was such a lovely man. I didn't know him that long, but he always took the time to talk to me. And when he asked me to drive him that night… Oh, I know I was scared. I was even scared that I might be in trouble with the police. Do you remember?" She did, all too well. "But he, well, he made me feel useful."

He'd done that for a few people, Marvin Hole for one. Her for another.

"I miss him," Albert told her.

"Me too."

"If he were here," the old man continued, "he'd know what to do."

And then, suddenly, Deborah knew as well – as if Albert had been sent to her. Maybe he had been. Finally, she knew what needed to be done.

Knew exactly what to do.

CHAPTER TWENTY-EIGHT

It hadn't been easy to do.

Not at all. And it had taken faith. A summoning of all her belief, ridding herself of all the doubt clouding her mind. Because there was so much at stake. Christ, her children were at stake! It would take peace and quiet, so she'd switched off her phone – her mum had been trying to reach her again, but Deborah didn't know what she'd say to her right now, and she certainly didn't want to deal with Izzy's nonsense. Not tonight.

It would take peace and quiet and a particular room. Her room at *The Imperial*; a very special room. She'd turned off the light and left the curtains drawn, with a view of the stars, sat back on the bed, cross-legged, and she'd called out to him.

"Jack. Jack, I don't know if you can hear me – but I need you. God, I need you *so much*. And I need you to be real, not a figment of my imagination or a fantasy – but real. You've appeared before, hell I wouldn't even be here if it weren't for you. I wasn't even going to come." Deborah let out a sigh. This was no time for pointing the finger, for blame. It wouldn't do any good – and Jack must have had his reasons.

"Jack, *please*. Are you there?" This was like some kind of stupid, half-arsed séance. Knock once for yes, twice for—

"*He* has our kids. Your sons. I need you to hear me. I need you to tell me what to do next."

Nothing. Not even a knock.

She tried again. And again. She tried for hours. Sat there waiting, but not patiently. She'd tried begging, tried being sorry, getting angry. Had even apologised about Clark in case that was the problem. In case Jack might be upset about the kiss. She'd been lost, that was all. Wanted not to feel the way she was feeling, like she'd let them down. James and Jack.

She'd cried. She'd wiped away the tears, before crying again. She'd grown exhausted, so tired she could hardly keep her head upright, her eyes open.

Then, just when she thought nothing would happen, he was there. Sitting on the edge of the bed again, like he had done the night of the Whittaker attack – bathed in silver light from the stars. "Jack," she said in a low voice, and he turned. "Jack, please help me."

He opened his mouth, frowning. Looked like he was in pain. The cords in his neck were straining, he was pointing with a finger to his mouth. This ghost was trying to speak.

Trying to tell her something.

It was taking all of his concentration, all the effort he could muster. But he did finally get something out, wheezing it into the air. It was a name: "G-Glover…"

"Glover? What about him?"

Practically a whisper: "G-Glover is… is the… key…"

"What? It's Glover?"

Jack gave a half-nod.

"Where, Jack? Where are the kids? Where are our sons?"

He was trying again to speak, sounding like someone who'd had a tracheostomy. "Return… Back… go back…"

"Back? Back where?" To Armitage Bay? It was true that's

where she thought she'd seen someone outside their house, where Izzy had thought she'd been followed, but—

"Back... back to the start... To the beginning..."

It still wasn't making any sense. For The Gemini, for Maxwell Craine, this had all begun in a village called Cambley, just outside Brenton. That's where he'd been brought up, where he'd taken his first life. Was Jack saying she needed to go there, had The Gemini returned home? "Jack, I don't understand." She crawled forwards on the bed, as much to be near him as anything. But he was fading, even she could see that. He'd helped her as much as he could, and it'd taken everything he had.

"Jack, what are you saying? Go back where, to Cambley?"

Knock.

"Jack?" He was fading fast. Vanishing, not able to hold his form.

Knock.

"Jack, I love you!"

Knock!

"Housekeeping!" a woman's voice said, and Deborah snapped to on the bed. It was light, and the cleaner was already inside the room – she'd forgotten to put a 'do not disturb' on the door, the first rule of a séance, surely. "Oh, I'm sorry. I did knock, love." Twice for no, three for – what? Not Jack, it hadn't been Jack.

Deborah tried to focus on the name-badge the woman was wearing: 'Miriam', she thought it said. "I..."

"Are you all right?"

Probably not. Deborah couldn't remember the last time she had been, certainly not in the last couple of weeks. "I... please, could you come back..."

Go back. Return. Just a stupid dream, wasn't it. Had she been awake, asleep? One thing was for sure, it was daylight now, sort of – overcast – the next day definitely. And Deborah still didn't know what to do.

"Of course," said the woman, still watching her intently. "No worries at all."

"T-Thanks."

Miriam dragged her trolley back out, one of the wheels squeaking and setting Deborah's teeth on edge. She had no idea what time it was, her head was still spinning. It felt like all this was coming to an end, but she was none the wiser about anything. Apart from maybe Glover.

Glover being the key.

The Gemini rising again, coming back. Back through his sons... She thought about Luke Simpson, how he'd looked. He'd looked like Maxwell Craine, like... her former boss. But Glover. He looked nothing like either of them, did he? Had he altered his appearance somehow, plastic surgery?

"I'm pretty much done here anyway."

Then again, The Gemini was a person of many faces. Could wear two. Could wear the face of a victim if he chose to, someone who'd been a twin and he'd—

No, no. That was too outlandish, even for her. Just tapping into her mistrust of the inspector, but she was beginning to think maybe a DNA test might not go amiss. Beginning to think about all that when she felt the twinge again, the headache she'd experienced in the car with Clark yesterday.

The vision James and Jack had shared with her. What they'd been seeing then, The Gemini coming for them. What they... they were seeing now?

The flash hit her so fast and so hard, she almost cried out, nearly called for the cleaning woman to come back again. But she didn't, Deborah bit it back – tried to concentrate on what she was looking at. What she was being *shown*.

A place. Dark. Lit by candles. She was seeing all the jars, the ones with body parts in them, preserved. Bones, polished. A collection, just like last time. Not the same, because that had been damaged, taken away or burned. No, this had been built up again, starting from scratch. But with the same intention.

Was she seeing it from *His* point of view, though? The Gemini. Were her kids showing her this because they were already—

No, again. Because there *He* was, busying himself. Getting things ready for the final push. One of her sons would be the last sacrifice to complete this collection, the final twin – she realised that. Which meant Deborah had to find them in time to prevent that from happening.

Which meant she needed to know where they—

It was then that she saw it, the clue telling her where she should go.

Back to the beginning. Jack – whether he'd truly been here or not – had been right. It made perfect sense now.

She had to go back to where this had all started.

Where it would finally end.

CHAPTER TWENTY-NINE

It was the place Vinny Hole had been looking for.

The sacred place, where those sacrifices had occurred so long ago – even before Norchester had been created. Been named. The slaughter that had happened to bring this all about, to create the conditions to bring this *day* about. To make sure that if you conceived on this land, you stood more chance of giving birth to twins. Not a coincidence, but by design. A method of bringing about the existence of The Gemini – and his brother.

Separated at birth, brought up apart, only coming back together when it was time for the endgame to begin. Pretty obvious when you thought about it, or it had been once Deborah realised where her sons were.

And she had to go alone, she knew that, too. Couldn't risk dragging Clark into this, she'd done that once before with him and his friend, Peel. She'd had to live with the guilt of that man's death on her conscience for so long, she wasn't going to live with Clark's blood on her hands, as well. That's if she lived at all.

When she got there, when she confronted him – The Gemini – she had no idea what she'd do. How she'd defeat him. Get close enough to grab that fork, use it the way Jack had done? Didn't matter if she was killed in the process, as long as her kids were safe.

There was no way she was reporting this to the police, either, or the bloody SCI! If what she suspected about Glover was true, then who knew how far the corruption had spread? Not to mention the fact he'd pulled this off right under their noses, how he'd hidden it all in plain sight.

No, this was something she had to do on her own. It was her business, always had been. It had taken almost a decade for it to come around again, but this would conclude today.

It had to.

She knew the best way to get into the place, as well. Not out the front, because that actually was where some of the press were camped out. A few vans here and there scattered about, but if they caught a glimpse of former Detective Sergeant Deborah Harrison, caused a ruckus, then everything really would be lost.

So she carefully snuck around the back, down the alley to where the fenced-off car park had once been. Now it was just a cracked concrete square, with weeds poking up through the holes in the ground. When she got there, she looked up at the building with its boarded windows, signs plastered all over it; some yellow, some red, all with exclamation marks stating 'KEEP OUT' or 'UNSAFE BUILDING'. It was sad to see. The new had its place in the world, but so did the old. So did history – and this land was steeped in it, whether anyone realised or not.

Deborah thought back to those illustrations in Vinny's book, how the priests had conducted their rituals by murdering people – right here. The population of this city might think they'd moved on, left all of that behind, but nothing had really changed, had it.

She found the back door, one that had needed a card to access it before but now was just a piece of wood. A piece of wood that had already been pulled away from the frame, she found. If you pulled on it enough, it left a gap to squeeze through, so she did.

It was dark inside, and she reached for her phone… then realised she'd left it behind, switched off in her hotel room. Should have brought a torch, but she knew the layout like the back of her hand anyway. The further up she got, the more light there would be. She'd seen it. The candles, the oil lamps.

Seen it along with the clue as to where her boys were being held. What was left of the desks in the bullpen, the papers and posters still pinned to walls. A cup that she'd always used during her time here, chipped and cracked now, dirty but with the logo 'coppers like it blue' on the side still clearly visible.

Obvious when you thought about it, because The Gemini had been drawn to this place before. Back then it had been underground, in the cells under Yardley Street nick, a dungeon before it had been a police station. As below, so above. A reversal of the norm. Because this time he'd chosen the abandoned building itself to perform this final act.

Oh, it had been searched – from top to bottom, so Glover had said. But afterwards, she was willing to bet nobody had really bothered. Either that or they'd been ordered to steer clear. The perfect opportunity to move that grotesque 'collection' of his in here, probably under cover of darkness one night.

Up she went, not as far as you needed to go in the new station, and certainly not by lift – because she wouldn't trust those now, wasn't even sure she trusted the stairs – but far enough. High enough you wouldn't be disturbed by anyone, even if they did choose to ignore the warning signs and venture in.

Deborah reached the floor she was looking for, poking her head out and peering down the corridor. She still had the element of surprise here, thanks to her sons. If she played this right, she could grab them and get out, alert the press, the authorities. Get the bloody army in if need be!

Slowly she made her way along that corridor, wincing every time the floor creaked. Wondering if it would give way before she even reached her destination; they wouldn't have put those signs up outside for nothing. Already she could see the flickering of those flames, though. The only light inside, because wood was covering every smashed window.

Deborah reached the doorway, risked a quick glance inside to confirm where the kids might be: towards the back of the room. She froze when she saw them, two small forms curled up on the ground. They looked—

"Your children are already dead."

No, no, they couldn't be. They were the ones who'd brought her here – unless something had happened in the time it took to get here? She would have felt that too, surely? Seen it, even?

Her instinct was to rush across to them, gather them up in her arms and just run. But not without trying to find out where The Gemini was first. That meant leaning in further, craning her head – and catching sight of the collection. As horrendous as the last one, memories of that nightmare flashing back to her more clearly now: limbs; organs; bones. So many, each representing a twin that had been killed, culminating in the parts he'd taken from Felicity, Geoffrey, Vinny...

Of the person she was looking for, though, there was no sign. She might actually get away with this, snatching her kids – try not to think about the fact they're not moving – and getting the fuck out of there.

Deborah made her move, dashing over to where they lay. She hadn't been planning on spending too much time bending, checking on them, but when she got there she couldn't help it. She was their mother.

They were still breathing, their chests going up and down.

She let out a breath of her own, then immediately sucked it back in. The shock of hearing someone speak behind her.

"They're sleeping. Wore themselves out… screaming. Or maybe it was the drugs I gave them a little while ago." She whirled, standing at the same time; responding to that strange, echoing voice. "A mild sedative, nothing more."

There he was, standing right there. Where he'd come from, she had no idea; how could you hide anywhere when you were that big? Behind the door? No, she thought she'd checked that: the first place you were taught to look when clearing a room. Then again, she had been in such a hurry to get to the kids, to make sure they—

"Your children are already dead."

Wrong, you fucker! But they would be soon if she didn't do something about it. Yet it was also like he'd known, had been waiting for her to enter. Had he heard her after all and got out of sight? So much for the element of surprise.

"I'm… I'm not scared of you," she replied, her pitch and the fact she was shaking saying otherwise.

"Oh?" he said, moving more out of the shadows – this creature *of* the shadows with his two faces, both male, neither of them familiar to her. "You should be."

"N-Not my first rodeo."

"I suppose not." He clasped his hands behind his back as he walked, not in any hurry himself, it seemed. "A little different this time, however, no?"

She shrugged. "All I see is another psycho, pretending to be a god."

He laughed. "Pretending? Soon I *will* be a god, woman. Just one more to go. You can help me decide if you like."

"Decide?"

"Which one of your children to gut."

A chill ran down her spine, but he'd already turned away – was wandering over towards that hideous jumble of jars; of flesh, blood and bone. The Gemini stooped to pick one particular container up, turning it this way and that so it glinted in the light from a nearby candle.

It was an eye.

"I need a matching pair, you *see*." He chuckled at his own bad joke, looking over at Deborah with two sets of eyes himself. One half of his 'face' was female now, and this one she did recognise: it was Felicity Bailey. "We learnt, though. This time kill the other twin when you take the first eye. Wait and take the second one last." He nodded over towards the boys behind her. "No chance of anyone spying then."

"Except they did!" she barked at him. "Someone did see what you were doing, you bastard. My kids. Jack's kids."

Another laugh. "They saw only what I wanted them to see, woman. What I *allowed* them to see, and from a distance, off to one side – my interpretation. In a way they could understand, like watching a TV show. Like cartoons! The final phase." The last few killings, when it was too late to do anything about it. Not even her coming to Norchester had made a difference. Or had that been the point? The intention all along? Getting her here, the kids here?

"They weren't the only ones who saw," she told him. "I saw too, through them."

"And I allowed that to happen as well, *when* I wanted it to."

Her visions, the one of the apartment, of this place? The Gemini had let her see what Jack and James were seeing, but only on his terms. No wonder he'd known she was on her way, he'd set it up.

"What's that phrase, controlling the narrative?"

That phrase? Glover's phrase about the press... His bad jokes...

"I'd have thought someone like you would be able to understand that, a writer?" The Gemini cocked his head. "You think you know me, I can tell. You don't know me."

"I know enough," she told him. "Inspector. You've been

controlling everything from the start, haven't you?" The narrative, events. Just like those priests in the past, and all the other Geminites. His little helpers. Steering everything to this day, this moment. The Gemini reborn in his own son. "Too bad about your brother Luke, though. No head for heights."

"My brother—" A belly laugh, this time. "You show your ignorance, woman." She really wished he'd stop calling her that. Of all the things to be pissed off about in this scenario, it was rapidly reaching the top of the list.

"Yeah?"

He nodded, placing the eye down and stepping closer. "I know something you don't know," The Gemini chanted. "A secret. Something not even your little friend Vinny knew. Isn't that right, Vinny?" And as he called him, The Gemini's face changed again, Vinny Hole's countenance appearing on the left-hand side: trapped, helpless. Being worn as a Halloween mask.

"No," Deborah whispered. She had to free him. Had to free them all somehow, just like Jack had done before. All those prisoners inside this monster, the spirits empowering him.

"You see, my brother is still alive. You know him. You'll meet him again soon enough."

Deborah paused, her brow furrowing. "What the fuck are you talking about?"

"Not the man you call Maxwell Craine. Not his twin sons – they're both dead. Well, now they are anyway. You made sure of that, we saw to the other one a long time ago. He's in here with me, safe and sound. My cousin."

"Wha—"

"Mason. We're *his* sons, you see.

"Inspector Roy Mason's sons."

CHAPTER THIRTY

Deborah wasn't sure what had thrown her the most.

The fact that this wasn't the child of The Gemini, the son becoming his father, but instead… Or was it the mention of that man's name?

"Mason." He said it again, as if knowing it caused her pain; but then he would. "Of course, the family resemblance isn't quite there. Not like it was with Luke or his brother. But sometimes it goes that way, right? We take more after our mother. Look more like her."

"Your… Holy shit."

"It's a sad tale. I won't bore you with it."

"No," she said, "I want to know. I want to know everything."

All four of this Gemini's eyebrows shot up. "It won't change anything, stalling for time won't alter a thing."

"I genuinely want to know," said Deborah. It wasn't a lie. She wanted to know what the hell was going on, how they could have got it so, so wrong.

"A drunken fumble, that's all. Mason and an older woman he picked up and screwed, back when he was only a DC. One night, that's all it took. But then I don't have to tell you about that, do I?"

"No." It was such a surreal situation, this monstrosity in black with its two faces – so much like the first Gemini, yet not – chatting away to her like he was telling a therapist his problems.

"I think on some level our mother even loved him, but all Roy wanted was the sex. To scratch an itch. Couldn't stand to even look at her afterwards, said if she kept following him around he'd fit her up for something. Make sure she never saw the light of day again. Yeah, he was a prince, our father."

She thought about saying something like 'takes one to know one' or 'the apple didn't fall far from the tree', but quite apart from the fact he could put her through a wall she really did want to know where all this was going.

"Then she fell pregnant. Didn't tell him because she was frightened of what he'd do, so she went through it all alone. Didn't even have any family to help her out, had never really had much money – so no fancy doctors or hospitals for her." He sighed, the first sign of real emotion he'd shown since she got here, and she almost – almost – felt sorry for him. Couldn't help comparing it to her situation, except she'd had her mum on the scene in both instances. "She had a terrible time, almost died having us. Dangerous you see, in your forties. As it was it left her with serious health issues, ones that would get her in the end.

"But not before she told us the truth. Told us who our father was."

"And so you went out and found him? Discovered what he was doing with his own brother, what that man could do?"

He nodded. "But I always knew I was different, destined for something beyond all this. Special, like Mother always said. That I could... sense them. Twins. I only had to be near to one to know. That apparently did run in the family. Dear old Uncle..."

"So what, when we killed him, you wanted revenge?"

"Revenge? Hardly! We'd already started our own quest by then, my brother had joined the police force to help facilitate things. Grease the wheels. Although I hadn't quite perfected— The fork makes it much easier, definitely. It was the missing piece of the puzzle." He gestured with his hand like he was a character doing a monologue in a Shakespeare play. "What you did actually helped, you and that interfering idiot of a boyfriend. We'd thought about doing it ourselves, eliminating Uncle. But weren't anywhere near strong enough; he had a head start on us, you see. But you… you cleared the way for us to take over, finish the job properly. Take the crown."

"All these years, you've been doing the same thing? Going around and killing twins?"

"Well, yes." He said it like it was a normal thing to do, but then to him it probably was. "For a purpose. When this is all over, I'll bring order to the world. Nobody will be able to stop me."

"And we'll all be your slaves? Serve you, just like those—" Deborah pointed to his chest, his face. "Like the people you murdered serve you now, whether they want to or not."

"There will be peace. Isn't it all that matters?"

"Peace always comes at a price," she said.

"You don't understand. Perhaps you will listen to my brother when he gets here."

"Is he going to help me decide which of my kids to let you stab?"

The Gemini laughed. "Perhaps he will. I'm not sure what's keeping him, though." He cocked an ear. "Ah, talk of the devil. Here he comes now."

Deborah looked over towards the door, could hear the footfalls. Then she saw him, the face she'd been expecting. Twin not to Luke Simpson as she'd thought, which totally explained why he hadn't looked like him, but to this brute in front of her. Hands down like father like son. Glover.

Fucking *Detective Inspector* Mike Glover.

CHAPTER THIRTY-ONE

She knew it!

Had known it from the start, never trusted this man standing in front of her. Even Jack had said it, "Glover is the key". He was the key, all right. Had covered up The Gemini's shit for... how long, more than eight years? Since before they'd killed his uncle.

"Deborah, I—"

She held up a hand. "Save it."

Fucker. Absolute fucker! He was the reason she was here, her kids were here, on the pretence of saving lives when he was responsible for so many deaths! The reason Rosy was in hospital, Kiz – shit, how was Kiz? she hadn't even asked – had needed surgery. She'd been right not to believe a word that came out of his mouth, the lying, conniving—

"You?" This was The Gemini talking, asking, sounding shocked, surprised even. "What are *you* doing here?"

"I found him outside, sniffing around." Another figure joined them all, this one armed.

Deborah's first thought was: *We're saved!* But the more she did think about it, the more she couldn't understand why the second man was talking to The Gemini as if he knew him. "Press almost spotted the twat."

"That would have been… premature," uttered The Gemini. "And disappointing. For them. Soon they'll have something *to* report. Something to spread around the world. Something glorious."

Deborah was barely listening, she was still fixated on the man behind Glover, now pushing him into the room. "Robbie?"

"Debs," he answered. "How're you doing?"

"I'm… What's going on? Why're you…" She looked from him over to the huge figure in black. Then at Glover. "But you're…" The inspector shook his head.

"I'm sorry, Debs," said Clark. "Truly I am."

"*You don't understand. Perhaps you will listen to my brother when he gets here.*"

"No… Robbie…" Deborah's mouth fell open. It couldn't be, it couldn't have happened – not again. This man had made her care for him, when all along he was… "But you were there, with me, when… Peel, your friend Peel!"

Clark's eyes glistened. "I tried to save him, Debs. You saw me! I loved that guy, and our uncle just…" He shook his head sadly.

"So your father was—"

"Regrettably, yes. The worthless turd."

Her mind was flashing back now again, not just remembering the collection in those underground cells – the cells that were below them right now – but what had happened after those sparks of light, after those spirits escaped and attacked The Gemini. How she'd realised his face was the same as her superior's; as, yes, Mason's. How Clark had attacked the man, distracted him long enough for her to bring up that knife and—

The fury on his face, Clark's face! Hadn't just been because Peel was dead, he was taking something else out on that guy.

Revenge for how he'd treated their mother, how he'd threatened her. For how she'd had to go through labour alone, then eventually died as a result of that.

"I thought maybe, when I joined the force, came to work here, that I might see something in him. Something our mother once loved. But all I saw was weakness, selfishness. Deceit. Look at the way he treated you, what he did to you."

"What *he* did to me?"

Like father like—

"I'm glad you killed him. I just wish it had been me who'd got to do it." Clark's face was scrunching up like he had a sour taste in his mouth.

"You had such a huge impact on my life and my career. I don't think you quite realise…"

Another thought occurred to her now. "Like you killed Luke Simpson, you mean?"

Clark shook his head more forcefully. "An accident. He slipped, that's the truth."

"But you would have killed him anyway, right?"

"What for? He didn't know anything about all this. Just a druggie criminal, a distant echo of his brother. We wouldn't even have been there if it wasn't for you, for your friend Vinny." And there was something in that statement, a jealousy that still betrayed his feelings. But how could he still care about her? After everything, after all this.

"I trusted you," she said.

"I know. It wasn't misplaced, though."

"Not… Jesus Robbie, that guy's a mass murderer!" Deborah swung an accusatory finger back at The Gemini.

"I haven't killed anyone," Clark stated.

"You *helped* him!"

"It was all necessary, for the cause."

"I can keep a secret."

"Your colleagues at Rosy's place, that was necessary was it? Kiz? My kids? Robbie, he's talking about killing Jack or

James, about making me choose. How can you stand there and—"

"They won't really be dead," he cut in. "They'll be part of something bigger than themselves, Debs – can't you see? None of those people… Those twins," he changed it to, "are really gone. They're working towards the greater good. They—"

"They're being *used*. They're being held against their will, just like the first time! Christ, they shouldn't even have been killed – they had no choice in that, either!"

"None of this will matter in the end," he told her.

"All of it matters, Robbie! It *has* to!"

"Not if you know what we know, about what comes afterwards."

"Yeah, yeah. I've seen the books, the prophecies. World peace, with him running everything – that sound about right? Thinks he's fucking Zeus or something!"

"Enough!" bellowed The Gemini, causing them all to flinch. Then, more quietly, "Enough. This is pointless. It will happen, nothing can prevent my ascension now."

"We'll see," whispered Deborah.

"You didn't answer my question," said the giant next. Deborah hadn't realised he'd asked one, but she saw he was directing it at Glover. "What are you doing here?"

Glover didn't reply.

"Probably following her. He's done it before," said Clark, and again there was a whiff of jealousy about his words.

"My, aren't we popular," said The Gemini. "I think even my brother's taken a shine to you."

Clark was going red in the cheeks.

"He can fuck right off," spat Deborah.

"Not what you were saying, or doing in the car, Debs." Now he seemed hurt more than anything. "If I remember rightly, I had to put a stop to that or—"

"That was just… I was confused. Upset. *He'd* just taken my kids!"

"Bullshit," said Clark. "It had nothing to do with all that, and you know it. I'm the one who's been trying to hold it back, trying not to make things worse. It's why I made up Helen, so that things wouldn't get more complicated than they needed to be."

"Ha! Now we're getting to it, an imaginary girlfriend! Bloody brilliant!"

"So things wouldn't go too far. Because you—"

"Can you even hear yourself? Okay, yeah, I admit I was flattered. I'd be lying if I said I hadn't considered it – back when I thought you were a good guy."

"I *am* a good guy!" Clark argued.

"But I felt so bad about that," she continued, ignoring him. "Taking advantage of your crush."

"My—"

"Just like our father, he wanted you too – didn't he?" The Gemini butted in.

"Don't," said Deborah.

"But in our case it would have been a little too… Do you want to tell her or shall I?" the man with two faces asked Clark.

"What?" Deborah's shoulders slumped. "What now?"

"Another secret," hissed The Gemini. "Another twist in the tale, writer lady."

Clark rubbed his forehead furiously. "Our mother."

"What about her?" asked Deborah. She'd already heard the full story, tragic as it was – hadn't she?

"We only found out later, when she'd passed and we were going through her things. Found her birth certificate, found out about her real family, the one that hadn't wanted her. That had shunned her, just like our dad did."

Deborah was starting to get a really bad feeling about this.

"Get ready for that final shocking reveal!" shouted The Gemini, arms outstretched.

"You see," said Clark, struggling to get the words out. "Our mother and Jack Foley's mother were sisters."

"Twin sisters," The Gemini completed for him.

CHAPTER THIRTY-TWO

No, it couldn't be.

Yet it made perfect sense. Like everything else: orchestrated, arranged. Since those first rituals began, there was always going to be a backup plan – people who wait centuries were never going to leave things to chance. The Geminites, it was all down to them, pulling the strings. Deborah looked from Clark to his brother. They were the substitutes, always had been. But did they know that?

Were they aware that they were the 'also rans'? It certainly didn't seem like they knew. But before she could say anything, something else struck her. "That makes James and Jack…"

"Our cousins," said Clark. "First cousins once removed actually."

"And why things might be a bit… messy between you and my brother," The Gemini said. He was talking like that was still an option; it made Deborah feel sick. But not as sick as the next thought made her.

"That's why it has to be one of them, isn't it? James or Jack. The final sacrifice." Vinny had said it himself: *Sometimes they even killed members of their own family, the ultimate offering.*

"I'm afraid so," Clark confirmed. "But like I said, they won't really be—"

"Go fuck yourself, Robbie," she snapped. It was the real reason why they were here, why she'd been coaxed back to Norchester. Why the twins were here.

"All one big happy fucking family!" The Gemini announced.

But why… why would Jack send her back here? Come to her with that message back in Armitage Bay? Had she misinterpreted it? Had it been a warning? No, it had been pretty clear… He wouldn't have put them in harm's way unless it was necessary, would have known their people were everywhere as the Geminite priest had said. Must have thought there was a way of stopping it, for Deborah to stop it.

There was a moaning from behind her, and Deborah turned to see her boys rousing. Waking up slowly, the drugs still in their system but the noise in here disturbing their slumber.

A way for her to stop it, for her boys to stop it.

And 'Glover is the key'.

She looked over at the inspector, who'd been watching this whole thing play out with fascination. "Please tell me the cavalry is on its way, that you didn't come here alone."

He stared at her apologetically. "It's as I feared, I'm off the case. It's just me, Miss Harrison. I did come armed, but, well…" Glover gave a small laugh. "I'm not even a twin."

"We can't all be special," said The Gemini.

"No," Deborah replied. "Just you." She turned to Clark. "Just him, right? He gets all the power, the glory? And what do you get out of all this, doing his dirty work for him? Doing what you're told. Lying for him? What kind of life will you have… afterwards?"

Clark thought about this for a second or two. "There will be a place for me, he's promised. For us all."

"You never gave a shit about me, or my kids."

"That's not true, Debs."

"Stop calling me that!" she shouted. It felt wrong now, felt like another life – which of course it had been. One built on falsehoods and deception. Just like— "Mason, your father. You *are* just like him."

"Don't say that," Clark pleaded with her.

"Weak, spineless. He's the dominant one, right? Always has been. It's his plan, I'm guessing. All this was his idea? The Gemini? Do me a favour. *A* Gemini, maybe. A copy of the original. More like Twinkle, though, I reckon."

"You dare!" rumbled The Gemini.

"Why, what are you going to do about it?"

Then she saw. The Gemini rose.

He is rising, has risen!

But it wasn't just a drawing up of himself, standing tall. He was taller than ever now. And when Deborah looked down, she saw he was off the ground. Floating. Tiny sparks of electricity were visible, creating static. Deborah realised now where he'd been when she entered, why she hadn't been able to see him. The fucker could fly! Or float, levitate, whatever you wanted to call it: was lifting himself higher and higher. Like directing those visions, this was another trick the first Gemini hadn't mastered. Hadn't even attempted. Perhaps he was superior after all.

But it was taking a hell of a lot of concentration, she could tell. A summoning of a lot of his power. She turned and bent towards the kids, leaning in to whisper to them. "James, Jack, can you hear me? Are you awake?"

They were mumbling something she couldn't quite catch. Then James said: "N-Nightmare… about the Bad Man."

"Yeah, that's right. You were having a nightmare about him, but I want you to do something for me."

"W-What?" asked Jack, bleary-eyed.

"I want you to think about the Bad Man, the one with two faces. Concentrate on him."

"It's time to end this!" The Gemini's voice boomed out. Clark was watching this spectacle, awestruck. It was obviously the first time he'd seen it. Glover, for his part, didn't really seem surprised at all.

"Do it, do it now, boys. Please, for Mum."

They both nodded in unison, scrunching up their eyes. The Gemini dropped. Just a little, but he dropped. "No, what is—" Then he fell some more, plunged to the ground again with a thud.

"That's it, that's it boys! You're doing it, just think about the Bad Man." It was working, just like Deborah had hoped it would. If the link was there, maybe it ran both ways. If The Gemini could open it up at his end, maybe her sons could do the same and pitch it back at him. Weaken him somehow, distract him long enough to—

The huge man in black fell to one knee, clearly in distress.

"No, Rich!" said Clark. Then to Deborah, "Stop it. Stop it, you're hurting him!"

"Good!" she shouted back.

Clark shifted the gun, away from Glover, and pointed it at the trio towards the back of the room. "Stop! I-I'm warning you!" Whether he was going to fire or not wasn't clear, and Deborah didn't really want to test if he cared enough about them to find out; certainly not compared with his own flesh and blood, his twin as opposed to distant relatives. But in the end it didn't come to that.

Glover grabbed his arm, shoved the gun upwards, which went off with a bang that they both reeled at, deafening them. Clark looked more shocked about this than seeing his only brother defying gravity, but snapped to and started wrestling Glover for possession of the firearm.

They spun around, Glover bringing the gun back down again – then Clark headbutted him and the inspector almost let go. Instead, he pressed himself up closer to Clark and the two men began their strange tango again. Which ended when the gun went off a second time.

Deborah's hand went to her mouth.

Glover stepped away, revealing that Clark's shirt was stained red. The inspector turned, smiled. Deborah smiled back. Then the man dropped over sideways, dead weight, and it was clear whose blood that was on Clark.

Hand shaking, Clark walked over to Deborah, who was now shielding the kids. "I said stop it. Whatever they're doing, get them to stop, Debs. Deborah. I *mean* it."

She didn't know if she even could. But when he raised the gun at her head, it happened anyway – the boys more worried about their mum than the Bad Man.

The Gemini grunted. Got up off his knee. Used a desk nearby to help himself stand, then grabbed the underside of it and flung it against a wall. The cracked cup, Deborah's old cup, fell to the floor and completely shattered. The Gemini trod on the remains and stalked towards them.

Clark smiled, then said to either her or the twins, "Thank you."

A shadow fell over all of them, The Gemini only metres away – still on foot. He pulled out his twin-pronged fork – another copy, a replica, like Vinny's but real; merely a tool fit for purpose – and held it aloft. "Time to finish this. Which one?" he asked again.

Deborah shook her head.

"Which one? Decide!"

How? How could she decide that? Which one of her sons was going to die, to have an eye plucked out of his head? No, she couldn't do it.

"Which one, or I kill them both!"

Clark looked from his brother to Deborah and the twins. "No. They don't both have to..." The Gemini shoved Clark aside, just the latest obstacle to getting his way. Then he reached down and grabbed Deborah, lifted her up off her own feet – a twisted parody of what he'd been doing himself not long ago.

"No... no please," whimpered Clark. "I promised. You promised."

The Gemini was ignoring him. "Choose, or I'll kill all three of you."

"Robbie," said Deborah.

"Please. I said she could live," Clark breathed. "We could—"

"The whore doesn't want you!" snarled The Gemini.

"Don't call her that," said Clark.

"When this is over, you can have any woman you want, little brother." Little. Brother. Probably the second one out, Deborah imagined. Certainly the submissive one in this relationship, and she could see Clark thinking about her own words earlier. Weak. Spineless. Doing what he was told.

"Put her down," Clark said. No please this time. Not asking: telling. "Richard, put her down."

The Gemini smirked. "I don't take orders from you. Never have done, never will."

"Put her down, right now."

"I was always Mother's favourite, the special one."

Clark bared his teeth. And then he leaped on his brother, the surprise attack sending the huge man sideways a little. Causing him to let go of Deborah. The Gemini spun round and faced Clark now. "What the fuck do you think you're doing?"

He didn't answer, just kept trying to wrestle the man.

"We're almost there, Robert. We're—"

The gun went off again. Almost certainly another accident, but too close for comfort – too close to The Gemini's head, anyway. From her position on the floor, looking up, Deborah felt sure she saw it ricochet off – maybe just skimmed the surface, but definitely didn't do any permanent damage.

Enraged, The Gemini put down his fork and grabbed

Clark with one hand and the gun with the other, snatching it out of his grasp. He crushed the metal object like it was a pop can, folding it up on itself, his strength incredible. Electricity crackled once more, as he tossed the gun aside and took hold of Clark now with both hands. She could imagine that maybe they'd done this as kids; James and Jack certainly did, play-fighting. But now Richard had the distinct advantage over Robert.

Clark gritted his teeth, but still in anger rather than terror. He was giving it a good go, she had to admit. Right up until the point that she heard the crack of bones, which were almost as loud as those gunshots.

The Gemini was folding his brother up like the gun, like a concertina more accurately, putting pressure on that body where pressure shouldn't have been placed. Blood was bursting from various places, mingling with that of Glover's. He looked over her way, face contorted in a weird kind of smile. Deborah turned away, unable to face it anymore – then saw James and Jack, almost fully awake and watching the scene unfold.

She gathered them in her arms, pulling their heads to her shoulders and forcing them to look away. Knelt there amidst the carnage until The Gemini was done. Until he dropped the remains of Robert Clark into a disgusting heap.

He turned slowly to gaze at them, all four of those eyebrows stooped. "Look," he echoed. "Look at what you made me do, bitch."

Deborah said nothing. She just sat there holding her boys, shaking. Could feel them shaking, too.

The Gemini faced front, loomed over them. The electricity was sparking off him even more. This was it, the end. "Don't look, my babies," she whispered. "Mummy's got you."

At least they would all be together. All apart from Izzy, and her own mum, she suddenly thought. But what could she do about that? There was nothing left to do but succumb to this.

"Deborah."

She heard the voice calling her name, knew that voice. It belonged to the only man she'd ever really loved. "Jack?" she replied. The boys stirred in her arms.

"Deborah, it's going to be okay."

She looked up and saw him, saw Jack standing there behind The Gemini. He was smiling that sweet smile of his, and somehow she knew whatever happened it was going to be all right. Everything would be fine. He was here to be with them at the end, to collect them.

No. Something else.

Jack faded, just like he'd done every time before. Someone else replaced him, a figure she couldn't make out.

The Gemini realised there was somebody behind him, but it was already too late. He jerked, spasmed. Deborah jumped too – and so did the boys, even though she was still holding them to her and they couldn't see a thing.

When the prongs came through, it was still a jolt. The fork had been rammed in through Richard's back, right in and out the other side, piercing the heart. Deborah could hear glass breaking, realised it was the sound of the jars exploding back there in what had once been the bullpen.

The Gemini touched the sharp tips of his own weapon, then looked down. Looked down with one face: an exact duplicate of Robbie Clark's. Already the sparks that had been electrifying his body were escaping through the holes the fork had made, but they didn't stop there: the spirits inside him were fleeing through his eyes, liquifying them as he raised his head again; through his ears; his nose; his mouth, stuck in a screaming rictus. The souls of the twins he'd murdered were leaving any way they could, now that they weren't tied to that form anymore.

The Gemini – the second Gemini – shuddered and shook,

more violently than Deborah had been doing only moments before. Other parts of his body were exploding outwards, mirroring the jars of the collection. It wasn't long before he was a heap on the floor alongside his brother, revealing who it was who'd saved them.

Glover, looking like crap. Holding his stomach with one hand, his other empty where he'd shoved the abandoned fork into Richard.

He wasn't the only thing Deborah saw, however. Some of the candles, the lamps, must have fallen in all the chaos – not least when The Gemini was tipping over that desk. It had started fires. Fires that were spreading, fast.

Glover followed her gaze. "T-Time we weren't here."

Deborah rose, carrying one of her sons in each arm. "I think you're right." She led the way to the door, looking back at the inspector. He almost fell, letting his hand slip – and she saw the damage the bullet had caused. He needed to get to hospital, and soon. But he waved them on.

"Go, go. I'll be okay. I'm right behind you."

By the time they'd made it out and down the corridor towards the stairs, the fire was already raging – lapping out through the door to try and reach them. Another explosion sounded from inside, but they managed to get on the stairs.

Half stumbling, half-falling down them – the heat from above chasing them – they went down and down.

It seemed to take forever, and when Deborah risked a look upwards she saw only fire. An inferno devouring everything on those floors. It would eat the whole building, she knew that.

But at last they reached the ground level, tumbling out into the car park, getting as far away from the building as they could. Collapsing in a heap, they waited there. Because they could already hear people coming round the side. Press, reporters.

Rushing to see what was going on, to cover the story – but also to help.

By the time what had once been Yardley Street nick was ablaze from top to bottom, they were already safe. Already away from that place, delivered from the evil.

Inside ambulances and on their way to Norchester General.

CHAPTER THIRTY-THREE

Mornings were always gorgeous here.

No matter what time of year, no matter the season, regardless of how chilly or hot. Regardless of what she'd been through the past few months. Actually, it was nice to be returning to some kind of normality at last, whatever that meant. Nice to be back here, with the press having mostly cleared off once she'd given them what they wanted.

Deborah strolled a little further, looking for pebbles that she could skim into the ocean, mind wandering, thinking about all that had happened since Yardley Street. That, in itself, seemed like a million years ago now.

She'd spent so much of those first few weeks in the hospital. She and her boys were treated for smoke inhalation initially, but then Rosy was there a lot, of course, visiting Kiz – who'd come through the surgery but had been left in a coma. It was anyone's guess as to whether she'd wake up or not, and even if she did she wouldn't be the same as she'd been before. There had simply been too much damage.

"I'd give anything just to have her back," Rosy had said when Deborah dropped in one time. "Kids, whatever. She could have what she wanted." Tears were welling in her eyes as she sat there next to the bed, holding Kiz's hand, the machines bipping and pinging. "I hate the way we left things. I hate what…" The sentence tailed off with more crying.

"I know," said Deborah, placing a hand on her shoulder. Things might have been drawing to a close, but it certainly didn't feel like time for that champagne yet. Maybe when Kiz awakened – if she ever did.

But the look her friend had given her then said it all. She blamed Deborah for all of this, in spite of the fact she was the one who'd brought her back into it. That she'd agreed to the twins staying there, Rosy's loyalty to a department she didn't even know if she was going to join now swaying her decision.

An organisation the other person she spent time with still belonged to. He'd needed surgery too, but the bullet had done a lot less damage than The Gemini had with Kiz. Nicked one of his kidneys, and made a bit of a mess of his gall bladder, but he was recovering nicely, the doctors and nurses had told her. Had only played dead to fool Clark and The Gemini. They weren't the only ones who could pretend.

Glover had inched himself up when she first visited him, wincing but smiling at the same time. "Miss Harrison, it's really nice to see you."

"Deborah, please. Or Debbie, or," she said sitting down, "to my friends and people who saved my life – saved my children's lives – Debs."

He smiled again, much wider this time. It was during conversations visiting him that she found out why he'd been at Yardley Street that day, not because he was following her, but because of an anonymous tip-off. "It had just said that I should go there and take another look. So I did. I think someone out there was trying to help us, don't you?"

Deborah nodded, but had no idea who that could be. When he asked why she thought her boys might be there, she'd tried to fudge the issue, but he'd seen right through her. It was more than she'd been able to do with him. "This is all going to sound crazy but they showed me. After my Jack gave me a nudge in the right direction. Sort of."

"Jack, as in Jack Foley?"

"Told you it would sound crazy."

"Not as crazy as you might think. The dead try to help us as much as they can, especially when we're in dire straits. Like I said to you before, I have a little experience of ghosts. My old friend Charles, for example."

Something Vinny had said to her came back then. "Charles Mansfield?"

Glover seemed surprised at that and she had to explain where she'd heard the name.

"He was murdered by the X Killer," Glover said. "Cut from the same cloth as our guy, he was. All for power again, and in the end Charles died for nothing. He was my friend," Glover said again.

"But... but he came back?"

The inspector regarded her seriously. "It's not always easy for them to do that. But it's possible, especially if their work here isn't done."

He wouldn't be drawn any more on the subject, instead went on to tell her that the SCI were conducting an internal investigation to weed out any undesirables.

"Geminites, you mean?" she said.

"Well, yes. There's whoever stole the original Gemini's remains for a start," said Glover.

We're everywhere...

"Have you thought about what you want to do about that, you know, moving forwards?" he asked her then.

It was definitely a concern, but now that The Gemini was dead... Glover had offered a few suggestions, like more protection and security for her family, even relocation – a sort of witness protection deal. "I'm damned if I'm going to let those bastards drive me out of my own home!" she'd said, after running it past the others as well. Their lives were in Armitage Bay, and they couldn't keep running away from this forever. Wouldn't spend the rest of their lives looking over their shoulders. "I want to see them coming, if they ever do."

Strangely, now that the whole press thing had ramped up – and Deborah hadn't been able to avoid everything coming out, including her pseudonym which her agent and publisher had been more than happy about – it meant the Geminites were less likely to try anything. They operated behind the scenes, not in the public eye. Add to that the fact someone had been arrested for creeping about in the area, gawking into people's homes and stalking women, it threw doubt on whether there had ever been a Geminite on the prowl there in the first place. That night when she thought she'd seen somebody outside the house, or Izzy had been followed.

In any event, forewarned was forearmed. They would just have to be careful, that was all. She'd even been allowed to visit the Geminite priest before his transfer to a secure SCI Prison. "If any of your lot ever come near me or the people I love, I will personally track all of you down and end you," she told him. "Your 'god' is dead. Again. We killed him. Again. Do you really want to mess with the people who did that?"

Typically he'd remained silent, not even smirking this time. He'd been wrong about her children being… But maybe it had been a threat rather than a statement. All she could do was hope the message got back to the rest of his clan.

Glover had promised to keep an eye on them too, and she was oddly glad about that. Was never happier to be wrong about someone in her life. It kind of cancelled out Clark, her mistake in trusting him.

"I still can't believe you thought I might be…" Glover shook his head. "I'm older than I look you know, and have never, ever been a twin. Ask my mum. I think she'd remember something like that from when I was born."

"I'm sorry," Deborah apologised, not just for that but the way she'd treated him all along. The more time she spent with Mike, the more she actually liked him. And the icing on the cake? Jack, appearing again after one of her visits with more unfinished business. To tell her, speaking more easily now, that the inspector was 'A good man'. He'd smiled then, and she wished now more than ever she could just fall into his arms. But of course he'd already vanished, was already gone. Had been for a long time.

Her mother and Izzy had joined her not long after Yardley Street too, the family unit back together again and all of them staying at *The Imperial* (she'd even introduced them to Albert, who seemed to be rather fond of Wendy; he was on a hiding to nothing there, she was spoken for). It would help massively with the mental recovery of the twins, Deborah was told. Yet another reason to all go back home together, once her hospital visits were done with and she'd been able to attend the funerals of people like Felicity, Geoffrey Wilkinson – even though she hadn't known him – and Vinny Hole. As with the original killings, the other victims might never be found – especially now the collection was ash, burning away any chance of identifying who those body parts had belonged to.

In a bizarre twist, one of the officers that had been protecting – or trying to protect – her boys, the one that had been impaled on the railings, DC Gough, had pulled through. He'd got together with another survivor, DC Maple, and there was even talk of wedding bells.

Three funerals and…

Deborah found her pebble and skimmed it, making her way further along the beach. It was busier in this stretch, lots of families bunched together. Her own family there on the beach, the twins making sandcastles as her mum and Derek sat in deck chairs. They waved to her as she approached. Izzy got up and ran over to her, giving her a big hug.

Things had been much better since they'd seen each other

again, the shock of nearly losing all three of them apparent. The teenager had once again apologised for her behaviour. For what she'd said the last time they spoke. "Go to hell!" she'd told her, and in all honesty Deborah had. The twins had too. Even met the devil, or one of his demons at any rate. And made it out again.

"I'll try to do better," Izzy promised, and to be fair she had. They'd never see eye to eye on a lot of things, but these awkward years would be over soon enough and hopefully they'd end up being closer than ever when they came out of the other side of that particular hell. As close as she was with her own mum, Deborah prayed.

She'd even inspired her a bit apparently, Izzy had confessed. If her mum could face those terrors, then she could face the people at school. Face the consequences of that.

"You're pretty badass, you know," Izzy informed her.

Deborah laughed. "You're not so bad yourself."

As they walked back over to the family, Deborah asked if she fancied an ice cream. The girl looked at her, said: "What am I, six?" Deborah wished that she was again, dearly wanted to have those years back – but time moved on. Then Izzy grinned, laughed, and added, "Only joking, *of course* I do! When am I ever going to refuse a Mr Whippy?"

Deborah chuckled and pulled her in for another hug. The twins got up and rushed over, doing the same, wrapping their arms around their mother and sister – who was mock complaining about being crushed. They'd been through so much, those two, and there was still a long way to go with them before they were recovered fully, if they ever did. But they were all together. They'd deal with it together.

"Nice walk, love?" Wendy Harrison asked, having got out of her chair as well to join in with the group hug.

"Thanks Mum, yeah."

"And did I hear ice cream mentioned?"

Jack and James gave a cry of joy at that, and Deborah laughed harder. "Mr Whippys all round then."

More screams of delight; they were better than the alternative. And as Deborah leaned even more into the hug, she was thankful.

Gave thanks that for now, at least, they were happy, safe.

And the nightmare was over.

CHAPTER THIRTY-FOUR

It was only just beginning.

This part of the story, this final chapter of the whole thing. Mayor Tierney looked out over her city (the one she controlled – CCTV and all) then took a sip of the single malt, and grinned. Power. That's what she had, that's what she'd been granted in return for certain... favours. Tasks she had to complete, was happy to do so. She'd already arranged for the buffoon who'd got himself caught to have an unfortunate accident on his way to the SCI prison. Wasn't hard, their people were everywhere, after all. Shouldn't have been overstepping his mark in the first place. His job had been to observe, not get into a fight with the person being observed!

All of this had left a bad taste in her mouth, what had almost happened. And all because of another one of their kind who hadn't been able to follow orders. That woman Clark! A rogue Geminite who'd taken it upon herself to try and birth their leader, got herself pregnant by the twin of their one, true god.

She'd had to stamp on it, of course. Had been riding that useless Inspector Glover, pushing him to end this faux Gemini's reign before it began. She'd even had to send that anonymous message telling him where he could find Richard, never expecting him to go there alone – prat!

Luckily it had all worked out. Yardley Street police station had burnt to the ground, Robert and Richard Clark with it. Would save them having to demolish the place, because it had already been bought by a shell company. They had plans to build on the site, firming up the foundations not just of the church that would follow but the schemes they had in mind for the future.

Already their scientists were harvesting the DNA they'd need and were preparing the volunteer. Hand-chosen, good breeding stock, such as *They* deserved. The twins. Genetically engineered, replicating the originals down to the last cell.

This wasn't just the endgame they were playing now, it was a long game. She'd received the message that Deborah Harrison had given the inmate, the one she thought was a Geminite priest. *Pah!* He was far from that. But she and her family would remain untouched, not because of any threat that woman had issued, or because of her newfound fame. Simply because it wasn't the time yet.

Their one, true god was coming back. He would decide what to do with her, with her own children. The Mayor had a feeling she knew what their fate would be.

She wandered over to the robes hanging up in her chambers, reached out a hand that was not currently occupied holding the fiery liquid.

Mayor Tierney touched the chains of office she was proud to wear. Not because she 'served' this city – this special city of Norchester – but, as she turned them over and saw the symbol on the underside of the medallion there (two horizontal lines connected by two vertical ones) because of who she actually served. Like her parents before her, and their parents as well, stretching back and back. They were everywhere, but especially here.

And they could wait. Because *He* was rising, would one day be risen again. The one, true Gemini. Her lord and master.

Then they would all see, oh yes.

This was only just beginning. But one day it would end.

One day it would be…

The end.

EPILOGUE

Inside the womb, changes were taking place.

Since seed had first encountered egg, energising it with life. It had survived, against all the odds. Then the egg split: a consequence of the conception taking place under such conditions, as artificial as they were. Everything guided, everything controlled and manipulated.

Suddenly there were two identical eggs, genetically indistinguishable. Exact duplicates that would emerge in something like eight or nine months' time. Twins. They would be the same in appearance, in looks if not in personality... though they would be more alike than either of them might ever realise. And no matter how 'individual' they grew up to be, the fact remained that they'd started off as one.

Inside that womb the developing foetuses interact.

They nudge and kick each other, communicating in their own distinct and secret code. Working out which one would be the dominant of the two, as if that was ever in any doubt; who would take the most sustenance from the mother. And also probably trying to get back that which they had lost. The wholeness. Nevertheless, they would share a bond with each other that could never be broken. Not by time nor distance, nor even by the blackness and finality of death itself – which they had already experienced once, both of them.

But all that was in the future. For now they were nothing but clusters of cells, forming. Waiting, patiently waiting.

Because the miracle, the marvel that still remains a mystery especially in these times of scientific wonder and technological achievement, was only really beginning.

The miracle that some refer to as:

The Gemini Effect.

AUTHOR'S NOTE

If I can, I always try and link stories together – I've done it with the crime novels and novelettes, I did it with the *Hooded Man* series, and even in my Sherlock Holmes entries (see if you can track down Enola in *Sherlock Holmes and the Servants of Hell*)... And long-time readers of my work especially should be able to spot more than a few nods to some of my other characters and yarns in this sequel to *The Gemini Factor*.

I know that a few of you clocked the fact that in *The Storm* the main female protagonist – Gemma – referred to events in the first *Gemini* book, because her cousin was, is, of course, Deborah; something that gets another mention here (plus Bernie Noble mentions the other half of that pairing, Keegan, in his army reminiscences). Similarly, the strange things that went on in Armitage Bay with the blue-eyed man are a reference to *Before* and the antics of The Infinity.

I was able to tie together the history of both the *RED* and *Life Cycle* werewolf tales in a novelette called *The Curse of the Wolf,* and that gets another airing here when Vinny is talking about the history of Norchester. As does my Controllers mythos, when Vinny's spirit is being absorbed into The Gemini. While the SCI, only mentioned briefly in books like

Blood RED or short stories such as 'To the Power of...' (read this if you want a little bit of background on Charles Mansfield and the X killer), plus at the end of *The Gemini Factor* and in 'Gemini Rising', get to take much more of a centre stage here. I'm hoping to write further tales about them in the future, because there are lots of uncanny cases they're up to their necks in.

I even chucked in *The Wanderer's Rest*, from my short story 'The Procession' and my play *One for the Road* – which sees the Four Horsemen of the Apocalypse gathering there on the eve of Doomsday to have a pint and a natter.

You don't need to have read any of this material to enjoy *The Gemini Effect* – you don't even really need to have read *Factor*, though it will help, naturally – it's just a fun little thing some of us writers like to do sometimes. Interlinking stuff in what my old mate Steve Volk – he of *Afterlife* and *Ghostwatch* fame – has termed in the past 'Kane's World'.

Oh, and I wonder if you can guess which books Deborah writes? If so, give that person a cigar!

In any event, I hope you've enjoyed reading *Effect* as much as I did writing it. This is the first novel I wrote after a two-year gap (during which we had the pandemic, lockdowns, a house move, and my better half Marie O'Regan and I finally managed to put on the ChillerCon UK event in Scarborough – or perhaps that should be *Scare*borough?). A sequel to a novel I wrote over twenty years ago, it's felt a lot like coming home in many ways.

And, as you've no doubt now seen, I'm not about to leave it there. As they say at the end of the Bond movies, The Gemini will return…

Paul Kane
Derbyshire
March 2023

ABOUT THE AUTHOR

Paul Kane is an award-winning (including the British Fantasy Society's 'Legends of Fantasy' Award), bestselling writer and editor based in Derbyshire, UK. His short story collections include *Alone (In the Dark)*, *Touching the Flame*, *FunnyBones*, *Peripheral Visions*, *Shadow Writer*, *The Adventures of Dalton Quayle*, *The Butterfly Man and Other Stories*, *The Spaces Between*, *Ghosts*, the British Fantasy Award-nominated *Monsters*, *Shadow Casting*, *Nailbiters*, *Death*, *Disexistence*, *Scary Tales*, *More Monsters*, *Lost Souls*, *The Controllers* and *The Naked Eye*. His novellas include *The Lazarus Condition*, *RED* and *Pain Cages* (a #1 Amazon bestseller). He is the author of such novels as *Of Darkness and Light*, *The Gemini Factor* and the bestselling *Arrowhead* trilogy (*Arrowhead*, *Broken Arrow* and *Arrowland*, gathered together in the sell-out omnibus edition *Hooded Man*), a post-apocalyptic reworking of the Robin Hood mythology. His latest novels include *Lunar* (which is set to be turned into a feature film), the short YA novel *The Rainbow Man* (as PB Kane), the critically-acclaimed and award-winning *Sherlock Holmes and the Servants of Hell* from Solaris, the sequels to *RED* – *Blood RED* and *Deep RED* – *Before* from Grey Matter Press, *Arcana* from WordFire Press, plus *Her Last Secret*, *Her Husband's Grave* and *The Family Lie* from HQ/HarperCollins (as PL Kane)

He has also written for comics, most notably for the *Dead Roots* zombie anthology alongside writers such as James Moran (*Torchwood*, *Cockneys vs. Zombies*) and Jason Arnopp (*Doctor Who*, *Friday the 13th*, *The Last Days of Jack Sparks*) and as part of the team turning *Clive Barker's Books of Blood* into motion comics for Seraphim/MadeFire. His stand-alone comic *The Disease*, published by Hellbound Media, was also a 2016 Ghastly Award-nominated title in the 'One Shot' category. Paul is co-editor of the anthology *Hellbound Hearts* (Simon & Schuster) – stories based around the mythology that spawned *Hellraiser* – *The Mammoth Book of Body Horror* (Constable & Robinson/Running Press), featuring the likes of Stephen King and James Herbert, *A Carnivàle of Horror* (PS) featuring Ray Bradbury and Joe Hill, *Beyond Rue Morgue* from Titan (stories based around Poe's detective, Dupin), *Exit Wounds* – a crime anthology featuring the likes of Lee Child, Val McDermid, Dennis Lehane and Jeffery Deaver – *Wonderland* (a finalist in the Shirley Jackson Awards), *Cursed*, *Twice Cursed* and *The Other Side of Never*, the last five also from Titan.

His non-fiction books include *The Hellraiser Films and Their Legacy*, *Voices in the Dark* and *Shadow Writer – The Non-Fiction. Vol. 1: Reviews* and *Vol. 2: Articles and Essays*, plus his genre journalism has appeared in the likes of *SFX*, *Fangoria*, *Dreamwatch*, *Gorezone* and *Rue Morgue*. He also co-wrote the afterword to the latest edition of Stephen King's *Night Shift* collection. He has been a Guest at Alt.Fiction five times, was a Guest at the first SFX Weekender, at Thought Bubble in 2011, Derbyshire Literary Festival and Off the Shelf in 2012, Monster Mash and Event Horizon in 2013, Edge-Lit in 2014, HorrorCon, HorrorFest and Grimm Up North in 2015, The Dublin Ghost Story Festival and Sledge-Lit in 2016, IMATS Olympia and Celluloid Screams in 2017, Black Library Live (Warhammer 40k) and The UK Ghost Story Festival in 2019, plus the WordCrafter virtual event 2021 – where he delivered the keynote speech – as well as being a panellist at FantasyCon and the World Fantasy Convention, and a fiction judge at the Sci-Fi London Film Festival. He is a former Special Publications Editor of the British Fantasy Society, served as co-chair for the UK arm of the Horror Writers

Association from 2015 to 2022, and co-chaired ChillerCon UK in May 2022.

His work has been optioned for film and television, and his zombie story 'Dead Time' was turned into an episode of the Lionsgate/NBC TV series *Fear Itself*, adapted by Steve Niles (*30 Days of Night*) and directed by Darren Lynn Bousman (*SAW II-IV*). He also scripted *The Opportunity*, which premiered at the Cannes Film Festival, *Wind Chimes* (directed by Brad 'Hallows Eve' Watson and which sold to TV), *The Weeping Woman* – filmed by award-winning director Mark Steensland, starring Tony-nominated actor Stephen Geoffreys (*Fright Night*) – *Confidence*, directed by award-winning Mike Clarke (*A Hand to Play, Paper and Plastic*) which stars Simon Bamford (*Hellraiser, Nightbreed, Starfish*), and *The Torturer* directed by Joe Manco of Little Spark Films. Loose Canon/Hydra Films have just turned Paul's novelette *Men of the Cloth* into a feature called *Sacrifice* (aka *The Colour of Madness*), starring *Re-Animator* and *You're Next*'s Barbara Crampton. His work for audio includes the full cast drama adaptation of *The Hellbound Heart* for Bafflegab, starring Tom Meeten (*The Ghoul*), Neve McIntosh (*Doctor Who*) and Alice Lowe (*Prevenge*), and the *Robin of Sherwood* adventure *The Red Lord* for Spiteful Puppet/ITV, narrated by Ian Ogilvy (*Return of the Saint*). You can find out more at his website www.shadow-writer.co.uk which has featured Guest Writers such as Dean Koontz, Robert Kirkman, Charlaine Harris and Guillermo del Toro.

ALSO BY PAUL KANE

NOVELS

Arrowhead

Broken Arrow

Arrowland

Hooded Man (Omnibus)

The Gemini Factor

Lunar

Sleeper(s)

The Rainbow Man (as PB Kane)

Blood RED

Sherlock Holmes and the Servants of Hell

Before

Deep RED

Arcana

The Red Lord

Her Last Secret (as PL Kane)

The Storm

Her Husband's Grave (as PL Kane)

The Family Lie (as PL Kane)

NOVELLAS & NOVELETTES

The Lazarus Condition

Dalton Quayle Rides Out

RED

Pain Cages

Creakers (chapbook)

Flaming Arrow

The Bric-a-Brac Man

The PI's Tale

Snow

The Rot

Beneath the Surface (with Simon Clark)

Blood Red Sky

Confessions (as PL Kane)

Corpsing (as PL Kane)

Coming of Age (as PB Kane)

Murder on the Golden Sands Express (as PL Kane)

COLLECTIONS

Touching the Flame

FunnyBones

Peripheral Visions

The Adventures of Dalton Quayle

Shadow Writer

The Butterfly Man and Other Stories

The Spaces Between

Ghosts

Monsters

The Dead Trilogy

Shadow Casting

Nailbiters

Death

The Life Cycle

Disexistence

Kane's Scary Tales Vol. 1

More Monsters

Lost Souls

The Controllers

White Shadows (as PB Kane)

The Colour of Madness: Official Movie Tie-In

Traumas

Darkness & Shadows

The Naked Eye

Tempting Fate

Nailbiters – Hard Bitten

Zombies!

EDITOR & CO-EDITOR

Terror Tales #1-4

Top International Horror

Albions Alptraume: Zombies

The British Fantasy Society: A Celebration

Hellbound Hearts

The Mammoth Book of Body Horror

A Carnivàle of Horror: Dark Tales from the Fairground

Beyond Rue Morgue

Dark Mirages

Exit Wounds

Wonderland

Cursed

Twice Cursed

The Other Side of Never

NON-FICTION

Cinema Macabre (Contributor)

The Hellraiser Films And Their Legacy

Voices in the Dark

Shadow Writer – The Non-Fiction. Vol. 1: Reviews

Shadow Writer – The Non-Fiction. Vol. 2: Articles & Essays

Leviathan – The Story of Hellraiser and Hellbound: Hellraiser II
(Contributor)

Hellraisers

War is Hell: Making Hellraiser III: Hell on Earth (Contributor)

Stuart Gordon: Interviews (Conversations with Filmmakers Series)
(Contributor)